Be a F...

Randy

MW01064512

BRIDGE
—THE—

RANDY POOL

Bloomington, IN Milton Keynes, UK

authorHOUSE™

AuthorHouse™
1663 Liberty Drive, Suite 200
Bloomington, IN 47403
www.authorhouse.com
Phone: 1-800-839-8640

AuthorHouse™ UK Ltd.
500 Avebury Boulevard
Central Milton Keynes, MK9 2BE
www.authorhouse.co.uk
Phone: 08001974150

This book is a work of fiction. People, places, events, and situations are the product of the author's imagination. Any resemblance to actual persons, living or dead, or historical events, is purely coincidental.

First published by AuthorHouse 2/21/2006

ISBN: 1-4259-1277-X (sc)

Printed in the United States of America
Bloomington, Indiana

This book is printed on acid-free paper.

DEDICATION

To my father and step-mother, Herman and Susan Pool, who have believed in my writing and always made me feel proud of my work. A father's approval is a reward that every son seeks. I am indeed blessed and honored by the smile of my Dad.

To my sister, Patricia, whose unwavering support as well as medical knowledge made many portions of the book plausible.

Most of all, I dedicate this work to my partner in life, love, and missions – my beloved, Cindy.

Acknowledgements

I would like to thank Dianne Klutts, ministry assistant for the Gibson Baptist Association for her willingness to proof and edit "The Bridge". Her sacrifice and diligence is tremendously appreciated.

I would like to thank Mike and Kathy Kemper for their friendship and experiences on the mission field that have been part of my calling to missions since the beginning. May you both continue to follow God's leadership in His fields and find fruit in the Harvest.

I would like to thank Eddy Holmes, both meteorologist (in Jackson, TN) and Bible teacher, for his expertise with weather conditions and his prayers for a fruitful story.

I would like to thank Don Pierson, who has become my mentor in prayer, and to the many "Gerties" that I have met since "The Breach" who have affirmed the importance of prayer. May this volume continue to move others toward the "throne of Grace".

I would like to thank the countless readers of "The Breach", who repeatedly hounded me for the completion of "The Bridge". I hope the result was worth waiting for.

PROLOGUE

<u>Jackson, Tennessee</u>   *<u>Friday October 30, 1998</u>*

"OH, SWEET Jesus!" whispered the meteorologist to himself. The National Weather Service report was waiting for him on his desk, but the storm was not waiting to be read. Bob Houston was known for his folksy manner of delivering the weather to a twenty-eight county area. His greatest challenge was taking the technical information from the National Weather Service, translating it into layman's terms, and then finding a "down-home" way of presenting it to the rural counties of West Tennessee. Having "weathered" through tornadoes, flash floods, ice storms and even the dense fog of the delta, Bob had gained the respect of farmers and city folk alike. But how do you describe a category-five hurricane to rural people so far removed from any coast?

Bob picked up his earlier notes to refresh his memory over the slow and deliberate course of this tempest.

> *Tuesday, October 20* – "A tropical system appears in the southern basin of the Caribbean just north of Panama."
> *Thursday, October 22* – "The system gradually moves toward the north and strengthens."
> *Saturday, October 24am* – "The tropical system has grown to Hurricane force and is given a name: Mitch
> *Sunday, October 25* – "In the past twenty-four hours, the central pressure has dropped fifty-two milibars down to nine hundred and twenty four. By late afternoon, the hurricane reached categories four and five. Winds rose in excess of 250 miles per hour."
> *Tuesday, October 27* – "Hurricane forces are slowly weakening as the storm stations itself above Honduras and Nicaragua."
> *Thursday, October 29* – "Hurricane Mitch remains stationary for the second day off the northern coast of Honduras. The eye of the Hurricane is located just a few miles off the island of Guanaja."
> *Thursday, October 29* – "The eye has moved south dropping up to twelve inches of rain across the inland of Honduras and Nicaragua. Mitch is re-categorized as a tropical storm."

1

Bob sighed deeply and slumped into his swivel chair. Thinking to himself, he was relieved when the storm was re-categorized, but now the rains were increasing. He read of total accumulation in some areas of up to 48 inches of rain. Rivers were overflowing. Whole villages were under water. Hundreds were stranded on rooftops. Thousands were homeless. The capital city of Tegucigalpa, located well in the center of the country, had experienced severe flooding, lost major bridges and was almost an island.

"This is not good," Bob said out loud.

"What's not good?" asked Susie Elkins, copy editor for the news station.

"Hurricane Mitch," was all Bob could say in response.

"I thought that Mitch had down sized to a tropical storm yesterday," Susie replied in business fashion.

"When a hurricane moves inland, winds tend to diminish and it is no longer classified as a hurricane, but rains increase due to lift from the land masses. The higher the land masses, such as the mountains surrounding the capital, the more the lift is accentuated causing serious flooding. This is going to be a national disaster of epic proportions. Honduras and parts of Nicaragua are being destroyed as we speak. Today is going to be one of the darkest days in their history. How do I put that in a weather report?"

"Let me run some other sources and get some more information," Susie reacted, retreating from Bob's cubicle. Her voice grew faint as she walked away. "If this is as big as you say, it will be appearing in more than just the weather segments."

Bob turned to his computer and stared. What could it possibly be like to be in the middle of that storm? What would it be like to have to rebuild after such a disaster? What could he do to make a difference? He bowed his head and whispered again, "Oh, sweet Jesus, help them…"

El Porvenir, Nicaragua   *Friday October 30, 1998*

"Aye, Dios, mio!" Marta cried out as the wind lifted the thin sheets of tin halfway off the roof and then beat them hard against the rafters. The torrents of rain had already found their way through gaps in the walls and had softened the dirt flooring into a thick pasty mud. Heavy rains in October were not unusual, but the volume of water was getting dangerous for the mountain villages near the volcano slope of *La Casita*. Marta gathered her children into the center of their small adobe-block house and prayed to the Virgin for safety. What should have been a noon day sky was as dark as

twilight. The leaden gray clouds had oppressed the entire country for nearly a week and now their copious loads of rain were being mercilessly released.

Two kilometers above her village of *El Porvenir*, the cone of the volcano *La Casita* began to shudder. Fissures in the softened earth widened in jarring shifts. With a thunderous groan, the southern flank began to collapse being pulled by gravity towards the base of the mountain. As the cascading debris broke up older deposits from previous eruptions, additional water and sediment caused the slide to increase in size about nine-fold. Like a growing maelstrom of mud, volcanic sludge and rock, the landslide gained momentum and volume as it rolled over vegetation, roads, buildings and anything else in its path – including homes. There was no high ground to flee to. There was nowhere to run. Within minutes, the villages of *El Porvenir* and *Rolando Rodriquez* were completely covered by the fatal *lahar* of the flow. By the time the slide ended, over two thousand would be dead.

North of León, Nicaragua   *Saturday October 31, 1998*

"Apuraté Daniel!" Roberto cried out through the roar of the rain, trying to hurry his friend. The two strong young men had journeyed down the mountain to the city of León to learn what they could about the storms that had plagued their village for over ten days. They discovered it was no safer in the city. Before the electricity had gone out, there had been reports of landslides, flooding, much death and hundreds missing. Though much of the attention was being placed on Honduras, Nicaragua was receiving her share of suffering. The collapse of *La Casita* the day before was the largest site of sudden devastation and death recorded for both countries, as two whole towns were utterly destroyed. The storm was not through.

Daniel and Roberto had stayed the night in León. By early morning, they decided they needed to make their way back to their village. No buses would chance the mountain roads while the flooding and landslides continued. The young men had a long walk home. Determination to be back with their families drove them to brave the winds and rain. An hour-long bus ride took over six hours by foot as they trudged through thick mud and rested under many of the large trees. Roberto reminded Daniel of the dangers of trees and lightening more times than he could remember. They reached the small village alongside the road that sat adjacent to the path that would lead them to the river. Their village was just across the river.

"Hurry *Daniel*," Roberto called out again, "We are almost there. I can see the bridge. Hurry!"

The two men quickened their pace. Exhaustion could wait just three more minutes. Once across the river, they were less than a kilometer from home. The black baleful clouds hung ominously in the sky. Together they paused at the entry of the bridge and looked across. The river level was up ten feet since they left and was higher than either had ever seen it. The surging channel churned violently just four feet below the bridge. The two men paused long enough to cross themselves and then took careful, well-placed steps onto the slippery two-by-fours. They grasped the two-inch thick-rope on both sides of the support and held on tightly. They slid their hands along the rope with just a foot spacing between each man. They had run across this bridge several times before and it seemed like a short distance when in a hurry. Now each step felt like minutes. The sky above rumbled with distant thunder and the bridge felt like it moved. Roberto yelled to Daniel to walk faster.

Daniel quickened his stride leaving Roberto about three steps behind. Roberto felt the bridge move again and called out to Daniel to be careful. Daniel felt the slight rocking of the wood and increased his steps even more. Roberto knew that ten days of rain would leave mold on the surface of the wood. He called to Daniel to slow down. The bridge began rocking to each side with every stride of the men. Adrenaline and fear caused Daniel to disregard Roberto's warnings and he started to dart for the end of the bridge that was still over four yards away. His shoes began to slide on the slick wood and he suddenly fell on his right side.

"*Daniel!*" Roberto called out, but the young man couldn't respond. He was thrashing for the rope he had let go of and was sliding between the narrow posts through which the rope was threaded. Daniel grabbed at the post with both hands as he slid over the side of the bridge. His upper torso was barely supported on the planks and his feet dangled just over the water's crest. The bridge groaned and shifted to the left tilting Daniel closer to the current. Roberto tried to make his way to his friend, but could only watch helplessly as the post gave way and broke off in Daniel's hands. He watched his friend submerge once and then reappear nearly twenty yards down stream. Roberto couldn't hear due to the rain, but he knew Daniel was trying to yell. Regaining his own balance, Roberto looked intently at the opposite bank and the end of the bridge. He knew the structure would not stand much longer. He had six yards to go.

The bridge heaved hard to the left and Roberto heard the sound of cracking wood behind him. He didn't turn to look, but he knew that the bridge was giving way. He pulled on the ropes and guided himself towards the land ahead of him. Three yards away from the edge, the wood below his feet began to come apart. He knew he had only seconds before the bridge would be washed down river with Daniel. He arched his back, pulled hard

4

on the ropes and thrust himself forward taking several light steps and then leaping with all of his might. Roberto landed with his face in the mud, but his thighs and legs were still on the bridge. He felt the bank let go of the support beams beneath the bridge and felt his waist begin to twist with the rubble. He grasped at the rocks in front of him and found one buried firmly in the ground. With all his might, Roberto pulled himself towards it as the bridge disappeared from beneath his legs. He could feel the cold water swirling around his shins as he crawled up the new bank and away from the flowing death.

He was safe. He would return to his home to tell his family the story. He would have to tell Daniel's family the sad news, but he himself was safe. He did not know what his village would do now that the bridge was gone. They would need help. Surely there would be help. He crawled towards a small bush to recover. The rain didn't stop. He would have to continue on to his house soon, but he couldn't move - he had to rest. The sky was now black as night. Roberto cowered against the bush as curtains of rain fell over him. He looked in the direction of the path that led to the village. Lightning flashed and he saw a silhouette etched against the horizon. It was a small man with a large stick in his hand. Roberto knew the man with the stick. Suddenly, he no longer felt safe.

CHAPTER ONE

(About Ten Months later)
"THE BEGINNING"

THE TROPICAL rains had only slightly lightened since daybreak. The sky was still shrouded with a blue-gray canopy that darkened just over the top of the mountain. The lush vegetation of the hillside quietly wept from the early rainfall. It was as though the entire countryside was in mourning for the death of little Maria. The processional began at her uncle's small adobe shack where the little girl had been laid in state the night before. The two-kilometer march would grow in size as neighbors joined the grieving family members in carrying the small wooden box towards the edge of the village. Some spoke quietly amongst themselves out of respect, while others carried on normal conversations. As the crowd reached the main road, it had grown to nearly eighty. The mud did not deter them from the task.

Allen West slowed his *Land Cruiser* to a crawl as he approached the parade of people in the road. Allen was accustomed to delays and traffic when traveling in Managua, but aside from the occasional cattle herds, he seldom encountered road activity along the country back routes of León, one of the larger regions of West Nicaragua.

"What is this, you think?" Allen asked his traveling companion.

"I can't tell, *hermano*," José replied. "Could be a religious processional for a town Saint. I see them carrying something near the front, but I can't make out what it is. If you want, we can pull over, and I'll ask."

Allen shrugged his shoulders. They weren't going anywhere quickly, nor were they in a hurry. It wouldn't hurt to see what was happening. He pulled the large vehicle to the narrow shoulder and José jumped out to catch up with the procession. Allen looked around. He and José had not visited this community before. He saw a few houses along the road, but most were sprinkled among the mango trees and banana plants deep within the growth and away from the dirt road that wound its way up the mountain. As he rolled his window down, he could hear the sound of rushing water. There was a sizable river nearby. He could only guess by the crowd in front of him, that much of the community was involved in the processional. He stepped out of his truck and tried to peer into the foliage of the rain forest beside the road. It was difficult to determine just how far back the community had settled.

This was one of those hidden pockets of people that he knew existed and occasionally stumbled upon.

Allen and his wife Becky had been missionaries for twenty-two years. Their travels had included their year of language study in Costa Rica, nine years in Venezuela, two in Peru (where they had to leave due to health reasons), and their latest six years in Nicaragua. Their transfer to Nicaragua coincided with the last of their two children going to college. When they began their new life in Central America, it was as a couple again. Allen began his missionary career teaching in the seminary at Caracas. As theological education was phased into the hands of the national believers, he found his zeal for evangelism renewed. Allen accepted a Church Planter request for Peru, but found the altitudes difficult. He battled with his health for two years before accepting the fact that he needed to seek God's direction in where to serve. It was then that the request was discovered for rural Nicaragua. The country had only been reopened to Baptist missionaries for about three years when the request was made. Ten years of civil war and economic instability had made for a fertile ground for the gospel.

Allen glanced up to see José returning.

"It is a funeral procession," he reported sadly.

"What happened?" Allen asked sincerely.

"A little girl drowned trying to cross the river."

Allen dropped his head.

"There's more," José continued. "This is the ninth death this year and five have been children. It seems the river took out the bridge they had when Hurricane Mitch came through last year. They have not been able to rebuild the bridge, but the people still try to cross the river when they think the water is low enough or the current is not strong. The little ones can't judge as well. Now that the rainy season has begun, the river will be stronger."

"Are there no plans on the part of the government to rebuild this for them?" Allen asked incredulously.

"It seems the municipal leaders are still working on rebuilding homes throughout the regions. Major bridges are still not completed. No one cares about a small village like this losing its bridge." José explained exasperated.

"That's not true," Allen replied firmly lifting his head. "God cares. What is the name of the village?"

"*Pozo Negro,*" he said shaking his head in disapproval.

"Black well?" Allen thought to himself.

The new sanctuary of the Coronado Baptist Church was filled to capacity. Having been completed two weeks ahead of schedule, it was available for the special service that packed both the floor and balcony. The two-story facility was well positioned allowing the maximum parking available.

"Arnie was right," Howard Pennington thought out loud, gazing about the immense worship center.

"Beg your pardon?" his wife Donna asked innocently as they sat together on the front pew.

"I was just commenting that Arnie was right to go with the two story design. It is beautiful and it really does allow for all these people to park closer to the church. I'm so glad he took charge of this after we left."

"Feels a little funny being back here after almost a year, doesn't it?" Donna asked.

"That's an understatement," Howard said trying to keep his voice low. "This seems like a totally different church. Rusty has done a great job as pastor. I counted at least five new Sunday School classes that have started, and his new member's class was overflowing. I'm so glad the church decided to extend him a call after we left without waiting too long, especially since he's the first single pastor they have ever had."

"Did you notice who is singing in the choir?" Donna remarked softly.

Howard looked up into the new three-tier choir loft and scanned the faces. The men's section was twice the size it had been when he was pastor. He made a quick pass and stopped. There was Arnie Johnson, smiling and waving in their direction. When their eyes met, Arnie quickly motioned towards his right. Three basses down was a tall young man who looked only fairly familiar. Then Howard saw the resemblance. It was Arnie's son Alex. Howard would hear the story later of the months of counseling and probation that resulted in Alex's complete turn around. Arnie would always be thankful to his former pastor as well as his current pastor for that change.

The service began as the Pennington's sat together on the front row. Karen and Terry sat close – closer than they had been in years. Karen knew her going to college meant leaving home, but now her little brother was leaving the country and there would be no "drop in visits" on the weekends. She was going to miss him. Terry had turned eleven and was excited about the traveling. He had just spent almost two months at a missionary orientation center with his parents, where he had met several children – some older and some younger than himself – and all going to different countries around the world. He learned about the different kinds of food and culture of other countries and he knew he had some adjusting to do, but he saw it all as an adventure. The mission board did not appoint families with children over the age of thirteen for that very reason. The younger the child, the more flexible and adaptable they could be. Terry was ready for Central America, whether Karen was ready for him to leave or not.

Rusty Patterson stepped to the pulpit after the choir's robust call to worship. He welcomed the visitors while the ushers passed out the visitor's packets. Rob Billings jokingly offered Howard a packet as he passed the front row.

"Today we have a special honor," Rusty announced proudly. "The Coronado Baptist Church will be sending out one of her own to the mission fields of Honduras. Most of you know them, but for those of you who are new to the church, allow me to present to you our former pastor and his family."

The Pennington family rose to a spontaneous ovation. It didn't seem like they had been gone for nine months, but there were many new faces. Howard took Donna's hand and together they waved to the congregation.

"They served here for ten years before God called them both to serve overseas. It has been my pleasure to serve alongside Dr. Pennington here at Coronado and I mean this when I say that I have every respect and admiration for this man and his family. I wouldn't be with you all today, if it were not for him," Rusty shared from his heart.

"*Amen!*" came a husky voice from the choir.

Rusty turned and smiled at Arnie.

"And I am not alone in that statement, I see", he quickly added. "So without further delay, I would like to invite the Pennington's to come and join me here on the platform. We have a special surprise for you."

Howard led the way as Donna and the children followed in line. The instrumentalists began a quiet rendition of "*People Need the Lord*" and the doors at the rear of the auditorium opened. The congregation turned to watch behind them as flag bearers began to march in to the music. Two lines of young people hoisting flags of the nations kept in step as they paced themselves down the two main aisles. They reached the front together and crossed each other as they marched to the opposite walls and then back to the rear of the building along the outside walls. By the time they had all entered and taken their positions, flags from most every country of the world could be seen lining the church. The ranks formed two right angles that met at the communion table. By the time the last person was in place the congregation was once again on its feet in ovation. The applause swelled in proportion to the tears that formed in the eyes of Howard, Donna and one other.

The flag bearers stood motionless till Pastor Rusty resumed his place at the pulpit. They then placed their flags in the stands provided. Howard noticed the two flag bearers closest to the communion table. One he recognized, but the other, though unknown, seemed out of place. She was much older than any of the other young people that had marched in. Karen glanced down, saw them both and began to cry.

"I mentioned a surprise," Rusty continued. "But this isn't it. We have another honored guest with us this morning, and if you didn't notice, she was carrying the Honduran flag. Her daughter, I think you know. At this time, I would like to invite Mrs. Susan Eldridge to come and share with us."

The older woman placed her flag securely in its stand and turned towards the Penningtons. The young girl Howard had recognized began to tear up. As Susan stepped to the platform, Donna reached out her hand and Susan took it. The two women embraced and the tears began. Howard waited his turn to give her a hug. He wasn't sure if he could handle this.

While the Penningtons took turns greeting Susan, Rusty took advantage of the time to introduce her to the congregation.

"Susan Eldridge served with her husband Carey for over fourteen years in Honduras. Her daughter Anna is here below, and her sons, Joshua and Caleb are among our flag bearers this morning. Many of you may remember the Sunday morning service when Bro. Howard shared his decision with the church to go to the mission field. That decision was partly in response to a tragic accident that had occurred on the field. Carey Eldridge was the missionary who lost his life in that traffic accident. His work was just beginning in some strategic areas. This is his wife. She now lives here to be near her daughter who will be starting college at the end of this month. She still serves with our Mission Board by working with candidates who are considering missions. She goes to college campuses and speaks in churches through out the state sharing the vision of missions and counseling with those who may be sensing God's call. We count it an honor to have her with us today."

The Pennington's took their seat on the front pew and listened as Susan Eldridge shared the legacy of her husband's work and then moved past his death to the open doors that he left behind. Her words were both painful and at the same time therapy. Her strength was evident. As she had hoped, the congregation did not pity her, but rather admired the grace she displayed.

The Eldridges had left Honduras before the dreadful hurricane Mitch had tormented the land thrusting the country into total disarray. She had followed the stories closely in the news and called friends when it was possible. Susan related some of what she knew in order to call the church together in prayer for the area and for the ministry needs that would be awaiting the Penningtons when they arrived.

"There are so many needs in that country," she concluded. "I know God has great plans for you there. But before you can begin, you must humble yourself to that of a child in order to learn the language. Your first year in Costa Rica will be one of the most difficult years of your life. It will be the time when you will cross from one culture to another. You will learn more than just a language, you will learn the ways of a people that are not your own. You will embrace them or you will build walls that will prevent you from ministering fully to them. This next year will be crucial. But let me assure you, if God has called you to missions, 'faithful is He who called you – who also will do it.'"

Her final words carried both assurance and warning. The Penningtons would reflect on those words often in the months to follow. The service continued, including a special presentation of a monetary gift for the family and a commitment that the church would support them in prayer on a consistent basis. Near the end, Howard was invited to the pulpit to share a word.

Howard chose not to "preach", but to simply relate the activity of the family over the past nine months. He gave opportunity for Donna to relate her call to missions at an early age and then speak to plans for Karen to stay behind and begin college with Anna Eldridge. The two had grown very close in the past year.

"In closing," Howard began to conclude. "I know that the needs are going to be great where we are going. I also know that it will take skills and gifts I don't possess. I want to give you all fair warning, that someday, we may be writing home asking for a group of volunteers from this church to come and work with us on a special project. Across our nation and convention, thousands of volunteers travel around the world each year meeting needs that are beyond the reach of the local missionary. You may not be called to 'plant' your life overseas, but you can certainly 'visit' and bring a hammer with you. We'll be in touch – I guarantee it."

The congregation burst into applause once more. Howard took that for the support he was looking for. His words found fertile soil among several that morning. For some, the call to serve would come quicker than even they expected.

Pozo Negro had an unusual history. In Spanish, the name meant "black well", though there was no well near the small village. Some had suggested that the name referred to a "pit" rather than a well, since *pozo* could be understood as either. But no one had ever found a pit of any great size there either. The truth of the name was to be found in the deep darkness that pervaded over the community. There was no church, Catholic or Evangelical within the area of the village. Some said it was because it was too difficult to access since no road passed through the village. Only a narrow footpath for horses and walkers existed. All merchandise was carried in by mule-pack. Those who were raised in or near the village knew otherwise. For them, *Pozo Negro* was the dark pit of the devil himself. Don Tulio Bayardos was the reason. He was a witch.

Don Tulio had come to the area from the northern part of the country where he had studied witchcraft under Fernando Gadea, known throughout Nicaragua as "Nando". Nando lived near the top of a mountain in *Jinotega*. Situated near his home was a large cross that was visible to the people as they made their way up the mountain. The irony was that the cross gave an impression of Christianity though all recognized the true origin of Nando's practice. Don Tulio had followed many to seek the wisdom, secrets and magic of Nando. He stayed two years and learned all he could.

When the civil war broke out, Tulio sought refuge in the mountains above León to avoid taking sides. He carried his practice with him. He was called Don Tulio more from fear than from respect. During his first year, stories of witchcraft and strange deaths began to circulate. Tulio was quick to take credit for the events. From there, his reputation grew. To some, he was a healer, to others, he was a Satanist, to all he was powerful, and because of him, there was a cloud of darkness over *Pozo Negro*.

Don Tulio sat alone in his house. Most of the village had made their way across the river to be with the family that was burying their daughter. The smoke from the pot, which boiled on his clay stove, hung heavy in the air. It was not lunch. Tulio walked over to the black pot and stared into its contents. The brownish red stew bubbled furiously as fragments of bone, meat and hair swirled about. Taking a large ladle from the table beside the stove, Tulio scooped up a spoonful of the amalgam and poured it onto a clearing on the floor marked off with occult designs and candles. He squatted next to the spill and began to study it intently. He "read" the signs for nearly five minutes and then rose slowly. He walked back to his only chair, and sat down hard.

"This is only the beginning," he said sadly to himself.

———————————

The reception line moved slowly, as church members waited to express their best wishes to the Penningtons. It was an emotional time for everyone. As the last of the families gave their hugs, Howard noticed a familiar face standing patiently against the wall. When the opening presented itself, the man stepped forward and extended his hand.

"Billy!" Howard exclaimed. "I didn't know you were here."

"I wouldn't have missed it," Billy Eldridge, Carey's brother responded. "I was hoping Susan would be able to make it."

"That was a pleasant surprise," Howard added.

"It was Rusty's idea," Billy confessed. "I'm glad to see everything worked out well for you and your family. I'm especially glad to know that Karen and Anna will be starting together in college. I think the two will be good for each other. Anna will help Karen understand better what you all are experiencing. That should help her at this end."

"We can't thank you all enough for helping her get started while we were gone."

"It was nothing. By the way," Billy added changing the subject. "I've decided I'm going on a mission trip sometime in the next year. You don't know where I can find a good construction man to help out, do you?"

Howard looked at Donna and the two of them laughed out loud.

"His name is Arnie, and I think it would be great if you could get him overseas. Let's see if I can find him and introduce you two."

The rest of the afternoon was filled with phone calls and visits. The Penningtons had never expected such a send off. They knew that the church supported their decision to go to the mission field, but they never realized to what extent. This was truly a grand commissioning service.

For Allen, living in the city of León was wiser than locating in the capital, even though most of the missionaries resided there. With the children grown and gone, the need to be near schools, fast food, or theatres didn't exist. He and Becky were happy with their small house near the central plaza. León, one of the oldest cities of Nicaragua, was founded during the 16th century by Hernandez de Cordoba, (from whom the currency of the country was named). It became the seedbed for liberal politics while Granada in the south near Lake Nicaragua bolstered conservatism. The two factions had often spilled into civil war. The Wests determined early to glance blindly at the political factions, including the strong Sandinista influence still alive in León, and to concentrate solely on the spiritual needs of the people. It was difficult to separate the two at times. Confiscated and resold land caused legal nightmares as they sought property for church buildings. And yet, it was not uncommon to find former Contras and Sandinistas worshipping side by side in a spirit of reconciliation through the message of the gospel.

Allen worked on several levels of church development. In some parts of the region, he worked alongside established churches as they opened new works. He would help with evangelism through services, films, and special groups – such as medical teams – that could impact an area where human needs were great. In other parts of the region, he conducted workshops for equipping new leaders, teaching in areas of discipleship, doctrine, and leadership training. He also helped set up construction teams for the building of new chapels and providing Sunday school space. His plate was full.

Earlier that morning he had been on a survey trip with a local pastor, José Moralis, to check out a village where they were thinking of beginning a new work. It was on the way to that village, that Allen encountered the funeral procession. All that morning, the thought of the small casket haunted him. He had not traveled that road often enough to know that the hidden village of *Pozo Negro* even existed. But it had dramatically caught his attention. He parked the silver *Land Cruiser* on the street outside their home, and used his key to let himself in.

"You back already?" Becky called from the far end of the house.

"Yes, I carried José by his house on my way in," Allen yelled back. "It's just me for lunch."

"Good thing," Becky replied stepping into the front room to greet him. She kissed him lightly and smiled. "I made a small pot of chili, and that leaves more for you."

Allen enjoyed Nicaraguan dishes, but was especially glad to come home to "good ole-home-cooked" North American meals. His favorite was lasagna, but Becky's chili was just as tempting. They sat down to a quiet lunch together at the kitchen table.

"So how was the trip this morning?" Becky began after they had prayed over the meal.

"Very fruitful," Allen replied while breaking crackers into his bowl. "We didn't have any trouble getting into *Las Minas*, in spite of the morning rains. We found the brother that José had met and talked to him about starting a Bible class in his home. He was very receptive and I think José will be able to start taking some from the church up as early as next week to begin witnessing and holding classes."

"That's wonderful," Becky responded. "Are you going to be going with them at first?"

"Yes, I think I'll go and see how José does. I'll try to let him lead the way, then I won't be noticed as much when I ease out. I believe José is ready to start a church plant on his own."

"Well, that truly is wonderful," Becky repeated herself.

Allen took a few bites and then sipped his tea.

"I saw something else this morning that I would like to follow up on also."

"What was that?" Becky asked.

"About eight or so kilometers below the village we went to is another village I didn't even know existed. It is set back in the hills and is separated from the main road by a river. It seems hurricane Mitch destroyed their bridge and now they cross the best way they can – usually when the water is down. But sometimes, like this week with the heavy rains, the river swells and,...well..." Allen's voice trailed off.

"And?" Becky edged him on.

"And, well a little girl drowned trying to cross it."

"Oh no," Becky reacted alarmed.

"José checked around, and found that there have been other deaths due to the situation. Worse of all, there doesn't seem to be any church back up in there at all to speak of."

"Are you thinking about checking into it?" Becky asked.

"I intend to start praying about it – that's for sure," Allen said determined. "I don't know if we can work two areas at the same time or not. But I sure would like to get up in there sometime."

Allen and Becky continued their meal. God began planting seeds.

CHAPTER TWO

"THE ARRIVAL"

"IS THIS place going to have TV?" Terry asked cautiously while he buckled his lap belt.

"I'm sure it will," his mother replied helping him pull the strap tightly. He glared at her actions as being totally unnecessary. "Why do you ask?"

"Cause that place we went to in Virginia didn't, and you guys didn't even tell me till we got there." He pouted.

"That's because we didn't even know till we got there," Dr. Howard Pennington added from across the aisle of the LACSA airliner. "Besides, even if there is TV, it will probably be in Spanish."

"You're kidding," he exclaimed.

For Terry Pennington, this had been quite a sudden change. He was young enough to adjust, but old enough to question what was happening. Howard and Donna had taken careful steps to include Terry in their discussions and plans. For the most part, he was excited about living in a foreign country. Yet, as the Boeing 737 began its taxi across the Miami tarmac, he was beginning to realize he was now leaving the United States from the opposite side he had grown up on. Worse, this was the third plane he had been on in one day. He had flown more in the past three months than he had his whole life.

In the past eleven months, his family had lived in no less than four different places and three different states. The time in Texas with his grandparents was not too bad. Two months were spent at the Missionary Learning Center located on a large tract of donated farmland somewhere outside of Richmond, Virginia. It was there that his parents attended classes and studied in the campus library for hours while he attended school classes with other MK's (missionary kids) and then "hung out" at the playgrounds or ball fields. The biggest disappointment was the fact that there were no TVs in any of the apartments and some dumb rule that they were not to use the ones in the classrooms for network programming. They could watch a video from the library of African bushman or some other "National Geographic" type film, but they couldn't tune in *Full House* and definitely no *MTV*. Terry had made friends with another boy whose parents were going to Singapore and a young girl getting ready to go to India. He wondered what it would be like for them. Terry didn't know anything about Costa Rica, but he had heard the boys play soccer. Maybe it wouldn't be so bad, he thought, even if *Fresh Prince* spoke Spanish.

As the plane began to level off, Howard opened the briefcase he had carried on, and began skimming through some of the notes he had taken on the language school that he and Donna would be attending for the next year. The Spanish Language Institute of San José, Costa Rica had been in operation for several decades. It served various evangelical organizations as well as other groups needing a concentrated study in the Spanish language. Whether heading to the southern most tip of Chile or just across the border from McAllen between Texas and Mexico, San José Costa Rica was the ideal place to get the basics in Spanish grammar, phonetics, and practice. The style of the language institute varied depending on the amount of time devoted to the program. Most Southern Baptist missionaries stayed a full year and completed four terms. It became the buffer zone of culture shock between new missionaries and their destined fields.

For Howard, the language learning would be no new experience. He already possessed a fair ability to communicate. He was not fluent by any means, but he could hold a conversation, as he had with an illegal Honduran in a holding cell nearly a year before. Howard reclined his seat as far as it would go and reflected over that meeting that had changed his life. He could still hear the words of the skinny man in the cell who had traveled hundreds of miles only to be caught two hours after his illegal entry into the United States. When Howard had shared the gospel with him, his first response was total amazement.

"I have never heard this before," Flaco said. "Why have I never heard this before? Why did I have to come all this way to hear this news?"

Howard had thought about those words many times in the past year. Now it was he who was traveling. His mission was as clear as was his calling. No man should have to leave his home country to find Jesus.

Donna tried to contain her excitement during the flight. She was realizing a childhood dream and it seemed just too good to be true. She watched Howard read over materials concerning the language school, the city of San José and a little about the country of Costa Rica, but for her, it was an adventure to be savored and taken as it came. As Terry slept beside her, she began to reflect over the missionary stories she had heard growing up in Texas. She recalled with delight the native dress, the foreign currency and the large table with the colorful items from around the world. She remembered the very service when a young missionary from Uruguay shared her testimony and then gave a challenge to the girls present. That was the time Donna had first felt the tug of God to go to the mission field. She knew it was too soon to seriously consider going, but seeing this young woman had always encouraged her. She especially remembered how impressed she was with a *single* woman giving her life to the mission field. As Donna replayed the sketches her memory permitted, she could see the young face of the missionary who had just completed her first full term on the field. That had to be more than twenty-five years ago, she thought, and yet her face was as clear as if she had just met her.

"*You have,*" came an inward voice.

Donna gasped to herself.

"Marnie!" she said aloud. No one stirred, but Donna felt as though she had been lifted from her seat. How ironic that the missionary speaker that had been used by God a year earlier to confirm the timing of Donna and Howard's calling to missions was the very missionary that Donna had heard as a little girl that had prompted her heart towards missions in the first place.

"What are your plans for today?" Becky called from the kitchen.

Allen West had worked on chores around the house most of the morning, which was sure indication that he didn't have any pressing matters to attend to. After changing two burnt out bulbs, fixing the drip under the sink, and finally adjusting the hinges on the back screen door so that it no longer dragged along the ceramic floor tile, Allen decided to put his tools away.

"I guess it would be a good day to travel back up to that area I told you about last month," Allen said with surrender in his voice.

"What area?" Becky replied.

Allen entered the kitchen and began washing his hands at the sink.

"It's a little village off from the main road. José and I stumbled on it when we took that first trip up to *Las Minas.*"

"And how is the work progressing at *Las Minas?*" Becky interrupted.

"Oh, just fine," Allen responded. "I probably won't continue going with José much longer, he has taken full charge of the new work and that tickles me to no end."

"So what is this other area you were referring to?" Becky asked returning him to his train of thought.

"You may recall me mentioning a little town just off the main road, but across a river and that there had been a funeral procession that day we were traveling to *Las Minas.*"

"Yes, I do," Becky said, turning to look at Allen. "That was where the little girl had drowned, wasn't it?"

"Exactly," Allen confirmed. "Well, I kept saying I was going to go back there and I never have. Since I don't have anything going on for this afternoon, I thought I might drive back up there and investigate it a little."

"I have just finished the breakfast dishes," Becky said wiping her hands on the dishtowel near the sink. "Would you like me to get dressed and go with you?"

"That would be great," Allen replied enthusiastically. "José is not available today, and I would enjoy the company – especially yours!"

"When do you expect us to get back?" Becky asked.

"Before dark for sure, probably around 5:30 or so."

"Then let me throw some meat in the crock pot and we'll have some beef stew when we get back." Becky offered.

"Sounds like a winner! I'll go get changed."

The Wests enjoyed working together. With their children grown and with families of their own, Allen and Becky found ministry to be a joint adventure. Becky could still walk the long uphill hikes to some of the off-road churches and missions and preferred that to keeping the house. She would help new works by conducting children's classes and special women's workshops, such as teaching a small craft or preparing a special dish. She had to learn how to cook on a wood burning clay stove to be able to teach something they could do in their own home. While Allen taught Bible, Becky helped improve the home of the families that came. They were a good team.

The line outside the small adobe house of Don Tulio sat patiently. Inside the single dark room of his home, a frantic mother cradled her sick child. Don Tulio sat in his chair and listened to the mother sob.

"I have tried the soup you told me to prepare, but it hasn't helped," she cried. "His head is still hot, and he doesn't eat. He won't respond. Please help us."

"Do you have the twenty córdoba?" Don Tulio responded coldly.

"I have ten," she offered apologetically. "I had to borrow that from my brother's family. It is all I have, I swear."

"Maybe you should go to your sister's family," Don Tulio sneered. "How can I help you when you don't even do what I ask. The money is not for me, it is your demonstration of faith in what I offer."

The people of *Pozo Negro* had no idea what Don Tulio possessed, because much of it was kept in other communities. All they saw was his humble dwelling and small tract of property at the far edge of the village. No one knew of his *finca* (ranch) near *Posoltega*, or the amount of cattle he had grazing on it. Don Tulio was a man of material substance – most of which he gleaned from the pockets of the poor as they sought his miracles.

Perhaps overcome with a moment of compassion, Don Tulio rose from his chair and walked to a small bag near his stove. Taking a small handful of blended herbs, he poured them into a small folded paper.

"Try again, and be sure to boil the water well before you pour in the herbs," Tulio warned sternly. "Then give it to him at midnight while it is still hot."

The woman trembled as she took the small paper filled with herbs. She gently slipped it into her dress pocket and retrieved the crumpled green bill and offered it. Don Tulio huffed and took it from her. Before leaving, he gave other instructions and reminded her to return within the week to report the results. She could also bring the other ten córdoba at that time, he added firmly.

The lady thanked him and assured Don Tulio that she would return and bring his money. She then backed out of the front door where the next patient waited nervously.

"Where do we go now?" Donna called out frantically over the din of Spanish chatter.

"I'm not sure," Howard replied looking around as passengers filed past him. "Let's try following the crowd and see where that leads us."

Donna grabbed Terry's hand firmly and hoisted her carry-on over her shoulder. They merged into the crowd that weaved it's way through the terminal under construction till they reached a large room with floor lines passing through what appeared to be toll booths.

"Which line do we get in?" Donna asked helplessly.

Howard looked effortlessly over the heads of the ones in front of him to read the signs on the immigration booths. He thought how much taller he felt now among the short stature of the "Tico's", as they were affectionately called. He spotted the sign for "foreigner's" and led the family into that direction.

Howard gathered the three passports and instructed Donna to stand close. He chose not to reveal his limited Spanish to the immigration agent. For one, he was afraid of getting in over his head, and secondly, he had been advised to "play dumb" so that the customs agents would be less likely to pilfer through their bags. When asked questions, he simply smiled and pointed to his passport. He had filled out the necessary forms on the plane and they were all placed appropriately in each passport. The agent need only confirm each passport belonged to its holder and stamp the necessary pages to begin their tourist visa. The language school would later take up the passports and begin the process for student visas that would carry them for the full year.

For Donna, it was no problem acting confused. She took the opportunity to point out to Terry the palm trees that they could see through the windows. Terry was not impressed. He had seen palm trees before. Then he saw young boys climbing them with their bare feet to retrieve coconuts. He watched them shimmy up and down the rough curved trunks and wondered if he would ever be able to learn how to do that. This was a different world than the one he had left. The air was warmer, and the smell of rain was heavy. Costa Rica would take some getting used to.

Howard located the baggage claim area and they began looking for their footlockers. All their earthly belongings for the following year had traveled in the belly of that plane. Now they had to somehow manage them through the customs area and to the outer sidewalk where hopefully their "big brother and sister" were there to meet them.

The "big brother" program was sound in its philosophy and practicality. A family that had been on campus of the language institute for at least one full trimester would assist the entrance of an arriving family. The Baptist missionaries in particular had a working system that provided transportation from the airport and furnished housing for the new family as they stepped into the country. The "big brother" would help the new family learn how to use public transportation because no one owned vehicles while attending language school. They would orient them to banking, shopping, as well as the campus of the institute. The most important task of all – they would show them how to order pizza to be delivered to their homes as soon as possible. The bonding that would take place between new arrivals and their "big brother and sister" would be one of the most important relationships cultivated in the new land - and for good reason.

Albert Redding's rotund physique had barely passed the medical release four months earlier. Fortunately, during his first full trimester in San José, he had trimmed fifteen unneeded pounds due to the daily exercise of walking to and from class coupled with the fresh fruit available. His flush cheeks held a consistent smile that motivational speakers train to develop. For Al, life was to be enjoyed and that enjoyment was to be shared. He was truly a friendly face. His wife, Leanne, was a small petite woman who barely reached Al's shoulders. If there were ever personality opposites, it was the Reddings. But the combination was uncanny. The Reddings were four-month veterans of the language school on their way to Oaxaca, Mexico.

They stood along the railing outside the airport doors and scanned the faces of the weary passengers lifting their loads onto the customs tables. Al quickly dismissed any Latin faces and strained to see those still collected around the conveyor belt like expectant fathers awaiting their "little bundle" to emerge. In Howard Pennington's case, he was expecting sextuplets, Al thought humorously. Leanne Redding pulled the folded email with the attached photo from her purse and examined it for the fifth time. It was a black and white photocopy that the mission office had made for them, but the faces were still fairly clear. She handed it quietly to Al, who looked at it for the fifth time, nodded, then handed it back to her. She remembered how nervous they had been on their flight in, and how their "big brother and sister" had failed to recognized them for several minutes after they had exited the airport. It was scary and she didn't want the Penningtons to have to go through that.

The Land Cruiser worked its way across the cutbacks as Allen navigated the ruts and rocks. He took his time so as not to bounce Becky too much. His several trips to *Las Minas* over the previous month had taken him by the opening to *Pozo Negro* enough times to know where he could pull off the road and leave his truck.

"Did you bring your walking shoes?" Allen asked, squeezing the Land Cruiser as close to the shoulder's edge as he dare.

"Don't worry about me, dear," Becky responded with a smile. "Though I do think I would prefer getting out on your side."

Allen adjusted his ball cap and helped Becky out his door. They made sure the doors were all locked on the vehicle and then walked across the dirt road toward a small group of adobe houses obscured by the shadows of the large mango trees.

A small girl was sweeping the ground in front of the nearest home. She didn't notice the alien couple walking toward her until they were close enough to call out in a regular voice.

"Excuse me," Allen called politely in Spanish. "Are your parents home?"

The little girl quickly turned and stared mutely at the North Americans. She had never seen skin so light before. Allen was taller than most men she knew and Becky wore unfamiliar designs in her dress. She dropped her broom and ran into the open doorway of the house. The Wests exchanged glances and decided to wait for an adult to emerge from the dwelling.

After several minutes, a spindly woman with a loose hanging cotton dress peeked out the doorway and slowly advanced into the yard like a doe investigating a new meadow. Her cautious manner alerted the Wests to a need for slow diplomacy. Becky took the lead and stepped in front of her husband.

"Good afternoon," she began assuringly. "We didn't mean to frighten your little daughter – we are looking for a village."

The woman didn't respond.

"Do you know how we can get to *Pozo Negro?*" Becky tried again taking a couple steps closer.

"*Pozo Negro?*" the little woman echoed.

"Yes, *Pozo Negro,*" Becky repeated slowly taking another step. "My husband and I are looking for *Pozo Negro.*"

The woman held up her hand and Becky stopped. She wasn't sure what the motion meant, but Becky didn't want to make any misunderstood moves. The woman turned slowly to her right with her hand still raised and pointed in the direction of a small banana grove. Without looking back she spoke clearly enough for Allen to hear.

"*Pozo Negro* is through those trees about two *manzanas* to the river. But you will not be able to cross the river in those clothes."

"Is there no bridge nearby?" Becky asked, knowing the answer.

The skinny figure turned back towards the two strangers with a distant look in her eyes.

"No bridge," she said sullenly. "No bridge at all."

The finality of her words ended their conversation and she promptly returned to her darkened doorway and disappeared within the shadows of her home.

"Gee, so much for the welcome wagon," Allen commented, as he stepped up to join Becky.

"I don't blame her for being cautious," Becky replied taking his hand. "I doubt they get many visitors through here."

The two stared in the direction of the banana leaves and squeezed each other's hands.

"Are you ready for an adventure?" Allen asked toyingly.

"Why don't we pray first?" Becky replied.

Allen nodded and took her other hand in his. They stood quietly in the shadow of the mango trees and bowed their heads. From the darkened doorway, little eyes watched curiously.

"Father, we thank you for hearing us this day. Thank you for going before us and now leading us down this path. We don't know what lies ahead, but you do. We commit our steps to you. We pray for these homes that we can see around us. They seem to have been overlooked by many for so long and yet, Father, we know that you see inside every house. We're not sure what we will find when we get to the river, but we are going just the same. We pray Your protection over us. Open our eyes and guard our steps. We thank you for what You are about to do. In the precious name of our Lord, Your Son, Jesus Christ,…Amen."

"Amen," Becky agreed.

"Welcome to Costa Rica!" Al announced boisterous and friendly as the Penningtons lumbered through the glass doors of the airport. Howard brandished his computer case and carry-on while Donna tried to handle her own bag and Terry.

"You must be Albert and…"

"Leanne!" Al finished for him. "You got it, but you can call me Al. Come this way, we have a van and car waiting over here."

"You have a van?" Howard looked surprised.

"No, it belongs to the mission, we checked it out to pick you guys up," Al replied while motioning the luggage carriers toward the white Toyota twelve passenger van.

Three young Costa Rican boys followed the two over burdened baggage men to the rear door of the van in hopes of helping load the six plastic containers for an additional tip. Howard watched Al wave off the boys and then using his body as a wedge, block them from interfering with the airport luggage handlers. Howard thought to himself that Al was being a little rude to the young men who were just trying to help.

The baggage men hoisted and stacked the heavy containers behind the back seat and then turned to Al for their gratuity. As they rolled their empty dollies back to the passenger area, Al was promptly surrounded by the three boys chattering in blended phrases of Spanish and broken English. Howard picked up enough to understand that they were upset Al wasn't paying them also for helping load the luggage. He decided to stand aside and allow his big brother to handle the dispute.

Leanne took the opportunity to introduce herself to Donna.

"How was the flight?" Leanne started.

"It was long – but then there is no easy way to get here, I guess," Donna shrugged.

"Did you come through Miami?" Leanne continued in order to make conversation while her husband dealt with the unruly boys.

"Yes, we had to make connections from southern California, so we started very early. Do you have any children?" Donna asked to change the subject.

"We have three, in fact," beamed Leanne. "We asked our maid to stay with them tonight till we could get you guys settled?"

"You have a maid?" Donna responded surprised.

"Why yes, most of us here do. Did they not mention that to you at the Missionary Learning Center?" Leanne said opening the sliding door to the van so the women and Terry could get out of the dispute over the bags.

"I guess I didn't take that part too seriously," Donna sighed. "I figured that was just something some of the missionaries indulged in because they could afford it."

"Trust me, it's not an indulgence," Leanne replied with a smile. "You will be working eight hours a day easy on language study. You will not have time to clean house, cook and handle the wash – not the way you would have to do it here. Besides, the maid becomes one of the best resources for testing your Spanish. Most have worked for missionary families and are passed from home to home as students come and go. They understand why we are here and what we are trying to learn in the short time we have. They help with child care while you are out of the house as well as guard the house."

"Guard the house?" Donna sounded alarmed. "Guard the house from what?"

"Robbery is high here, as I suppose it is in much of Central America. You don't leave the house unattended at night if at all possible. They'll cover all of that at your orientation on Friday."

Donna got quiet. She wasn't sure she wanted to pursue that line of conversation in front of Terry.

The men jumped into the front seats and Al started the engine. Howard buckled his seat belt and took a deep breath. He was placing himself in the hands of others for the first time since this trip began.

"Folks," Al had reverted to his jolly demeanor, "sorry about that with the boys back there. You'll discover soon enough the difference between helping the poor and the manipulation of foreigners. You will want to give to everyone you see on the street at first. In time you will learn the difference between helping a need and funding a habit."

"That makes sense," Howard observed. "I can tell right now, I've got a lot to learn."

"That's the first real lesson you have to learn, brother." Al smiled. "Welcome to missionary life!"

———————————

Allen walked slightly ahead of Becky to clear away the undergrowth from the path. The smell of tropical foliage was heavy as they got closer to the river. Becky quickened her steps as she could hear the sound of rushing water before them. Part of her anxiousness was the desire to emerge from the foreboding shadows of the mango groves and banana plants that enveloped them. She had never sensed such heaviness in an area before. Becky reached out and took Allen's hand and held it tight. He turned back to assure her they had almost reached the clearing. He could see the relief in her eyes.

"It can't be much further," Allen promised.

Becky nodded.

The final turn in the path brought them to a small incline. Allen could see the mid-day sun now as he approached the crest of the climb. They exited the tree line border and stood on a fairly high bluff alongside a sweeping river. The expanse was about forty yards across to the other side. Allen could see where the tempestuous waters from Mitch had gorged into the opposite bank causing landslides and widening the river. Now that the rains were beginning again, the river was running swiftly. It was probably too deep to cross at the point where they stood without being caught in the current. Whether calmer pockets existed further upstream would take some investigation. It was obvious to Allen that they would not be venturing to the other side of the river that day. He would need to return, perhaps with José, to explore in both directions.

Becky peered across the river to find more trees and darkness. She could just barely make out the shape of a house within the tree line, when a figure caught her eye. She stared intently trying to focus on the features. It was short slender man. He held something that looked like a spear in his right hand, but something told her it wasn't a spear. He stood motionless as though he was guarding the village.

"Allen," Becky called softly. "Do you see that man over there?"

Allen had to glance at Becky to see which direction she meant. He had been accessing the river. He followed her gaze to the spot where the man stood. Instinctively, Allen raised his left hand up to wave in greeting. There was no reciprocal response. Allen started to lift his arm again, when Becky gently blocked it with her own and whispered.

"I don't think he is glad to see us."

"How can you tell that?" Allen asked. "Maybe he doesn't see us."

Becky looked around.

"Allen, dear, we are standing out in the open on this bank and he is in the shadows. We stick out like a couple of cherries on a cream pie."

"Maybe we stick out more like the cream pie," he corrected her. "Maybe he has never seen *white* people before. He's probably just being cautious."

"What is that he is holding in his hand?" Becky asked curiously.

"I can't tell from here. It may just be something to clear his way through the jungle on that side of the river, or maybe it's a gauge to measure the river and his job is to see if it's safe to cross - I really don't know."

"He doesn't seem very friendly, does he?" Becky offered in changing the subject.

"Give him time, like I said, maybe we are the first real foreigners he has seen. I can understand him wanting to be cautious. I think it would be better for me to come back with José and see if we can get across this river somewhere."

"I just have a bad feeling about him," Becky confessed.

"You're sounding like one of the Star Wars characters now," Allen laughed. "Listen, we'll head back and I'll get José to come back with me next week. Maybe we'll even get to meet this guy and find out his name."

"You just be careful," Becky responded. "Before we go, I would like to pray for this area – for the river and for the village on the other side."

The Wests stood side by side and bowed their heads. As the water rushed passed them below, Becky prayed for the entire area around her. She prayed for the few homes that they had passed as they made their way to the river. She prayed for the problem of crossing the river and for the village that lay on the other side. She prayed for the families of those who had lost loved ones in the river that year. She prayed for an opening for the gospel within the community that surely existed just beyond their line of sight. And she prayed for the man with the stick – whoever he was.

————————————

Don Tulio watched carefully as the *gringo* couple stood alongside the river before him. He could see them clearly. He watched them as they stood motionless with their heads bowed before him, though he knew it was not to him they bowed. He gripped the pole in his hand even tighter.

"And so, they have arrived," he said to himself with a tone of finality. "They have arrived."

CHAPTER THREE

"THE ADJUSTMENT"

THE SPANISH Language Institute of San José had been built on an incline. A concrete stairway served as a backbone to the campus joining three levels of buildings. The uppermost level was for administration and Chapel. The library, business offices, and student lounge were housed in the administration building. The Chapel was connected to the snack bar where fresh fruit and a small selection of warm Costa Rican dishes could be purchased. There was also a fountain coke machine. The chapel services were arranged and scheduled by the Student Body Chaplain who was elected each trimester. Given the interdenominational nature of the Institute, this meant Baptists and Pentecostals praising side by side. Mennonite speakers followed Methodist prayers, and all strained to understand Friday's Spanish only service.

The second level of buildings included classrooms, bathrooms and post office. The post office consisted of a large open room with a Foosball table in one corner, locked cabinet shelves against one wall and numbered cubbyholes along the adjacent wall. The actual mailroom was behind the wall of cubicles that allowed the school to post the letters and small packages from the back side of the compartments and then close the back panel so the mail wouldn't be pushed back through. Letters were posted between the second and third hour of class during the longer thirty-minute break. During that time, the locked cabinets were opened to reveal a modest book store that provided the students with school supplies, stamps, envelopes, Bibles and Spanish Christian music on cassettes. The bookstore manager was also a volunteer selected from among the student body. It was set up to perpetuate itself rather than create a profit. It was also open for the brief break that the students had in the middle of their arduous morning of study.

The lowest level of buildings consisted of more classrooms, restrooms, and an open-air Ping-Pong area where men and women alike relieved serious stress. Tournaments were regular and those who had spent much of their college time learning how to slice, slam and spin took charge. One of the greatest releases at the Ping-Pong table was the English – not the intentional spin causing misdirection for the small plastic ball - but the freedom to converse and curse (appropriately) in one's mother tongue.

At the base of the concrete stairway, a long sidewalk worked its way to the back gate. On the left was the gymnasium where special assemblies, bazaars and sports took place. The parquet hardwood floor was hand laid and could have been found on the ballroom floor of one of the more elegant hotels. In contrast, the walls were multi-colored with no distinguishable pattern. It was festive. Across from the gymnasium was a Kinder for the pre-school children of both the students and the teachers. "Playground equipment" that would horrify any OSHA inspector was brightly painted and positioned around the fenced courtyard. Children too young to know the difference learned new languages from their playmates. Costa Rican children learned how to say, "mine" while English speaking children learned how to say, "*baño*" meaning bathroom. Ironically, that was one of the first Spanish words their parents learned as well.

The daily schedule for the parents began with the twenty-minute hike to the language school up the hills around the park of *El Bosque*, pass the small market, and finally into the housing area known as *San Francisco de Dos Rios*. The "two rivers" of San Francisco were mere streams that flowed near the language institute. Both the upper and lower gates were manned by paid guards. Only students and teachers were admitted. Visitors and guests were escorted to the administration building. Street vendors were allowed near the gates, but not at the entrance itself.

Once on campus, husbands and wives usually separated to attend their individual classes. Though they would take the same subjects, they may not be at the same level. The formal Spanish training consisted of four hours of classroom spread over a possible six-hour schedule. Each first year student would take one hour of Phonetics, one hour of Grammar, and two different hours of Practice. The placement in the grammar and practice classes would depend on the level of Spanish that the student could demonstrate upon arrival. Sometimes, the wife would be placed in classes more advanced than her husband or vice-versa. Dr. Howard Pennington was placed in the most advanced classes for his practice, but Donna was actually better at grammar than he. They complimented each other well around the kitchen table doing their homework.

After the second week of school, the *practica* class began giving out homework assignments that carried the students outside the fences of the language institute. It was called *tarea* (homework), but was not to be done at home. Each student was given a small text to share with a designated number of Costa Ricans. It began simple and could be read from a small index card. The first text simply said (in Spanish), "my name is…and I am studying Spanish. I have been in Costa Rica for two weeks. I think the country is beautiful and the people are very nice". The idea was to go up to a perfect stranger and to read the card. Most Costa Ricans living around *San Francisco de Dos Rios* had become accustomed to this unusual ritual. Most students picked on the local vendors or store workers whom the students saw anyway. Occasionally, a brave *gringo* would share his text on the bus with a stranger who was unfamiliar with the language institute and their method of instruction. Realizing that the struggling student was trying to communicate from a written message and could not converse beyond the simple presentation, the polite listener would usually acknowledge with a smile and respond in a short and clear *"muy bién!"* and go back to reading their paper. The relieved student would relax into their seat and wonder when they would have to actually "talk" to someone.

Donna remembered how easy the first assignment seemed, until she actually began to speak out loud. Her Texan accent strained at some of the Spanish sounds. Like many learning the new phonetics, she had to remind herself constantly that the vowels never changed and that she had to lose the "a as in apple" sound altogether. Her *"gracias"* sounded more like "grassy-us" for the first few days. Donna soon realized why they told her in orientation that language learning meant "being a clown". You had to learn to imitate and not to be afraid of being laughed at. The humility of language learning is realizing that five-year-olds speak better than you, and are able to get what they want at the checkout counter.

Costa Rican weather was not unlike that of San Diego. Making the transition in late August was even less arduous for the Pennington family. Only the rain seemed unusual, but primarily for its regularity. Howard could almost set his watch by the two o'clock showers of the early afternoon. Since classes finished less than thirty minutes before this hour, couples scurried back down the hill to their homes like frightened sheep. Cheap street-bought umbrellas tended to have about a five-week life expectancy during the heavy raining season.

Donna worked on decorating the small apartment sized house they were placed in. She quickly learned that fresh flowers were an affordable commodity that brightened the home. A large glass vase of exotic bright orange birds of paradise adorned her kitchen table. Various jars of tinted carnations and roses decorated the end tables on either side of their cushioned Rattan couch. The living space was less than half the cubic footage of their former pastorium. Nevertheless, Donna was determined to make her tropical home beautiful.

Each house was designed for the average nuclear family with three small bedrooms. Howard converted the third bedroom into a small makeshift office where he could spread out his language books, vocabulary cards, his 501 Verbs, and Chicago Spanish Dictionary. Howard's limited experience with the language was an advantage at the first, but now he was having to study almost as hard as the ones without high school Spanish. He quickly flipped through his vocabulary cards.

"Are you busy, honey?" Donna called from the dining/ living room.

"Nothing that can't be interrupted," Howard called back. He laid down his index cards and joined her. Donna pulled out two chairs from the dining table indicating a serious talk was ahead. Howard had learned the drill. He was to sit down and listen attentively without comment for at least five minutes. When she reached a point where Howard sensed either a question or the need for an opinion, he would slowly wade into the discussion. He had learned much in the past year.

"This looks serious," Howard offered lightly, giving Donna the open door to begin without having to awkwardly work her way to the point.

"About a six on the scale," she said calmly. "Can I get you some lemonade?"

"Sure, sounds good," Howard smiled.

Donna went to the small refrigerator and pulled out a plastic container of natural lemonade. One of the perks of living in Central America was the plethora of fresh fruit available. Donna poured two glasses and rejoined Howard at the table. She cupped her hands around the cool glass and took a breath.

"I've been thinking about the maid issue," Donna started.

Howard sipped his lemonade to refrain from commenting. It worked.

"Leanne brought it up the night we arrived, and I didn't really take it seriously, but now, I'm beginning to think she may have a point."

Howard nodded.

"I mean, at first it was just getting used to the heat, and then it was having to learn what foods we could no longer buy. I've been tired more than usual, and I'm not used to studying so hard. And, well...maybe it wouldn't be such a bad idea to...well,...you know..." her voice trailed off.

Howard allowed the silence to linger. Donna looked up as though giving him permission to speak. It was a look of appreciation for his patience.

"Donna, we are not in Kansas anymore," he began, smiling. "For that matter, we are so far from everything you and I both were comfortable with that it's a wonder we haven't packed up and quietly flown home in the middle of the night."

"But they took our passports to get our student visas processed," Donna interrupted. "Believe me, I have had those thoughts."

Howard rose and walked around the table. He took her hand in his and knelt beside her.

"That's one of the reasons why they took them. It's natural to feel what you have been expressing," he said gently. "That's also why the mission recommended using a maid while we are in language school. It's not because the labor is cheap and we can afford one. It is because the rigors of adjusting to a new country, a new language, a new culture carries a tremendous emotional drain with it, not to mention the physical demands on your day. You can't just rush out to the grocery, sweep and dust and call it a day with the house. Hon, I've seen you work over an hour on these floors and there aren't that many of them. It takes twice as long to wash the clothes and you have to hang dry them whether it is raining or not. Preparing a meal from scratch and without a microwave is another hour at least."

Donna acknowledged.

"Then between your homework and trying to help Terry with his, your day is past spent and so are you. I'm not much help with my errands into the city. It takes all day just to go to the bank, post office, and buy the supplies we need in San José. Let's face it Honey, the hours are just not there to do it all. I know they covered all of this at orientation a couple weeks ago, but like you, I thought we could do without a maid. I guess there is more to adjusting than just the language and the food. To be honest, I'm surprised we made it this long."

Donna looked deep into Howard's eyes.

"You really do understand, don't you?" she said.

"More than you know," Howard replied. "I'm just as exhausted as you are at times. But more than that, I have been curious about tasting some of the Costa Rican dishes I have been hearing about from some of the other students. I love you, Donna, but your tuna fish sandwiches have reached their critical mass. I don't know what kind of Mayonnaise you are buying, but it didn't come from a Kroger."

They laughed and then hugged.

"Can I talk to Leanne tomorrow about helping us find a maid?" Donna asked.

Howard reached across to the Rattan end table and picked up the phone receiver.

"Don't put off till tomorrow what is desperately needed today. My guess is she has some names already lined up."

Donna took the phone and began dialing. Howard walked back to his office. They were going to make it. At least for another week.

Terry Pennington stared ahead as he walked down the steep sidewalk that bordered the park area of "El Bosque", which was Spanish for forest. In reality, there were only about five trees on the entire lot. Much of the park slopped downhill, but there was level ground near the bottom used for soccer games, when the afternoon rains let up enough. Terry walked slowly downhill watching for the mold covered sections where the concrete never dried. He rounded the corner of the park and began counting streets till he came to the third lane from the guard's stand. That was how directions were given in El Bosque – so many blocks from a known landmark. The guard's stand was a small wooden structure where the neighborhood watchmen sat when it rained. When the weather permitted, he would ride a bicycle through the neighborhood blowing his whistle to alert potential thieves of his vigilant presence. In spite of this system, many homes were still burglarized.

Terry found his street and was about to cross when a soccer ball bounced in front of him and bounded into the road. Terry glanced to his left and saw a small car rounding the corner and into the path of the ball. Without thinking, he dashed into the road and kicked the orb the rest of the distance across the street following it with quick strides. The car's horn blasted and continued to whine even after it had passed Terry. He picked up the ball and turned back towards the park. Three Tico boys stood motionless on the sidewalk staring at him. One yelled with a barking command and held up his hands as though waiting for the ball to be returned. Terry dropkicked the white and black ball just over their heads and two of the boys ran after it. The stern faced third that had demanded the return of their ball looked hard at Terry. He then yelled across the street to the young North American in utterances that he hadn't learned yet. Terry recognized just two words: "*gracias*" and "*gringo*".

One of the tedious tasks Rusty Patterson ever had to assume as Pastor was sifting the mail that came across his desk. He never realized how much correspondence ministries generated. In addition to the flow of his own denomination's promotions and calendar events, the Coronado Baptist Church received newsletters, advertisements and brochures from most every non-denominational group in southern California. Some he filed, some he tossed, while some he delegated to other associates in the church. He could finally appreciate how much Dr. Pennington had edited down the stack before Dianne gave him his mail when he was Associate Pastor. He used to look forward to stopping by her desk. In many ways, he still did.

"Light bill,…literature bill,…water bill," Rusty mumbled thumbing through the stack. He organized the bills to his left, interesting advertisements in front of him, newsletters and brochures to his right to be later sorted, shared, filed, or tossed. Packets of bulk card mail-outs were passed immediately over the edge of the desk to the open mouth of the wastebasket, as were music or book club offers, credit card applications and other "occupant" garbage.

Two-thirds through the stack, a thick packet from the Baptist International Mission Board caught his eye. Rusty didn't have a stack for denominational material started yet, so he tossed it just above the stack of newsletters. He quickly sorted the remaining envelopes and gathered the bills together. He strode lightly across his office and stepped halfway through his door and handed Dianne the small stack. She would issue the necessary checks and contact the treasurer to sign them for paying the bills. He returned to his desk, and took the three-quarter inch stack of newsletters. Most he recognized and knew almost immediately which ones would contain information worth reading. He quickly divided the stack and set the ones he would not be reading on the corner of his desk. These he would pass to his youth director and singles minister. After reading the survivors, he laid them on top of the unopened pile to be shared with the others as well. This left the stack of advertisements in front of him.

Rusty was careful not to indiscriminately toss every ad. He had discovered good deals on office equipment, bulk tapes for their sermon ministry, and even some quality nursery furniture by reading such material. Like the newsletters, he could quickly separate the sheep from the goats by familiarity. Whatever remained, deserved his attention. After thirty-seven minutes of rifting, reading, and ridding, Rusty had cleared his desk of all but one thick packet. He had received a similar packet the past quarter from the same missions promotion department in Richmond, Virginia. Three months ago he had tossed it unopened. But then, three months before, they hadn't celebrated the commissioning of the Pennington's. Missions now had a familiar face. Rusty held the packet up as though divining what was inside. He had opened one before, but never really read the material through. This time he would. He adjusted himself in his chair and got comfortable. Rusty was not going to rush through this information.

Allen sat at the computer reviewing his email. He remembered when mail took weeks to arrive and the exchange of important information could extend over a month. Now he could request and receive information from his area office in the same day. He still did not "surf" the web, or "instant message" loved ones, because of the phone charges. Phone companies were set up on a "pulse" system, which calculated phone use and charged extra when the designated number of pulses were exceeded in a given month. Besides, the phone system in León was not the most reliable. It was enough for Allen to pull down his mail and to get off a few letters each day.

Becky wrote the two children. They had one married daughter in Jackson, Tennessee. She had returned to the states to attend Union University, a renowned Baptist College with a history of sound academics and a passion for ministry and missions. Pauline West chose Union for their excellent nursing program and generosity towards MK's (missionary kids). Finding a dynamic "preacher boy" was an unexpected perk. She was still working on her nursing degree. He was a bi-vocational pastor of a small, rural, West Tennessee church (a common redundancy, for most of the churches in West Tennessee were rural and small). There were still no grandchildren, which was a mixed blessing for Allen and Becky. As much as they wanted to hold a little one again, they knew they were too far away to enjoy them and would only see them grow every four years.

Allen West, Jr. had chosen a state school closer to their Appalachian home in east Tennessee and was enrolled at UT Knoxville, the home of the Volunteers. Their undefeated season of 1998 was his favorite conversation topic. But while the Vols were battering South Carolina 49 to 14, Allen JR's father was preparing for the worst tropical storm of all time to beat upon Central America. Before the Big Orange would clobber Birmingham one week later, Hurricane Mitch would clobber both Honduras and Nicaragua with devastation and destruction that would take more than a year from which to recover. Allen, Jr. was still single, still in school and still undeclared in his major.

The inbox showed just two new entries, a Spanish advertisement from their network provider and a *PrayerGram* from their mission board. Usually, Allen would scroll down through the prayer requests pausing at those countries where he personally knew missionaries. He was in no hurry and read each request slowly. The second to last paragraph caught his eye. It was a prayer request from Mozambique. He did not know anyone serving there, but the request was for prayer that God would send a team to assist the Church planters in a much needed water project. Space limitations would not allow for details, but it was not the project that interested Allen, it was the request. He and Becky had been praying for the village of *Pozo Negro* since their visit. This was an opportunity to invite more people to pray for the little village and to share the need of a bridge at the same time. Allen hit the reply button for the PrayerGram and began composing his own prayer request. He decided that he would also contact his Field Coordinator and begin the process for requesting a volunteer team for the construction. Who knows, he may get a group from his home state of Tennessee – after all, they were known for their volunteers!

Donna Pennington offered Juanita a cup of tea. She smiled and took it without comment. Leanne let Donna resume her place at the small dining room table across from the petite Costa Rican domestic.

"Where would you like to begin?" Leanne asked gently. She knew that both women were nervous and uneasy about not being able to communicate with each other. Leanne had been in the same position just about five months earlier. She and Al had not waited like the Penningtons had about hiring a maid. They had not put as much thought into the matter. It seemed like part of the orientation. Leanne realized now that it is a major adjustment for a family to admit a stranger into their home, handle their belongings, prepare their food, and many times to care for their children. For most, the experience of having a domestic was a little surreal. They would never have considered such a service living stateside. Some even equated the idea with slavery and simply did without. Usually they were single and required less household maintenance.

The Baptist mission kept a thorough file on women who served well among their missionary families. If a maid was unreasonably contentious or dishonest with a family, they simply did not receive a recommendation to future prospects. It was difficult to fire a Costa Rican domestic without solid cause and evidence. The government was very protective of the "*empleada*", requiring the payment of severance, holiday, and even the "thirteenth month". The employing family would even assume some medical costs, including pregnancy, should the *empleada* find herself with child during her year of service regardless of the source of paternity. Consequently, older women with thicker files were more desirable among the new missionaries. By the time the Penningtons had made up their minds to hire, the files were pretty thin.

Juanita Pérez was twenty-three. She was unmarried and still living at home with seven siblings, including a married brother who, along with his wife, had taken over her room forcing her to sleep with two teenage sisters.

Juanita wanted to attend the University in San Pedro, but her father couldn't afford tuition. So Juanita joined the ranks of young *empleadas* hoping to learn English from the American families. Her first and only experience among Baptist missionaries was with a childless couple two years before. She never understood why they only stayed for seven months. She received a pro-rated severance, and was told that they had returned to the U.S. and that she would not be needed for the full year. She had not been called back...until now.

"Why don't we begin with introductions," Donna replied. "I would like to know a little about her and her family."

Leanne nodded and turned to Juanita. In slow and deliberate phrases, Leanne asked Juanita to share about her family and her own background. Juanita responded in like form speaking clearly and at a rate that Leanne could easily translate. Leanne was actually sharper with Spanish than her husband, Al. When Juanita had finished, Leanne turned back toward Donna who sat straining to pick out words and expressions she could recognize.

"She says that she does not live far from here. She is able to walk to work in less than thirty minutes. Her father works for a local mason. He is a builder. Her mother stays home with her younger brothers and sisters. There are eleven of them in a small house."

"Eleven!" Donna exclaimed.

"Yes, but two are her brother and his wife. They take care of themselves. She has two teenage sisters, and two brothers under ten and a baby sister about three years old." Leanne recited from memory.

"She has a three year old sister?" Donna repeated.

"They don't stop till their bodies stop making babies," Leanne said softly, though it was unlikely Juanita understood.

"Ask her about her experience as an *empleeado*," Donna requested calming her tone.

"Donna, the term is *empleada*," Leanne politely corrected. "The file says that she has served only one Baptist family and that there had been some problems. The file isn't specific, but the couple actually returned to the states before finishing language school. I suppose they resigned from the Board...it doesn't say," Leanne summarized looking down.

Donna caught Leanne's eye.

"I know what the file says," Donna said confidently. "I would like to hear what she has to say."

Leanne turned back toward Juanita and thought about how best to frame her question. After about four minutes of Spanish exchange, Leanne looked back at Donna who sat patiently sipping her tea.

"Juanita says that she was asked to wash clothes, cook some of the meals, sweep and wax the floors regularly, dust, and help them with their Spanish," Leanne began. "She would stay some of the evenings to help the woman with her homework. The husband usually studied in the other room. She says, that she was never asked to help the husband study. He was *duro*."

"What's *duro*?" Donna asked.

Juanita heard the question, and scowled.

"*Duro* means to seem 'mean' or 'hard' with other people," Leanne explained. "It was like he didn't like being around Costa Rican people."

Donna nodded.

"So when they left the country, she guesses the Mission blamed her and that is why they have not used her since."

Donna nodded again.

"Ask her where she goes to Church?" Donna changed the subject.

Leanne posed the question and turned back to Donna.

"She used to attend the Catholic Church in her town, but she has been visiting the Baptist Church now."

"I guess I could have expected that answer," Donna smiled. "I don't suppose it would do any good to ask if she was a Christian."

"Not really," Leanne agreed. "If she was brought up in the Catholic Church, she would call herself a Christian, whether she had ever responded to the Gospel or not."

"Then ask her if she is honest," Donna said, sitting up straight and looking Juanita in the eye.

Leanne asked the question.

Juanita looked at Donna instead of responding to Leanne.

"Si, Señora, Soy bién HONESTA! Puede confiar en mí! no sé precupe!"

"I got the first part," Donna remarked. "What was that last part?"

Leanne smiled.

"She said, 'you can trust me! Don't worry'".

Donna looked deep into Juanita's dark brown eyes.

"I believe we can," Donna replied firmly. "I believe we can. Ask her when she can begin?"

The final details of salary, hours, and responsibilities took about thirty more minutes. They closed the deal with a second cup of tea. Howard purposely stayed away from the house with Terry while the women "ironed" out the details. He just hoped she could cook. He couldn't wait for his first authentic Costa Rican meal at home. This was another step into cultural adaptation. It felt good to be moving forward.

José Moralis pastored the small church of *Monte Hermon* located 5 kilometers outside of the city of León. It was nestled at the base of a small mountain outside the city towards Chinandega. The church took its name from "Mount Hermon" of the scriptures, though the "*h*" was silent when pronounced. Allen West had been instrumental in the development of the small mission from the First Baptist Church in León. When they began thinking about a name for the small congregation, José had remembered one of his lessons from *hermano* (brother) Allen. Mount Hermon meant "sanctuary" and was possibly the mountain upon which the transfiguration of Christ took place. What was certain was that the high peaks of Mt. Hermon always had snow (something the missionary had tried to describe). It was the melting snow that flowed down the mountain that first formed the harp-shaped fresh-water Lake of Galilee, then continued southward forming the Jordan River until it rested in the basin of the Dead Sea. Unable to exit, the water became useless to man and creation alike. The missionary had once drawn the comparison between the Sea of Galilee being fresh and full of life because it both received and gave. The Dead Sea was stagnant and unable to sustain life because it only received and never gave. The illustration was directed to the difference between the two bodies of water, but José was more interested in the source – the mountain. Christians may be like the Sea of Galilee or the Dead Sea, but God was found in the "sanctuary" of Mount Hermon, where the "dew" formed and provided the life that would flow to the faithful believer. To José, the name of their church should reflect the majesty and activity of God. *Monte Hermon* was "high and lifted up" as well as the source of "living water".

José began traveling with Allen when *Monte Hermon* decided it was time to open a mission in *Las Minas* further up the mountain. The missionary served as a catalyst in the Church Planting, but much, if not most of the work was conducted by the national church itself. Allen never ceased to be amazed by the time and dedication with which the pastors in his region gave themselves towards new church starts. One of the great differences he had noticed between the international churches he had worked with and the stateside churches he had been involved with in the U.S., was the desire to start new work. It had been his job as an international Church Planter to start missions that would in time produce viable works that would reproduce themselves. This was built into their DNA from the start. *Monte Hermon* was less than two years old, and already had started a new congregation at *Las Minas*. In less than a month, *Las Minas* was already growing in new believers through a home Bible study and a week night service. Not all church starts progressed at the speed that *Las Minas* had. Allen had worked with some areas for over half a year, only to show no lasting results and new directions had to be taken. The mission of the First Baptist Church of León was now mothering her own mission. That was what a missionary lived to see.

José knocked at the West's large metal door that faced the street. It had been three days since Allen and Becky had visited and prayed at the riverside across from *Pozo Negro*. Allen had asked José to his home so that they could discuss *Pozo Negro*. The sound of heavy deadbolts could be heard scraping across the metal from within the house. Another job for his WD-40 Allen thought to himself as he opened the strong protective entrance to his home.

"Buen dia, hermano!" José exclaimed, wishing his brother a good day.

"Igualmente!" Allen replied, wishing him the same in return, extending his hand for a firm greeting. "Won't you come in?"

José entered the sitting room and was immediately greeted by Becky with a glass of ice tea. José liked the American tea that he drank when visiting his missionary friends. Though many in Central America didn't drink with ice, José had no problem with it. He accepted the glass and the hospitality with a large smile.

"I wanted to see how things were going at *Las Minas* and to approach you about a possible new work," Allen said, jumping right into the topic on his mind.

José took his seat in the nearest rocker and sipped his tea. Allen took the other rocker across from him and sat down. Becky retreated back to the kitchen to let the men speak.

"*Las Minas* is doing well. We began with three believers that we discovered on our initial visit," José began.

Allen nodded.

"Then you brought the *JESUS* film, and more people came to know the Lord. Of those, I would say that we have about thirteen adults and twice that many children coming to the Thursday night service that we conduct. Not all of those are believers yet, but they are coming regularly."

"That is encouraging, my brother," Allen smiled. "How many of your people from *Monte Hermon* are going with you now?"

"About five of us, including my brother-in-law Simón," José replied beaming. "He has really grown in leadership since he has been attending your seminary classes. He will preach some of the time also. I believe God is preparing him for ministry."

"I believe you're right," Allen affirmed. "He has good insight into the Word of God and a tremendous servant heart."

The two paused and sipped their tea. They were friends and comfortable with moments of silence. After a minute, Allen sat his tea down on the table beside his rocker.

"I'm glad to hear that things are going well at *Las Minas*. Now I need to ask you a favor," Allen began in a softer tone. "I know you remember the little town we passed on the way to *Las Minas* sometime last month where there was a funeral procession of a little girl that had drown in the river"

José nodded.

"You may remember the name *Pozo Negro*," Allen reminded. "That was the name of the village on the other side of the river that we couldn't see from the road. Well, Becky and I went a couple days ago, found the river, but we didn't cross it. We could just barely see a house or two and then there were more trees blocking our view of the village. I have no idea how many people are across the river."

Allen took a breath and continued.

"I was just wondering if you would have time for us to go up and see if we could cross that river and see what kind of area they have back in there."

José shifted in his rocker and sat his glass down also.

"I knew you would want to go back there the day we stopped. I just was waiting to see how long it would take for you to ask. I don't know if *Monte Hermon* could take on another mission point at this time, but I would like to be a part of seeing *Pozo Negro*. I believe God has plans for that area. I don't know what, but the people at the funeral procession seemed so abandoned and without hope. The heaviness of their sorrow was greater than I see at our funerals. I felt an absence of God that day among them."

"Then you will go with me," Allen asked excitedly.

"It will take an adjustment in my schedule, but I believe God is always adjusting our lives. He did not leave us as He found us, and He doesn't plan to just keep us the same as we are. We are always adjusting our lives to conform to His purpose, His will, and His Son," José proclaimed.

"Sounds like a sermon," Allen joked.

"I learned it from you, my brother," José said seriously. "Now let us see, if we are able to live those words."

"Amen," said Allen.

"Amen," echoed Becky from the kitchen.

"*Amen, so be it*" was heard within the three of them.

CHAPTER FOUR

"THE OBSTACLE"

TERRY PENNINGTON was well within the age limit that the mission board accepted for appointment. Mission policy strongly recommended that families with children over the age of thirteen not be appointed for concern that older children would have a harder time adjusting to the changes in culture and life, as well as their resistance to leaving friends behind. Terry had turned eleven while Howard and Donna were in the process. His age was not a concern to the Board. But Terry was not racing to embrace his new home. He was still apprehensive about playing with Costa Rican boys. He was intimidated by their skill on the soccer field. Terry wondered why he didn't see more football and was confused when they called soccer "futbol". The french-fries didn't taste the same at the McDonalds in downtown San José, and he didn't even want to discuss the sweet-tasting ketchup. In one restaurant, to his horror, they had brought out his french-fries covered with Mayonnaise! Terry attended an English school, but all of his teachers were Costa Rican. He had difficulty understanding some of their English, and when they got upset, they chattered in unintelligible tongues. He also missed his old stuff. He had to pack his bicycle and larger toys in the crates his parents prepared before leaving California. He was told they were sitting in a warehouse in New Orleans for the year they would be in Costa Rica. Sometimes, Terry wondered if he would ever see his things again, if life would ever be the same again. Though he never said it out loud, Terry didn't like Costa Rica.

Sunday morning was his least favorite time. The Pennington family, like the other Baptist missionaries, were expected to become part of a local church while in language school. They would be given an opportunity to visit some of the congregations before choosing. Although no family was assigned a church to attend, it was understood that the Big Brother would assist in the process.

Al and Leanne Redding had three young girls, and had chosen a small church located in *El Bosque* to attend because it was only three blocks from their assigned home. Unfortunately, six other Language School families had done the same, and the word was put out that no more students should attend there for obvious reasons. It was not obvious to the Penningtons. The Baptist Language School coordinator explained at a monthly meeting when the question was put forth, that the small Costa Rican churches face a tremendous blessing and problem with North American students. On the one hand, the students bring a tithe/offering that is many times greater than the churches annual budget. This is a blessing for the small struggling congregation for the time that the student attends. But the same blessing causes jealousy on the part of other churches. It also creates a sense of dependency on the student's offerings and sometimes the church would enter into long term financial obligations that would create hardship when the student leaves or decides to attend a different church. Another major consideration was the tendency for the student family to not take an active part in the life of the Church when other students, doing better in the language, would rise to the challenge. Part of the church experience was to prepare the missionary for taking leadership roles in the church when they reached the field. It was ideal for a wife to become a teacher's assistant or for the husband to have the opportunity to preach before their year of language study was completed. When many families attended the same church, this became impractical. The most obvious reason, they explained, is the danger of forming a *gringo* cell within a congregation that would cling to each other and therefore not mingle with the Costa Rican believers. This would defeat the purpose of experiencing cross-cultural worship and hinder language development. Howard got the message. The *El Bosque* Church was saturated with students and wisdom dictated they look elsewhere.

Al agreed to carry the Penningtons to another church that he had heard was good for language students. One of the Baptist missionaries assigned to church planting in Costa Rica attended there, so they would not be alone. At the same time, it was quite a distance from their home and would require either a taxi or two bus rides. Most of the people in San José traveled the city by bus. Sometimes the buses could become very crowded, with two lines of people standing in the aisle. Personal space was non-existent and modesty was challenged regularly. The bus was always picking up more passengers even when seating and standing capacity was full. The joke at the language institute was, "how many *Ticos* could you fit on a bus?" The common reply was obvious, "Three more!" When they rode the buses, they did not know exactly where they were when they changed from one bus to the other. Donna just followed her husband when he said to get off. Terry moped behind his mother. That was one reason why Terry disliked Sundays. He hated the ride.

The *Primera Iglesia Bautista de Moravia* was located outside of San José. It was a small congregation of about sixty members, including the children. The bus rides took about forty-five minutes for them to arrive. A taxi could do it in twenty. It was the second week that the Penningtons visited the church in Moravia that Donna noticed Terry was unhappy. He hadn't spoken much on the buses and wasn't mingling with the other boys before the song service that preceded Sunday School. Terry had learned how to tune out the Spanish around him. Donna had learned how to recognize it. The song service began with the typical greeting song inviting the members to "take the hand of their brother" in Christian love.

"Why don't you sing?" Donna asked softly.

"I don't know the words," Terry replied curtly.

"At least you can shake hands with some of the church members," Donna chided, stepping past Terry to greet the ladies in the main aisle. Howard was already pumping palms vigorously and exchanging Spanish salutations with the men. The ladies greeted with a polite peck on the cheek to both men and women. Howard accepted the greetings, but seldom initiated one.

After the greetings and kisses were graciously exchanged, each one took their place beside family again for the chain of choruses led by a young enthusiastic worship leader at the keyboard. The congregation remained standing for the entire fifteen minutes of singing. Even Terry recognized some of the tunes, such as "Seek Ye First" and "I Love You Lord". It helped for him to hear familiar music even with the strange words. He could at least hum along as they sang, but he got tired of standing. The small church had printed the words of all the hymns and choruses that they sung in a small songbook. Though they stayed at the church, the pastor had let the Penningtons carry one home the first week. Donna decided she would try to pick up a new chorus each week. She started with the ones with familiar tunes.

Once the song service was concluded, the people took their seats and the pastor made the weekly announcements. Even Howard was lost as the pastor, Don Benito, spoke rapidly about the various services being held that week. The Pennington's knew to listen for their names and to be ready to smile and wave if they were introduced. Aside from that, they understood very little of what was being shared during the opening assembly.

The small group was dismissed for their Sunday School classes and Donna carried Terry to his room. She felt the reluctance in his steps and watched as he slumped into his chair. He wouldn't understand a word that was going to be said. Donna eased into her class smiling. She wouldn't understand much either, but she was determined to get something out of the class. She was determined to overcome the obstacle of language.

Allen and José drove up the mountainside in silence. Neither felt comfortable about making the trip during worship time on a Sunday, but then neither could find an open time during the week and Allen needed to be in León for the evening service. God would understand, they thought together. The Land Cruiser rounded the bend and the small village along the road came into view. It occurred to Allen, that he did not even know the name of the small settlement this side of the river of *Pozo Negro*. He had been so intent on learning about the community across the river, that he had not asked about the homes that were scattered along the road. Were they a part of *Pozo Negro* also? He would make a mental note to find out.

Allen showed José where he and Becky had asked directions and the small path they followed through the mango groves and banana trees that led to the river. Allen remembered how uncomfortable he and Becky felt as they walked. It hadn't gotten any better. The two men emerged at the riverbank and stopped.

"How do you get across?" José asked.

"That's why we are here," Allen replied. "I thought we would look for a narrow and calm place to cross."

"*Buenos suerte!*" José replied sarcastically.

"We're not relying on luck, my brother," Allen smiled. "The Lord will show us a way."

They chose a direction and began walking downstream.

Fall in southern California was affable. The early morning breeze set a pace of leisure that made for a pleasant prelude to church. The Coronado Baptist Church opened her doors early on Sunday. Rusty arrived two hours before Bible Study time to pray, and to make last minute preparations for the morning worship service. He still worked like an associate, though he had been the senior pastor for over a year.

Rusty finished his rounds early and returned to his office to read over his notes for the morning sermon. It occurred to him that he had not been in the office since Thursday due to a special conference he had attended up the coast in Oceanside. He turned on his computer and began pulling down three days of email. While the server squealed out its incoherent resonance of computer talk between machines, Rusty glanced at the mail neatly stacked on his desk. He sifted his piles mechanically, setting the bills aside for Monday, the newsletters went to the corner of his desk, and the advertisements were divided like sheep and goats with the ones worth attention placed next to the bills for Monday as well. He was about to open a thank you note from one of his Church members, when the familiar tone announced his email arrival was complete. Rusty quickly set aside the paper correspondence in deference to the miracle of cyber mail that just seemed more important because it had come through his computer.

Like most, he was still fascinated that two people could write and answer one another in moments instead of days. He quickly scrolled through the forty-two new entries to determine how many were spam. Three days worth of advertisements, forwards, daily mail-outs from selected web-sites, and personal correspondence looked like a lot, but was quickly reduced to seven meaningful emails. Rusty was once again thankful for the filter they had installed that kept the porno-ads out of eye-range. Now, all he had to delete with regularity was mortgage rate ads, Virus controllers, chains and urban legends from friends, and the same old jokes that make the rounds every six months. Of the winning seven emails, two were replies, three were inquiries that he would have to address Monday when the staff was present, and two were received weekly from mission organizations. One was the weekly PrayerGram from the Southern Baptist International Mission Board that he was scheduled to receive, and the other was from World Vision. Rusty glanced at the update from World Vision and decided it was similar to his last letter and decided to delete it. He was about to delete the PrayerGram as well, when his eye fixed on a word in bold print - NICARAGUA.

"I don't see anywhere to cross this way," José said after the two had walked for nearly thirty minutes. "I suggest we go back and look upstream."

"Maybe you're right," Allen acquiesced. "I haven't seen anything that looks like a crossing point either. You would think we would find a trail on the other side where people come down to cross."

"Come to think of it, we haven't seen anyone since we left the trail to the river," José observed. "I would like to think it is because they are all in church, somewhere."

"But we both know that that is not the case, hermano," Allen said firmly. "That is why we are here. And I am not about to let a little obstacle like a river stand in our way."

"Now you are talking like a man with a vision," José said positively. "I like that. I believe God has us here today for a reason. I know it is Sunday, and I would like to be in His house worshipping Him today with my church, but I believe that the Lord is going to show us something important today."

"Amen, hermano," Allen affirmed. "Let's find it."

The Sunday School class seemed to last for hours for young Terry. He couldn't get out soon enough. The Penningtons took the same bench for the worship service they had for the opening assembly. Now the long part came. Terry tried to get comfortable, but everyone was asked to stand. There was the scripture reading from the book of Psalms to open the service. The same young song leader stepped to the front and asked each of the children's classes to come forward one at a time and recite the memory verse for the week. Each teacher lined up her students and led them in the Bible verse. When Terry's class went forward, Donna elbowed Terry, who decided not to resist. He stepped up alongside a pretty Costa Rican girl, his freckles emphasizing his distinction from the rest in line. He successfully pantomimed the memory verse and quickly took his seat. Donna put her arm around him smiling. Howard was not oblivious to his son's feelings, he just knew that time could make a difference. Young boys were quickly motivated by some of the strangest things. He prayed something soon would catch Terry's attention. In the meantime, he would try to spend more time with his son. He had learned his lesson.

The worship service quickly moved into singing. The Penningtons shared the printed songbook and tried to pronounce Spanish lyrics to songs they thought they recognized. They would eventually memorize the songs even before they understood their meanings. It was all part of language learning.

Rusty read the prayer request three times. It was as though it were personal.

"NICARAGUA – Missionary Allen West reports of a village in the mountains of Western Nicaragua that is in desperate need of assistance. The only bridge linking the village with a primary roadway was washed out by Hurricane Mitch last year and several drownings have resulted. The village is also without a gospel witness. Pray for a bridge and open doors to reach the village of *Pozo Negro*."

Rusty took his hand from the mouse and stared at the screen.
"Do not delete this message" Rusty heard deep within his spirit.

He turned his eyes from the computer and looked back at the pile of mail on his desk. In the short stack of newsletters that he had set aside, he found a brochure from the International Mission Board. He had just assumed it was a tri-fold newsletter. The front cover called attention to "Priority Volunteer Requests". Rusty remembered the packet on volunteer missions that had come the month before. He quickly glanced at his watch. He had twenty minutes before the first arrivals for Bible Study would be filling the halls. He located the thick packet that he had placed on the bookcase near his desk, and began reading about volunteer missions.

———————————

Allen and José reached the point where they had begun their journey along the river when Allen noticed a man on the bank about twenty yards up tying a small dugout canoe to a fallen tree. The two men looked at each other and then trotted towards him.

"Excuse us, sir," Allen began. "Is this your canoe?"

"Si, Señor," the man replied cautiously.

"We were wondering if you could carry us across the river to the other side," José continued for Allen. "We would be happy to pay you."

"How much?" the man asked.

"Fifty córdoba!" Allen responded enthusiastically. José looked quickly at his friend.

"That's too much!" José whispered.

"It's worth it," Allen countered. "Besides, we need a friend in this area."

"He will expect that much every time," José said through clenched teeth while smiling.

"We'll cross that bridge, when we come to it," Allen said taking out his wallet.

José didn't understand the expression well enough to argue. He understood the words, but there was no bridge. That was why they were negotiating with a man about a canoe.

The man agreed and untied his canoe while José shook his head at the missionary. They climbed in carefully and Allen felt the excitement he always experienced when he began a new adventure. José talked to the man and discovered his name was Beto, which was short for Betaño. Beto lived on the side of the river near the highway, but was hired to carry supplies across the river for people in *Pozo Negro*. He had just returned from a delivery when they discovered his canoe. He admitted that fifty córdoba was a great deal for the trip and promised to wait till they were ready to come back. José felt he could be trusted.

"Does Don Tulio know that you are coming?" Beto asked, as they approached the other side.

"Who is Don Tulio?" José asked.

"You do not know Don Tulio and you are going to *Pozo Negro*?" Beto exclaimed.

"No, we do not know Don Tulio," Allen replied. "And why does he need to know if we are coming to *Pozo Negro* or not?"

"Because Don Tulio knows everything that goes on in town," Beto said solemnly driving his canoe onto the riverbank.

"Is he the mayor?" Allen asked.

"No, *señor*," replied Beto jumping onto the ground and tying off the canoe. "He is the *hechicero*."

"*Hechicero*?" Allen asked, turning to José.

"*Brujo*! Witch Doctor!" José said softly.

"And I thought the river was the obstacle," Allen said to himself.

The knock on the door startled Rusty.

"Pastor, are you in there?" came the voice from the other side.

"Yes," Rusty replied emphatically. "I'll be right out."

Rusty gathered the packet, the brochure and the email that he had printed out and stuffed them all into a loose folder. He quickly snatched up his Bible and notes and darted for the door. He turned and looked back at his desk. He was feeling that excitement of beginning a new adventure when God breaks into the comfort zone and stretches the borders of one's experience. He knew that morning worship was not going to be as he had planned it. His morning message on Cornelius in Acts 10 would have to wait.

Thirty-five minutes of congregational music was followed by fifteen minutes of impromptu specials. Aside from the occasional hymn or praise chorus taken from North American worship, the Penningtons understood little of the worship music, but it did not keep Howard and Donna from praise. The offering time was similar enough. Then it was the preacher's turn. Howard understood the Bible reference and quickly showed Donna and Terry where the pastor was reading. Donna and Howard read along in Bilingual Bibles that had the English on one page and the Spanish on the other. Terry just read his New International Version.

The message was about as long as the song service. It was exhausting trying to pick out words they understood and joining them together with some semblance of meaning that was consistent with the scripture that he was reading. Howard knew he was not getting the illustrations, but he felt he could keep up with the main points because the pastor was seminary trained and had learned the same Homiletic principles that Howard once studied. But after thirty minutes, even Howard gave up and just listened to the voice of his pastor. He began to think about the day when he would be able to preach in Spanish. It seemed so far away.

Allen and José found a footpath near the spot where Beto tied up the canoe. Beto thought it would be better for him to stay with the canoe. He didn't explain why. Allen and José followed the path up a small hill that led to a wider road. Allen was beginning to feel uneasy about the lack of human activity when suddenly three boys came from nowhere chasing a soccer ball. They stopped in front of Allen and stared. José stepped forward and greeted them. They spoke slowly and with little extra comment. José asked where they lived and they all turned and pointed up around the bend in the road. José asked where they were playing soccer. Again, they pointed up around the bend. As the boys turned, Allen and José followed slowly. The five of them walked around the edge of the tree line and Allen stopped short in his steps. The village was larger than he expected. There were buildings, shops, and homes clustered in what would look like a town square. Other roads connected with the central area and spread out in several directions with houses lining both sides. In a large open area, several boys and young men stood waiting for the ball to return to the game. The three boys broke into a run to toss the ball back into play. Suddenly, there was the noise of life. It was a wonder that the two men had not heard them playing as they approached.

"Something is not right here," José said deliberately.

"What do you mean?" Allen asked.

"Look about the square," José directed. "There is not even a Catholic Church here. We should have heard more noise before we got to this point. I don't know what it is, but something is not right about this town."

"Let's look around and talk to a few people," Allen suggested.

The two men walked slowly through the town amidst stares. Some of the younger children that had been playing ran like frightened kittens in different directions. The older boys stopped their soccer game.

"Which one of us do you think they are staring at?" Allen asked sarcastically.

"You would think they had never seen a North American before," José replied. "Or they never thought one would come to their village."

Allen looked around carefully studying the structures and the homes. Then he realized something significant. Of all the small areas he had ever visited, he could count on two things wherever electricity was found: Coca-Cola and television. The empty bottles along the street was evidence enough for the presence of one, but Allen saw no antennas above any of the homes. He also heard few radios going in town.

José led them towards an open door that looked like a home store called a *pulperia*. Inside, the men found two couples seated quietly around a table eating. They looked around at the two strangers and one of the men seated rose to greet them.

"*Buenos Dias*," he said politely.

"*Buenos Dias*," José returned in kind.

"With your permission," Allen added, requesting entrance into the home.

"It's yours" was the customary reply of courtesy.

Allen and José could tell they were surprised to see them, but they sensed no real objection to their presence. The man who greeted them motioned them towards the small table. His wife rose to bring two wooden chairs from against the wall into the middle of the darkened room near the table. The other couple remained seated and quiet. Allen tried to read their faces. There was still a distance he felt that was a little unsettling.

José took his chair and began talking. He introduced himself and Allen as visitors from across the river. He explained how they had been in the area back in the rainy season about four months before and had witnessed a funeral from their area. They were concerned about the number of deaths that had taken place since they lost their bridge. Allen noticed that José had not mentioned that they were ministers, but thought it best not to interrupt.

"Is there someone we should talk to about the possibility of building a bridge?" José asked cautiously.

The two couples looked at each other with a slight alarm. The friendly one finally spoke up.

"You will need to speak to Don Tulio," he said firmly.

Allen and José had heard Beto speak of Don Tulio, but wanted to know more from the ones who actually lived here in town. They decided to play ignorant.

"Who is Don Tulio?" Allen asked.

"He is the…" the man began and then stopped abruptly. He thought for a moment. "He is the one who makes the final decisions in *Pozo Negro*."

The others in the small room nodded in agreement.

"Where would we find Don Tulio?" José asked with respect.

"He lives in the house at the end of this road," one of the women said finally, speaking out. "There is usually a group in front of his house seeking help. You won't have any trouble finding it."

She quickly turned back toward the table as though she had said too much. The others just looked down. Allen glanced at José with a questioning look on his face. José shrugged his shoulders and pointed toward the doorway with his head.

"We thank you for the directions," José said backing toward the door. Allen followed close by. "We hope that we will be able to help the community."

The two men quickly exited and were relieved to be in the sunlight again.

Allen whispered, "That was the strangest conversation I think I have ever had in Nicaragua. It was as though the people were afraid to speak."

"They were," José replied with all seriousness in his voice.

The service ended between 12:30 and 1:00. The Penningtons were exhausted. Howard had tried to catch as much of the sermon as he could understand. Donna had tried to keep Terry interested, and Terry had tried to sleep between pokes. The departure from the church was also lengthy. Greetings and kisses were exchanged again. Howard spoke with the pastor briefly at the door and then led his family to the bus stop. Terry was a little more enthusiastic about the trip home, because that would include a stop at one of the American restaurants for lunch. They had been to the McDonalds and the Pizza Hut downtown before on Sundays. Maybe they would take the bus through San Pedro and stop at the Taco Bell across the highway from the University. Terry had been there one other time with his school.

They waited about twelve minutes for the first bus to come around the corner to their stop. Howard quickly looked at the name printed above the windshield and decided that they could take that one into downtown. Terry sighed. It would not be Taco Bell today. The price of the bus was printed on a sign in the front side window. Howard quickly counted the fare times three out in the Colones and centavos that he had in his pocket. The family mounted the diesel Mercedes and walked toward the back. Howard found one seat for Donna and Terry. He then stood beside them holding firmly the long hand rail overhead.

The bus lunged forward and swiftly took its place in traffic. Howard leaned with the curves and tried not to make physical contact with the ones sitting across the aisle from Donna and Terry. He had been "brushed" more than once by inconsiderate passengers on buses. The buses tended to fill the standing aisle in two distinct lines facing the seats. Occasionally, a passenger would face the center of the aisle and "back into" seated riders accidentally. This was not a wise stance to take considering the possibility of having your wallet lifted by someone staring at your back pocket. Howard always tried to face his family.

After three stops, a small group boarded causing the center aisle of standing riders to shift. Though one short man eased past Howard to take a position closer to the back of the bus, two larger men just began pushing those in the center aisle farther to the rear. They were too large to squeeze past the other passengers, so the whole center aisle took the cue and stepped backwards. This caused Howard to have to move about four seats behind his wife and son. The two large men took the space where Howard had been standing forming a human blockade. Donna looked back at Howard, who just shrugged and gave her a reassuring smile. She turned back to Terry and put her arm around him.

Howard gave his attention to the roads as the bus neared the downtown area. He recognized the fancy four story Hotel, the grocery store with the American cereal, and the corner where they would get off this bus. It would be just a three-block hike to the McDonalds across from the National Palace.

"*Parada!*" Howard yelled, calling out for the bus to stop.

The drive mechanically eased the bus towards the curb as other passengers began to rise from their seats. Donna and Terry stood and looked back at Howard who was beginning to maneuver his way towards them. The two large men took a forceful step backwards and made a space for Donna and Terry to step out into the aisle. Without thinking, Donna took Terry's hand and mumbled a "gracias" to the men and began walking towards the front of the bus. Howard eased himself past a woman with a large bag of groceries, keeping Donna and Terry in sight.

Suddenly, the two larger men turned around to face Howard and stood motionless blocking his way. Howard stepped up to the men, but they did not acknowledge him or his desire to pass. Howard struggled for the right phrase, but suddenly felt uncomfortable.

"*Perdón,*" Howard said sheepishly. But the two men did not budge.

"*Perdón!*" Howard said more forcefully, but they continued to ignore him deliberately.

Howard began to feel the sudden rush of panic as he looked over their shoulders and saw Donna about to disembark from the bus.

"Donna!" Howard shouted. "Wait! I seem to have a problem back here."

The passengers looked in Howard's direction as he was yelling English. The two men did not move, but continued to look to the rear of the bus as if they did not even see Howard. Then one of the men turned his eyes down on Howard and smiled. Howard knew this was not right. He was about to cry out for help, when the short man behind him began pushing on Howard to move him out of the way. Howard let the short man pass and watched as he began yelling rapidly at the two men. The anger in his voice was unmistakable. It was quite a show for the rest of the bus. The man spoke so fast Howard only understood the word "*gringo*".

When he finished, the two men looked at each other and turned inward. One stepped beside the other leaving a space for Howard to pass. Dr. Pennington wasted no time getting through the obstacle and rejoining his family. He quickly ushered them off the bus and the driver promptly closed the door and drove off.

"What was that all about?" Donna asked.

"I don't know," Howard replied, still shaken. "I'm just glad that little man came to my rescue."

"What do you suppose they wanted?" Donna asked again, trying not to show too much alarm in her voice for Terry's sake.

"I have no idea," Howard repeated. "They didn't try to grab me or even touch me. It was as though they just wanted to keep me from passing."

"That's strange," Donna remarked. "What could they have expected to gain from that?"

Howard suddenly stopped in mid-stride. His shoulders sunk and his head dropped. Donna turned and looked at him. There was a sickening feeling rising from the pit of his stomach and it showed all over his face.

"My wallet is gone!" Howard said slowly.

"Oh, my gosh!" Donna exclaimed.

Howard dropped his mouth and mumbled to his own dismay.

"It was the short man behind me!"

———————————

Allen and José continued on down the road through town making little contact with the people. As they passed the small houses along the street, they could scarcely make out curious faces in the doorway peering through the darkened shrouds of their adobe homes.

"This place needs lots of prayer," José said breaking the silence.

"I was thinking the same thing," Allen agreed. "We should plan to have a Prayerwalk for the area."

"The sooner the better," José said nervously.

As they reached the end of the road, they saw a house surrounded by shade trees. A small group of people sat patiently in front of the house, some with small children and a couple with animals. José looked cautiously at the missionary.

"I believe this is the place," José said.

"I believe you are right, my brother," Allen nodded. "Why don't we have a word of prayer now before we go up."

The two men bowed their heads and Allen began in praise thanking God for bringing them safely to *Pozo Negro* and for leading them faithfully to this point.

"Now, Lord, we pray Your wisdom in speaking with this man. We ask you to bind the powers and principalities that we sense in this place. We pray for an open door for your Gospel to be presented unashamedly. We ask you to soften the heart of this…Don Tulio so that no obstacle can stand before Your Word going forth."

"Amen," José inserted in agreement.

"And we pray for your protection over our lives, as well," Allen went on.

"Si, Señor," José added with emphasis.

"May the Spirit of the Lord Jesus go before us…strengthen us from within…and give us the words to speak. For we are nothing without Him. I pray these things in the name of Jesus Christ, Who has sent us to this place…Amen."

"Amen," echoed José.

When the two men looked up. They saw a man with a large stick staring straight at them from the portal of his home. His piercing eyes glared from over thirty feet away and there was no mistaking the look. He was upset.

The small gathering at his door quickly dispersed and left the three men facing off like an old Western. Allen straightened his shoulders and took a step forward. José found it difficult to move. He watched his colleague walk slowly towards the house. José felt fear swell in his chest. He had heard many stories of witch doctors from his grandmother. Much of their practice was helpful, but they did have power – she said – and you didn't want to anger them.

The stern man held up his heavy rod.

"That's far enough," he said in a strong educated voice.

"My name is Allen West," the missionary began. "I am from…"

"I know where you are from!" he said angrily. "I know why you are here! I have seen your coming and I tell you now that you will fail."

"But I believe we can help YOUR village," Allen responded respectfully.

"What makes you think we need YOUR help?"

"I think I can help you get a bridge," Allen replied carefully.

"What makes you think we need a bridge?" Don Tulio questioned.

"There have been deaths, have there not?" Allen asked.

"What concern is that of yours?" Tulio toyed with the missionary.

"I was present when one of the daughters of your village was buried," Allen began. "I was concerned for other children of your village."

"Why?" Tulio asked as though interrogating the man before him.

"Because I, too, have children. They are grown now, but I remember when they were little. I would do whatever was necessary to protect them from danger. I want to do the same for the children of your village."

"But these are not your children, just as this is not your country," Don Tulio said sharply. "You have no business with my village, just as you have no business with my country. Why are you here?"

Allen held back from responding. Then the words came to him.

"You have already said that you know why I am here," Allen said strongly. "You have also said that you have seen my coming. If that is true, then my answer is not necessary for you. If you know why I am here and have seen my coming, then you should know that I do not come alone and that the one with me is strong. If you did not see him, then how do you know that I will fail?"

Don Tulio looked at José who still hadn't moved.

"He doesn't look that strong to me," Tulio said tauntingly.

"He is not the one I speak of," Allen said with finality.

Don Tulio turned quickly to face Allen.

"We are finished speaking here," Tulio spewed angrily. "You will leave *Pozo Negro* now."

With a sweep of his staff, Don Tulio retreated into the darkness of his home. Allen and José thought it best to return to the riverside as well. They prayed that Beto was still waiting for them.

"I think that went as well as could be expected," José commented sarcastically.

"Oh, I think it went better than expected," Allen smiled.

"What do you mean?" José questioned.

"He knows what he is up against, and it angers him."

"And that is a good thing?" José asked.

Allen stopped and looked at José.

"Look at it this way. We did not tell him we were believers, or that we wanted to start a church in this town. We presented only a humanitarian concern for his village. He resists us because he knows we represent more than just humanitarian concern. He has made a spiritual connection with our coming and he doesn't want to talk about that."

"I don't get your point," José said confused. "He is still the most powerful man in the village. He opposes our presence and kicks us out of town. To me, he is like a giant before us and we have no way around him."

"Stop comparing yourself to the giant, and start comparing the giant to God!" Allen said with a smile.

The two men resumed walking out of town and back down the path towards the riverside where Beto sat in the canoe waiting patiently.

"José, there is no doubt in my mind," Allen said confidently. "God wants to build a bridge to *Pozo Negro*. Not just a transit across this river, but a connection between the town and heaven. This Don Tulio is not our obstacle - the devil is. Don Tulio may just be our opportunity."

CHAPTER FIVE

"THE BREAK-IN"

"LET'S GET a late lunch before we go home," Allen suggested to José as they reached the road leading back into León. There had not been much conversation between them for much of the trip back from *Pozo Negro*.

"That sounds good to me," José agreed. "The *comedor* at the edge of town is fine."

Allen knew that the Nicaraguan *comedor* would serve a simple meal with several selections. *Comedors* were small restaurants that prepared typical dishes and were common for most class of people. They were also much less expensive than the American style restaurants that had found their way into the emerging middle class of Central America. José knew that the missionary had no trouble paying for either, but he just resisted being treated to a meal that would cost more than he would earn in a day.

"The *comedor* is good," Allen concurred.

They drove another kilometer staring forward. José broke the silence.

"*Hermano* Allen, did you notice heaviness in *Pozo Negro*?"

Allen West paused before answering. He knew what José was asking. It was more than just coldness on the part of the people and the rudeness they had received from Don Tulio.

"Yes, I did," Allen started slowly. "I believe we are dealing with more than just a powerful man in a community that has had little contact with the outside world. I believe we are dealing with what the Bible calls, 'principalities and powers'. There is definitely a heavy spirit over the town."

"Have you had much experience with this?" José asked with a little concern in his voice.

"Not very much, my brother," Allen confided. "But I know enough that it is going to take some serious prayer and fasting. We are not dealing with just a man with a stick. We are facing the influence he holds over the people and that influence is spiritual. But praise God, 'the weapons of our warfare are not carnal, but mighty through God to the pulling down of strongholds, casting down imaginations, and every high thing that exalts itself against the knowledge of God,'" Allen quoted from 2 Corinthians chapter ten.

"So we must prepare for battle." José commented.

"My brother, we must always be prepared for battle...for such a day as this. We should never be caught unaware of the battle around us. The devil is not dormant and the moment we forget about him, is when he strikes the hardest," Allen replied with full conviction. "I believe we are about to be involved in something difficult. But at the same time, I believe it will be exciting to see what God is going to do. Do you still want to be a part of starting a new work in *Pozo Negro*?"

José paused before answering. He knew the missionary was asking a serious question, and he didn't need to make an empty commitment.

"*Si, hermano*," José said solemnly. "I too believe God is going to do some incredible things."

"Good," Allen said soberly. "I'm going to need your help to understand a little more about why the people turn to a witchdoctor. I will need to know some of the beliefs that are common among the people that open them up to such demonic suggestion and lies. The greatest weapon we have is the truth found in the Word of God. I want to know how best to use that truth."

"Did you not also mention prayer and fasting?" José asked sincerely.

"Yes, I did."

"Then maybe it would be better if we didn't stop at the *comedor* in town," José offered humbly.

Allen West smiled at his companion.

"You learn quickly, my brother," the missionary said proudly. "Perhaps you would like to lead us in a time of prayer as we complete this journey?"

"With much pleasure," José responded.

As Allen maneuvered through the narrow streets of León, José carried the duo to the Throne of Grace.

"Lord, Jesus, we come to you this day with a great burden on our hearts for the town of *Pozo Negro*. We know it is a town of darkness, even as its name suggests. We pray for the people that they will know the Truth and come to the Light. We pray for Don Tulio, that he might come to know You as the Lord of both Heaven and Earth. And Lord, I pray that you will raise up others who will join us in both prayer and work. We need help to build a bridge to *Pozo Negro*. I pray that you will send workers and send them soon.

"Amen," Allen whispered in agreement.

———————————

Rusty Patterson took a deep breath as he took his seat on the platform of the church. The Praise Team had already led the congregation in an opening chain of Praise choruses. Rusty was still enjoying the "honeymoon" season of his pastorate – that undetermined period of time when the congregation is so much in love with their new pastor that they overlook any minor mistakes or deviation from the routine. His was a slightly different situation, in that the Church had known Rusty for several years before he became their pastor. The time had only enhanced Rusty's relationship with the people. They had come to trust him as an Associate, and now they trusted him as their leader. Rusty knew that the honeymoon period would not last forever. He had seen other men outlive theirs. That was when the complaints began to surface.

The morning service had been fairly routine till the message. The Church was accustomed to her order of worship that included congregational singing, announcements, scripture reading, the collection of tithes and offerings followed by a resonant special in song that would lift the heart, if not the rafters. Such praise was designed to prepare the worshipper for a powerful declaration of God's Word to the wayward, the wanting, or the wistful. As Pastor Rusty took the pulpit, his steps were slow and deliberate. Some in the choir noticed the change in demeanor...especially Arnie. He narrowed his eyes as Rusty began to speak.

"There are times when God breaks in," Rusty began, looking down at his Bible. "When I read the scriptures, I see some of those times. I see him breaking into the life of Abraham and calling him to a land he didn't know so that some day his people could possess it. I see him disrupting the life of Joseph and literally carrying him to a strange land for a divine purpose. I see him relocating a whole nation to establish His people. I see him moving Ruth from her homeland to follow her new God. I see him moving the parents of our Lord from their country and then bringing them back at the appointed time."

"Oh no," Arnie whispered to himself. "Here we go again." It had barely been a year since Bro. Pennington had begun a similar type of message. All Arnie could imagine was that they were about to lose another good man.

"I had planned to bring you a message entitled 'Even a Good Mans Needs Jesus', about the conversion of Cornelius in Acts chapter ten. But this morning God broke in."

Rusty paused, then opened his Bible.

"I want you to see what I saw," he began without the flare in his voice that usually marked his preaching. His sincerity came through and the people opened their Bibles.

"In Acts, chapter ten, you will find the story, but instead of Cornelius, I want you to focus on Peter. To understand what God is going to do with Peter, we need to see Cornelius in the background."

Rusty read the first four verses of Acts ten. He was comfortable with this part of the message, because he had prepared to share this information in his typical sermon style.

"Cornelius was truly a man seeking God. Acts 10:1-4 describes him as a man of devotion, a man of deeds, and a man of dedication. His devotion to the God of Israel was communicated to his entire family so that they too, shared his faith and reverence. His good deeds were noted by both heaven and earth. He was a man God could talk to, because he was a man accustomed to talking to God. There was but one problem. He was a Gentile. It is to this man, a roman centurion of the Italian Cohort, that God sent his angel with instructions and directions for locating his nearest messenger - Peter. Cornelius promptly dispatched his two most trusted servants and a devout soldier to find the man who could share with him and his household the good news of eternal life."

Rusty stepped away from the pulpit and his notes. He began to picture the event out loud.

"I can see the three men quietly approaching the gate of the house glancing at each other in awkward silence, wondering which would call out for the man none of them knew. It was surprising enough that they even found the house. Having traveled overnight along coastal roads, they must have ventured through the small harbor town of Joppa seeking the home of a local tanner. Lesser men would have given up sooner, gone home and offered the excuse that he wasn't there. But these men lived in loyalty to a leader and master that commanded obedience and expected results. He was a man of power, of authority, and he had had a vision. So they followed their limited directions and stood before a gate with just a stranger's name."

"Inside, Peter was being prepped by God. Peter was a man whom God was seeking. As the prominent spokesman of the twelve, Peter had seen tremendous waves of holy activity throughout Palestine, including Samaria, where many were slow to believe that God had entered and touched lives as He did in Jerusalem. But even Peter was not prepared for the revelation and call that was about to come upon him."

Arnie leaned forward, wondering exactly where this message was going. Others listened intently, being drawn in by the story. Rusty returned to the pulpit and began reading the verses about Peter's vision on the rooftop of the house. He read the passage slowly as though still drawing insight from the verses. He read Acts 10:9-16 and then looked up. There was a brief pause while Rusty took a breath.

"The account of Acts 10:9-16 is a call to change. But change is challenging at best and many times is met with the same resistance that Peter demonstrated when he declared his defiance, 'Surely not, Lord.' Such words can not be taken seriously. For if He is Lord, you can not tell Him 'no.' Peter simply uttered his personal objection to change."

"For one thing, it was contrary to his training. Though an uneducated fisherman, Peter was a strong Jew, trained since childhood to hold certain laws and rituals as part of his personal heritage and belief system. The Jewish dietary laws were not a means to grace, but a mark of a people, much like circumcision. They were not universally binding. The Seed of the blessing of Abraham was about to be planted among the Gentiles and Peter had to get past his own Jewishness to serve as the sower."

"It may have been contrary to his desire, but it was time to change. The prophetic words of Simeon as he held the Lord Jesus in the temple were about to find their fulfillment. The 'glory of thy people Israel' was about to become 'a light to lighten the Gentiles'. And Peter was called to be the change agent."

Rusty took another breath and continued. No one moved. No one even cleared his or her throat.

"Perhaps, the greatest point of resistance was in the fact that it was contrary to his routine. Like many modern day disciples, Peter had lapsed into a routine and was at rest in his ministry. He was content with touring Palestine, filling synagogues and marketplaces with the fulfilled prophecies of the Messiah, and the presentation of the Nazarene who was the sacrifice for all men's sins. But up to this point, he had not proclaimed it to all men. Then one day, God broke in and awakened him through a mid-day trance."

"I am afraid that we, too, have grown comfortable with sermons, activities and an occasional revival. We adjust worship styles and follow the trends. We know our demographics and projected growth. Our five and ten year plans are chronicled with goals and committees, but what if God should lower a sheet filled with raw fish, rice and beans and say, 'go, stay and eat!' Talk about a wake-up call!"

There was a low response on the part of some throughout the congregation. Rusty was hitting a nerve and the Holy Spirit was driving it home.

"We celebrated the mission calling of the Penningtons earlier this year," Rusty continued with conviction. "And maybe with a small sigh of relief, that the church was now involved in 'hands-on' missions vicariously through one of their own. But,...what if God were calling more than just one family from this church to go on missions."

Arnie sat up. Rusty had said "family" not "person". He had something more than just himself in mind.

"There are ways to overcome resistance to the call to change. We must see other people groups for their importance to God. Peter needed to see Cornelius, not with the same disdain he may have held for the centurion who crucified his Lord, but with the same love that Jesus demonstrated in word and deed as He forgave the Roman from the cross. We must see the nations of the world without their drawn borders and differences. If they are precious to God, they must be precious to us."

"Amen," resounded several throughout the pews.

"We must see that God's call is the guarantee for the grace necessary to minister. If Peter were to enter a Gentile home as a Jew and proclaim a love beyond belief, it would not be in his own strength. We must never lose sight that the Lord, who calls us to come to Him walking on the water, is already there. He is our grace to do what He has called us to do in His name. If that call involves change, rest assured, He is willing to make the transition with you."

Rusty stepped back behind the pulpit to emphasize the importance of his final words.

"The Lord broke in on me this morning as I was making final preparation for the service. He showed me a need that I believe He wants us to help meet. I don't know who else He may be leading, but I believe He is. I don't believe in telling other people what God's will for their life is. When I read this story I see God preparing both Cornelius and Peter at the same time. It was no coincidence in timing between Peter's vision and the arrival of the three men. It is no coincidence that you are here this morning."

Rusty closed his Bible. Several glanced down at their watches.

"Has the Lord broken in on your life lately? I know you came expecting the typical service. Instead, you have gotten a ten minute message and maybe the challenge of your lifetime."

Rusty held up the printed *PrayerGram.*

"I am holding an invitation in my hand to go to Nicaragua on a week long volunteer mission trip. I extend this invitation to you this morning. I don't know all the details. I don't know what it will cost. I don't know where I am going or exactly what I will be asked to do. But then,…neither did Peter. If you would like to find out more about this with me and say this morning, 'I am ready to go wherever God calls me.' Then, I would ask you to join me here at the front. If you are willing to pray for this need and this trip, but cannot go, I ask you to stand where you are. Let us pray."

"Loving Father and Gracious Lord, we bow before you this morning in humble submission to Your will. We have gathered to praise Your name. We have celebrated Your mercy and grace towards us. Now we offer ourselves for your service. Speak to us clearly and point us to Your fields. Help us get past the confines of our walls and ourselves and see the harvest You are preparing. Show us unmistakably that You will provide for whatever you require of us and that we need not fear, and dare not say, 'not so, Lord.' May Your will be done with us and through us. In the Holy name of our Lord and Savior, Jesus Christ, AMEN."

Several "amens" echoed through the sanctuary.

Rusty instructed Steve, the Worship Leader, to come to the pulpit and to lead the instrumentalists in playing softly, "Wherever He Leads, I'll Go".

"I am going to ask just Steve to sing. Sometimes we fail to hear God because we are using the invitation to gather our Bibles, make our lunch plans, or we just listen to ourselves sing. I want your full attention to be upon God this morning. If you have heard God's voice breaking in on your life this morning – I invite you to join me here at the front."

As the keyboard player and the pianist began to play, Rusty took his place in front the Communion Table and bowed his head. One by one, members began to stand in their pews indicating their commitment to pray for the mission trip. One whole row of young people stood in unison and joined hands. Rusty stood nervously alone at the front.

Betty Johnson had stood with the first to rise in support through prayer. She was proud of her young pastor for his strong conviction and for the powerful challenge that he had set before the church. She had felt that they could have been doing more in ministry, but the emphasis on the building program in the last few years had consumed most of the people's resources. She was about to give Rusty a reassuring smile, when something caught her eye. Two of the choir members that had stood to show their support in prayer had both exited the rows they were in and made their way to opposite side aisles. She watched as they left the platform without even noticing each other. They met almost simultaneously on either side of the pastor. Only then, did the two men become aware of the other. Rusty reached out his arms and took Arnie Johnson on his left and Alex Johnson on his right. There was spontaneous laughter and then the tears.

The coming of the father and son opened the door. By the end of the second stanza, two more men and a young woman had stepped from their pew and made the faith-filled walk down the aisle to stand with their pastor.

Rusty was feeling the exhilaration of watching God do a mighty work when his heart suddenly sank. He watched cautiously as Stan Henly, the Chairman of Deacons, step out of his normal seat near the back row and walk around the rear of the sanctuary to where the Church Treasurer sat. Stan knelt down beside the end of the pew, so that the two men could speak quietly. Rusty's mind rushed through a torrid scenario of reprimands that would be coming after the service. He braced himself and continued smiling, though he kept his eye on the two men exchanging opinions and nods. To Rusty's amazement, both men then stood and walked towards the front. Rusty watched helplessly as they marched straight toward him. He wondered if they would ask for his resignation there on the spot. Steve had just completed the third stanza and motioned to the instrumentalists to continue playing, but he refrained from singing. He wanted to hear what the two men had to say. Stan Henly stood before Rusty without emotion.

"May I address the church?" Stan asked firmly.

Rusty nodded. He swallowed hard.

Stan took the wireless mike that was kept on the Communion Table for testimonies. The keyboard and piano players found the nearest measure to close the hymn. Bro. Henly waited for the silence.

"As most of you know, I am the Chairman of the Deacons, and I have served in this church for many years. I believe we have a good solid foundation. We have had good pastors who have led us through many difficult times. We have been faithful in giving and in supporting local missions. We have been strong in our cooperative giving and the special mission offerings that we take throughout the year. We have just been through a successful building campaign and we are seeing the fruit of several hard years of sacrifice to be where we are worshipping today."

Arnie looked down. He too, feared the direction that this was going.

"We were stunned last year to hear our pastor say that he was going to leave us for the mission field, but we supported his decision whole-heartedly," Stan continued. "It is one thing to let your pastor go, but what we have been presented with this morning is taking missions to a new level – one we have not been prepared to take. . ." Stan looked hard at his young pastor and then finished his sentence, "...until now!"

Arnie looked up. Stan and the Treasurer were both smiling.

"I believe our pastor is right on target," Stan continued. "But I think something more needs to be said,...y'all."

Rusty was suddenly reminded that Stan was not a native Californian. He had come from Mississippi and was one of the founding members of the Coronado Baptist Church. He was a Southerner at heart, who had found the weather of the West Coast more agreeable in his retirement years. He had been a cotton farmer as a young man and a navy man later in life.

"Growing up, my brothers and I got up about four in the morning. We had cows to milk, chickens to rob – that's getting eggs for you city folk – and pigs to feed all before breakfast. We would put in a good two to three hours hard labor before most of you ever got out of bed."

The congregation snickered, though they knew it was true.

"After breakfast seemed like a good time to take a nap, but the truth was, that the work hadn't begun yet. You see, on the farm, what you do before breakfast was the chores. The work was in the fields. When I look at how well this church is doing, I can smile and feel good. But the truth is, everything we do behind these walls are just the chores – to keep this household of faith going. The real work is in the fields, amen?"

"AMEN!" came a resounding chorus across the congregation from those standing and sitting alike.

"I believe its time we move past the chores and see what God wants us to do in the fields, and I for one am ready to go," Stan declared to everyone's amazement.

Rusty held his comments, but inwardly was shouting praises.

"And furthermore," Stan led on. "I have asked Richard, our treasurer, if he could set up a special fund for the church to contribute to this volunteer trip. He is in full agreement. If this needs the church's approval, we will present it at the next business meeting. But if the contributions are voluntary, I don't see how we are taking anything from the church budget. If we need to, we'll cross that bridge when we come to it."

Rusty thought how ironic Stan's final words were. For he had not yet shared the details of the request.

"That's all I have to say...for now," Stan said and took his place next to the others standing at the front.

Rusty took a deep breath. He looked out over the congregation. Over two hundred people were standing in commitment to pray for the project and the team. Beside him stood five men and one woman. His treasurer smiled reassuringly from the front pew. Rusty could contain himself no longer.

"Whooo!" he shouted.

"Amen!" came the response.

"Praise the Lord!" added Arnie.

"Is there anyone else that would like to share a word this morning?" Rusty asked.

From the mid-section of the congregation a hand went up.

"Would you like to step forward so that everyone else can hear?" Rusty asked, offering the wireless mike.

Stepping past three or four others, a middle-aged man eased himself out into the center aisle and slowly made his way to the front. His face was unfamiliar. He was not a regular in attendance. As he approached the front, Rusty felt a peace about his presence. He offered him the mike without asking his name.

The man spoke humbly.

"I am not a member here. In fact, I have only visited this church on two other occasions. This morning as I was preparing with my family to attend our church on the other side of town, I felt a strong impression from the Lord to come here. I explained to my wife and children what I was doing, though personally, I was not sure why I was to come. They agreed that I should come alone."

The man took a breath and swallowed hard. He continued.

"My name is Billy Eldridge."

Rusty gasped.

"It was my brother, Carey, who died in Honduras last year that led your pastor to sense God's calling to the mission field. I was here just a few months ago when this wonderful church commissioned Howard and Donna Pennington for the mission field. Before that, I was with you as a Gideon speaker during the time shortly before my brother's accident. I was unsure why God wanted me here this morning, until now."

Billy looked at Rusty.

"God is truly doing a work in this church today. Your Chairman of the Deacons is absolutely right. God is taking you to a new level of missions. I have been on the mission field of Honduras with my brother. You cannot go and return the same. For those who take this trip, you will see sights and people that will grip your heart and never let go. I know. I suppose that is why God brought me here today. With the permission of this church, I would like to go with you on this trip."

Rusty looked at Stan. There was no doubt God was moving at Coronado Baptist Church that morning, and Billy's presence seemed to confirm the direction. There would be no objection.

"I see no reason why not...church?" Rusty asked looking at the congregation.

"AMEN!" they replied in unity.

"What a day! What a day!" Rusty exclaimed. "Truly, God has broke in on us today. And we are the better for it. I invite the rest of you to stand as we pray together in one accord. Let us ask God to provide for what He has called us to do."

As Rusty led the church in prayer, the assembly moved together in agreement. The Spirit of God confirmed in the hearts of all present that this was a divine course. When the Amen was pronounced, Steve began to lead out in a familiar chorus of "Shout to Lord". Without accompaniments playing, the richness of their voices grew stronger with each line to a crescendo that could be heard in the parking lot. Billy gazed heavenly as the praise grew. He broke off from singing and whispered to God, "Thank you that the seed of my brother's death is still bearing fruit." For it was.

The Penningtons finally arrived in *El Bosque* completely exhausted physically and emotionally. After discovering Howard's wallet had been robbed on the bus, they had continued on to the McDonalds. They had to eat something; it was almost 2:30 in the afternoon. Donna had found some Colones in her purse that she had since her trip to the market the day before. She had enough to feed them and to catch a bus to the top of the hill where the language school was. They had walked the three-quarters of a mile home downhill without conversation. When they unlocked the gate to let themselves into their home, they soon discovered that the day held more surprises.

Howard looked into the patio/carport that led to the front door of their house. Something was wrong. Donna's makeshift shopping cart that she used to carry her groceries home from the market usually sat in the right corner of the carport. It was gone. Terry's muddy tennis shoes that his mother made him leave by the screen door were also missing. Howard motioned for Donna to keep Terry at the gate while he checked the door. It was unlocked.

Howard quickly disappeared into the house moving from room to room. Donna held Terry's hand for several moments, when Howard burst back through the doorway.

"We've had a break-in!"

CHAPTER SIX

"THE RESPONSE"

THE BAPTIST mission at the language school was like a large family. It didn't take long for the news of the Pennington's "break-in" to circulate through the prayer chain. They had not been the first family in the institute to have been robbed and most likely would not be the last. Sunday "break-ins" were more common than at any other time, because many missionary families didn't think to have someone watch the house in their absence. Local thieves knew which houses were used for North American language students. They also knew that the majority of these families attended church. They would watch a house for a couple weeks, to determine how long the family was away at church. The Pennington's did not return from Sunday lunch until nearly mid-afternoon.

Experienced missionaries who lived in country knew to either have a watchman stay outside the home with a machete or small arm, or they would have their maid stay inside the house while they were away at church. The language school director for the Baptist mission, Buddy Weatherton, was an "in-country" missionary. Buddy arrived at the Pennington home within an hour of the phone call.

"Have you been able to determine what all is missing?" Buddy asked gently. His wife Sandy was comforting Donna in the bedroom.

"Best I can tell," Howard stated, still a bit shaken, "they got the little TV we were using, Terry's SEGA and games, my 35mm camera, the video camera, some of Donna's jewelry, which was not that valuable, and what little money was on my dresser."

"What about your laptop?" Buddy asked.

"Praise the Lord - Al borrowed it last night to do some homework on, so it wasn't even here."

"I know you're glad of that," Buddy sighed. "It looks like they had plenty of time to look for anything they wanted."

"I know," Howard sighed. "It was almost 3:30 when we got home – they had every bit of six hours to break in the back door – open the front door, let anyone else in and take their time."

"You know we probably won't be able to recover any of your things?" Buddy said apologetically. "I think we will be able to get a police report for you – so you need to fill out the insurance claim."

"I may have to get another copy of the form from you," Howard said. "They made a mess of my files in the bedroom."

"Speaking of which," Buddy replied, looking in the direction of their bedroom. "How is Donna holding up? I know Sandy is with her, but this sort of thing is very traumatic for the wife. A robbery is a personal violation, you know."

"She was pretty shaken up," Howard said softly. Terry's bedroom door was cracked open and Howard didn't want him to feel insecurity over the day's events. "You know, I was also robbed on the bus today. Some men got between me and Donna and Terry. A little fellow behind me lifted my wallet while pretending to help me get by the two larger men on the bus."

"I heard," Buddy replied looking down. "I'm really sorry for all you guys have gone through. But, there is a way to prevent home break-ins, or at least deter thieves enough so that they look for an easier place."

"Let me guess," Howard said. "We have our maid watch the house on Sundays while we are at church."

"That's right," Buddy nodded looking back into Howard's eyes. "We covered this in orientation."

"Don't rub it in," Howard replied smiling just enough to let Buddy know that he wasn't offended. "We are still getting used to this 'maid' idea in the first place."

"We know," Buddy agreed. "But now you know another reason why we encourage new students to hire a maid. It is more than just cooking and cleaning. It is for language assistance, cultural help, as well as home security. Talk to your maid, I'm sure she wouldn't mind the extra hours and income."

"I guess we just thought she would be going to her church also," Howard reasoned.

"Some do, but most attend on Sunday evening."

"We can't get back on Sunday night," Howard admitted. "Even if we could, after today, I doubt I'll ever get Donna out on a bus after dark."

"That's understandable, and nobody really expects you to try to get back out on Sunday evening.'

"That's what is so hard to get used to sometimes," Howard sighed. "I'm accustomed to being directly involved with church and ministry seven days a week. Here I get to church once, maybe twice a week and I can't even pray out loud in a service yet. Do you know what that is like for a pastor?"

"Yes, I do," Buddy confessed. " Do you think I could always speak Spanish?" We went through the same class schedule, the same adjustment time, the same frustration and inability to communicate that you and Donna are going through right now. And let me tell you something – it's going to get worse before it gets better. That's what is called 'culture shock'. Oh, you may think things are different and maybe difficult, but trust me, the realization hasn't hit you yet. You don't have a ticket home."

Howard let Buddy's words sink deep. He didn't respond, but he glanced at Buddy as though looking for words of comfort.

"The important thing is that you take one day at a time. To be honest, this was a rough day to take. The question facing you is how are you going to respond to today? You can pack it in and say, 'we don't have to take this!' or you can thank God none of you were hurt and then pray for those who 'despitefully used you', and stole from you today. This stuff happens here – and I will venture to say that this won't be the last time you will be robbed."

Buddy was beginning to sound like a coach as well as a friend. Howard listened closely.

"I have known new students who begged to get their passports back so that they could go home. I have known some that I thought needed to go back home. I have known some that have weathered heavier storms than what you faced today, and were stronger in their resolve to stay. I believe the strength to stay comes from the call to go. If God sent you here, God will take care of you here, and to be honest, there is no safer place to be."

"I believe that," Howard replied humbly. "If I didn't, I think I would be in that room with Donna packing our things. I appreciate you and Sandy coming by to be with us."

"Think nothing of it, Brother," Buddy smiled. "We have been down this road before, and we have survived. You will also. If I know Sandy, she and Donna are finding something to laugh about. Before too long, they'll be out here and we can all have a time of prayer."

"Should I go ahead and get Terry?" Howard asked.

"That would be a good idea," Buddy said rising from the table with Howard.

Howard knocked on the door lightly and stepped inside. The door closed behind him and Buddy waited patiently. After a couple minutes, Howard stepped back out into the dining room area and closed the door behind him.

"Terry isn't quite ready to pray for the robbers," he explained.

"Give him time," Buddy assured. "Younger children watch to see how Mom and Dad are going to handle things first. Feeling vulnerable as a child is a fearful thing, especially if Mom and Dad are afraid."

"I'll remember that," Howard said, taking his seat at the table again. "I guess that describes it. I have never really felt vulnerable until today."

"All the more reason to draw your strength from God," Buddy replied. "He resists the proud and gives grace to the humble."

"Well, we have certainly been humbled today."

The two men continued to chat till the ladies emerged from the back bedroom laughing lightly. As the two couples joined around the table, Buddy led out in prayer. Howard followed, then Sandy and finally Donna through tear stained eyes. The peace of God was felt as each one lifted their heartfelt cries before the Throne of Grace. Terry listened from behind his door. He wanted to go home.

———————

Allen West dropped José Moralis at his house with just enough time for the pastor to change clothes and get to his evening service five kilometers outside of León at *Mt. Hermon.* Allen was always amazed by the degree of dedication that the local pastors demonstrated. Without a vehicle of his own, José would make it to the service and home again that night without complaining. Allen admired José.

The Land Cruiser weaved its way back through the narrow streets of León. Allen was glad to be home. He was not scheduled to preach anywhere that evening, and was thinking seriously about spending the evening at home with Becky. They had much to discuss and pray about. As he let himself in the front door, he felt suddenly tired. Allen had not realized just how much emotional energy he had discharged that day. When Becky met him, it was noticeable.

"You look beat," she commented.

"I am," Allen confessed. "That's strange, because I felt OK for the trip home. I just let José out and came straight home. I suddenly feel like I have been hiking for hours."

"What happened?" Becky probed. "Did you make it into *Pozo Negro?* What did you find there?"

"One question at a time," Allen sat down hard on the couch. "It was quite a day."

For the next twenty minutes, Allen related the events of walking the bank, finding the canoe, walking to town, the first family and eventually meeting Don Tulio. Becky nodded with interest, refraining from interrupting.

"I have never been anywhere like it," Allen summarized. "It was as though a heavy cloud hung over the town. And the people just seemed to exist under it. It was Sunday morning, but you would never have known it. There wasn't a single service going on anywhere. José felt it too. I believe we were in a stronghold area of oppression."

"It sounds like it," Becky agreed, taking the cue from Allen's pause. He leaned back and she continued. "I think that is why you are so tired right now. You have had harder days of activity and travel, but today you battled spiritually."

Allen nodded.

Becky continued with conviction in her voice. "You faced off with someone who obviously has allowed Satan to use him to cast spiritual blindness over an entire village. You said it yourself. He knew you two were believers without you stating it. He resisted you and you didn't back down. I'm not saying that there were angels and demons wielding spiritual swords all around you two today, but you have to admit, that spiritual warfare is real. Paul gave us some pretty sound advice and warning about it."

"You are so right," Allen replied, drawing strength from his wife's words. "I told José basically the same thing as we were leaving. I admit that I have not had much exposure to this sort of thing before, but if God is preparing a work in *Pozo Negro*, I have full confidence that He will prepare those of us for whatever it's going to take."

"So you are planning to go forward with the project?" Becky asked.

"I'm planning to keep going till God closes the door," Allen answered raising forward. "I have already put out the prayer and volunteer request through the Board. We'll wait and see if God touches some hearts to come and help. It will take a pretty solid construction team with some talented people, but God can put that together."

"He sure can," Becky said, sliding her arm around his shoulders. "In the meantime, we'll do some spiritual groundbreaking on this end. I'm like you, I believe God has some exciting things in mind for *Pozo Negro*."

They sat quietly together on the couch for a few moments. Allen broke the silence.

"I don't think I will be going back out tonight. I think I'm going to spend some time in prayer for *Pozo Negro*. Then I'm going to get my study Bible out and start looking up some passages about spiritual warfare."

"That sounds like a good idea, honey," Becky said softly. "I'll join you in prayer and then start us some supper while you do your Bible study."

"You can join me in prayer, but you may be eating alone tonight."

"Why?" Becky asked surprised.

"Oh, just a discussion José and I had on the way home today. I think we will both be giving ourselves to fasting tonight."

"Sounds like you are already getting yourself prepared. I won't tempt you, so I'll just re-warm some of the soup I had for lunch."

Becky rose from the couch and offered her hand to help Allen up. He jumped to his feet apparently refreshed. They walked together to the back-porch where they often went for special prayer time together. The late afternoon sun began to slip behind the distant hills. As they bowed their heads, they raised their spirits and prayed till nightfall.

———————————

Usually, Howard Pennington found Mondays at the language school to be surprisingly refreshing. When you struggle in a new culture and language, routine suddenly has its appeal. But when you are violated twice in a single day – especially on Sunday, even the return to the familiar is difficult. It was hard enough getting Terry onto the bus for his classes. The long walk up the hill through *El Bosque* seemed to take forever. Howard and Donna had less conversation than normal between them as they toted their backpacks drearily to the lower entrance of the language school. Howard acknowledged the Costa Rican guard at the gate, but didn't speak.

"*Buenos Dias*", Donna offered and smiled as the uniformed Tico opened the gate for them both.

"*Buen Dia*", he replied smiling back.

Howard just nodded and continued up the sidewalk, past the gym and to the first level of classrooms. Donna quickened her pace to keep up.

"I'll see you at the break," Howard said curtly and rounded the corner to his grammar classroom. He left Donna standing at the corner of the building. She had hoped for his kiss and reassuring smile that everything would be all right. She knew he was still hurting from the robberies, but so was she. She needed her kiss. Donna pivoted on her heel and headed into the opposite direction for her first of two *practica* classes.

Practica was where the elements of the other classes of phonetics and grammar came together. It was mostly oral, though there was some reading. The instructor tried to pull out the language from the students by getting them to explore ideas, tell stories, to relate personal experiences using all the Spanish they knew. When a word was unfamiliar, the teacher would coax the students into finding a way around using that word, by using whatever terms they did know. This resulted in some humorous descriptions. Sometimes a student would experiment with a term in hopes that it would be correct. When it failed, it was usually passed around for the amusement of others. Donna remembered how Paul, one of her classmates in *practica* tried to tell the class that his wife enjoyed mountain climbing. He was very enthusiastic in his description of her hobby. He wanted to tell how she was able to "free-climb" without the use of harness or rope. He didn't know the word for harness and guessed at the word for rope. To his embarrassment, he announced to the class that his wife would climb hills without *ropa*. The instructor quickly stifled her laughter and corrected Paul. *Ropa* was the word for clothes, not "rope".

Donna took her seat quietly while the other five students continued chatting of the weekend. The bell was heard and the instructor quickly cleared her throat.

"*Solo Español!*" she said sharply, reminding the class that they were to only speak Spanish in *practica* class. The students quickly grew silent.

Doña Gonzales was petite but forceful. Her dark brown eyes were closely set together and commanded respect. Her diction was filled with the tone of perfection that she desired from her class. Like most language school instructors, she was stern and demanding at first. Some would soften as the term progressed, while some kept the taskmaster reputation throughout the trimester. Doña Gonzales was one that waited mid-trimester to lighten up. She was actually a compassionate teacher, who loved her Lord greatly and wanted to see these missionaries succeed. But experience had taught the instructors that leniency on the front end was disastrous. The soft side of the instructor may only be practiced after respect was established. A teacher cannot go from soft to hard as well as they can the reverse.

"Let us begin with something about the weekend," Doña Gonzales began in perfect Spanish.

Two chairs left of Donna sat Ernesto. Most thought he was fluent by his appearance, but Ernesto was third generation Hispanic American, raised in Louisiana and had never learned the language. It was almost comical watching him struggle with pronunciation. His Cajun twang was very prominent.

"*El fin dea semana,*" he began.

"*El fin DE semana,*" Doña Gonzales quickly corrected.

"Oh, yeah, dat's right," Ernesto replied, slipping into his English.

"*Solo Español!*" she quipped.

"Sorry," Ernesto said unthinking. "I mean, *lo siento, mucho.*"

Ernesto took a breath and tried starting over. It was tedious working with limited vocabulary. He wanted to talk about going to the National Plaza after church and feeding the pigeons in front of the Catholic Cathedral, but he had no idea what the word for "pigeon" was. He ended up calling the birds – "*pajas*". Unfortunately, Doña Gonzales had to inform Ernesto that he had just said that he enjoyed feeding the *straw* in front of the Church. Rather than asking him to further embarrass himself by elaborating what he fed to straw, she quickly moved on to the next student trying to hide from view.

Donna kept her head low praying silently that the discussion would become lively with someone else and that they would never get around the table to her. The minute hand of her watch seemed to slow unmercifully as she glanced repeatedly at her wrist. The instructor noticed and decided that

Donna would go next. She was obviously unprepared for class and needed to be corrected.

"Señora Pennington, tell us about your weekend," Doña Gonzales enounced with commanding diction.

Donna looked up with pleading eyes. "Please don't call on me today," they said. The instructor saw, yet persisted, not with malice, but with professional authority. Her job was to "pull out" the Spanish that the unconfident possessed.

"Señora Pennington," she repeated.

Donna sat for an eternal moment, first looking pathetically towards her instructor, and then at the table. She took a breath and began forming words.

"*Somos robos,*" was all that came out of her mouth.

Doña Gonzales looked stunned. She knew what she heard, but couldn't believe it was correct. Giving Donna the benefit of the doubt, she softened her tone and spoke in English.

"Did you mean to say, *robos* or *robados*?" the instructor asked carefully.

"I'm not sure," Donna replied honestly. "What does *robos* mean?"

"You just said – 'we are robbers!'" Doña Gonzales said slowly.

Donna gasped and shook her head no forcefully.

"And *robados*?" Donna asked innocently.

"Robbed," the instructor said.

"That is what I meant to say," Donna sighed. "But not, 'we are'. Rather, 'we were.'"

Suddenly the table came alive with conversation. The "Spanish Only" was understandably suspended and the other students were allowed to ask their questions without reprimand. Donna broke down and began to cry as she answered. Doña Gonzales gave way for the class to minister to one of their own. She too cared, but her opportunity would come later.

The knock was faint.

"Come on in," Rusty called from behind his desk without looking up from his keyboard.

"Don't mean to bother you, pastor," came the husky voice from the doorway.

Rusty swiveled around to face Arnie.

"No bother at all, come right in," Rusty replied smiling.

"I stopped at Dianne's desk, but she wasn't there," Arnie said politely.

"She takes an early lunch on Mondays. What can I do for you, Arnie," the pastor offered.

Arnie swaggered into the office with a big grin on his face. The large barrel- chested construction worker reached in his shirt pocket and produced a small thin dark blue notebook and held it up for Rusty.

"I found it," he said proudly.

"Found what?" Rusty smiled, sharing in Arnie's enthusiasm.

"My Passport," Arnie replied. "I took Betty to Europe for our twentieth wedding anniversary about four years ago and had to get one then. I am ready to go!"

"That's great Arnie, what about Alex?" Rusty asked.

"I just went by the Post office and picked up his application – they say it will take about three weeks."

"That's not bad, I need to get on the ball and get my application in as well," Rusty said making a note on a yellow Postum.

"How many do we have going?" Arnie asked putting his passport away.

"So far we have seven from the church plus Billy Eldridge," Rusty said smiling.

"How many do you think we need?"

"That's a good question," Rusty thought. "I may try to make contact with the missionary and let him know we are praying about this project and get an idea of what he is looking for."

Rusty took out a legal pad to make some notes.

"In fact, Arnie, while you're here, why don't you help me with the construction questions."

"I can do that," Arnie said taking a seat.

Rusty cleared a place on his desk while Arnie scooted his chair closer. They began with a prayer.

"Lord, we thank you for this open door," Rusty began. "We pray your direction in each step we take. We pray for those who have made this request. We pray that You can use us in meeting this need and making a difference in the lives of those we will meet. Lord, most of all, we pray for ourselves as we prepare for this mission trip. May we be spiritually and mentally prepared for what lies ahead."

"Amen."

Allen and Becky did not look forward to their trips into Managua. The capitol was congested and the traffic was so much heavier than León. Fortunately, the mission office had been moved from the business district to the hills leading out of the city to the south. It was located on the campus of the MK school. The school for the missionary kids had grown to include the bilingual children of middle-upper to upper class Nicaraguan families. The mission had moved its office to the campus as development began expanding in the late 90's. The West's combined trips to the mission office with major shopping days so as to make as few trips as possible. Their Land Cruiser easily held groceries for a month and most times, that was as often as Allen wished to make the trip.

The trip home was usually late afternoon. The only good part of the return drive was that the traffic improved shortly after getting out of the city limits and that left two hours of relaxing talk.

"Did you get to see Aaron at the mission office while I was at the store?" Becky asked after the final checkpoint just outside the city limits.

"I did," Allen nodded. "We have a meeting with the rest of the mission in March concerning some new directions that the mission board will be taking."

"More new directions?" Becky mused.

"No, just *newer* new directions" Howard replied sarcastically.

After a couple kilometers of silence, Howard continued.

"He also had some emails for me that came to the mission office. I slipped them into my satchel. Why don't you pull them out and we'll look at them together."

Becky reached between them and opened the worn leather satchel that Allen carried with him at all times. It had his calendar, his Bible and whatever pertinent folders of material he was working on at the time. She sifted through the folders and found some loose sheets wedged between his sermon notes and some paperwork on some mission property.

"I think I found them," Becky said pulling out the creased pages. "Was there about three?"

"That sounds right, look at the subject lines, I think one of them is about a volunteer team," Allen replied concentrating on the road.

"Let's see," Becky began as she read the top of each email. "One is a memo from the area office to all Nicaraguan missionaries – I guess Aaron just made you a copy and put it in our box. One is from Aaron himself giving the dates about the meeting in March, which you already know about first-hand. And the third is…oh yes, this is about a volunteer team."

"Who's it from?" Allen asked.

"Let's see…it looks like 'corn' something," Becky answered squinting and then fumbled for her reading glasses. "The font is small, I'll need some help."

"Corn?" Allen said to himself.

"That's just the first part, let's see…that's better. I'm sorry, it wasn't 'corn', it says 'coronadobc@aol.com'."

"That must mean 'Coronado Baptist Church'," Allen thought out loud. "Who do we know there?"

"I don't even know where 'there' is, sweetie." Becky said looking over the rim of her glasses.

"See if the letter indicates where they are." Allen pursued.

"Why don't I just read the letter and then maybe all of our questions will be answered," Becky offered.

Allen chuckled. "O.K."

"The email says," she began to read. " 'Greetings in the Matchless Name of our Lord and Savior, Jesus Christ'."

"Good beginning," Allen interrupted.

"…My name is Rusty Patterson, and I am pastor of the Coronado Baptist Church near San Diego, California."

"Well, that answers that," Allen interrupted again.

"…Recently, I received a PrayerGram from the Mission Board that spoke of a need in a small town in Nicaragua named, *Pozo Negro*."

Allen sat up straight and let Becky finish without interruption.

"…Our church has never been on a mission trip to my knowledge, but I believe the time is right. We have some tremendously talented people wanting to come and help build a bridge. Please let us know what we can do. I am working now on making sure everyone is getting a passport. We were thinking about sometime in the early spring of next year. Let us know what your timetable for building is and the best time to think about coming. Most of our people are flexible.

"I am assuming we would need to help with the building materials also," the email went on to say. "If you have an idea of the costs for materials, let us know. Again, we are willing and excited."

"Now that's a combination – 'willing and excited'," Allen exclaimed.

"Wait, there's a little more," Becky said enthusiastically. "…Last year, the pastor of the church answered the call to missions and he and his wife are currently in their second month of language school in Costa Rica. They will be going to Honduras sometime next year. We hope to someday work with them on a project. This will give us a little experience. I pray you will consider our offer and contact us soon. In His Name, Rusty Patterson."

"When was the email received?" Allen asked anxiously.

"Just this past Monday, about three days ago."

"I'll write them as soon as we get back home," Allen said confidently. "I guess this trip to the capital wasn't so bad after all. It would be great to get a team to *Pozo Negro*."

"Are you going to tell him about the witch doctor?" Becky added.

"I think I will. This team will need to be planning for more than construction. They will need to be preparing themselves for spiritual warfare. Five to six months should be just about right."

"So you're thinking maybe April?" Becky asked quickly adding on her fingers.

"I think so, the rains will have stopped, it will be in the mountains so the heat shouldn't be too awful, and it will be near *Semana Santa*."

"But not during?!" Becky exclaimed, knowing that Holy Week was the time before Easter when most businesses closed and supplies and materials were difficult to purchase.

"I wouldn't think so," Allen agreed. "But then, I don't always think as God does."

"Let's make that a real matter of prayer," Becky suggested, nervous that her husband would choose the most exhaustive holiday of the year to bring in a volunteer team.

"Oh, we will make the whole project a matter of prayer," Allen concurred. "In fact, why don't we begin now."

Becky took his hand. As he drove, she bowed her head and took the lead in praying for the people of *Pozo Negro*. She prayed for the little man with the big stick. She prayed for the new pastor who wanted to lead his people on a venture that would most definitely test the metal of their spiritual strength as well as their ability to build in a third world country. She prayed for her husband as he would lay the groundwork for the team and faced the challenges of logistics like food, transportation, and housing for the team. There was much to do. And Becky prayed for the family in Costa Rica, as they prepared for the mission fields of Honduras. She prayed for their ability to learn the language, their adaptation to the new culture, and for their safety. Without knowing them by name, Becky prayed for the Penningtons and the Penningtons needed their prayers.

Juanita worked quietly around the Pennington home. It had been almost a week since the break-in, and Mr. and Mrs. Pennington still did not talk much, to her or each other. She was relieved that neither had accused her of being involved in the break-in. It was not unheard of for the *empleada* to be accomplice to a robbery since she knew the family schedule, but Juanita knew she was not involved. Working for North Americans was not easy. There were misunderstandings many times due to language, customs, and personality differences. Juanita learned to do her work without "talking" any more than was necessary, even though her desire was to learn English. There were times when Donna would invite Juanita to join them at the kitchen table for a meal, but even then, she was not asked about her family or other personal matters. They usually practiced their text for the week and asked her to correct their pronunciation.

Donna eased behind Juanita in the small kitchen so she could carry some dirty clothes to the small washer that was stationed on the back patio. Juanita would start the wash load and hang the clothes on the nylon lines that were strung under the plastic roofing when it was raining. The clothes would dry throughout the night if there wasn't too much humidity in the air.

Donna stepped back into the kitchen and leaned against the doorframe.

"Juanita," she started slowly.

Juanita looked up from stirring the rice and beans she was preparing on the small cook-stove.

"*Si, Señora*," she responded turning her full attention toward the lady of the house.

Donna struggled with her words, and relied on her limited vocabulary to express herself. "You know what happened last Sunday while we were at the Church?"

"*Si, Señora,*" she replied nodding.

"Mr. Pennington and I have been talking about this. We are concerned about leaving the house alone," Donna continued, deciding to get right to the point. "We need someone who can stay at the house on Sundays while we are at Church. We could try to hire a watchman, but I wanted to ask you if you would be interested in coming to the house and Sundays."

Juanita refrained herself from correcting Mrs. Pennington's mistakes with the language. She could tell that her employer was trying to communicate and was trying to share something serious. Now was not the time for a Spanish lesson. Juanita looked down and paused long enough to show that she had understood what Donna was asking.

"*Señora Pennington,* I am sorry for what happened to your family. I am sorry that my people have taken from you. I am sorry if this has made you feel bad about my country. Please know that not all my people steal. Please know that I do not steal."

"Oh, I know," Donna inserted quickly.

"I would like to thank you for giving me this job," Juanita continued, looking Donna in the eye. "I would like to thank you for asking me to watch your house. You CAN trust me. I would be pleased to help you watch your home on Sunday."

Donna relaxed her stance.

"We would pay you, of course for the extra day, AND make sure to include the amount in our *aquinaldo* which we will pay you before we leave."

"I trust you to do what is right," Juanita said smiling. "I just want to help your family."

Donna finally smiled. She wanted to reach out and hug her maid, but still felt cautious. There was still some healing to come for her. She took Juanita's hands into her own as a tear began to form.

"Thank you, so much," was all Donna could say.

"*A su orden,*" Juanita replied smiling back. Donna understood the response well. It simply meant, "at your order". It was a welcomed response.

CHAPTER SEVEN

"THE LESSON"

DIANNE WINTERS had served as church secretary for over three years with the Coronado Baptist Church. She was hired right out of college and loved her job. She rented a small house in Oceana and commuted each day along Harbor Drive. The church paid her toll to cross the Coronado Bridge to the beautiful church that was located just south of the Naval Installation of North Island.

Dianne had enjoyed serving under Dr. Howard Pennington, except during the early days of the building program that almost cost him his family. She rejoiced with the rest of the church over their family's decision to go to the mission field and she prayed for them often. Now that Rusty had moved from the associate's office to the Pastor's Study, she wondered if their relationship would continue to develop as it had been before he took leadership of the church. Propriety was important, and she did not want to jeopardize Rusty's role as pastor. Though he was as friendly as he had always been, she knew he was also holding back from the little comments he used to make. He hadn't even asked her to lunch since he became pastor of the church. She wondered if he longed for the opportunity as much as she did.

Rusty was not a coffee drinker, but he did enjoy a diet Dr. Pepper each morning. Dianne took advantage of the routine and would bring him one from the staff refrigerator shortly after he arrived. She would wait till he had prepared his desk from the day before and sifted through the mail. Sometimes, he would already be engrossed in study or interesting correspondence, but most of the time he was unoccupied and could respond in conversation. She hoped for the short time of conversation.

"Ready for your D.P.?" Dianne asked softly tapping on the open door.

"Absolutely!" Rusty replied, obviously in a good mood. "Have you got a minute?"

Dianne tried not to show too much enthusiasm.

"There's nothing pressing this morning...sure," she replied nonchalantly.

"I was doing some study at home last night on the computer about Nicaragua and came across some interesting information on the area we are going to go to in April."

Rusty cleared a space on the side of his desk and invited Dianne to pull one of the leather chairs alongside. He spread several pages with blocks of highlighted areas before him on the desk and started arranging them in order.

"Do you remember hurricane Mitch?" Rusty began.

"Vaguely," Dianne admitted. "When was that?"

"Just last year, about this time," Rusty stated. "It hit off of the coast of Honduras, but did a lot of damage in El Salvador and Nicaragua as well."

Dianne squinted as if trying to remember more.

"Don't worry," Rusty smiled. "I had almost forgot about it as well. I guess that is the way we take news in America. If it doesn't happen to us, it has about a two-month life span. For us, if it is not current, it's not news. We forget quickly the aftermath of disasters in other countries."

Dianne nodded.

"I got interested because the missionary we are going to work with wrote that we would be working on a bridge that was lost during hurricane Mitch. I was curious about how Mitch affected Nicaragua. Most of the news we heard was about Honduras. So I went to the Internet and found some interesting items."

Rusty pulled one of the sheets from the stack and sat it between them so that Dianne could see.

"This is just a statistical report that came out after the disaster. Over 6,500 Hondurans died and about 2,500 Nicaraguans," Rusty stated handing her the sheet.

"I didn't remember it being that many," Dianne remarked stunned. She took the sheet to read more.

"In addition, over one million lost their homes."

"Over a MILLION?!" Dianne exclaimed.

"That's right," Rusty replied shaking his head. "There are people still living in tent cities a year later. Efforts are being made by several church groups, including Baptists, to build small homes for these people, but there are still thousands living under plastic sheeting and in tents."

"That's terrible," Dianne sighed.

"Here is an article I found on health needs," he said pulling out another sheet from the stack. "The flooding carried a great deal of dead bodies, animals and people through the living areas and disease followed."

"What kinds of disease?" Dianne asked cautiously.

"Malaria, Cholera, dengue,…"

"What's dengue?" She stopped him.

"As best I can tell, it is like malaria. It's carried by mosquitoes and has no real treatment, once you have it," Rusty replied, trying not to sound like an expert.

"Is it deadly?" Dianne asked.

"There are some instances of death, but mostly among young children and older people with poor immune systems," Rusty explained searching for another document. "I had the same questions, so I looked it up also." Handing Dianne a third sheet, he continued. "This site gave me the information on dengue."

Rusty could tell Dianne was interested, but was also being overwhelmed by the lesson. He decided to shift gears.

"All this to say,…we are going to see some disturbing sights on our trip. Let me share a piece about Nicaragua."

He pulled out another heavily highlighted report and slid it across the desk so that they could both see.

"I just see a mountain," Dianne said studying the picture on the page.

"Actually, it is a volcano," Rusty said correcting her. "Do you see those bare spots down the side?"

Dianne studied the picture closely and nodded.

"That is called a *lahar*," Rusty said pleased with himself and his new word.

"A what?" Dianne asked.

"A *lahar*. They are usually formed by a volcanic flow. They destroy anything in their path and cover the ground with a hard crusty covering that prevents vegetation from growing back."

"You said, 'usually'," Dianne probed.

"That's right," Rusty confirmed. "But when you read the article, you will find that this volcano is *La Casita* in western Nicaragua. Those bare patches were caused by landslides that took place during the hurricane. What happened was that part of the cone of the Volcano collapsed and began to slide down the side of the mountain. The *lahar* was formed by the volcanic rock, the mud and sludge, as well as some pretty good sized boulders that were caught up in the slide."

Rusty paused to make sure that Dianne was with him, then proceeded delicately.

"Those larger bare spots mid-way up the mountain were villages that were covered by the *lahar*. Two villages were destroyed and about two thousand people died with them."

Dianne shuddered.

"Of the nine-thousand fatalities recorded among the four countries of El Salvador, Guatemala, Honduras and Nicaragua, over one fifth of the deaths took place on this mountain."

Rusty pulled out a map from his stack and laid it before Dianne.

"This is where *La Casita* is located…" Rusty pointed to a spot on the map. "…and this is where we are planning to go." His finger moved less than an inch on the map. This is the city of León and *Pozo Negro* is just outside this city up another mountain."

"But not another volcano?" Dianne asked with a touch of concern in her voice.

"I don't think so," Rusty chuckled. "…but I will find out. One other thing worth mentioning," he said collecting the pages together.

"Many of the people in the mountain areas are very superstitious. They have blended animism and religion in their belief system."

"What does that mean?" Dianne asked.

"They look at natural disasters like Mitch as having supernatural significance. Whether it was God punishing or the devil afflicting, many have attached religious meaning to the results of this storm. Unfortunately, some blame themselves or their village for the disaster. In some places, this has opened the door for the gospel, but in others, it has hardened the people against a message of love."

"Now look at this," Rusty continued, leaning toward Dianne. "Hurricanes are named in alphabetical order beginning with 'A' and so forth.".

"I knew that," Dianne replied confidently, but not insulted.

"Well, guess which hurricane of the season that Mitch was?"

Dianne thought for a moment and began counting to herself. She reached "L", the twelfth letter of the alphabet and suddenly realized what conclusion Rusty was leading her towards.

"Mitch was the thirteenth hurricane of the season!" she exclaimed.

"That's right, now look at this breakdown of the hurricane's activity." Rusty added quickly, presenting a report on the storm itself.

"The greatest damage took place on the 30th and 31st of October. According to an email from the missionary, *Pozo Negro* lost their bridge on the 31st."

Rusty paused for the significance of the date to sink in.

"Halloween!" Dianne declared.

"To be specific, 'The Day of the Dead' as the people call it in Central America," Rusty replied, proud of his research.

"Yuck!" Dianne repelled.

"Exactly," acknowledged Rusty. "Imagine how that looks to a superstitious people – a national disaster on the Day of the Dead from the thirteenth hurricane of the season."

"I see what you mean," Dianne nodded. "So what does all this have to do with your trip?"

"I suspect we are going to be dealing with some people who will see the loss of their bridge as a supernatural phenomenon with spiritual implications," stated Rusty leaning back into his swivel chair. "In other words, we may have some serious spiritual warfare involved with this trip. I think our team members need to be prepared."

"How do you mean prepared?"

Rusty opened his Bible to a place where he had placed a bookmark earlier.

"Paul writes in 1 Corinthians 10:3-5, *'For though we live in the world, we do not wage war as the world does. The weapons we fight with are not the weapons of the world. On the contrary, they have divine power to demolish strongholds. We demolish arguments and every pretension that sets itself up against the knowledge of God, and we take captive every thought to make it obedient to Christ.'*"

Rusty quickly turned to a second passage he had marked and continued reading.

"Then in Ephesians 6, he wrote – *'For our struggle is not against flesh and blood, but against the rulers, against the authorities, against the powers of this dark world and against the spiritual forces of evil in the heavenly realms. Therefore put on the full armor of God, so that when the day of evil comes, you may be able to stand your ground, and after you have done everything, to stand. Stand firm then, with the belt of truth buckled around your waist, with the breastplate of righteousness in place, and with your feet fitted with the readiness that comes from the gospel of peace. In addition to all this, take up the shield of faith, with which you can extinguish all the flaming arrows of the evil one. Take the helmet of salvation and the sword of the Spirit, which is the word of God. And pray in the Spirit on all occasions with all kinds of prayers and requests. With this in mind, be alert and always keep on praying for all the saints.'*"

"Did you notice in both places he talks about our 'weapons'? This is not something to take lightly. Believe me, the devil doesn't take it lightly."

Rusty closed his Bible and looked hard into Dianne's eyes.

"We better know what we are heading into, and we best be prepared. I have a feeling that this is not going to be just a construction project. I plan to start having some team meetings that will prepare us *spiritually* for the trip."

"How many do we have going now?" Dianne asked.

"We have a solid dozen," Rusty replied quickly. "After Arnie shared with his Sunday School class, two more men with construction experience said they would go. Alex, Arnie's son recruited two young men from his college. It seems their spring break lines up with the dates of the trip. There's Billy Eldridge and the other four that came forward the morning of our big service last month."

"Which four is that again?" Dianne asked trying to remember their names.

"There is Ty Andrews, who is a welder. He has done some repair work on the Coronado Bridge from time to time. There is Willis and Rhonda Beamen. I think he is an auto-mechanic. They have no children and are able to go together. And Stan Henly is still planning to go. That makes twelve."

"I would offer to go, but that would make it thirteen," Dianne teased.

"No thanks," Rusty laughed. "Besides, I need you here while I'm gone. You keep this office running."

Dianne smiled. She enjoyed being appreciated. More important, she enjoyed being noticed by Rusty.

"Well, I better let you get to work," she quipped. "It sounds like you have some serious preparation in mind for the team."

"Thanks, Dianne," Rusty said as she stood and headed for the door. "I appreciate you letting me share my findings with you. Sometimes, I just need a listening ear."

Dianne smiled as she walked through the doorway leading back to her desk. "Anytime," she said to herself. "Anytime."

Donna Pennington walked briskly out of phonetics class and began looking for Howard in the hallway. Because of the distinct levels in their language ability, they had been placed in different classes. Howard clearly had a better command of the language, but was learning the intricate rules of grammar.

She found him with the crowd checking their mailboxes for the precious correspondence from home. Though they had their laptop, they had not subscribed to an Internet service and were not receiving email during their year at Costa Rica. A letter from the United States took about seven days to arrive and was as prized as peanut butter, (which was also a rare commodity). Today was a special day. The return address included the name Pennington. It was a letter from Karen.

"Did we get something?" Donna called while still several feet away.

Howard looked up and smiled. He waved a special airmail envelope so she could see.

"A letter from Karen," he beamed.

"Well, its about time," Donna chuckled. "It's been at least two weeks since her last letter."

"Remember, she's a busy college girl now, and has lots of study time to think about," Howard said in humor.

"Like we don't?!" Donna reminded him.

"No argument here," Howard laughed. "Let's see what she has to say."

He read the opening lines of family greeting out loud and then trailed off. Donna stood anxiously beside him waiting to hear of any news. Was it a boyfriend, a hard class, or maybe an accident?

"Is everything OK?" Donna finally asked, breaking Howard's concentration.

"Oh,...yeah!" he simply responded still in thought. "It's something else that she thought we would like to know."

"WELL?..." Donna asked at a higher pitch.

Howard handed Donna the letter and smiled.

Donna began to read aloud.

"Dear Mom and Dad..."

"Start at the second paragraph break," Howard instructed.

"Uncle Billy is excited about going on a mission trip next April. It seems that the Church is taking a team to Nicaragua. Billy was at the church the morning they decided to go. It was really neat. He doesn't know much about what they are going to do, except that it involves some construction work. Rusty will be having some team meetings closer to time and Uncle Billy will learn more at that time. Anyway, he's really excited and wanted me to let you know – so I have."

"Imagine that," Howard mused.

"What?" Donna questioned. "I think its great that Rusty is taking a team overseas, and its exciting that Billy Eldridge will be going with them."

"Oh, I quite agree with that," Howard replied. "But did you see how Karen referred to Mr. Eldridge? - *Uncle* Billy. That means they are treating her like family."

Donna looked back at the letter and smiled also.

"You're right, that was a good arrangement for her."

As they savored the moment of a good letter, a small gathering started to form at the opposite end of the hallway. Howard noticed the group first and began stepping toward them to see what was happening. Donna continued to read the letter, and soon realized she was standing alone. She saw the growing group and could hear the voice of Al Redding. She walked over and stood next to Howard as Al spoke rapidly. She wasn't sure what he was telling, but it had obviously distressed him. Donna quickly looked around to find Leanne, but she wasn't with him. She pressed forward to hear better.

"Over one hundred and sixty dollars!" Al said sharply. A quiet gasp waved through the group.

"Did you tell the school administration?" a voice called out.

"I just left the office," Al responded, as though he were the center of a press conference. "They basically rebuked me for trying to change money on the street. They said, that was why they told us to ONLY make our exchanges at the bank."

"I remember that," someone said half-heartedly. "It was during orientation. They said that black market money changers may offer a better rate, but there was always the risk of being taken."

"What are you going to do?" another voice called out.

"I'm going to learn my lesson," Al called back. The perpetual optimism was lost in his voice. Howard had never seen Al distraught like this before. It was discomforting. "I'm also going to be careful about trusting *Ticos*," he quickly added.

Howard looked up alarmed. That didn't sound like Al. The Reddings had been in country for almost eight months. They had been language students four months before he and Donna arrived. Now was not the time to be losing trust in their host-country – not as a people.

"You don't mean that, Al," Howard offered reassuringly.

"Look who's talking," Al snapped back. "How long ago were you robbed, both at home and personally?"

The group suddenly turned their eyes on Howard.

"Is that true?" someone near Howard asked earnestly. "How much did you lose?"

"The Robertson's home was broke into last weekend," came a voice from near the back of the group.

"We've been robbed," another added.

The group was quickly turning into a mob. Howard raised his hand and tried to gain the attention of the group.

"Yes, we were robbed. I had my pocket picked on a bus on our way home from Church, while at the same time, someone or *some ones* were breaking into our home. We lost some things and some money. So have some of you. But it was some *ONE*, not the country. There will always be bad people wherever you live – wasn't that the case back in the States? Would you want the Costa Rican people to lump you and me into the same category as those who commit similar crimes in our country?"

"But Howard, look around you," Al interrupted. "how many victims do we have in this small group alone? Doesn't that tell you something about this country? Theft is more common here than where I come from."

"Look at this group around us," Howard replied firmly. "We are targets because of the perception that, and I repeat, *some* have about North Americans. Some think we are all rich and can afford to have what we possess taken, because we can easily replace it. But I do not believe that the majority of the Costa Rican people we walk around each day want to take advantage of us – just because we appear to have something they don't."

"Then you're naïve!" Al shot back abruptly. Then softening his tone unapologetically, he added, "Like I was – but not again."

Howard looked hurt, but refrained from striking back. "I'm sorry you lost your money, Al. If we can help, let us know."

Others expressed similar sentiments. The group began to slowing dissolve back to the mailboxes and down to the ping pong area. There was still ten minutes left to the break. Donna led Howard away while two or three remained in conference with Al.

"Wow!" Donna said softly. "That didn't sound like Al."

"I know," Howard concurred. "I know he's upset. I know how he feels."

"But that's no reason for striking out at you," she said defensively. "I mean, you were only trying to help."

"I don't think he saw it that way. He wants to be angry with the people right now. He'll get over it"

"How did it happen?" Donna asked, slightly changing the subject.

"It seems that Al and Leanne were trying to change some money over the weekend. The banks were closed so they decided to use a money changer downtown."

"They should know better," Donna interrupted.

"They needed money, and figured everyone else did it, so why not? Anyway, they exchanged about four hundred dollars for their monthly expenses, and you know what that means."

"A huge stack of five thousand Colon bills," Donna inserted.

"That's right. Only problem is that his money changer was low on five thousand bills and wanted to give Al the balance in one thousand Colon bills"

"How many?" Donna asked knowing that meant a large stack of money to carry around.

"About seventy or so," Howard replied. "Anyway, he gave him the five thousand first and counted them twice. Then he began counting out the one thousand bills even quicker. Do you know what color the one thousand Colon bills are?" Howard asked.

"Red," Donna replied succinctly.

"That's right. And guess what other currency is red?"

Donna thought for a moment and came up blank.

"The One-*Lempira* bill from Honduras. And do you know what it is worth?"

Donna shrugged again.

"Less than eighteen cents – and that's if you can get any value for it in this country in the market. No merchants will take it."

"But the one thousand Colon is worth just about $3 dollars apiece!" Donna exclaimed.

"That's right. Today, when Al was getting some money out to take to town, he noticed that more than fifty of his bills that he exchanged on Saturday were not Colons, but Lempiras. He lost nearly one hundred and forty dollars in the exchange. They mixed the Lempiras in with the Colons and because they were both red, Al didn't notice the difference until it was too late."

"That's terrible," Donna sighed.

"I think it is worse than just the lost of money," Howard said softer. "I think it marked a lost of trust that they were building over seven months to establish."

"Is he that upset?" Donna asked looking in Al's direction.

"I think so," Howard replied with a sorrowful tone in his voice. "It wouldn't be hard for some to get very discouraged here."

Donna sighed. She knew the feeling all too well.

Becky West closed her Bible and bowed her head. The warm early morning sun bathed her gently as she sat in a small outer court of their home. Sometimes she missed the front porch in Knox County, but had found her quiet spot in a small open-air court within the compound of their home in León. Outfitted with just a rocking chair and small table stand, she escaped the world and could still see a patch of sky. The mountains outside of the León were not the Appalachians, but they were still mountains. That's all a girl from east Tennessee needed sometimes to get her day started.

Becky began to pray for her children. She listed each by name before the Lord. She prayed for her parents and their health needs. She prayed for Allen's father, who lived alone in West Virginia. She prayed through the prayer calendar of those missionaries with birthdays that December morning. Becky then turned to her personal prayer list. She prayed for the women's Bible study she was leading in Chinandega. She prayed for different women by name. She prayed for her husband, as Allen would be traveling that week to check on churches near the Honduras border. She then prayed for José, as he would be traveling with Allen those two days. She paused in her prayers and waited. Becky had learned that not all prayer needs were on her list. As she sat in an attitude of prayer, many times she would be led to pray for people and needs that she had not anticipated. This was one of those times.

Allen started his day checking out the Land Cruiser. He was never much of a mechanic, and newer vehicles were nearly impossible to "tinker" with, but some things were still basic. Allen checked his belts, his fluids and tires before every major trip. One time he had broken a fan belt while in the mountains and learned that one of Becky's panty hose was strong enough to make a provisional repair till he could get back to his mechanic in León. Since that time, he never traveled without them. He also kept a small air compressor in the back for tire leaks. Allen cleaned off his oil stick and replaced it satisfied that the level and color was good. Mileage was not the best indicator for determining an oil change when you traveled as many dirt roads as he did.

Allen closed his hood and went back into the house to find Becky kneeling beside her rocker. He paused long enough to determine if she was in pain or in prayer. He could hear her soft voice, though not what she was saying. Convinced she was ok, he quietly went to the kitchen so as not to disturb her. He reheated his coffee in the microwave and sat at the small dining table they had gotten after the last of the children had returned to the states. He was about to pick up the *Prensa* for the daily news, when Becky joined him.

"Some serious prayer time this morning?" Allen asked smiling.

"Definitely beyond the routine," Becky answered, then added thoughtfully, "As if any prayer time should be routine."

"Anything you care to share?" Allen probed.

"The Lord really brought that village across the river to mind this morning – the one we visited where you are going to take that team next April." She paused and sat down across the table from him. "I don't always get such strong impressions, but this was definitely from the Lord. I believe He wants you and the team to be prepared for something. A phrase kept coming to my mind – maybe it will mean something to you."

Allen gave his wife his full attention.

Becky took a breath, and simply spoke the words, "Bind the strong man".

Don Tulio stepped out of his darkened abode, brandishing his twisted staff. Children playing soccer in the road a block away quickly gathered their ball and stood against the building till he passed by. His face was set and he quickened his stride as he walked toward the Town Square.

Roberto Espinal watched the little man with the big stick pass by. He wasn't as frightened as the children, but he understood why they were. The stories surrounding Don Tulio were not all good. He could reduce a fever, cure a hurting back or limb, and even stop some diseases from spreading to other family members. There were stories of him healing bad teeth, reversing infections, and even lengthening shortened legs. But at times, Don Tulio was thought to use his power in more malevolent ways. If a family failed to pay what they promised for a cure or gave poor crops or animals in exchange for his service, Don Tulio had been known to curse the man's crops or cause one of his primary animals to die unexplainably. If the town upset him with a decision to hold a festival without consulting him, he would assure them that the weather would be bad and sometimes even out of character for the season. There was talk that one year he held the rain for two months during the critical growing season because they observed the festival of the Patron Saint. Some even rumored that Don Tulio was responsible for the bridge being washed away. Roberto didn't know if he was responsible or not, but he knew that the little man was there. He remembered clearly seeing him silhouetted against the sky as the bridge and his friend, Daniel, were both swept downstream. Roberto never told a soul about that day. He simply tried to avoid the little man with the big stick.

Roberto Espinal worked for his uncle two to three days a week in *Pozo Negro* when he was not hiring himself out for different jobs that he found each week down in León. He hoped to some day be able to leave *Pozo Negro* altogether, but for now, he had family that needed him and that meant that he had to be around Don Tulio.

The healer made his stride more deliberate as he entered the main square. Don Tulio marched to the two-room building that served as the city hall. The *Alcalde* sat on a hard wooden chair at the front door, because it was too hot inside the building. Two men of the village stood around as the trio talked about crops, rain, and the rising cost of rice that needed to be brought in from other markets. Their heads turned toward Don Tulio as he approached the mayor and quickly grew silent.

"*Alcalde!*" Don Tulio snapped indicating a desire to speak alone with the political head of the village. The two men immediately sensed the tone and dismissed themselves.

"Don Tulio," the *Alcalde* replied with the dignity he could muster. Solomón Garcia had been elected mayor for his business experience and his gentle manner. Those who wondered why Tulio Bayardos had not been elected *Alcalde* of *Pozo Negro* soon recognized that Don Tulio did not need a political position to wield power. He could even tell the mayor what needed to be done when it pleased him.

"What brings you to my office today," Solomón continued amiably.

Don Tulio sneered sarcastically at the suggestion that this man actually held an office that mattered.

"I am troubled by some things I see," Don Tulio remarked. The mayor looked surprised. To his knowledge, nothing different had taken place in the village for months. The last incident out of the ordinary was the death of the small girl who drowned during the rainy season over four months ago. It was not the first of such deaths. The town had mourned and much time had passed – what could be bothering Don Tulio? Rather than try to guess, Solomón simply asked.

"What trouble have you been seeing, Don Tulio?"

"It is not what I have seen, it is what I see," Don Tulio began cryptically. "I see men coming to *Pozo Negro*. I see men bringing strange ideas that will hurt our people. I see men pretending to help us, but really they have come to steal from us."

"What men?" the mayor questioned. "What men would even have interest in *Pozo Negro*? What do we have here to steal?"

"Our souls," Don Tulio quickly replied. "They will come to rob us of our souls."

"Our souls?" Solomón asked incredulously. "How can they steal our souls?"

"They will come with lies that will cause the spirits to be angry with us. They will cause the spirits to strike us. There will be more death. I have seen this."

"What should we do?" Solomón asked sincerely. Though he was the mayor, he both respected and feared Don Tulio's council, as did most of the village. He had heard the stories, and thought it prudent to believe them.

"I will tell you when the time comes, but you must listen to me completely at that time. Don't be deceived by their words. They will talk good words, but they are not good men."

Mayor Garcia simply nodded with compliant numbness. Don Tulio returned the mayor's acknowledgement with a firm rap of his rod on the flooring of the porch. Without a further word, the healer turned and began his march back to his darkened hutch. Solomón exhaled slowly and deeply. He knew better than to argue with Don Tulio. It was a hard lesson he had learned just a year earlier.

CHAPTER EIGHT

"THE PACKAGE"

"WE HAVE a package!" Howard Pennington called enthusiastically from the screen door as he pushed his way into the small open living/dining area of their language school housing. Juanita turned and looked up from her mopping. She had not understood the English expression "package", but she could tell it was good news. Donna appeared from the kitchen where she had been pealing a pineapple.

"A package?" she repeated with equal zeal. "From who? Karen?…Where is it?"

Before he could reply, Terry bolted from his room.

"Did you say a package?" he squealed. "What did I get?"

Dr. Penning held up his hands.

"Slow down, it's not here,…yet."

"But you said,…" Donna protested.

"We HAVE a package," Howard repeated slowly. "We just don't have it YET!"

"I don't understand," Donna replied confused. Terry stood silent waiting for the explanation.

"I have a notice that a package has arrived," Howard began calmly. "I just have to go to the post office and pick it up. They couldn't deliver it to the language institute."

"So where is the post office?" Donna asked anxiously.

"I asked around at the Language Institute, and they said it's in Zapote, not too far from here."

"When can you pick it up?" Terry spoke up.

"I'm not sure. The folks at the school office seemed to indicate that there was a procedure to getting packages. I'll just have to go and see."

"Can I go with you?" Terry asked.

Howard and Donna exchanged glances. This was the first time in weeks that Terry had expressed any interest in going anywhere outside of the immediate neighborhood. He hadn't been making friends among the local boys. His contact with the other MK's was becoming less and less. He would see them in school, but seldom visited their homes. Howard and Donna were getting concerned about Terry's acclamation to their new host country.

"Why sure son," Howard replied quickly. "When will you be home from school tomorrow?"

"I only go half-day," Terry answered enthusiastically. "I can be ready by 1:00."

"Well, let me see," Howard thought aloud. He was finishing exams that week before Christmas break. He would also be free early the next afternoon.

"I think I can be ready around that time as well. Why don't we plan to take a taxi from here to the post office around 1:30 tomorrow."

"A taxi!" Terry squealed. He hated the walks up the hill to the bus stop almost as much as he hated riding the buses. A taxi meant they would leave from the house and go directly to their destination.

"I think so," Howard said nodding toward Donna for approval. "After all, they will know exactly where to go."

"Great!" Terry replied looking up at his mother's smile.

Donna thought to herself, it was good to see Terry excited about something for a change. She turned her attention back to Howard, who was also smiling. It was beginning to be a good day.

For several weeks, Allen West had been meditating on Becky's statement to "bind the strongman". He knew the direct reference was 'to Jesus' statement to the scribes and Pharisees when accused of casting out demons by the power of Satan. He knew the reference was directly related to spiritual warfare. As he studied the passages in Matthew 12, Mark 3, and Luke 11, he found significant insights among the differing scriptures.

On the one hand, Matthew had Jesus responding to Pharisees after healing a blind and mute man. Mark mentioned scribes coming from Jerusalem to accuse Him of casting out devils by Beelzebub. Luke had unknown agitators seeking a sign. The constant between the three accounts was the reference to "binding the strong man" in order to plunder his house. Allen had to confess to himself it was not an easy passage to interpret or to apply.

According to the Gospel of Matthew, it appeared that the healing was an invasion of Satan's domain. Allen knew better than to ascribe all sickness and disease to Satan as he had heard others claim. Some sickness was a simple result of disregarding God's natural laws for health (like proper diet, rest, or sexual activity). Some sickness was genetic (like the man born blind). Some were results of natural accidents (both avoidable and unavoidable). Satan could not be blamed for human negligence and ignorance. Nor could Satan be credited for the plagues and sickness that God himself visited on rebellious people like Pharaoh, Egypt, and Miriam or even the crippling of Jacob. No, Satan was not the source of all sickness and disease, though he certainly caused his share. The healing ministry of Christ was the demonstration of his authority over sickness as was his authority over nature when He calmed the storm, cursed the fig tree, walked on water and multiplied food. The healing ministry of Christ, like His other miracles, gave proof of His Deity and identified Him as the Messiah that was to come. It was the kingdom of darkness He was invading, not just the realm of disease.

Allen concluded that Matthew was presenting the Messiah to the religious leaders that resisted His claims in the face of the people's question, "is this not the Son of David?" As he studied Levi's account, he discovered that Matthew is the only gospel to return the accusation, by asking through whom their children cast out demons. Clearly, the issue was not just about sickness, but about power and authority. Allen thought it interesting that Jesus referred to the activity of their *children*, rather than the Pharisees themselves. The statement "they will be your judges" especially intrigued him. What was Jesus trying to say? Would the followers of the Pharisees finally see them for their hypocrisy? Was Jesus likening the household of the strong man to the household of those religious leaders, as well as to the kingdom of darkness? The questions just kept leading him deeper into study.

Allen spread two English Bibles and his Spanish Reina Valera 1960 out on the dining room table. Though he had a good Bible program for his computer, he still preferred turning the pages of God's Word. He opened the two different English translations, locating Matthew twelve with one and Mark chapter three with the other. He noticed that the Gospel of Mark referred to the statements as being parables. The picture of a house being divided by itself was more than a figure of speech. It was an image. It was like one family member ordering another family member out of house. Such a home could not remain intact. Allen made a few mental notes and then bowed his head in prayer.

"Father, it's obvious that there are some that will not understand our work and will oppose it. Lord, I know that one in particular hosts the kingdom of darkness in *Pozo Negro*. He has created a stronghold against the kingdom of light. In less than five months, a team from the United States will be coming. I begin now praying that you will bind the strong man that holds *Pozo Negro*. May we have entrance and authority to proclaim Your name and declare Your glory. Now prepare me with the Sword of Your Spirit. May your Word equip me with truth and light. I pray for the team that is coming, as well. May you begin now preparing them for the battle that will be waged next April in *Pozo Negro*."

Allen continued to pray. He knew there was much to learn from both God's Word and from national believers. As he prayed over his open Bibles, Becky joined him silently from the kitchen. Together, she prayed, they would ask the Lord to bind the strong man.

———————————————

Rusty was so glad he no longer had to deal with any aspect of the Christmas Cantata. For the two years that he served under Dr. Pennington, he had had to work closely with the Worship Leader in preparing any drama or children's portion for the annual musical. Now, with such responsibilities delegated to the new Youth and Children's minister, Rusty could approach the holidays with less stress. This December that was good, because he needed to put a travel package together for the mission trip in April.

For three days, Rusty had called the airlines checking prices and connection times. He still didn't trust online price groups that promised the best deals. He was meticulous about getting the best rate, but not at the risk of having too little time to reclaim luggage, pass through customs and make the next flight. He would decide on the carrier and purchase the tickets before the end of the month. Some of the members had designated a special gift for the trip and wanted to give it before the year's end. He figured it was for tax purposes. In some cases, he was right.

In addition to the airline tickets, Rusty had to be thinking about housing and transportation costs while they were on the field. There would be other logistics as well to consider. For that very reason, Rusty had contacted Billy Eldridge and invited him to come and together they could sit down and determine what were other logistics that the team needed to consider. Rusty was excited about going and he didn't want to overlook something basic to the trip. Surely a missionary's brother could help him plan.

Billy Eldridge was more than happy to take part of a workday and meet with the young pastor of Coronado Baptist Church. As he pulled into the parking area near the church offices, he was reminded of his visit over a year before with the former pastor. So much had happened with this church since his invitation to come as a Gideon speaker. Billy reflected over the conversation he had with the former pastor after the service and how he had to defend the calling and sacrifice of missionaries to an educated man who felt that those who went to the mission field were wasting their gifts. How ironic that the man who questioned the wisdom of taking a family off to a third world country was now learning the Spanish language with his family for that very reason. How ironic that his call to missions was realized by the death of Billy's own brother. And now how ironic that Billy would be going on a mission trip with that same church.

"Mr. Eldridge, it is good to see you again," Dianne greeted Billy standing to extend her hand in greeting.

"Call me Billy, please,"

"Billy, then," she smiled and paused. "Rusty…uh, I mean, Bro. Rusty is waiting for you."

"Rusty is fine, Dianne," came the pastor's voice from behind her as Rusty stepped out of his office. Billy joined him in a chuckle as Dianne blushed and quickly sat back down. "Billy, thanks for coming. I could sure use your help. Come on back."

The two men left Dianne to her embarrassment.

Rusty picked up his notepad and took one of the two chairs in front of the large oaken desk that usually separated him from his guests.

"Have you heard from Bro. Pennington lately?" Billy began taking the other seat.

"Well, let's see," Rusty started. "They have been robbed, both at home and personally. They have taken turns with parasites, though not serious. Donna is struggling in one of her classes. Terry has not been making very many friends and is spending a lot of time at home alone, which concerns his Mom and Dad. Oh yeah, and Howard is missing 'real' ketchup".

"Real ketchup?" Billy laughed.

"Yeah, it seems the ketchup in the stores are all local brands that have a particularly sweet taste – far from stateside brands. Bro. Howard said he would settle for any generic brand over what they have there. I can't imagine ketchup making such a difference."

"I can," Billy replied with a quieter tone in his voice. "I remember when Carey would write us letters from the field. He said the first year was the hardest. For them, it was spent in Costa Rica also while they were in language learning."

Rusty could tell it was not easy for Billy to talk about it.

"At that time it was just Carey, Susan and Anna. Caleb and Josh were born on the field, both during the first term. In fact, I think Susan was pregnant with Josh before they left Costa Rica. Anyway, the first few months were filled with exciting news of the sites and foods. They took right up with the buses and started visiting areas whenever they had the chance. Carey was adventuresome and Susan trusted his judgement."

"So what happened? What went wrong?"

"Nothing specifically. In fact, it was more like Bro. Howard's ketchup."

"I don't follow you."

"It's called culture shock. It begins with the "tourist stage" where everything about the new surroundings and culture are fascinating. The adventure has begun; the money is different – doesn't seem real. The sound of the language, the music, and even the environment seems filled with a curious newness that enchants. I have experienced the same thing on my short trips abroad."

"And that's culture shock?" Rusty asked surprised.

"No. In fact, what most people think of as culture shock is just the tourist stage. They think that because some of the sites like the poverty or the crime are indeed shocking, that they are going through a culture shock. The shock comes much later, usually about three to four months into the stay."

"Wait a minute," Rusty interrupted. "Three or four months? Why so long?"

"Because the shock is not that things are so different; it's the point when you realize that they are not going to ever change while you are *there* and you are going to be *there* for a very long time. That's when the person tends to slip into different degrees of depression. Some it hits hard, some barely notice. That is the culture shock."

"How long does it last?" Rusty asked concerned for his pastor.

"It depends on the individual and how deep their depression may go. In most cases, the individual can begin laughing again anywhere from six months to a year later."

"What if they don't start laughing again?"

"Carey said that he knew some that went home before they finished language school. It's not common, but it's not impossible, either."

"Wow! You mean there are missionaries who never even get to the field? How can that happen after all the work and training that is done to get them there?"

"That's a good question. The bottom line is – how strong is the call? I believe God is able to carry us through some real hard times when He is in control and leading. The Bible says, 'Faithful is He who calls you, who also will do it'. It's the call that gets you through. But sometimes, people mistake the call for their own personal reasons. Those are the ones that can buckle when it gets tough," Billy sighed. "As you know, Susan is now working in this area with new candidates for the mission field. She has told me that one of the first things she tells couples is that the struggles of adapting to a new culture are tremendously hard on the marriage. If there are cracks in the armor, it will be amplified by culture shock. A couple better be close to the Lord and close to each other before they try to adjust to a new culture."

Rusty thought deeply on those last words. He knew that Howard and Donna had been a bit strained together in the months leading up to their surrendering to the mission field. He quietly hoped that all of that was resolved before they left. Rusty shook his head to clear the thoughts and turned his attention back to the list in front of him.

"I know that must be true. Personally, I haven't had to face the marriage issues in my own country yet. I can't imagine what it must be like to work through problems in unfamiliar waters. But let's change gears and let me pick your brain about what our team is going to need when we travel to Nicaragua."

Billy got comfortable in his chair and leaned back.

"OK, how can I help?" he replied politely.

"I have been trying to put a package together of what the trip will cost each member. I know about the obvious expenses, but need to see if I am overlooking something."

"What have you got so far?" Billy asked.

Rusty leaned forward to show Billy the list. It was handwritten on yellow legal paper. There were only a few items listed.

"I have the air travel, an estimate on lodging, a rough figure for building materials, and food for the week. I know that is not all I need to consider. What can you add?"

Billy took the list and looked at it, even though it said exactly what Rusty had just stated. He thought for a minute, and handed the list back.

"I would include at least the following," he began leaning back again in his chair. "Insurance from the mission board will run you about two dollars a day per person – that will be about $16 dollars per person for the duration of the trip."

Rusty made a note.

"Then I would consider taking some Bibles and literature if you can. Remember, each person has two pieces of luggage, but you don't need to carry two big bags for yourself, so designate one piece for materials to help the field."

"That's a great idea," Rusty said, writing it down. "We can use some of the space for our tools, but then use the rest for material donations."

"Now I can supply some Gideon New Testaments, but my brother always liked to have the whole Bible when possible. I think there are Bible Societys here in the states that can get you a good price on whole Bibles in paperback. You might want to budget for that."

"Good idea," Rusty agreed.

"Then you need to think about transportation also," Billy continued.

"I have air-fare and I even included tips and the trip to the airport," Rusty defended.

"Yes, but what about travel from the hotel to the worksite? I doubt the missionary will have sufficient means to carry everyone out and even if he did, you would need to consider paying for his gas as well. I suspect he plans to rent a van or small bus for the team while you are there, and you will need to pay the expense for it, or at least offer to."

"You're right!" Rusty said writing it down. "I am really glad I brought you in. I would have overlooked all of these things."

"We're not done yet," Billy smiled. "You will need bottled water each day to carry out to the worksite. It would be impractical to carry enough in your luggage, so plan for about $1 to $2 dollars a day in bottled water, depending on how hot it is when we go."

"What about snacks?" Rusty asked.

"You can carry some, and just have everyone prepared to buy a little through the week. The missionary can help with the exchange of money, but I would just make that a personal preference for expense. Some people "snack" more than others, but everybody will need water."

"Gotcha!" Rusty said making a note. "What else?"

"Let me see," Billy said reaching for the legal sheet. He glanced down the list that had more than doubled. "I can't think of anything else at this point. I am guessing that you have talked to someone about material costs."

"I have a contractor, Arnie Johnson, who is going with us. In fact, I think you met him at the commissioning service we had for the Penningtons and again at the service where we began preparing for this trip."

"I think I remember who you are talking about," Billy replied. "Big, barrel-chested fellow with red hair."

"That's him."

"Will he be able to get a design for the bridge drawn up before we go?"

"That's the plan," Rusty nodded. "I want to get him on the phone with the missionary, Allen West, and let them talk dimensions and come up with a plan we can complete in a week."

"I suspect that will be pushing it, but if the missionary can get some help on the front end before we arrive with some foundation posts, we should be able to span the river within the week," Billy thought aloud. "Provided we can get some good help on their end."

"That brings me to one other matter. I'm not sure how well received our team is going to be," Rusty stated in a lower tone. He rose from his chair and pushed the door completely closed. He hoped that Dianne would just think it was for privacy in prayer. The truth was, he did not want to worry her.

"I have been sensing a spiritual battle in connection with this project. My impressions were supported by a recent email from Allen West. It spoke of the presence of a witch doctor in the village of *Pozo Negro*. Allen didn't seem overly concerned – he was just informing me, but I couldn't help but read caution in the email."

"What kind of caution?" Billy asked.

"That our team be thoroughly prepared spiritually for this trip. After the first of the year, we will start having regular meetings to prepare us and I plan to provide some Bible study for spiritual warfare along with the orientation material."

"That sounds very wise," Billy nodded. "You had a good mentor."

"Well, right now, he's trying to fill some pretty big shoes."

Billy smiled at the inference to his brother, Carey.

"I'm sure Howard and Allen would both appreciate our prayers about this time," Billy commented leaning forward again in his chair.

"I'm sure you are right," Rusty replied. "Would you like to lead?"

"I would be honored," Billy answered with strength in his voice. For the next ten minutes, the two men offered prayers and intercessions for both the Wests and the Penningtons. They prayed for the April trip and for God to prepare the ground before them. They prayed for the team members and how God would keep them close to Himself in the face of the battle before them. They prayed for their own families – at least Billy did.

Dianne glanced up from her desk and noticed that the door had been closed.

"They must be praying," she thought to herself. At her desk, she joined them in spirit.

"Terry, are you here?" Howard called, as he stepped in the doorway. He closed the door behind him as Juanita stepped out of the kitchen.

"Oh," Howard stumbled, and quickly switched his mind into Spanish to greet the housekeeper.

"*Buenos tardes*, Juanita," he began cordially with the afternoon greeting. "*Donde está Señora Pennington?*" he asked, wondering where his wife was.

Juanita replied slowly that she had gone to the meat market for ground beef. Juanita felt comfortable talking with Mr. Pennington. He obviously understood more Spanish than Mrs. Pennington, and he was patient when he didn't get it the first time and had to ask her to repeat something. She enjoyed working for the Penningtons, even if the young boy didn't speak much and stayed in his room most of the time. Juanita had thought of bringing one of her younger brothers with her to work on a day when Terry would be home, but she didn't want to embarrass either one of them. She would keep watching to see when the time was right.

"Gracias," Howard replied, thanking her for the information. He struggled with the words to tell her that he would be taking Terry with him to the post office. He told her they had a package to pick up.

Juanita smiled almost sympathetically, Howard thought. What was the big deal about going to the post office? It was like the Costa Ricans felt sorry for you when you received a package in the mail.

"Do you have your identification card and passport?" she asked Howard.

"Will I need both of them?"

"It would be a good idea to have all of your identification information,... just in case," she explained in Spanish.

Howard shrugged and went to his bedroom to retrieve his passport. He kept it safely tucked in a drawer after the language school finally returned it. Stuffing it in his front pants pocket for safety, he called Terry again, who was now putting on his shoes in the living room. While Terry finished lacing up his sneakers, Howard sat down beside the living room phone and dialed the first of several numbers that were posted near the phone for local taxi services.

He had memorized the greeting and request for a taxi. He would have to give the street directions in so many meters from neighborhood landmarks, like the local guard shack where the community security sat when not making rounds on his bicycle. So many meters west of the guard shack to their street and then so many meters south to their house. He would give the house number and which side of the street it was on. Howard then waited for the familiar reply.

"*No, no hay,*" meant that there was not a taxi in their vicinity and that he should try another number on his list.

"*Si, ya viene,*" meant "yes, one is coming now".

Once the answer was neither of the familiar expressions and Howard got confused. So he called a second company that said they could send one. After three minutes, two taxis drove up at the same time and Howard learned that there was more than one way to say that a taxi was on its way. He promptly paid both drivers, but took only one to his destination. He also learned the new Spanish expression. That was language learning.

On his third attempt, Howard found a taxi that could pick up him and Terry and carry them to the post office. Howard knew it was not far to Zapote, but he didn't know exactly where the post office was located. He trusted the taxi driver was from this area and knew where to go.

Within minutes, a small vehicle was blowing its horn in front of the house. Howard finished his quick note to Donna about taking Terry with him. He knew he could tell Juanita, but Donna may not understand the word for post office. He thought a note would be safer. He sent Terry out to let the taxi driver know that they were both coming out. He gave a quick but courteous farewell to Juanita and jaunted out the swinging screen door himself. The taxi driver was a middle-aged man who nodded confidently when asked about the *correo en Zapote*. Howard checked his wallet for sufficient *Colones* and jumped into the backseat with Terry who was already looking around in vain for a seatbelt. He looked up at his father for reassurance. Howard managed a smile and lipped out the words, "hold on".

The post office in Zapote was a maze of several small buildings. Howard led Terry as they wandered from one worker to another, seeking directions to the packages. Finally, Howard began holding up the postal slip and finally a worker pointed them to the smaller building in the back. They journeyed across the gravel lot to the open door. A uniformed guard met Howard with the typical M-16 that most security men carried. Howard was undaunted by the sight of the armed worker and held up his postal slip. The man stepped to one side and motioned to a small caged opening along the wall.

Howard and Terry stepped inside the warm building and found the window and the seemingly bored young female employee preoccupied with a *novela* magazine. Howard slid the wrinkled slip through the opening in the cage and she gave it a perfunctory glance. Without looking up, she asked for his papers. Howard reached into his pants pocket for his passport and student ID from the Language Institute and slid them through the hole. She looked up once to check his face against the picture on the passport and then pounded the slip several times with different stamps she had before her. She pushed the slip back through the opening and returned to her magazine.

Instinctively, Howard continued down the passageway that opened to a larger room with floor to ceiling cages. Brown paper packages were stacked like small quadratic mountains. Howard looked around till he could find another employee standing behind a large counter. He held up his slip to the worker, who gave a nod and motioned him toward the counter. The first stop was to assure his identity, this station was to retrieve his package. He handed the certified slip to the worker who quickly disappeared. Howard looked down and smiled at Terry as though to say, "it won't be long now". After a warm three minutes, the attendant returned with a well-wrapped box about a foot-and-a-half-square. He handed it to Howard, who immediately checked the return address. It *was* from Karen. Across the bottom, she wrote in red magic marker, "FELÍZ NAVIDAD! DON'T OPEN TILL CHRISTMAS". Howard smiled and showed the writing to Terry who almost giggled out loud. With that, Howard turned to find his way out of the hot building.

"*Espere!*" the man called out loudly, asking Howard to wait.

The two Penningtons turned to see the attendant motioning for Howard to carry the box to the far end of the counter where a second man had suddenly appeared.

Howard looked a little confused but complied. He carried the package back to the counter and walked to the far end where the second man stood with a box cutter in his hand. His uniformed shirt had the name "Manuel" embroidered above the pocket. Howard swallowed hard. He suddenly realized what was about to happen. Karen's specially wrapped Christmas presents were going to have to be opened for inspection. Howard held the package against his chest and looked into the man's eyes as though to plead, "please, this is special. It's from home. It's for Christmas. Please don't make me open it here, not now...not in front of my son."

"*El paquete, por favor,*" demanded Manuel, motioning to the tightly held box in Howard's arms.

"What is he going to do?" Terry asked.

"I think he needs to see what is inside," Howard said loosening his grip and extending the package to the man with the box cutter.

"But that's our Christmas presents from Karen," Terry replied defensively. "We're not supposed to open that until Christmas morning."

"I know, son, but they have their rules. We have to let them see what is in the package."

Terry wasn't sure if he wanted to watch or wait till Christmas and be surprised. Before he could decide, the box was open and four neatly wrapped presents were tossed onto the counter. The paper was festive and the bows were still attached and intact. The postal worker looked at the four obvious gifts and looked at Howard.

"*Para Navidad.*" Howard offered, as though the worker needed to be told they were Christmas presents.

"*Si, Señor,*" Manuel nodded. "*Hay que abrirlos!*"

"What did he say?" Terry asked.

"He said we need to open them," Howard said apologetically.

"Why? Don't they know they are for Christmas?" Terry repeated.

"Yes, son. They know," Howard replied in surrender.

The worker picked up the largest of the gifts and began tearing away the colorful wrapping. When the front was pulled away, Howard could see the title of the hardback Christian novel. It was the latest in a series that Donna had been reading. Howard knew that she would love that. Manuel turned the book around several times looking carefully at the front and back cover. He opened the thick volume and fanned the pages to see if anything had been inserted. Satisfied that it was just a book, he set it aside and picked up another gift.

This time he chose a long rectangular shaped box which was also carefully and lovingly wrapped with festive paper. Without pause, Manuel opened one end and tore the paper away without any attempt to preserve the gift-wrapping. Terry stared in disbelief as the thin paper fell to the counter revealing the latest version of a popular handheld video game with two game cartridges taped together. Terry was filled with both excitement and disappointment at the same time. He would be getting something he really wanted, but for now, someone else was in control of it. Terry picked up the cartridges from the counter to look at them closer.

"Do you think that's mine?" Terry asked his father, trying to say something.

"I hope so," Howard replied watching Manuel examine the game and cartridges scrupulously. "I'm not too good on those things."

"I can't wait to get that home." Terry stated as the disappointment waned.

"It's still two weeks till Christmas," his father reminded him.

"Aw, Dad! Come on,…they're already open. Do we really have to wait?"

Before he could answer, Manuel picked up the third surprise and in one swipe, removed the paper completely from the box of a new computer program. Howard strained to see the title. He could see the logo of the Bible program he used on his laptop from the side panel, but he still couldn't tell what the program was. Manuel turned the box over several times and finally laid it on the counter face up with the other gifts. Howard could read the title, "*Reina Valera 1960 – Spanish Bible Translation*".

"Oh, Karen!" he thought out loud. He could think of no better gift. In addition, the program contained three other Spanish translations that Howard would learn were popular versions and used commonly with those who had limited reading abilities. He was beginning to think that waiting for Christmas may not be absolutely necessary.

Manual picked up the final package. It's shape and size was obvious. It was a videotape. Howard wondered what new movie Karen thought that they couldn't live without. Or better yet, maybe it was one of those tapes of old TV programs that they enjoyed. The paper was once again tossed aside mercilessly revealing a recordable tape and a hand printed label. Howard took a bold step extending his hand in an effort to read the label. Manuel, convinced it was personal material, handed the tape to him. Howard held the tape low enough for Terry to see the label. Together they read, "To Honduras with love – Karen". Father and son exchanged fond smiles. Home movies!

The patient postal worker let the Penningtons savor the moment and then reached out his hand. Howard didn't understand. There was obviously nothing dangerous or illegal in any of the gifts. He had been compliant in allowing this stranger to take their Christmas surprises and pour them out on a hot dirty counter, why did he need to reclaim a personal videotape?

"*Qué pasa?*" was all Howard could think to say. He knew it wasn't the best way to ask what the worker was doing and why, but he was confused.

Manuel explained in short and slow sentences that the post office must now take the items and assess their value. A tax would be placed on the items and that he could return tomorrow or the next day and pay the tax and then pick up his items.

"I have to pay for my own mail?" Howard tried to ask in Spanish. It was close and Manuel understood the question. He had dealt with language students before. He tried to explain that it was like an import tax for items brought into the country.

Howard felt heat on the back of his neck and knew it was not from lack of air conditioning in the building. He held his words and let the feelings wash over him. There was nothing to gain by getting angry. In fact, there was much on the counter to lose.

Terry stood alongside the counter watching helplessly as each of the gifts were placed back in the box they were mailed in. Manuel even picked up the gift-wrap and placed it inside the box on top of the items. He picked up a wide tape roller used by moving companies and resealed the carton. He filled out a form attaching one part to the box and handing Howard the other half.

"*Hasta mañana!*" he said firmly, and turned to carry the box into a new set of cages.

For about two solid minutes, Howard and Terry stood stoically at the counter, as though Manuel would change his mind and bring their Christmas gifts back to them.

"I guess that's that," Howard said finally, looking down sullenly at Terry.

"When do we get them?" Terry asked, showing his disappointment in full force.

"Tomorrow, I hope. I guess I better come back by myself tomorrow."

"Yeah," Terry agreed. He didn't want to be disappointed again...so soon.

The two took their claim ticket and walked out of the warm building and into the heat of the afternoon. Shielding his eyes from the sun, Howard thought to himself, "why does it have to be so hot all the time?" but he didn't say anything – not in front of Terry.

The ride home was not as near as exciting as the trip to the post office. Howard felt more than disappointment, he felt robbed again. He had to accept that he could see his property but could not keep it. He had to defend to his son the laws of their new country as being different than the one they knew and yet he didn't agree with them either. When the taxi let them out in front of their house, Terry was quick to run through the door.

"This country stinks!" Terry blurted, letting the screen door slam behind him.

"Terry!" Donna retorted in shocked surprise at her son's attitude as well as his words.

Terry just ignored the reprimand and went straight to his room.

Donna rose to follow him as Howard entered the house a bit calmer, but visibly agitated as well.

"What was that all about?" she addressed toward her husband.

"Let's just say, I know now why the nationals were sympathetic about my trip to the post office. It is not an experience to relish."

"What happened?" Donna asked, turning her attention from Terry's bedroom.

"You know how we have to go through several people to make a purchase in the stores?" Howard began, trying to calm himself.

"Yes, one to show you the product, one to write the ticket, one to make the sell, and one to give you the package, after it has been bagged," she replied by rote memory.

"Well, turn that into a package delivery process, only instead of showing you a product, they open your package. Then leave off the last step where they give you the package."

"I don't understand," Donna said confused.

"We had to show our identification, pick up the package, then have a postal inspector open the package," Howard began explaining.

"So you were able to see what was sent," Donna interrupted.

"Oh, yes," Howard said sarcastically. "We watched another man open our Christmas gifts from Karen."

"Our Christmas gifts? Isn't that a bit personal? Why did they have to open them?"

"I thought it was to assure that nothing dangerous or illegal was being shipped into the country, but it appears I was wrong."

"Why then?" Donna inquired.

"It appears they are going to charge us a tax on the items and then I can pay and pick them up tomorrow or maybe the next day." Howard said in a tired voice.

"How will you know which day?"

"I won't. I'll have to just do back down there and hope for the best."

"That stinks." Donna said softly, so that Terry wouldn't hear her.

"I have been trying to find another way to express it – Terry has already taken that one."

"I'm just glad Juanita wasn't still here working when he came in. He was very angry. He's in his room now. Should I go in and talk to him?"

Howard took a seat at the kitchen table.

"No, just give him a few minutes. He is going to have to get past the anger before he will hear us. I'm afraid I don't blame him, especially after seeing what Karen sent him."

"What was in the package?" Donna asked changing the subject slightly.

"Don't you want to be surprised for Christmas?" Howard teased.

"Why? You all won't be. That's not fair, now is it?"

They both tried to laugh. Donna stepped beside him and gave her husband a reassuring hug. At least she could comfort one of them.

Two days later, Howard traveled alone back to the post office. He went straight to the building in the back. He repeated his steps past the armed guard to the cage and the young girl who was now reading a different magazine. He was directed to a new area where he could pay the *impuestos* or taxes on the items in the package. Howard refrained from speaking any more than necessary. He presented his new claim slip to the new man behind the new counter and waited. The postal worker with Antonio embroidered on his shirt walked behind a wall behind the counter and returned in less than a minute with the familiar package and some new paperwork. Antonio perused the multicolored handwritten invoice in front of him and then looked up at Howard and stated firmly.

"16,000 Colones!"

Howard's mouth dropped. At an exchange rate of 310 Colones to one US dollar, that came to just over $50 dollars. Howard opened his wallet and counted his bills. He had the money, but it just didn't seem right. Antonio was unmoving and seemingly uncaring. The two stood motionless for a moment and then Howard counted out three multi-colored five-thousand Colon bills and one red thousand Colon bill and reluctantly laid them on the counter. Howard was sure there was no way to know how much tax they were charging, because value was being assessed on the price of what the different items would cost in Costa Rica rather than the US. Howard would just bite the bullet. He told himself he was paying for the video of Karen more than anything and that was worth the price.

Antonio quickly collected the money and slid the package towards Howard. It was taped both lengthwise and then across the sides. Howard wasn't sure, but he thought he remembered them only taping it across the opening after it was examined. He let go of the thought and quickly snatched up the box and made his way to the door before anyone could think of another reason to detain him or the precious package.

Now that school was out for Christmas holidays, Terry and Mrs. Pennington were at home waiting together anxiously for Howard to return. The taxi pulled up in front of the gated home; Donna and Terry eased into the carport anxiously. Howard stepped out on the driver's side away from the house. They could see him pay through the window and then step back so the taxi could pull away. They held their breath as the small car moved from between them and their view of Mr. Pennington. The brown package was held securely in front of him. Terry squealed and Donna exhaled with relief. She didn't think she could take another disappointment.

"Christmas – eight days early!" Howard called from the street.

Terry opened the gate to let his father in. Donna held the screen door open. Howard gave her a peck on the cheek as Terry ran past and squeezed between them so as to get to the kitchen table.

"So are we going to open it now, or wait till Christmas?" Donna asked, following Howard into the house. It was a rhetorical question.

"I can't think of any reason to wait, we already know what it is. We might as well start enjoying it now." Howard was thinking about the video from Karen more than anything else.

"Well, some of us know what it is," Donna corrected. "Some of us are still in the dark."

"Oh, I forgot," Howard replied smiling. "Well, not for long. I doubt they rewrapped anything."

Howard retrieved a knife from the drain board and began cutting through the sealing tape. Without fanfare, he opened the lid. He first noticed that Donna's book was on top of everything else. Then he realized that, not only was nothing rewrapped, but that the paper he had put back in the box had been removed.

"Didn't the fellow at the post office tape up the box while we were there?" Howard asked Terry.

"Yes sir," Terry answered.

"They must have reopened the box because the wrapping paper I put in the box is not here."

Then Howard remembered how the box had been retaped in both directions. A sickening feeling came over him, but he tried not to show it. He handed the book to Donna and gave a hearty "Merry Christmas".

"My video game player next," Terry almost shouted impatiently.

"A video game player?" Donna asked excited for her son. "What a nice gift."

"Yeah, and Karen sent a couple extra cartridges also," he added with equal excitement.

"Let's see," Howard said, fishing in the package past his computer program and the home made video. "Here it is!"

He pulled out the video game player and passed it to the outstretched hands of Terry.

"And the cartridges?" he quickly added without looking up from his new electronic pastime.

Howard moved the two remaining items around inside the box and then finally took them out completely. His Bible computer program and the homemade video sat on the table beside the box, but nothing else could be found. Howard paused before speaking.

"There seems to be something missing," he said quietly.

Terry looked up from his new game at his father who was returning his gaze with sympathetic eyes. The young boy tilted the box toward him and stared in every corner. It was gone. The two additional cartridges that had been taped together that he had held in his hands just two days before were gone.

"Where are they?" Terry said slowly.

"I don't know, son," was all that Howard could bring himself to say. He wanted to say more. He wanted to curse the workers and the system that allowed pilfering. He wanted to return immediately to the post office and demand his son's game cartridges, but he knew it would not happen. He knew they would deny any loss. He felt helpless in defending his son, just as he felt helpless defending his home or even his own wallet. Dr. Howard Pennington did not like feeling helpless. But it would not be the last time that he would feel that way.

CHAPTER NINE

"THE NEW YEAR"

"I'M SORRY, I don't agree!" Howard Pennington said firmly and with finality.

"Look, I didn't say you had to change your plans, or even agree with me," Al Redding replied calmly. "I'm just saying that the rest of the world is wrong and I am right."

"So you are going to dismiss everything the rest of the world is saying? You are going to say that all the media attention, all the global celebrations, all the literature and even the greatest threat to civilized man in this modern technical age were incorrect in their premise?"

"Just about. We'll see if Y2K does any real damage as the day wears on. I'm just saying that the third millennium didn't start TODAY! THIS year, the year 2000, is the last year of this millennium. You don't have one thousand years till you completed one thousand years, and you don't have two thousand years until you complete two thousand years and that won't be till the end of THIS YEAR!" Al explained for the third time.

"I hear what you are saying, and it makes sense. I just can't see how the rest of the world could be wrong," Howard said shaking his head for the fourth time.

"You might as well save your breath," Leanne Redding inserted while passing glasses of Papaya punch to the two men. "When Al sets his mind to something, that is all she wrote."

"Only when I'm right," Al said defending himself.

Leanne and Donna Pennington exchanged common smiles. They both knew the wisdom of letting their husbands believe what they wanted when it really didn't matter.

"Then I toast to Al's extra year *till* the new millennium," Howard stated raising his glass of papaya punch into the air. "May it be as prosperous as the end of our last millennium – whenever that was – and may we set our course on completing the task we have been given. May we be found faithful in the fields of the Lord. May we draw strength from His grace, may we confirm direction in His calling, and may we learn this language – come *heaven* or high water."

"Howard!" reacted Donna jokingly, since Terry wasn't present.

"I said, *heaven*," Howard smiled.

"Yeah, well you could have said the other," Al said lowering his glass. "After all, that is what it has been like."

"Al?" Donna responded with a more serious tone.

"I'm sorry," Al replied with a touch of calm. "All I'm saying is it hasn't been what we thought it would be."

Leanne eased down at the table next to Al and laid her hand on his forearm. Al looked at her reassuringly. He took a deep breath and continued.

"Leanne and I have been talking more about it lately. We thought it would get better after the trimester ended and we had time to relax during the Christmas holidays. We even took the *paseo* with the school to go to the beach at *Manuel Antonio* the week before Christmas."

"We ended up making trips to the post office," Howard interjected sarcastically.

Al paused long enough for the comment to pass over.

"We took the girls with us as a special Christmas present."

"That was nice," Donna offered.

"It would have been if the bus ride hadn't made Margie sick. She never got in the water the whole first day. It rained the whole second day. The rooms were cramped and Alison didn't like any of the food. We spent a couple hundred dollars for the most miserable trip of our lives," Al concluded.

Leanne patted his forearm and never looked up. She was avoiding eye contact with Donna.

"What are you saying?" Howard prompted.

There was an unsettling pause between the foursome.

"Al and I are thinking about returning to the states," Leanne said softly without looking up."

Howard and Donna looked stunned at each other. Words didn't come.

"I know what you're thinking," Al offered defensively. "You're feeling sorry for us because you think we have had too rough of a time of it. You think we are giving up."

"No, Al!" Donna responded quickly. "We are just caught off-guard – that's for sure, but we know you have prayed about it."

"You don't understand," Al explained. "That's the problem – we haven't been praying about it. We assumed more than we prayed about."

"What do you mean?"

"Oh, we prayed about missions enough when we were in the states. We knew that the need was great and that the Lord had commanded us to be a part of global evangelism. We just assumed that that meant going."

"What convinced you otherwise?" Howard asked sincerely.

"First, it was the little things, but then it became apparent as Leanne and I began arguing more and more."

"I haven't had a very easy time this past trimester," Leanne added. "I have not been able to pick up on the language as well as I did at the first."

"But you did great when you helped me interview the maid," Donna objected.

"That's because you knew so little," Leanne countered. "I was still using the wrong declensions. I suspect you can speak as well as I do at this point and I should be a full trimester ahead of you. I'm just not getting the language like I should."

"On top of that, our girls have not been adjusting as easily as some of the other children," Al commented.

Howard and Donna refrained from voicing their similar concerns about Terry.

"Alison won't eat any of the typical food here and the American products are so expensive. We try to get her to just taste even the chicken and rice, but she says it looks too dirty. We can barely get her to eat the familiar cereals that have Spanish labels."

Al took a breath and then continued.

"I know all these things sound small, but together, they have built up to show us that we may have made a mistake coming to the field. Even the mission board had some questions left unresolved about our candidacy before our appointment, but they felt it was simple anxiety and would pass soon after we got here. Well, it didn't. It has been magnified to the point that we are now questioning our call."

The two couples said nothing for a moment, letting the words sink in. After a significant silence, Howard took the opportunity to probe.

"Didn't you have to relate your call to missions several times during the appointment process – I know we did."

"Yes, and at the time, we were as convinced as you were that God was calling us to missions. Afterall, I had been a pastor in Oklahoma for seven years and was building a very mission minded church. We had been on several trips to nearby Indian reservations, we did disaster relief in and outside of our state and I had personally led at least five volunteer trips to Mexico. That's why I felt God was calling us to Oaxaca."

"What has changed that?" Howard asked sincerely.

"Since being here, I think I have learned an important lesson about calling." Al began with a strong sense of assurance in his words. "There is a difference between being called to be pastor with a missionary heart, and being a missionary with a pastor's heart. I believe I am the former. I will always want to be involved with missions, but God hasn't called us to be missionaries – does that sound strange?"

"Not at all," Howard replied nodding. "So what are your plans?"

Al and Leanne exchanged reassuring glances. They could trust their "little brother and sister".

"We are planning to return home before the next trimester starts!"

Pozo Negro celebrated the New Year like most of the towns in western Nicaragua with the exception of the Mass. There were the same fireworks, the same feasts, the same drinking, and the same "old man" made of clothing stuffed with paper and explosives. As close to mid-night as possible, the effigy was lit and allowed to blow apart and burn signifying the passing of the old year.

Don Tulio did not lead the festivities, but he didn't overtly oppose it. Don Tulio regarded the New Year as the time to appease the spirits through personal sacrifice. He would fast for three days leading up to the New Year isolating himself from the community. On the first day of the year, he would kill and dismember a chicken. He would cook the entrails and clean several of the bones. From secret ceremonies learned while apprenticing with Nando Gadea, Don Tulio would "read the bones" and seek visions into the coming year. Though few predictions were made public, Don Tulio took the rites seriously and the townsfolk held a healthy respect for his privacy. No one wanted to anger Don Tulio at the beginning of a new year.

The witchdoctor bent over his pot of boiling entrails and stirred slowly. The pungent aroma couldn't deter him from his trance. He continued repeating two words like a deliberate mantra.

"*Muestra me, muestra me, muestra me...*" meaning "show me, show me, show me."

A puff of smoke suddenly bubbled from the satanic soup and Tulio leaped backward nearly losing his balance. He regained his composure and resumed his position. The ruddy mixture was beginning to move with the boiling activity in a discernable manner for the witchdoctor.

"*Si...,*" he said confidently to himself. "*Si, yo se...*" he began to chant meaning, "yes, I know". The smoke hung dark near the ceiling of his small room like ominous clouds announcing a storm.

"NO! No! No!" Arnie yelled at the 27 inch screen.

"Calm down," Betty responded in like-decibels from the kitchen. "It's only a game!"

"Only a game?" he shot back without taking his eyes from the jubilant Wolverines descending on the field after the missed PAT (Point after touchdown) by Alabama. "Bama just blew their extra point and lost in overtime to Michigan."

"Good," Betty replied in a lower tone emerging from the kitchen with a tray of snacks and soft drinks. "Now maybe we can turn that thing off and visit a little while."

Pastor Rusty refrained from comment while Arnie Johnson brooded over his remote. They had spent more than a third of the day between the Rose Bowl and the Orange Bowl. Neither had cared much for Stanford but enjoyed watching the "Great Dane" of Wisconsin and their awesome defense lead the Badgers to a 17/ 9 victory over Cardinal. The tension was greater during the face-off between the Wolverines and the Crimson Tide. Twice Michigan had trailed by fourteen points and twice they had rallied to tie Alabama. In an overtime showdown, Shawn Thompson had scored and the extra point was successful. Alabama effectively reached their endzone, but then kicker Ryan Pflugner failed to connect solid and the extra point sailed wide to the right.

"Cheer up, Arnie!" Rusty ventured. "We still have Tennessee in the Fiesta Bowl tomorrow."

"May I remind you two that tomorrow is Sunday?" Betty teased handing her pastor a Diet Coke.

"Oh yeah," Rusty chuckled. "I probably need to be getting home so I can put a sermon together."

"It's a little late for that, don't you think" Arnie kidded back.

"You're right, I'll just pull out last year's New Year's message and preach that. I doubt any of you folks would remember."

They all laughed together. Each knew better. Rusty Patterson was a dedicated pastor and a diligent preacher who never left his office on Friday until everything was ready for Sunday – even on New Years Eve.

"Well, before you leave, tell us where we are on the mission trip." Arnie said settling into his recliner.

"Well, for starters, we are about four and a half months away, but we already have airline reservations and I will start gathering the ticket money from the group after we get past the holidays. I met with Billy Eldridge about three weeks ago and he helped me put a package together that will help us know what our expenses will be while on the field. I have to admit, I would have overlooked some things if he hadn't been there. I'll share the package with the group at our next meeting. It's looking like just a little over $1,000 a person."

"A thousand dollars?" Betty asked with a slight show of concern in her voice. "That's over two thousand for Alex and Arnie."

"Yes and no," Rusty replied reassuringly. "Do you remember the special account that Stan Henly mentioned setting up when I first shared about the trip?"

The Johnsons nodded.

"I haven't been making a public announcement about it, but we already have over six thousand dollars that has been donated toward the trip."

"Praise the Lord," Arnie nearly shouted.

"And I believe that that is just the beginning." Rusty quickly added. "I am thoroughly convinced that God provides for His work. We have twelve people signed up at this time. That is already a five hundred dollar share towards each person going. We can use that money toward the tickets and then see what comes in."

"Now, we can pay our share," Arnie injected strongly.

"I know you can," Rusty explained. "I also know that this involves more of our people than just those who are prepared to go. 'Holding the ropes' is an important part to mission endeavors, whether we are doing it cooperatively for our denomination, or collectively for our own church members. I think it is not only positive, I think it is healthy for the church to participate in this manner, especially when we haven't even asked for it."

"What have you heard from the missionaries?" Betty asked.

"I get emails now and then. Again, I have been waiting till we get past the holidays to share them with the team. But I suppose I can let you guys know, so we can start praying."

"Praying about what?" Arnie asked.

Rusty took a breath. He wasn't sure how to put in his own words what Allen West had been sharing about *Pozo Negro*.

"As you know, we are going on a construction project. We will be helping the missionary build a bridge across a small river."

Arnie nodded intently.

"It seems the village that we are building the bridge for doesn't have any church at all, not even a Catholic Church."

"That's great," Arnie responded, as though the news was better than he anticipated. "So we are going to be part of a church plant as well as a construction project. I think that's great!"

"I do too," Rusty added cautiously. "But there is more. The reason there is no church in the town is because there is a witch doctor that has kept anyone from starting one."

Betty and Arnie looked at each other.

"A real witch doctor?" Betty said.

"Like a Voo Doo witch doctor?" Arnie added. He knew it sounded silly when he said it, but he had no other point of reference from which to draw. Southern California knew of Satan worshippers and bizarre rituals, but it was usually looked upon as just a form of rebellious counter culture behavior.

"I'm not sure just what all it means," Rusty replied, trying not to patronize his friend. "All I know is that he is opposed to the project and we may encounter some resistance."

"On more levels than one I bet," Arnie quickly added.

"That's right, and for that reason, I would like for our team to start meeting to prepare spiritually for the trip. I'm going to work on a few Bible studies to help us. This is new territory for me as well. But I tell you, I would much rather know this going in than finding it out after we get there."

"You have got that right, pastor," Arnie agreed. "To change the subject, I just want you to know that I have been working on some ideas for laying that bridge. That is if the missionary hasn't already put a plan together."

"I don't know. I haven't written about that yet," Rusty confessed. "Why don't you let me check with him and you go ahead and draw up your plans. Better to have it and not need it…"

"…then to need it and not have it!" Arnie finished his sentence. "I know. I keep that one right up there with 'measure twice and cut once'."

"I'm glad you are on this team," Rusty said patting his hand on Arnie's shoulder. "I really believe God is going to do something amazing with us and through us while we are down there. It may be the bridge, the lives we touch, or even this witch doctor – I don't know, but I do know that God has been involved putting all this together."

"Amen!" Betty whispered aloud.

"This New Year's Day marks more than a New Year; I believe it will mark a new era for our church. We are never going to be the same after this trip."

"I believe you're right, Pastor," Arnie replied.

The three of them sat quietly sipping their sodas and staring in different directions. The somberness of the moment seemed to overshadow the whole afternoon and evening of televised sports. It was obvious where their priorities were placed.

Allen West closed the first day of the New Year at home with Becky. They had called their children, eaten their "black-eyed peas" from Tennessee, watched some of the parades pass by their home and listened to the sound of fireworks and gunshots ring through the streets. Home was the best place to observe the New Year considering the drinking and revelry that took place during the holidays. It would be nearly a week before the businesses would all be in full operation again.

Becky turned off the kitchen light and joined Allen in the den taking her place in the rocker across from his. The soft selections from an instrumental CD of praise music played softly in the background. As the two rockers glided in unison, the couple sat in silence enjoying the music.

After three pleasant tracks, Becky broke the silence.

"What are you thinking about?"

"What this New Year has in store," Allen responded without pausing.

"Anything in particular?" Becky asked.

"I suppose the volunteer trip in April is mostly on my mind right now."

"Isn't it coming together?"

"Oh yes, nicely in fact," Allen admitted. "I'm just not sure what we are going to run into with the witch doctor. I feel responsible for the team, and I don't want to put them in any unnecessary danger."

"Do you think the team could be in danger?"

"I don't know," Allen said honestly. "I guess that's what is bothering me. I know that he opposes us being there. I suspect he will try to influence the municipal powers. I'm just not sure what he can do personally to the team."

"What do you mean personally," Becky asked concerned.

"Well, you know…," Allen started to falter. He wasn't sure how put his concerns into words. "I really believe that we are going to face some serious spiritual warfare."

"What else do you REALLY believe?" Becky prompted.

Taking the cue, Allen began to reassure himself and her.

"I believe that 'greater is He that is in us than he that is in the world'."

"Amen."

"I believe that 'the weapons of our warfare are not carnal, but are mighty in God to the pulling down of strongholds, casting down imaginations and every high thing that exalts itself against the knowledge of God'."

"Keep going," she prodded.

"I believe that God will go before us and 'show Himself mighty on our behalf'. I believe that the gospel will go forth and 'light shall shine in the darkness and the darkness will not be able to comprehend it'. I believe God will be our 'shield and exceeding great reward'."

"Sounds like you're preaching now," Becky giggled.

"Just drawing strength from the Word," Allen replied confidently. "I plan to study even more in preparation for this team."

"I'll study with you," Becky said softly reaching across from her rocker to take the hand of her beloved.

"This is going to be a great New Year," Allen proclaimed.

"This is going to be a year to remember, that's for sure," Becky added.

The next morning, Don Tulio rose early and traveled to the bank along the small river opposite the mango groves that shaded the other extreme bank. He squinted as though trying to peer through the shadows to the other side. After some time, he moved his eyes slowly to the rushing water below him.

"They think they can build a bridge," he said aloud to no one visible. "They are wrong."

He clenched his jaw and remembered the words of an earlier conversation in his mind. "You have also said that you know why I am here," the gringo had said. "You have also said that you have seen my coming…If you know why I am here and have seen my coming, then you should know that I do not come alone and that the one with me is strong. If you did not see him, then how do you know that I will fail?'"

" 'He doesn't look that strong to me,' Tulio had said tauntingly, looking as José."

" 'He is not the one I speak of,' the stranger had said with finality."

"This one does not know how strong I am," Don Tulio said to himself. "I have faced others like him and they too were defeated. Their words, their lies, their pretension is no match for the might of true power."

He gripped his rod with both hands and lifted it over his head.

"These…missionaries will fail," he declared voraciously.

With a sweeping motion, he swung the rod in front of him and brought it back into position over his head. At that very moment a heavy cloud passed before the morning sun and dimmed the sky. A northerly wind swept through the river basin and the water beneath the bluff where he stood began to swell and agitate. The normally quiet current became erratic and choppy. However, the mango trees and banana plants on the far bank showed no evidence of wind. Whatever was happening, was happening on the river alone. The small tempest churned for about two minutes before subsiding. Don Tulio lowered his arms and smiled.

"I thought so," he said confidently. "Let them come and they will see the power."

Chapter Ten

"The Circle of Chairs"

CONTRARY TO the song, it does rain in Southern California. Sometimes it even storms. Mid-January has its share of precipitation. The team members had parked as close to the Church office as they could to avoid getting drenched as they scurried from their cars. Willis Beaman held an umbrella over his wife's head as they trotted through the open door. Rusty stepped aside to let them pass and then closed the door behind them.

"Sorry we're late," Willis apologized shaking the umbrella over the welcome mat and then placing it in the corner where at least six other umbrellas stood drying.

"No problem, we're still waiting on Alex and his buddies from USC," Rusty smiled. "There's some coffee set up in the conference room, down this hall and second room on the right past my office."

"I need to stop at the 'little girl's room' first," Rhonda said softly.

"Then just keep going down the hall and it's on the left just past the water fountain," Rusty responded politely.

Willis walked with Rhonda down the hall as far as the conference room and then turned in the doorway as she continued on down to the restroom. Rusty went back to watching out the glass door for the final stragglers to the volunteer team members meeting.

Willis Beaman joined the other men gathered around the coffee pot. He recognized most of them from the church. There were two men with Arnie Johnson that he did not know and a third man already seated that looked familiar, but he couldn't place. Stan Henly was pouring a cup of coffee as he approached.

"How do you like your coffee?" Stan asked Willis.

"Oh, is that for me?" Willis replied surprised. "Just one sweetener if you have it. Just enough to take the edge off."

"We have it," Stan replied, picking up a pink packet from the glass bowl next to the coffee maker. "You sure you just want one, though? I can't vouch for how well it tastes, Bro. Rusty put me in charge of making the brew."

"Beats the sludge we got in mess hall," Arnie interjected.

"Roger that!" called out the stranger from the chairs. Billy Eldridge then stood and joined the group.

"Not sure we have met, but you look familiar," Willis said extending his hand to Billy.

"Billy Eldridge, I'm not a member here, but your pastor has graciously extended the invitation to join you."

"Same here," replied one of the men standing with Arnie. "I'm Robert Winston, a friend of Arnie's. I sell insurance."

Billy jokingly withdrew his hand from Winston's direction.

"I sell insurance for construction workers and new buildings. That's how Arnie and I met," Winston added quickly. Billy smiled and offered his hand firmly.

"Let me introduce my other friend," Arnie added. "This is Peter Moralis. Peter manages a Mexican restaurant in Imperial Beach. Nice location just below the Silver Strand."

"Nice to meet you," Willis greeted shaking hands. "I think my wife and I have been there. 'El Puente', right?"

"That's right," Peter smiled, appreciative of the recognition. His accent was barely noticeable. Peter was born Pedro Alejandro Betancout Moralis. He legally changed his name after completing college. He was second generation Mexican/American and had been born an American citizen, but still fought the stigma of being "Chavo" in the restaurant business.

"Speaking of which," Arnie interrupted. "Where is your wife? SHE'S still going, isn't she?"

"Yes SHE is!" Rhonda responded from the doorway. "SHE wouldn't miss it." Mrs. Beaman sauntered confidently into the assembly of men. Rhonda was one of five who came forward at Pastor Rusty's initial call for volunteers. She had stood at the front without her husband. It was a week later, before Willis agreed to go with her. Rhonda's determination was matched only by her desire. She was strong in will and character. She would be the only woman on a twelve member team, but she would not be the one to hold them back.

"Glad to hear it," Stan Henly spoke up. "Can I get you some coffee?"

"Thank you, Mr. Henly," Rhonda replied a tone softer. "That would be nice. It is miserable out there today."

Stan let her 'doctor' her own cup, and the group began to break into various conversations. Billy introduced himself to the new couple. Rhonda had remembered his face from the service and was impressed that he was the brother of the missionary that had died in Honduras. The small group broke into two cells of differing conversations. After about five minutes of candid banter, Rusty led three rain soaked young men into the room.

"Here's the stragglers," he announced as Alex Johnson, Billy Littleton, and Matt Preston dripped through the doorway behind him. Arnie winced as he watched his son lead the others to a trash can where they collectively wrung the excess water out of their T-shirts.

"Why don't we grab our coffee cups and circle up the chairs," Rusty quickly commented before Arnie could express what he was feeling.

"ALRIGHT!" cried out Billy Littleton, the computer major studying at the University of San Diego with Alex and Matt. "CAFFEINE!"

"Now that's what I'M talking about," Matt joined in following Billy to the coffee pot. Matt's two hundred and eighty five pounds of muscle and grit ambled past Rusty dwarfing the young pastor.

The others quickly made a hole for the young turks and began rearranging the chairs into a small circle. Stan Henly, the oldest of the group took his place next to the pastor. As the Chairman of the Deacons, Stan's presence on the team showed strong support from the church. Stan had been a Flight Officer on the helicopter carrier, the USS Iwo Jima during late 60's. He also boasted of being on board in April of 1970 when the carrier was needed to pick up the ill-fated Apollo 13 flight. Until the Ron Howard film in 1995, Stan could hardly get people to listen to his story. Now friends and family seemed interested. When the Iwo Jima was reassigned from San Diego to Norfolk in 1972, Stan decided to retire. He definitely didn't want to go back to Mississippi where he had been born. He enjoyed southern California weather too much. Stan and his wife Virginia had been charter members of the Coronado Baptist Church even through his tours of duty at other locations. Now at the age of sixty eight, he wanted to prove to himself he still had the "right stuff" to be on mission with God. There was a natural leadership quality to Stan that others noticed. He was not overbearing or intimidating, but he carried a confidence that inspired follow-ship. Bro. Rusty welcomed him.

Arnie Johnson took the chair next to Stan. He knew his part in the meeting would involve addressing the group about the style of bridge they would be building. He wanted to be able to hand plans to both Stan and Rusty without having to get up, but he didn't feel comfortable taking the other seat next to the pastor. Arnie didn't like center stage. Next to Stan seemed like a good place to be. He carried his coffee in one hand and the plastic cylinder with his plans in the other and took his seat.

Arnie's friends, Robert and Peter, followed behind and took the chairs next to him. Neither man had been very involved with Church activities or committees in the past. Robert Winston, like Arnie, had been in construction most of his life, learning from his father. A fall from a second-story scaffold had caused Winston to change professions but not passions. His hospital bills and near bankruptcy convinced him that construction workers needed reliable insurance. He sold policies out of conviction rather than commission. His family had been attending Coronado Baptist for about seven years.

Peter Moralis, on the other hand, was new to the church. His wife, Angelina, and he had been attending for just over a year. It was Arnie that had invited them. Peter remembered well the night that he met the Johnsons in his restaurant. As he took his seat, he reflected over the memory.

It seemed Arnie was celebrating something with his wife and son Alex. They seemed so very close as a family. Peter had seated them personally and was about to find them a waiter, when Arnie spoke up.

"What's your name?"

"My name is Peter...Peter Moralis." Peter had replied somewhat surprised.

"Well, Peter, my name is Arnie Johnson. It is good to know you."

"Thank you, sir. It is nice to have you with us tonight."

"If I may ask," Arnie continued candidly. "Are you the owner or manager?"

"I am both, sir, and I trust you will enjoy your dining." Peter looked around to find someone who could come and take this family's order so he could get back to greeting customers.

"I'm sure we will," Arnie replied and then quickly added, "Peter, my family and I will be ordering in a moment and before our food comes, we plan to have a brief time of prayer for the meal. We would like to pray for you and your family as well. Is there a special need we can pray for you or your family?"

Peter turned his head suddenly into Arnie's direction. The request had caught him completely by surprise. He had dealt with comments and compliments about the food. He had fended off complaints and he had even had to expel unruly patrons, but he had never been asked for a prayer request. He looked hard into Arnie's eyes for insincerity, but all he saw was warmth.

"You want to pray for me?" Peter responded. "That is nice. I have to admit, that is the first time anyone has ever asked me that. You must be a preacher."

Alex almost laughed, but he caught himself realizing the seriousness of the moment.

"No, I'm a construction foreman," Arnie said humbly. "We just know how important it is for people to pray for our family. We have just been through a real crisis and the Lord has been good to us. This time last week, my son was sitting in jail in El Cajon. Our pastor and his associate came to visit him while we were there. It's a long story, but bottom line – God has helped put our family back together. We owe Him everything. For that reason, we pray as a family and we include those God puts in our path. So, I'll ask again, is there anything we can pray for you and your family?"

Peter's eyes began to well up with emotion and appreciation.

"May I ask you, sir," Arnie said softly. "Do you personally have a relationship with the Lord Jesus Christ?"

"I do," Peter nodded. "And you don't know what it means to me to find someone who takes their Christianity so seriously. May I ask you where you go to church?"

Peter and Arnie continue talking as the waitress came to take the order. Arnie shared about his church, his pastor and how God had just that past Sunday called his pastor to the mission field. Peter listened intently to the story about the missionary that had lost his life, about the illegal alien from Honduras in the same jail with Arnie's son, Alex. Arnie shared quickly about the conflict that had turned to fellowship between him and his pastor, and the exciting future that the church sensed was ahead. By the time the food arrived, the two men felt like brothers. Peter decided that night he would carry his family to see what God was doing in this church. They had been attending it ever since.

The Beamans took the next two seats available. Willis and Rhonda had been married just a little over three years and still without children. Willis worked as an auto-mechanic for his father. Rhonda was a LPN who pulled rotating shifts at the County Emergency Clinic. Though petite, she was strong. She once held down a Mexican construction worker whose arm was being reset without anesthesia. She could subdue a hallucinating junkie and still manage to look feminine in the challenge. Willis respected her beauty as well as her strength.

Alex and his two friends, Billy Littleton and Matt Preston, took chairs next to the Willis', cradling their hands around the warm Styrofoam cups of coffee. The three young men came from differing backgrounds and families. Billy enjoyed the challenges of Calculus while Matt and Alex struggled with applied Math. Matt was a second string half-back who saw little play, while neither Alex nor Billy even attended the games. Alex worked with his father in construction while not attending school, while neither Billy nor Matt could remember much about their fathers. What drew the three young men together was the campus Bible Study. The Baptist Student Union had changed its name to Baptist Collegiate Ministries about the time that Alex, Billy and Matt started their freshman year. They met at a small fellowship with guitars, girls, and study guides. Alex had shared his testimony of waywardness, rebellion and "jail-time". Billy and Matt both identified with Alex's experiences in their own way, and each had recently made a recommitment of their lives to Jesus. Their friendship grew and strengthened each other like the "three strand cord" of Ecclesiastes 4:12.

Ty Andrews sat next to Matt. The two were comparable in build and size - Matt the football player and Ty, the welder. Ty was divorced and living alone. He was a quiet man who seldom imposed himself into conversations. It took several months after the divorce for him to even return to his Sunday school class. He felt embarrassed by the fact that his wife had left him after twenty three years of marriage. Their one daughter had left home right out of high school and now lived somewhere in the San Fernando Valley. They had little contact with her, even before the divorce. Ty sought "family" in the church and rejoiced to find those who saw him as a "brother" and not a "leper". His decision to take this mission trip was one of the first visible movements he had made since his wife left. They had not been strong "church-goers". Maybe that was their first mistake. Arnie had been very encouraging to Ty, as had Bro. Rusty. He took his seat feeling part of a team.

Billy Eldridge took the seat next to the pastor and the circle of chairs was complete. Like Arnie, Billy didn't particularly want to appear in a place of position by sitting at Rusty's side, but it seemed appropriate to the rest of the group. Billy was the only one who had traveled to Central America. If there were insights to be gained, Billy would be the best source.

"Well, I thank you all for coming out on such a rainy morning," Rusty began. "I would like us to start with a word of prayer."

Turning to Billy, Rusty invited the brother of the fallen missionary to lead the team in prayer.

"Father God, it is by Your hand that we are gathered together this morning. We confess our insufficiency. We affirm Your sovereignty. We seek both Your face and grace to know our direction."

"Lord, I thank you for the privilege of serving alongside this fine group. May You take each one of us and make us a team. May we set aside any personal agenda or wrong attitude and completely abandon ourselves to Your will."

"We pray that we may be found faithful and fruitful in the place where you send us. Prepare us now for what You have purposed. In the mighty name of our Lord and Savior, Jesus Christ,…Amen!"

"Amen!" resounded the group.

Rusty opened a manila folder he had been carrying under his arm. Inside was a sheaf of emails, forms, and his handwritten checklist. He sifted the sheets till he found his checklist, and slipped it on top. Taking a deep breath, he began to address the troops.

"Well, I guess we should start with introductions. I'm sure some of you have already introduced yourselves to some of you while some of you were waiting for some of you to arrive."

The small group chuckled at Rusty's attempt to break the ice.

"Why don't we just start at my left with Billy Eldridge who has just led us in prayer, and go around clockwise."

The others nodded in agreement and Billy began. He remained seated which set a relaxed pace for each one to follow. Billy was brief in his introduction while still mentioning his brother Carey. The group acknowledged his loss with sympathetic smiles that reflected respect more than pity.

Ty was even briefer, though he did take the time to say that he was very grateful for the opportunity to be a part of the team. He had not felt a part of anything for a long time. More sympathetic smiles.

Matt, Billy Littleton, and Alex played tag team in their introductions, interrupting each other with quips and "friendly fire". As Alex completed the trios' presentation, Rusty took the floor.

"In that we have two Billy's among us," he began, motioning to Mr. Eldridge. "I hereby dub young master Littleton, 'Little Billy'."

"Wait a minute," young Mr. Littleton objected in his strongest adolescent voice. "Why do I get the nickname?"

"All in favor?" Rusty continued with parliamentary skill, ignoring the objection.

"Aye!" resounded the group, including his collegiate comrades, who were now poking his ribs in fun.

"And it is unanimous," Rusty continued without missing a beat. "Mr. Billy Littleton will be called, 'Little Billy'. Now let us continue with the introductions."

The laughing subsided while the Beamans took turns sharing about their different jobs and excitement about taking the trip together. They were a young couple, but not young Christians. Each had a testimony over ten years old in the Lord. They were active in their Sunday school class and various local ministry projects of the Church. They had even worked together in soup kitchens before. Rhonda had always wanted to take a mission trip. Willis agreed after they had prayed together about it for a week.

Peter Moralis gave his name, paused, and then gave his full birth name.

"I am completely bi-lingual and I hope God can use me and my Spanish on this trip," he added. He shared briefly about his work and his love for the church and missions.

"His restaurant also makes a terrific quesadilla," Arnie was quick to add.

Robert Winston followed Peter. His face was well known as one of the regular ushers. Winston apologized for some of the limitations he would face on the construction site, due to his accident, but he felt his contribution would be his knowledge of materials.

Arnie added his own comments of confidence in Winston's abilities and then quickly gave his own introduction. He mentioned the plans but didn't bring them out at that time. He knew Rusty would get around to it soon enough.

Stan Henly spoke gently, but firmly. His deep voice praised the Lord for bringing the team together and for seeing "his" church respond so well to the project. He gave his name for the new faces, but didn't mention his title as Chairman of Deacons. He was just another team member.

Pastor Rusty re-welcomed the group again and took a deep breath. This was new for him.

"Let me thank you all again for being sensitive to the Holy Spirit and becoming part of this team. I pray that God will bring us together into a close-knit team as we spend time together in preparation. If you are like me, this is your first mission trip outside the United States. From what I have been reading from our missionary and getting from Billy Eldridge, here, the first word we will all have to learn is…FLEXIBLE."

The group repeated the word as if on cue. Rusty smiled and continued. "I would like to take a few minutes now and introduce you to the missionaries we will be working with in Nicaragua."

The group looked around.

"I meant by email," Rusty sighed. "I have several messages here that have come over the past two months. I won't read them all, but I would like to hit some of the highlights so that you can hear the heart of Allen West. Allen and his wife Becky are veteran missionaries of over twenty years. They have served in two South American countries and have been in Nicaragua for about six years; they are half-way through their second term. Shortly after they started this new term, hurricane Mitch came through Central America. It hit hard in Honduras, but did plenty of damage in El Salvador and Nicaragua. That was a little more than a year ago."

"I remember Mitch," Peter spoke up. "Some of my wife's people live in Chiapas and were affected by it also."

"I'm afraid too many of us here in America have all but forgotten about Mitch," Rusty added sadly. "There was a great outpouring of aid that went out months after the hurricane, but now, I doubt most people even remember the disaster and deaths. Somewhere between nine and ten thousand people died as a result of Mitch, the flooding, the mudslides, and disease."

The group shook their heads in sympathy.

"In addition to the loss of life, there was tremendous loss of property, road ways and bridges. That brings us to our request. Allen West discovered a small village just off a main road he traveled regularly. He learned that the village was on the opposite side of a river that lost their only bridge during Mitch. The government has been slow to help replace the bridge and consequently, several people have drown trying to cross the river in the past year or so."

"That's terrible," Rhonda sighed.

"So they need a bridge," Ty added.

"They need more than that," Rusty continued. "After visiting the area, the missionary discovered that the village has no church – not even a Catholic church, which is pretty unusual."

"No church at all?" Little Billy asked.

"No church at all!" repeated Rusty. "What they do have is a witch-doctor who seems to be antagonistic to Christianity."

The team was quiet for a moment taking in the information.

"So this is more than just a construction team," Billy Eldridge finally said breaking the silence.

"Yes, it is," Rusty replied firmly. "I pray you all are up to it."

"Bring him on," Matt Preston nearly shouted.

"This is not a football game," Rusty quickly replied, trying not to rebuke Matt in front of the others with his tone. "It just means that we will be engaging in some serious spiritual warfare and hopefully some meaningful evangelism while we are there."

The team acknowledged the seriousness of the assignment.

"With those few words of introduction to the request, we need to look today at some of the logistics about the trip. We will probably meet about four times before we leave in April. I should have all of your phone numbers and email addresses. If not, please make sure I get them before you leave today."

The team nodded and Rusty took out his legal pad and began looking at his notes.

"Let's start with passports," he began. "Has everyone been able to get their passport or at least start the process?"

Eight hands went up displaying their stiff navy blue booklets of fresh and empty pages. Rusty kept his in the folder. He was embarrassed by his picture. Billy pulled out an older worn version of the same color. Even Stan had a new copy. He had never needed a passport to travel abroad in the Navy, just his military ID. Matt and Little Billy looked at each other as though they had forgotten a major homework assignment.

"We didn't know we would need them today," Matt explained, turning towards Rusty. "We both have them, we just didn't bring them."

"That's OK," Rusty assured them. "We can get copies later, but I do need to make a few copies of your information page. You will want to put one in your luggage, one in your wallet or fanny-pack, and I'll keep a copy of one in my folder."

"What's a fanny-pack?" Little Billy almost giggled.

"You know, one of those carry pouches that strap around your waist," Alex explained.

"Like the tourists wear to Sea World and Disneyland," Matt added.

"Gotcha!" Little Billy replied giving a thumbs-up.

"As I was saying," Rusty continued. "Rather than carry your passport around, you will want to have a copy of it. Putting one in your luggage is just a safeguard in case you get separated from your luggage. I also need a copy before I order the plane tickets. They want your name as it appears on your passport for the ticket."

"What are we going to do with our passports while 'in-country'," Stan Henly asked.

"My brother always collected them and kept them safe for the team," Billy suggested. "I'm not sure if the Wests want to do the same or not. It will depend on where we have our lodging."

"Give my passport to someone else?" Winston questioned with a hint of concern. "I'm not sure I'm comfortable with that. No offence to your brother, but I'm not sure I want to be separated from my passport while in a foreign country."

"I understand your concern," Billy Eldridge responded. "But it is actually safer in a missionary home than on your person. It would be a nightmare to lose it while on the work site, or to have it stolen while in the market."

Winston refrained from expressing any further concern, but he was not convinced it was a good idea.

"But we ALL have passports, right?" Rusty returned the discussion back to the issue.

Everyone nodded.

"OK, how about shots?" Rusty continued on his list.

"What shots?" Matt blurted. The group was getting used to looking in his direction.

Rusty read from his list.

"It is suggested that teams going to Central America consider Hepatitis A and B, and Tetanus, especially if you are going to be involved with building.

The fact that we will be working close to a river may mean considering something for Malaria as well."

"But that can be a pill, right?" Stan added, remembering his days in Panama.

"Yes," Rhonda spoke up. "And I may be able to get us some samples from the clinic I work at. I'll look into it."

"Let's get back to these shots," Matt spoke out. "Are they required?"

"No, they are SUGGESTED," Rusty repeated.

"They will also require some time between shots," Rhonda added. "You need to plan a couple months in advance if you are going to get the Hepatitis shots, and they are not cheap either."

"But they are just SUGGESTED," Matt said again with emphasis.

"Yes, Matt – you don't have to take the shots if you don't want to," Rusty replied. "For those of you who wish to take the shots, I believe you can do that through the health department. And Rhonda is right about spacing out the doses, so be looking into it."

He looked back at his list.

"OK, let's talk about what we are going to do," Rusty announced. Eyes turned towards Arnie.

"I have asked Arnie to communicate with the missionaries in Nicaragua and he has put some ideas together on how we can construct a sturdy foot bridge across the river. Now we know that we can't build something strong enough for a vehicle, but it should hold a horse with a load."

"That's right," Arnie jumped in. "Since hardly no one in the village has a vehicle, it wasn't necessary to make it that wide or so strong it would require support posts placed in the river. That is the good news. It will require two foundational platforms on both banks though."

Arnie began pulling out his drawings from the plastic tubes. He had made legal size copies that he was able to pass around the circle, while he spoke to the large blueprint in his lap.

"These two platforms will require some footing and time to set up before we can even start the expanse. We will be using a combination of rope and wood. If time allows, we will work on a wood railing, but by the time we leave, the bridge will be functional."

Nods of agreement bobbed around the group.

"How wide is the river?" Stan asked, studying his miniature of the plans.

"Thirty-five to forty yards is the best the missionary can estimate without survey equipment. He plans to measure the river some way – I'm not sure how, but then we will know how many sections we are talking about. It won't be exact, but it will be close enough

"What about those of us that are not too skilled with a hammer?" asked Little Billy, the computer geek. "I mean, I've tried and they call me 'lightning', not because I was fast – I just never strike twice in the same place!"

A chuckled erupted from the group.

"I know what you mean," Rusty conceded. "I'm not a carpenter either, but we can make sure the ones that are never run out of materials to work with. There are plenty of tasks that are, if I may use the phrase, 'unskilled labor', that we can plug into."

Little Billy nodded, and Arnie continued.

"Now, let me try to explain what we will be doing the five to six days that we will be working," Arnie said, returning to his plans. For the next ten minutes, he outlined the construction ideas and procedures. Consideration was given to the river level, the rainy season, the festivals and holidays that might be observed during their stay.

"Why do we need to know about the holidays?" Matt asked.

"Because businesses close down for some holidays and we want to be sure that we can get the materials and supplies we need while we are down there," Rusty explained. "Also we plan to use some local help, and we would like them sober during those days."

"You're kidding," Rhonda exclaimed.

"I wish he was," Rusty followed up. "Local labor will not come from the church, because there is no church in the area. We'll have to contract workers that live near *Pozo Negro*."

"More opportunity to share Christ," Stan remarked.

The group asked a few more questions about the bridge and then Arnie put his plans away. Rusty resumed the leadership of the discussion.

"For lodging, we will be staying in León. That will mean an early morning wakeup call and quick breakfast in order to make the hour trip to the worksite by 8:30am."

Groans were heard from the University trio. Stan and Arnie snickered.

"We will be shutting down each day by 5:00pm to give us time to get re-packed and down the mountain for supper by 6:30pm. On at least three of the evenings, we will be going to church at night," Rusty shared reading from one of the emails. "At least that is the plan. Like I said, the catch-word for the week will be…"

"FLEXIBLE!" the group responded in unison.

CHAPTER ELEVEN

"THE BROKENNESS"

HOWARD PENNINGTON was glad the rainy season was behind them. Mid-January brought cooler temperatures, almost sweater weather in San José, Costa Rica. The walks to and from the Language Institute were brisk and invigorating. With the winter break past and the second trimester starting at full force, the pressure of language study came with a vengeance. Howard knew that the process of cultural adaptation was not easy. He had experienced the gut-churning stress of not knowing how to get back to a familiar bus stop from downtown after dark, the utter confusion of trying to ask for a particular battery for their camera, and the sheer helplessness of trying to understand a joke being told after church one Sunday. It didn't help that his Big Brother and family had packed up and returned to the states before the end of the winter break. The Penningtons had two trimesters left to go, and in some respects, they were going to have to "go it alone".

Donna had finished classes earlier than Howard with the new trimester schedule and had already made the trip down the hill to their home. Some days she would decide to stay after her classes to walk with him, but today she was anxious to return to the house. Howard looked in the snack bar to make sure she wasn't waiting and then swung his back-pack over his shoulder. Before leaving the upper level, he decided to check the *correo*, just in case Donna had not picked up the mail.

There was always a twinge of excitement to find a thin envelope with the special colored markings indicating an airmail letter from the states propped up against the side wall of the mail compartment. Howard snatched the envelope and quickly checked the return address, hoping to find Karen's handwriting. The word "Texas" caught his eye first. Then he read the town - "Parsons", Donna's hometown. The letter was from her parents. He toyed with the idea of opening it, but decided against it. This was the first letter she had received from them since they left the states. And it was addressed to Donna alone.

Donna's parents had not completely been in favor of her leaving Texas to go to California after she and Howard were married. They were even less thrilled about them taking their youngest grandchild out of the country. Even though Donna's father was a retired minister himself, they had maintained a cool distance during the whole missionary process. Inwardly, they had hoped that the Board would have found some reason to turn them down. They had talked at Christmas by phone, but no letters had been exchanged – till now. Howard began to wonder if the letter carried some bad news. He stuffed the envelope into his shirt pocket and moved quickly to the gate leaving the Institute.

Juanita knew how to use a washer and how to iron "permanent press" shirts before she came to work for the Penningtons. She was careful not to put away the clothing when family members were not at home. She didn't want to give any cause for the family to be concerned about her presence in their house. She only spoke when spoken to and for the first couple weeks, that was limited to greetings and basic questions. With time, Mrs. Pennington began to open up more. After the break-in, there was a long period of little conversation. Now that they were pass the holidays and their language skills were getting better, Juanita was being included in more conversations.

"How is your family?" Donna asked while Juanita ironed.

"They are all well, thank you," she replied politely. "They wanted me to thank you for your Christmas gift. The box of food and money was very helpful during the holidays."

"You are very welcome," Donna smiled. She and Howard had not only given Juanita her Christmas bonus and "thirteenth month" pay, but an additional amount for her parents to use for Christmas gifts, bills, or whatever they needed. Howard had wanted to deliver the food and envelope personally and to meet Juanita's family, but Donna was not ready. She was still nervous about personal contact with Costa Ricans. She was OK in church where the conversation was casual and surface, but she still felt self-conscious about her Spanish and her ability to understand their customs. Christmas time especially was filled with so many different practices, foods, and unfamiliar songs. She knew it would take some getting use to. Maybe next year it would be easier.

"Señora Pennington," Juanita began softly, trying not to sound invasive. "Do you miss your family in the United States?"

Donna was caught off guard by the question. The tone was more than curiosity, it reflected thought and insight. Donna wasn't sure what was meant by the question. She decided not give a glib response.

"You know, Juanita, sometimes, I'm too busy with school to even think about how much I miss them. Then I feel guilty when I do think about them. I haven't seen my family much in many years because we moved away from them when I got married. But I always knew that they were just a short plane ride away. Now they seem so much farther. It's like they are a million miles away."

Donna knew she hadn't used the correct grammar and tense and that she may have mixed up a few words. She didn't know the word for guilty and had just said that she felt "bad". Juanita understood every word perfectly.

"It must be hard living away from family," Juanita responded softly. "Especially at Christmas."

Donna couldn't respond. But her eyes thanked Juanita for her understanding.

The moment was interrupted by Howard making his way through the front gate. Donna quickly dabbed her eyes, straightened her blouse and skirt and headed toward the door.

"Hey sweetie," she called as he pulled back the screen door to let himself in. "How were your classes?"

"I think I'm getting the hang of the subjunctive," he laughed. There was nothing harder for second trimester students to master than the subjunctive case in Spanish.

"Yeah, right!" she joked back.

Howard set his backpack carefully on the kitchen table and pulled the letter from his shirt pocket. He paused long enough for Donna to realize that he had a letter. Her eyes lit up with anticipation.

"Is it from Karen?" she asked excitedly.

"No, honey," his tone dropping a little. "It's from your parents. I haven't opened it yet."

She took a breath and then the letter. The thin airmail envelope opened easily. The letter was handwritten, meaning Donna's mother had prepared it. Her father liked his computer too much to ever write out anything by hand. She scanned the opening lines of introduction and pleasantries. The letter then took a serious turn and Donna's forehead furrowed.

"What is it?" Howard asked.

Donna raised her hand to pause his question. She then moved it slowly to her mouth and began to quiver.

Howard realized that the news was not good and swung a kitchen chair around behind her. She took a seat and Juanita stopped ironing. She could tell something was very wrong.

After a moment, Howard rephrased his question, "Who is it?"

Donna lifted her eyes from the letter that were now filling with tears.

"Aunt Clare has passed away...the funeral was last week. She's gone, and I didn't even get to say good-bye, or see her or anything." Donna began to sob.

Howard put his arm around her.

"Oh, Donna, I'm sorry," he said softly. "I know you were close."

"AUNT CLARE!" Donna repeated loudly.

"I know," Howard reiterated for comfort.

"She's my Mom's only sister. I grew up with Aunt Clare. She was more than an Aunt, she was a close friend."

"I know, sweetheart."

"She was the one who prayed with me when I accepted Christ. She helped me in college when Mom couldn't. She taught me how to drive. She…" Donna's voice trailed off.

Howard stood next to his wife and gently rocked her with his arm. He could feel her shoulders heaving with grief. Juanita sat the iron down on its rack and stepped to Donna's other side. She knelt down beside her chair and gently placed her hand on Donna's elbow. The three huddled for several moments without speaking. Donna rocked and cried.

"I've got some news," Allen West called from his computer screen. "The group from San Diego just sent an email."

"What's it say?" Becky yelled back from the kitchen.

"They had their first meeting as a group, it looks like…twelve in all."

"Twelve. That's a good size for a group. Have you thought about transportation?" She asked, walking into the study, wiping her hands on a dish towel.

"I can check with Raul about his van again," Allen replied nonchalant. "We still have over three months till they come. I'll set up reservations at the *Pinolero* though, now that I have the final number in the group."

The *Pinolero* was a small hotel in *León* titled after the nickname given to Nicaraguans. It was clean and a fairly good distance from the square with its night time activity and noise. The team should be able to sleep through the night at the *Pinolero*.

"I guess I'll be preparing some of the meals?" Becky asked.

"It will save them money if we do," Allen reminded her. "Besides, we have plenty of room in the court area for tables."

Becky enjoyed cooking for volunteers. It gave her the opportunity to get to know them better than just seeing them pull out in the mornings or trying to talk around a loud banquet table on their final evening. She could prepare chicken and rice economically for large groups as well as spaghetti.

"Are there any women coming?" she asked.

"One wife will be coming. Let's see, her name is…Rhonda Beaman."

"Just one woman?"

"Looks that way," Allen replied still reading. "It looks like they have a good lineup of construction help and even one bilingual team member."

"That will come in handy," Becky exclaimed. "What nationality?"

"I guess Mexican, but it shouldn't matter. The basics of the language will be the same even if there are some different expressions used here. As long he doesn't bring 'attitude' and a chip on his shoulder about Nicaraguans with him, it should be fine and even helpful to have another Spanish speaker."

"Did you tell them about the witch doctor?" Becky inquired.

"I was very upfront about the possibility of opposition and spiritual warfare involved with this project. I can only hope that they will take time to prepare themselves at that end. We will have opportunity to prayer walk the area before they arrive."

"Who do you plan to take with you?"

"I have asked José to bring some down from his church. We plan to do that in late February. Between now and then, we will have special prayer meetings at his church."

"What will you do if the witch-doctor mobilizes the city officials against the project?"

"I'm not sure they can stop us legally from building the bridge. The little settlement on this side of the river is actually closer than *Pozo Negro*."

Becky stood next to him and waited till Allen looked up into her eyes. They were tense with concern.

"I'm not talking about what they can do legally!" she said firmly.

Allen understood her comment and concern. He softened his eyes to reassure her.

"The enemy would like nothing better than to defeat us before we start. The truth is, he has no real authority in *Pozo Negro* or anyplace else for that matter. He was defeated on the cross and has been bluffing his way into the hearts of men ever since. He can stir up trouble through those who allow him, but he cannot overcome the work of God. John says, 'you are of God little children and HAVE overcome them, for greater is He that is in you, than he that is in the world.' This team may not be made up of super saints, but then neither was Gideon. If I read my Bible right, Gideon was pretty much a coward with his own doubts, but the angel called him as a 'mighty warrior of valor'. God sees what He can be through us, not what we may be at the moment. This team just needs to bring the light and a willingness to break the clay pot that covers it."

"I'm not following you," Becky replied.

"Gideon was sent into battle with two items – one in each hand – a torch covered with a clay pot and a trumpet. In which hand did they carry their sword?"

"I never thought of that," Becky said amused.

"At the signal, they were to break the pots that hid the light of the torch and blow the trumpet and shout, 'the sword of the Lord and of Gideon'. The light, the trumpet and the shout were their weapons. The Lord fought the battle. The enemy destroyed itself. That's the picture of spiritual warfare. We enter the battle with the light of Jesus Christ, but it is covered in a clay pot. We are the clay pot. We hold the trumpet to announce and we shout to proclaim, but only after we have broken the clay pot and let the light be seen. Paul said, 'we have this treasure in earthen vessels, so that the excellency of power may be of God and not of us'. I believe we need to let God break the earthen vessel in such a way that the light – the treasure – can be seen and that God is glorified."

"How does God break the pot?"

"Different ways. He may choose to use calamity or blessing."

"I can understand calamity. How does God use a blessing?"

"Remember the woman who came into the home of Simon the Pharisee and anointed Jesus at the table?"

"One of my favorite stories," Becky smiled. "A display of true extravagant worship."

"Yes, but also a picture of true brokenness. Remember her weeping and washing of his feet? That was a result of having had her sins forgiven. Jesus showed mercy and forgiveness to someone who later became so overwhelmed by grace that it broke her. I have met people that God spared in a miraculous way to draw them to Himself in brokenness. They knew they didn't deserve such a blessing from God and it humbled them. Granted, not many respond that way. Perhaps, that's why we think more of God humbling through hard times, but the 'rain falls on the just and unjust alike' with the same purpose of drawing men and women to Christ."

"So what do you think will happen this spring?" Becky said, drawing the discussion back to the mission team.

"I have no idea. But if we are going to see a breakthrough in *Pozo Negro*, I am convinced we are going to see brokenness take place as well."

———————————

The first wave of grief had passed and Donna sat calmly at the table with a glass of warm tea. Juanita had returned to her work and was in the back hanging out clothes to dry. Howard sat with her and waited for her to speak. His presence was her greatest comfort at this time. The news of her aunt's death had been amplified by her own tensions. Donna imagined what it would have been like to receive the announcement while in California.

She would have been saddened, made immediate calls and looked for an opportunity to return to Texas for the funeral. The fact that the letter arrived a week after the funeral made it hard to accept. Why hadn't someone called? What if she had wanted to come back for the funeral? What if it had been one of her parents? Was the distance and separation too great? Had coming to the field been a mis…She stopped herself.

"Should I call home?" she finally asked Howard.

"Of course you should," he replied supportively. "They need to know that you got the letter and that you now know."

"Why didn't they call me?"

"I don't know for sure. Maybe they thought you couldn't return for the funeral anyway, so there was no need for urgency. Maybe they thought it would be easier telling you in a letter."

"Easier for who?" Donna almost started crying again.

"I know what you mean," Howard consoled. "But maybe they didn't realize how close you and Aunt Clare were."

"How could they not know?" Donna objected. "I was always visiting her while growing up. She taught me piano. We talked about everything. She and Uncle Adam didn't have children and she treated me like a daughter when I visited. I remember her praying with me to accept Christ and when I told her I wanted to get married, she was the one that talked with me about…well, you know."

Howard shared a smile with her.

"So, do you want to call before Terry gets home?"

"Maybe I should. But I can't right now. I'll just start crying all over again."

Howard put his arm around his hurting wife. He knew Donna had been holding in much of her struggles with the language and adjustments. This news had burst the dam. He wasn't sure how much more she could take. For that matter, neither did Donna. They sat in silence for the next forty-five minutes.

"Mom, can you hear me? This is Donna…Donna…in Costa Rica.… We're fine, Mom. How are you and Dad?…Yes, we got the letter…Yes Mom, but…."

Howard listened from a distance and finally decided it would be better to let her talk alone. Donna was angry and hurt. Someone else had made the decision for her about how to handle her Aunt's death. There would be no closure, no good-bye, no final viewing. She would simply not ever see her again, even when she went home. It was more than a disappointment, she felt robbed all over again. He decided to pray that Donna would not say something bitter while speaking to her parents. It was not in her nature to do so, but the months here had brought many things to the surface that are usually kept in check.

The call lasted just under fifteen minutes. When Donna emerged from the bedroom, she was drying her eyes. The letter had not given the details of Aunt Clare's passing. Howard was sure Donna knew what had happened and about the final arrangements. He decided to let her talk about what she was comfortable with sharing.

"How do you feel?" he asked.

"I'll be OK," she replied with a clear voice. "Mom was helpful. She explained why they decided on the letter. I guess it was hard for them to even write the letter. Mom knew how close we were. It was difficult for her to talk about it, even after I knew. Clare was her only sister."

Donna paused a moment and then composed herself again.

"It was sudden. Clare had not been sick. When Adam died three years ago, she determined to get active and become involved with her church and community. She did just that. She was sixty-nine and still walking three miles each morning. Her blood pressure was fine, and Mom said even her cholesterol was where it should be. She just had a fatal heart attack walking one morning and no one can really tell why. The funeral was held in the First Baptist Church of Parsons and the place was packed. There were flowers…"

Donna trailed off thinking about how they didn't even get to send flowers. Howard put his arm around her. It would take time. He hugged her and thought to himself, "what else could go wrong during this year?" It was the wrong question to ask.

Terry Pennington was older than he looked. He had inherited his mother's gene as a "late bloomer" and though he would be turning twelve within the month, he still looked ten. He had been placed in the fifth grade and was one of the smallest boys in his class even though most of the Costa Rican children were also short in stature. The other MK boys were all bigger and stronger. Terry was seldom picked for playground games and his lack of involvement reinforced his desire to keep to himself. This was affecting his ability to pick up the Spanish language. He did fair in learning his classroom Spanish, but language was something you gain through interaction and Terry wasn't getting it.

Terry preferred to walk home from school rather than take the bus with the younger children that weaved through all the streets of El Bosque, dropping each child off at their home, sometimes making three stops to a street. He figured he could walk home about as fast as he could ride the bus. His father had found some cartridges for his Christmas Gameboy in a downtown store. The covers were different and there was Chinese writing all over the front, but they fit and the games were the same. Terry really didn't care where they came from, as long as he could play. Walking the same path home, focusing on the LCD screen in his hand was just the distraction he needed after a long day at school. Unfortunately, it was all the distraction a small gang of bicycle riders needed as well.

Terry never saw them coming. The first rode past him on the sidewalk about six feet and then did a power slide turning his bike lengthwise blocking the width of the sidewalk. Terry looked up to see dark brown eyes glaring at him. Within seconds, Terry felt his backpack pulling him to the left and he was swung around falling on his side in the grass. They flew from his hands and landed on the opposite side of the concrete. Another bicycle rider appeared, and the handheld game was scooped up from the grass with a single sweep of his arm. The rider that had jerked him off his feet now poised over him looking down.

"*No diga nada!*" he snarled, demanding that Terry say nothing.

Terry stared blankly at his assailants and then rolled over on his stomach. He had no fight in him. The boys rode off as quickly as they had appeared, leaving Terry shaking from adrenalin. He picked himself up, examined his torn backpack, and knew that he would have to tell his parents something. As he walked the rest of the way down the hillside of the park, he wondered why no one came to help him. These boys robbed him in broad daylight and no one tried to stop them. No one cared. He hated Costa Rica and he hated Costa Ricans. As he walked, his anger robbed him of his tears.

CHAPTER TWELVE

" THE TURF "

IT WOULD be weeks before Terry would walk home again. He hated the bus, but he hated more the thought of meeting up with the bicycle gang. In early February, an MK, whose family was preparing their way to Venezuela, took up with Terry at school and offered to walk home with him. Eric Cartwright was a year older, but was much bigger than Terry and very protective. The truth was, his father was in Howard's grammar class and heard about the ambush. He encouraged his son Eric to try and make friends with Terry. Once the boys got to know each other, it wasn't hard. Donna spent the same time working through her grief and regaining her focus for language study. It was difficult for both of them and Howard was keenly aware of the situation.

Howard Pennington sat in Chapel reflecting over the many hardships they had already faced. It seemed like they had endured more than their share. He could understand being robbed once or twice, but "no one had been hit as many times as the Penningtons" seemed to be the whisper around the language institute. Howard began to feel the real presence of spiritual warfare going on against his family. How much permission was Satan to be given, he thought to himself.

"Aren't we praying, Aren't we reading our Bibles. Why so much attack? After all, we're doing all we can to prepare for the mission field that You have called us to".

"That's the problem" Howard heard from within. *"You are looking at this time as only for preparation. I have work for you while you are here."*

Howard's eyes went wide. It was a familiar voice, but one he hadn't heard in a long time. He looked around the chapel and saw the faces of fellow missionaries and language students listening intently to the devotion being presented. No one else seemed to have heard the voice of God. Howard paused, as if waiting for more. At least he was listening. What he heard was the closing prayer of the chapel speaker and the heavy steps of the Institute director making his way across the platform.

"Thank you, *hermano* Richard for that word. I must admit, I haven't looked at Amos that way before."

The director cleared his throat and continued, "Before you make your way to your next class, let me remind you of the 'off-campus ministry fair' in the gym. Each trimester, we provide opportunities for ministries that can use volunteers to present their work to our students. These ministries take into account your limited use of Spanish. If you did not participate in a ministry last trimester, let me encourage you to take a moment during one of your breaks today to go down and talk to a representative. There are all kinds of opportunities, such as prison work, refugee ministry, orphanage visitation, street evangelism, and campus ministry, just to name a few. May the Lord speak to you in one of these areas. You're dismissed."

Howard sat motionless as the other students began to file out and make their way to the post office before class. He had a free period for the next hour. Donna would be finishing her classes and then would either hang around for him or make her way back home to get an early start on her homework. Howard waited and listened.

"OK, Lord…I hear You!" he finally said to himself and rose obediently to make his way to the gym.

Howard found several small tables set up, some with hand drawn posters, some with tri-fold cardboard displays, and some with just flyers and handouts scattered across the top of the table. He took a couple minutes to walk around each exhibit to see what ministries were being represented. He could tell which ones were promoted each year by the quality of their display. He could also tell which ones were being supported by outside agencies. Some were manned by students, while others were being staffed by off-campus personnel, many of whom were Costa Rican. After one complete round of the gym, Howard decided to walk back to a small card table with one lone representative who was obviously not a student.

"*Buen Dia!*" Howard said in greeting.

Immediately the enthusiastic ministry promoter extended his hand and began returning the greeting with a volley of Spanish, some of which Howard was unable to understand.

"*Mas dispacio, por favor!*" Howard returned quickly asking the young man to please speak more slowly.

"Sorry," the young man smiled. "I forget. My name is Mateo."

"Hello, Mateo," Howard replied, shaking his hand. "I don't mind trying in Spanish, but just take it a little slow with me."

Mateo laughed and brandished a large toothy smile. He was part Costa Rican and part Jamaican. Howard soon felt at ease. They exchanged simple family information that Howard learned how to share in his first month. After a few minutes of introductions, Mateo turned Howard's attention toward the brochures and handouts on his table. Mateo didn't have a professional display and didn't appear to have had very many takers at his table.

"These are called '*Los Cuatro Leyes Espirituales*'," Mateo said, picking up one of the brochures. "They are like your…"

"Four Spiritual Laws," Howard said, finishing his sentence.

"That's right. We use them on the University campus to share the gospel with students."

Howard pointed to the hand drawn sign on the front of Mateo's table.

"What does this mean, *Alpha y Omega*? I mean, I know how we use those words in the U.S. They stand for the beginning and the end."

"In Latino countries, *Alpha y Omega* is the title given to the ministry that is called,…how do you say, '*Campus Crusada for Christ*'?"

"Campus Crusade for Christ!"

"Jes!" Mateo said with his accent. "Campus Crusade for Christ – that is correct."

"I know this organization," Howard said excitedly. "In fact, I have met the founder, Bill Bright, while I was in California."

The two talked about the ministry, the *JESUS FILM*, and the impact that Campus Crusade had made over the years.

"So what does the university ministry involve?" Howard finally asked, realizing that he only had about fifteen minutes left to his free period.

"I use language students to come with me on campus and to share the pamphlet, *Los Cuatro Leyes Espirituales* with students."

"But my Spanish is not good enough to talk to University students, let alone present the Gospel. I would be doing good to read the tract myself and understand everything I was reading."

"That is the point," Mateo said, smiling big again. "We will ask the student if you can read the tract to practice your Spanish, BECAUSE you are a language student. They will allow you to read *anything* to practice your Spanish. Most are polite and will listen. We will ask them to correct your pronunciation and any words you may have gotten wrong. Then I will ask them what they thought of what you read."

"Kind of like a tag-team witness," Howard added enthusiastically.

"I'm not sure what 'tak-team' means," Mateo confessed.

"TAG-team, but don't worry about it, we will be working together."

"*Jes!*" Mateo replied.

"Put me down!" Howard asserted.

"*Perdon?*" Mateo looked confused.

"I will do it," Howard said slowly, forgetting that fluency didn't always include idioms, even in English.

Mateo handed him the clipboard to sign. Howard noticed his was the only name so far. He hoped there would be others, but if not, he would still enjoy working with Mateo. He could tell that just the conversations would be a boost to his Spanish work-out. Wouldn't it be something to be able to lead someone to Christ while in Language School, he thought to himself. Howard couldn't wait to finish his classes for the day and to get home and tell Donna. Maybe she would see the opportunity for service as good news.

Rusty finished his hospital visits early and returned to the Church before lunch. Dianne was still at her desk working on the upcoming newsletter waiting on Steve's article. Steve Allison was not much younger than Rusty and had served as Worship Leader for the Coronado Baptist Church for about the same amount of time as his young pastor. He had no problem with the transition from Dr. Howard Pennington to Rusty. If anything, he felt freer to try some of the newer worship choruses he was hearing on the Christian radio station.

"Who's ready for lunch?" Rusty called out from the hallway between Dianne's and Steve's office doors.

"That depends," came a voice from within Steve's office. "Who's buying?"

"Dutch treat!" Rusty called back lightly, but seriously.

"Thanks, Dutch," Dianne responded first. It was an old joke. She was just excited about eating with Rusty, even if it was a threesome.

"Let me check," Steve responded, while grabbing his sweater. He emerged from his doorway looking at his watch. "Looks like I'm free for about ninety minutes. I have someone coming at one. Where did you have in mind?"

"I'm feeling a little Mexican today," said Rusty. "And I know a great little spot, but it's about twenty minutes from here."

"Maybe I should take my own car, just in case," Steve offered.

"If you like. Dianne, you want to ride with me or Steve?"

"I've seen Steve drive the church van. I'll take my chances with the preacher," she replied playfully. Inwardly, she was jumping at the opportunity to accompany Rusty.

The cars traveled in tandem through the city heading south towards the beach area of the Silver Strand. Traffic was cooperative and they were never separated.

"Where are we going?" asked Dianne after they were on the open road.

"A little place called El Puente" Rusty replied. "The owner is on the Nicaragua mission team."

"The Bridge," Dianne commented.

"Right," Rusty replied. "We got some plans from Arnie and it is looking very do-able."

"What are you talking about?" Dianne asked puzzled.

"The bridge we are going to build in Nicaragua. Arnie has some plans that he shared at the meeting last month and they seem do-able to the group."

"I just meant the name of the restaurant is called, 'the Bridge'. El Puente means 'the Bridge' ".

"It does?" Rusty replied a little impressed. "How did you know that?"

"College Spanish...two years. Some of it stuck."

"I'm impressed," said Rusty smiling.

"Oh, there's more," Dianne returned cryptically. "You just need to get to know me better."

"Maybe I do," Rusty agreed. "Why don't we start with lunch."

Dianne turned and looked out her window at the seaside so Rusty couldn't see her smile.

El Puente had a good lunch menu and the crowd reflected it. Peter Moralis tried to greet each patron when he could, but the hour before and after noon was an exception. Steve pulled in right behind Rusty and Dianne and they were able to walk in as a threesome. Peter was in the kitchen and missed their entrance, but he soon spotted Rusty seated next to the three foot plaster statue of the classic sleeping Mexican with the huge sombrero resting on his shoulders and knees. Peter pointed a waitress with a large tray of drinks towards a table of construction workers and then made his way to their table.

"*Qué sorpresa!*" Peter exclaimed expressing his surprise. "But a nice surprise. Welcome to my restaurant."

"*Buenas tardes!*" Rusty attempted with an obvious accent.

"Very good," Peter smiled. "But its not quite noon yet, so it should still be Buenos dias."

"OK, *Buenos dias*, then. Let me introduce you to some of my staff from the church. This is my worship leader, Steve Allison. And this is the church secretary, Dianne Winters."

"*Con mucho gusto!*" Dianne remarked, extending her hand.

Peter smiled taking her hand in greeting. "*Muy bién,*" he replied.

"Two years of college Spanish," Rusty whispered toward Steve.

"I'm impressed," Steve conceded.

Without voicing it, so was Rusty.

Peter presented the group with menus and made a couple personal recommendations. Steve stuck with the taco plate. Rusty tried the quesadilla, but Dianne ordered the full fajita platter.

When the food came, the three took turns trying each others' cuisine. Dianne had the most to share. Rusty traded his guacamole for one of her flour tortillas filled with peppers and some of the roasted beef. Steve was cautious of trying too much of Rusty's quesadilla. He preferred the chips and salsa in the center of the table. For the most part, they enjoyed their meal tremendously.

A lull in the lunch crowd allowed Peter to rejoin them at their table. Taking a seat beside Dianne, he scooped a chip through the small bowl of salsa and quickly popped it in his mouth.

"May I join you for a minute?" Peter asked, wiping his mouth.

"I was hoping you would have time," Rusty replied. "That's one of the reasons we came by here today."

"I have been talking to my wife about the trip. She is very excited for me to go."

"I'm glad to hear it."

"I told her about the witch doctor, though," Peter said then paused.

"What did she say?" asked Rusty edging him on.

"She knew of a witch doctor in a village not far from her parents in Chiapas. She remembers some real scary stories."

"What kind of stories?" asked Dianne.

"Animal sacrifices, mysterious deaths, natural mishaps, missing children, you name it," Peter said seriously.

"Mysterious deaths?!" exclaimed Steve, holding a chip in midair.

"Mostly older people, but there were stories of young men who tried to oppose the witch-doctor. It was said that they died suddenly, some in their sleep, some while working."

"Peter, do you believe the stories?" Rusty asked.

"What I believe, is that there are powers at work around us that do not fall neatly into psychological or sociological explanations. It's not all suggestion or self-fulfilling prophecy. It's more than chance and it's more than many people want to admit."

"These powers," Rusty probed. "Do you think they are the powers mentioned in scripture when the Bible speaks of 'principalities and powers'?"

"I'm not the Bible scholar. But I know what I have heard. If the devil can blind the hearts and minds of men with limited power, then I believe these men have made themselves channels of that power, whether they know it or not."

"That's scary," Dianne commented half-way to herself.

"That is why Angelina and I have been praying for the team every night since our last meeting," said Peter, rising from the table. "We have a battle before us, and I want to be ready for it. I also better be ready for this next wave of guests. So if you will excuse me."

"By all means," Rusty acknowledged. "And thank you for dropping in with us. The food was excellent...wasn't it, gang?"

Steve and Dianne voiced their appreciation for the food convincingly.

"Trust me, we'll be back," added Rusty. "It was worth the drive."

Peter thanked them again and quickly turned to greet a couple who had just entered. When he had left the area, Rusty leaned into the table to speak.

"I wanted you to meet Peter," he said. "I think he is going to be a strong asset to our team. He has some insights into the latin culture that we need. He also has a strong faith."

"He's also very generous," said Dianne smugly. She pointed with her eyes to the empty space next to Rusty's drink where the waitress had laid the bill between him and her at the end of the table. Rusty looked down and then glanced back towards the front door where Peter stood smiling at them. He held up their bill and slowly tore it in half.

Donna was not as excited as Howard had imagined about his beginning a new activity away from home – even if it were ministry related. She was beginning to feel less and less secure about their surroundings. The attack on her son was still fresh on her mind, even if it had been over three weeks since the boys stole his Gameboy. What bothered her the most, was that she was beginning to feel uncomfortable around Juanita. Her trust was waning and she couldn't explain why. It affected how much she talked to Juanita and that became noticeable.

It was the first Tuesday after Howard and Mateo met in the gym. Howard took the San Marcos bus to the University entrance and looked around. Mateo had arranged to meet Howard at 3:00pm at the POPS ice cream parlor adjacent to the entrance. This would give them about ninety minutes before most of the students made their way from the campus to their homes.

Mateo was actually enrolled in classes at the University. This gave him access to the campus and ability to wander freely when he wasn't attending his one class of the day. The fact was, that Mateo had enrolled in a single class for each semester of the past five years. He was not working toward a degree, and the University didn't seem to mind taking his money.

Howard spotted Mateo waving his hand and smiling from the entrance of the ice cream parlor. He looked both ways and quickly made his way across the busy street to Howard.

"*Buenas tardes, hermano,*" Mateo called out, extending his hand.

Howard shook it vigorisly and returned the greeting.

The two turned and walked past the guard post onto the campus. Mateo spoke pleasantly to the guard on duty who seemed to know him. He then led Howard briskly to the main administration building pointing out the various other structures along the way. Howard knew he wouldn't remember each one from his first trip, but he tried to make mental notes along the way.

"I'm going to show you where one of the student lounges is located, then we will walk out to the lawn area where many students study and visit on the grass."

Howard followed dutifully.

"When I locate someone for us to talk to," continued Mateo, "I will only speak Spanish. If you have a question, ask me aside."

After pointing out the student lounge, where several students stood around smoking and talking with friends, the two men left the building and walked around the side to a large area of open lawn. Students sat in small groups chatting. Some were paired off embracing amorously in the open. Howard saw few books opened. He doubted that much studying was going on. He was right. Mateo spotted a young man alone laying on his back in the grass. His shoes were off and he was staring into the sky in deep contemplation. Mateo motioned for Howard to follow behind him.

They approached the young man and Mateo gave a toothy greeting. After a brief interchange of greetings, Mateo introduced Howard, who stood motionless beside his companion.

"This is my friend, Howard Pennington," said Mateo with impeccable Spanish. Howard did recognize the introduction expressions and was ready to extend his hand in typical greeting. "He is from the United States and is in our country studying Spanish. He has a brief text that he would like to share with you from a written script that he has been asked to practice. Would you be so kind as to allow him to read the script to you and then to make suggestions about correcting any words he may have had trouble pronouncing?"

Howard had to admit, that such an approach to sharing a gospel tract would never find its place on an American campus. He was amazed to see the young man sit up and agree to hear the presentation. What followed was not an act. Howard was nervous. He struggled to make sure that his pronunciation was clear. It was indeed a Spanish exercise for him. The young man listened intently and nodded at several of the difficult words. Howard had practiced the scriptures repeatedly.

He read the first law about God's love and wonderful plan for the young man sitting on the lawn. Without comment, he read the scripture and turned the page. He mechanically read the second law about man's sin and separation from God. He could quote the verse that accompanied this page since it was quoted at almost every church service he had attended since arriving. Howard resisted the temptation to stray from the text and add his own comments, partly for fear of engaging a conversation he couldn't carry, and partly because Mateo had instructed him not to. He read the third law about God's provsion in the person of Jesus Christ. Normally, he would have injected his own personal testimony at this point. Maybe in time, Mateo would allow him to do that. The final law spoke of the need to receive the free gift of God by faith through prayer. Howard decided to pause after the printed scripture. He looked up at Mateo for direction.

Mateo promptly took over.

"Muy bién," said Mateo. Then quickly turning his attention toward the young man, he asked, "And what did you think? Don't be afraid to correct anything, that is why he is here. It doesn't help him if you just act polite."

The young man lowered his head as in thought and then lifted it and looked at Howard.

"I think his pronunciation is pretty good," he offered slowly. "He needs to work on some of the larger words. He still has an American accent with a couple of his vowels. Other than that, I think he did pretty good."

"Would you have any suggestions for him on how he could improve?" asked Mateo.

"Not really, I understood him pretty well."

Howard felt a little awkward listening to the two men discuss his language ability as though he wasn't even present.

"One other question," Mateo posed smoothly. "What was your impression of the material that he read?"

"I found it fascinating," the young man replied. "I recognized that some of it was from the Bible, but I had not heard the other before."

"Do you read the Bible much?" asked Mateo, following up on the young man's comment.

"Not really. I received catechism at a young age and pretty much let the church fall by the wayside."

"What about God? Did you let Him fall by the wayside also?"

The young man dropped his eyes and paused.

"I guess so," he confessed.

"Would you be interested in knowing that He has not allowed you to fall by the wayside – and that is why we are here talking with you on the grass today."

The young man's eyes began to water. Howard couldn't believe how quickly he was responding to the simple message that Mateo was sharing. He looked around to see if anyone else was watching. A young man's heart was being turned toward his Creator and no one seemed to notice. There on the lawn of a University campus, a life was being reborn and Howard had been a part of it. He felt his chest swelling with anticipation. Mateo continued to apply the scriptures that Howard had read to the young man's life. Within minutes, the two were bowing their heads together in prayer. Howard bowed his head and listened to Mateo pray. There was a brief pause, and then the voice of the young man began crying out to his God in repentance. It was not the model prayer that was printed in the pamphlet, but the heartfelt longing of a soul reaching out for salvation. When the prayer was ended, Mateo embraced the young man. Howard quickly looked around the campus to see if that would attract any attention. No one seemed to notice.

Mateo presented the young man, Alberto, to Howard as a new hermano in Christ. Howard shook his hand with congratulations, but Alberto pulled him close and gave him a strong brotherly hug. Mateo took out his little notebook and asked Alberto for his address and phone number. He would contact him within the week about attending a Bible study off-campus at Mateo's apartment. Mateo was insistent on follow-up and discipleship. He would later help Alberto find a good evangelical church close to his home that he could attend. Before leaving, he gave Alberto a copy of the New Testament in Spanish and encouraged him to begin reading the Gospel of Mark to learn more about the life of Jesus Christ.

Walking away from Alberto, Howard whispered in English to Mateo.

"That was incredible. You really didn't need me at all. You have such a natural way with students."

"I may be comfortable in my sharing, but they would never be open to listen to me if you didn't first introduce them to the Word of God. No, my brother, I cannot do this without you – or someone like you. You open the door for the Gospel to be presented. In time, I hope you will be just as comfortable in talking to them."

"Me, too," Howard sighed.

Mateo smiled broad.

"I believe you will, and soon, my brother."

Allen West sat quietly in his den. The street noises just outside their front door seemed distant and immaterial. Allen was in a different world altogether. Becky passed by on her way to the bedroom to put away some laundry and noticed Allen sitting still without a book. He was looking outward beyond the room itself. She stared for a moment and then decided to inquire.

"Whatcha thinking about?" she asked playfully.

Allen looked in her direction, but took a moment to speak.

"Oh,..." he faltered as he began. "I was just thinking about tomorrow."

"What's tomorrow?"

"José and I are returning to *Pozo Negro* to begin preparation on the platforms for the bridge. The team comes in less than two weeks and we need to have the platforms ready for them. I meant to get to it sooner, but the special team meetings on this new mission organization structure put me a little behind schedule."

"Are you worried you won't have the time to get the platforms done before the team arrives?" asked Becky.

"I hadn't really given that part much thought," Allen confessed. "I was thinking more about the opposition we might face tomorrow from Don Tulio."

"Who?"

"The witch-doctor...the little man with the stick that you and I saw the day you went with me. I know he will be trying to dissuade the mayor from working with us."

"You've run into opposition from local priests before, why should this be any different?"

"Because we could always find some common ground based on the Word of God to appeal to the priest for the opportunity to provide a ministry that would benefit the people. Here, there is no common ground. It is just HIS ground. We are on his turf and he doesn't seem inclined to share it."

"How can he object to the building of a bridge if it helps the people?" Becky reasoned.

"He probably doesn't object to the bridge – just to US building it. He knows that such selfless service on the part of foreigners carries the opportunity for influence. When those foreigners carry a message that has the potential of undermining his influence, then he will oppose it with every fiber he possesses. He will use the authorities against us and if that is not enough, he may even incite locals to rise up and destroy our work. There is a potential for some real confrontation and danger if he feels threatened."

"At what point do you put the safety of the team above the project?"

"That's a good question," Allen replied honestly. "Sometimes, volunteers don't understand the seriousness of a situation until it is already out of control. Some come with this kind of "Superman" syndrome that makes them think their passport excludes them from mishap in a foreign country. They imagine themselves immune from laws they don't understand or folkways that are different. I have tried to share about the seriousness of this witch-doctor in my emails. I can only pray they are preparing themselves."

"WE can only pray," Becky corrected him.

"Of course," Allen smiled, taking his wife's hand. "WE can pray!"

"Getting back to tomorrow," Becky injected, kneeling beside his rocker. "How do you plan to approach the mayor if Don Tulio is with him?"

"That is partly what I have been sitting here thinking and praying about. It seems very unlikely that Don Tulio would miss such a meeting. It's a small town and word travels very quickly. He will know we are there before we even get to the mayor's office."

"Then don't go to the mayor's office," offered Becky. "Send someone to bring the mayor to the river's edge and have your meeting there so that you can show him what you have in mind."

"What if Don Tulio is in the mayor's office when the messenger arrives?" Allen asked.

"Pray that he is not," replied Becky simply.

"For that matter, why not just pray that he's no where around when we go?" replied Allen with just a twinge of sarcasm.

"Why not, indeed?" Becky countered. "Our God is mighty and NOTHING is impossible...AMEN?"

Allen smiled and nodded.

"Amen."

"Oh, ye of little faith," she taunted. "I'm going to pray that the witch doctor is not even in the village when you arrive. Do you care to join me?"

"Sure, honey."

Allen turned in his rocker to face her and to take her other hand in his. Together they bowed their heads and prayed for what Allen inwardly believed to be a miracle. He had been praying for wisdom, for words, for a strategy. She was praying for a movement and an open door. Morning would determine if either of their prayers would be answered. That night, Allen slept sound.

CHAPTER THIRTEEN

"THE FOUNDATION"

ONCE A year, Don Tulio oversaw the movement of part of his cattle in Posoltega to slaughter houses near Managua. He was usually away from the village for about two weeks. The money brought in by his cattle enterprises was then deposited into accounts in Managua. He was careful not to bank in León or even Chinandega for fear of other's learning of his affairs. Like the Scrooge of London, he maintained a wealth that he seldom allowed himself to enjoy. Rather, he chose the self-imposed poverty of *Pozo Negro* so that he could enjoy the aura of power he exercised over the town. People didn't fear the rich as much as they did the mystical. Don Tulio fed off of their fear, more than he did off of his material possessions.

For all of his divinations, Don Tulio had failed to "see" the date of the team's arrival one week before Semana Santa. Had he known that preparation would begin during the time of his "dealing", he would have postponed it. He wanted to conduct his business and return before the holidays began. He had been gone only two days when Allen West and hermano José made their way through the mango grove to the river's edge. Allen had sent a young boy to find Beto and his canoe to meet them at the place where he had carried them across before. Allen was prepared for a wait, but barely got comfortable when José called out and pointed. Beto could be seen paddling toward them from up river. He waved and quickened his strokes toward them.

For a few more córdoba, Allen paid the young boy to accompany them across the river. He needed a runner to find the mayor and ask him to join the missionary at the river's edge. In the meantime, Allen and José would take their measurements and study the terrain for the location of the two platforms that would be needed before the bridge could be constructed. They had twelve days before the team arrived.

José secured one end of a heavy rope that Allen had prepared to a tree stump, carefully letting it out from the canoe as they were carried across the river. The current was not very strong at this time of the year and Beto was able to make a straight course. When they arrived on the opposite side, Allen quickly jumped out with the rope in his hand and pulled it as hard as he could. José joined him and together they were able to pull the line up from the water's surface so that the rope extended from one bank to the other about two feet above the water. Allen pulled the rope as tight as he could and then looked for the markings he had made before they left the house.

"Thirty five and a half meters," Allen called out after finding his mark.

"That's about what I guessed," replied José.

"Do you think this is the narrowest point?"

"It looks like the narrowest point from this part of the bend. There may be another spot further down river, but this is the point where the road is closest to the river. I suggest they build here."

Allen passed the rope to Beto, who put it in the canoe, and started back across the river to untie the secured end. They didn't want the rope snagging a passing branch or some other form of debris. As Beto pushed off from shore and began to paddle, Allen began looking around.

"Qué pasa?" asked José.

"Oh, nothing," replied Allen still looking around. "I was just checking to see if the little man with the stick was around."

"I haven't seen him. Do you suppose he will come with the mayor?"

Allen had not discussed with José his conversation with Becky the night before. He was a little embarrassed. He wasn't sure if he was embarrassed by his lack of faith or of her naiveté. Strangely enough, Allen had a quiet peace about the meeting. He still didn't have any idea what he would say if Don Tulio began to challenge the project, but he decided he would trust the Lord when the time came.

The young boy was nearly out of breath when he ran onto the porch of the small city hall. Solomón Garcia, mayor of *Pozo Negro*, sat leaning back against the outer wall balanced precariously on two legs of his chair. Two other men rested with him on the wooden porch.

"*Alcalde*," the young boy gasped, calling for the mayor.

Solomón jerked up in his chair and had to catch himself before the legs slid out from under him.

"What's the matter?" he managed to say while composing himself.

"Two men would like you to meet them at the river's edge," he panted.

"What two men?" the mayor questioned suspiciously.

"One gringo and someone traveling with him. They both speak Spanish."

"A gringo?" asked Solomón. "What does a gringo want with me? Why doesn't he come to where I am?"

"They are doing some measuring," the boy added. "They were talking about a bridge."

"A bridge?" replied one of the men sitting on the steps of the porch.

"They want to build a bridge?" asked the other seated next to him.

Suddenly, Solomón remembered his conversation with Don Tulio. He began to feel nervous.

"Come, let's go," cried one of the men as he jumped to his feet.

"Yes, let's go talk to the gringo," said the other joining him.

"Wait," ordered the mayor.

The two men stopped and turned to look at Solomón Garcia still standing next to his chair. The mayor was trying to decide how to tell the men that he couldn't talk to the gringo about his bridge. While he hunted for the words, Roberto Espinal stepped out of the mayor's office where he had been reading a week old newspaper.

"What is the matter, *Alcalde*?" Roberto asked.

"Some men want to talk to him about a bridge and he doesn't want to talk to them," one of the men replied before the mayor could speak.

"Why don't you want to talk to them about a bridge?" Roberto continued calmly addressing Solomón directly.

"It is not that I do not want to talk to them," mayor Garcia began nervously.

"Good, then we will go with you," Roberto quickly inserted. "We will support you as representatives of the village."

"But,..." Solomón tried to say something, but it wouldn't come.

"But, WHAT?" Roberto replied firmly, knowing what was producing the fear in the mayor's eyes.

"But, Don Tulio warned me about their coming," he said quickly. "He said they would bring trouble to our village."

"And where is Don Tulio?" Roberto asked, knowing that he was away and had been for the past two days. Roberto hated to see anyone fearful of Don Tulio, especially someone the village was supposed to look up to.

"He is not here," Solomón admitted. "But when he returns, he will not be pleased."

The other two men looked at each other, unsure that they really wanted to get involved in a matter with Don Tulio.

"And when did he talk to you about these men?" Roberto pushed.

"Last December."

"Then how do you know that these are even the men he was referring to?" Roberto asked.

"He said they would come offering to help us," Solomón replied trying to remember the conversation over three months before.

"Did he mention a bridge?" Roberto interrogated.

"I don't remember him mentioning a bridge," Solomón admitted.

"Then, as far as you know, the men that Don Tulio was referring to could come later, and in the meantime, we have lost our opportunity for a bridge. Do you want to take THAT chance?" Roberto was pushing his point.

The two men rallied with Roberto and began encouraging Solomón to at least go out and talk to the men. With a shrug, the mayor agreed, and together, the three of them followed the young boy back to the river's edge.

Allen and José were surveying the bank for the best place to dig a footing that would support the platform. Allen was not the mason that José was, but he was a fair builder. He knew they would have to dig at least four feet for the posts without hitting water so that the concrete could set. After about ten minutes, they both agreed on a spot. As they were discussing the logistics for bringing in the materials and who they could find to do the work, José noticed four silhouettes above them heading down the hill along the path. The young boy ran ahead of the men.

"Here they come," José commented. "I count four."

"Do you see Don Tulio?" Allen asked nervously.

"I can't tell, but I don't see one carrying a stick. Maybe that is a good sign."

Allen swallowed hard and stepped out onto the path to greet the delegation. As their faces came into view, the missionary sighed. Don Tulio was not among them.

"Thank you, Jesus," he whispered to himself, though he realized that the little man could just be following behind and hadn't reached the ridge.

Solomón stepped to the front of the group and extended his hand. Allen grasped it firmly and greeted the mayor followed by Roberto, who promptly identified himself. The other two men shook hands, but didn't speak.

"This young boy says that you wish to speak with me about a bridge," declared Solomón in his official voice.

"Yes sir," Allen replied humbly. "I must confess, I meant to come by much sooner than this, but I have been busy with other projects and responsibilities. I work with many churches in this area. May I present one of the pastors that I work with?"

Allen presented José to the group and spoke highly of his work in Monte Hermon, below near León. He explained about the small mission in Las Minas, and how they learned of *Pozo Negro* earlier last year as they were passing by. Allen spoke of the visit they had made to the village and the burden that Allen had to help the village with a bridge that would provide a safe passage for the people to reach the road. Allen was careful not to mention his encounter with Don Tulio. He would learn soon enough if he would have to coordinate through him or not.

Solomón listened intently. He also decided not to mention Don Tulio at this time. He wanted to hear for himself why these men may be dangerous. So far, they seemed like good men intent on helping. He decided to ask about the church.

"So you are a priest?" he asked.

"No sir," Allen responded without showing any negative reaction to the inference. He chose his words carefully.

"I am a teacher. I teach God's Word, the Bible. I help people to worship God and I help train their leaders in how to serve God's people, the church."

Allen was careful not to patronize the mayor by trying to explain too much. The culture of the land would have included an understanding of the Bible, whether there was a church in his village or not. He wanted to emphasize the servanthood of his own ministry more than his position as a missionary. This was not a place for authority issues. He was coming to the leader of the village for permission, not acceptance.

"But not the Catholic Church?" asked Solomón cautiously.

"No sir, the evangelical church," Allen replied honestly. "To be specific, the Baptist Church."

Solomón knew very little, if any, about the evangelical churches in his country, much less one called the Baptist Church. He refrained from asking what the differences were. He just knew that Don Tulio resisted all churches. He sighed. This was probably the men Don Tulio had referred to earlier.

"May I ask a question?" stated Roberto. "Why do you want to build this bridge?"

Allen looked at the young man who seemed intent on having some input in the conversation.

"I learned about your bridge on a day when you were having a funeral for one of your children. It broke my heart to see her little casket. It broke my heart to hear she was not the only one to have drowned trying to cross this river. It broke my heart to know that your village has received so little attention. I believe God put the desire in my heart to help you build a bridge. I believe God wants to help *Pozo Negro*."

The four men from the village looked at each other. Solomón was impressed by the sincerity he was hearing in this foreigner's voice. It was true that their village had been neglected by the government. He did not sense danger from this man. Perhaps Don Tulio was mistaken.

"What would this bridge cost *Pozo Negro*?" Solomón decided to ask.

"Absolutely nothing," Allen was quick to reply. "I have a team that is preparing now to come from the United States to build the bridge and they are prepared to buy all of the materials. I just need your permission for them to work."

Solomón tried not to show his surprise. He found it difficult to believe that a group would come from the United States to build them a bridge. Most of Nicaragua didn't even know they existed.

"But you wouldn't refuse help, would you?" Roberto asked filling in the silence.

"Of course not," Allen replied smiling. "José had planned to be our master builder, but I'm sure he could use all the help we could get."

"Certainly," José affirmed.

"I believe I could get about three others to help us," said Roberto.

"Does that mean we can begin?" Allen asked the mayor.

Solomón Garcia looked into the eyes of the missionary. He knew that Don Tulio would be upset with the decision. Maybe his trip would take extra time to complete and the work would be done before he returned. If the Americans came and left, then maybe he wouldn't be angry – especially if there was a bridge.

"When does the team arrive?" he asked.

"A week from this next Saturday, twelve days from now," Allen replied. "We would like to begin tomorrow building a platform on both banks to have ready for them when they arrive."

"I can help with that," Roberto offered.

"Good, we will need all the help we can get," said Allen. "Mayor, what do you say?"

Solomón glanced at the small delegation that had traveled with him from the village. The two quiet ones nodded slightly. Roberto was more enthusiastic. For him, it was more than a bridge. It was reclaiming a part of his life that was lost the night of that great storm. It was also defiance against a darkness he felt had held the village for too long. Roberto had an agenda of his own. For Solomón, the decision was harder. He knew the repercussions that lie ahead. But he, too, needed to see this bridge rebuilt. The risk had to be taken. His pain had to end.

Don Tulio was not known for his patience in the village, even less when he had to journey outside of it. He despised using buses to travel. He despised staying in *Posoltega*. Even more, he despised being near the capital while his countrymen prepared themselves for the weeklong vacation of drinking and carousing in the name of a religious holiday. It was the epitome of hypocrisy and idolatry to watch his nation revel in indulgence and then to confess it to the priest before heading back to work. If he wasn't needed to make the legal transactions, he wouldn't make the trip. The first three days would be spent making sure all of his cattle were gathered, separating those set aside for sale and those to be kept for breeding. He would stay with the caretakers of his *finca* and then travel with the cattle to the small processing plant outside of Managua. With any luck, he would be back in *Pozo Negro* before the first hangover.

"So he wasn't there, huh?" Becky asked with a slight tone of justification.

"Not for the meeting, anyway," Allen explained. "I got the impression though that the mayor was still concerned about what Don Tulio thinks. If it weren't for the young man with him, we may not have gotten the permission."

"Did you say he even offered to help with the construction?"

"Yes. I'm anxious to see if he is there in the morning when we arrive with the materials."

"Well, God answered our prayer about keeping the witch-doctor away, why not pray for a good team of workers for the platforms?"

"I'm with you, sweetheart," said Allen humbly. He had learned his lesson.

The Wests had learned an important lesson about prayer. It was not to be underestimated. But the battle was far from over and the need for more prayer was about to present itself.

Allen and José led a small band of workers from Monte Hermon through the mango groves towards the river's edge. Each was laden with bags of fast drying concrete and digging equipment. An older man led a horse he had ridden up the mountain from his home. The lumber that was brought up by Land Cruiser was then transferred to the horse. He would make as many trips between the road and the river as was needed to move the wooden posts that would be set in the concrete. The small team was met by four others as they reached the river. Roberto had recruited his uncle and two others from the village. As long as Don Tulio was unable to object, they were able to help.

"*Buenos dias!*" called José to Roberto as they approached.

"*Buenos dias!*" replied Roberto, smiling and promptly introducing his uncle and the others with him.

Greetings were formerly exchanged and appreciation for their assistance extended. The four from *Pozo Negro* quickly relieved the arriving team of their loads and began stacking the bags of concrete together. Allen arrived shortly with the old man and the horse.

"It looks like we have help," Allen commented, pleased at the sight of Roberto.

"We are only happy to be of service," replied Roberto smiling.

"This may allow us to divide into two groups and work on both sides of the river at the same time," observed José. "We will be able to do twice as much work."

"Then let's get started," stated Roberto enthusiastically.

"Before we start," said Allen seriously. "Could we have a word of prayer?"

Automatically, the men from *Monte Hermon* removed their caps and bowed their heads. The four from the village looked at each other and reluctantly imitated the action. As Allen began to pray, Roberto stared at the gringo.

"Heavenly Father, we thank you for the opportunity to come this day and work side by side with these men. We thank you for seeing their need and sending help from so many directions. We pray for safety today as we work. We pray for the team that will be coming soon to build this bridge. We pray that this bridge will provide the Way to You for *Pozo Negro*. In Your Holy Name we pray…Amen."

"Amen," repeated several standing in the group.

Beto suddenly appeared from behind the group.

"Beto!" exclaimed the missionary. "So good to see you. Is your canoe nearby?"

"Sí, Señor, I saw your truck arrive and went and put her in the water. She is just beyond that point there," he replied pointing up river.

"We are ready for you now, we have four good men who can work on the other side of the river. I will go with them while José works on this side with his men."

José nodded and began huddling with the men from Monte Hermon.

"We will need to carry some of this concrete and a few of the tools to the other side."

"We have brought tools also," interrupted Roberto. "We left some on the other side for that very reason."

"It looks like you have been thinking ahead," Allen remarked.

"Yes…I have," Roberto said softly to himself.

It took over an hour to get men, materials, and equipment across the river so that the two teams were ready to begin. Shovels were handed to the young and strong. Others used long steel poles with flattened ends to loosen ground and break up some of the bedrock on the bank. The digging would be the hardest part and it would take most of that first day to finish: four post holes on each side, four-foot deep and about a foot in diameter. Allen didn't have survey equipment for lining up the platforms. They would just try to eyeball it the best they could. The foundations had to be deep, because the posts would stand over ten feet in the air. José had located discarded telephone posts that had been cut into fifteen foot lengths and carried to the site. Floating two of them across the river had not been an easy feat, but Beto guided while others pulled them through the water with ropes.

The digging went steady through the morning hours. Allen worked with the men from *Pozo Negro*. Roberto was a hard worker. He and his uncle would exchange comments occasionally. But, for the most part, there was little talking on the village side of the river. As noon approached, Allen had Beto carry him across the river to retrieve some sandwiches and drinks. When Allen returned, the men were still hard at work.

"Time for lunch!" announced Allen.

Tools were dropped almost immediately. Roberto's uncle began for the path leading back to town. His two friends fell in behind him.

"Where are they going?" Allen asked.

"You said they could stop for lunch. They are going home to eat," Roberto replied.

"Tell them to come back, I have some lunch for them here," Allen offered.

"They know, but they wish to eat in their homes. They will be back in an hour," Roberto assured Allen.

"I'm not worried about them coming back. I'm grateful for you men coming to help. Whatever assistance we receive will be helpful. I just wanted them to know that they could eat with us."

"If you haven't already noticed, the people of *Pozo Negro* do not mingle much with outsiders," said Roberto. "They do not know you well enough."

"What about you?" Allen asked offering Roberto a sandwich.

"I'm not shy of strangers. I work down in León some of the time," remarked Roberto, taking the sandwich. "I'm also not afraid of Don Tulio, like the rest of the village."

Allen paused from unwrapping his own sandwich and looked up at Roberto. This was the first mentioning of the witch doctor, since their arrival the day before. Allen didn't want to appear too anxious, but he needed information.

"Is that the man with the stick that I met on my first trip to your village last year?" he asked casually.

"I would think so – he is a small man in stature, but a big man in influence in *Pozo Negro*."

"Why is that?" Allen fished.

"Because the people believe he has great power."

"And you don't?"

"I believe he has power. I just don't believe it is as great as the people believe."

"Why is that?" Allen probed.

"Because he does not care for the people. He helps them only when it helps him and he threatens to hurt them if they oppose him."

"Hurt them how?"

Roberto paused taking a bite of his sandwich. He wanted to choose his words carefully.

"Do you believe in curses?" he finally asked the gringo.

"What kind of curses?" Allen responded, evading the answer.

"Crop failure, sickness…even death," Roberto stated matter-of-factly.

"I have to admit, I have not had much contact with curses where I come from," said Allen honestly.

"Where I come from, they are real. Don Tulio is an *hechicero*, a…*brujo*," said Roberto. Both terms referred to the names used for a witch-doctor. His tone was blunt with the North American. Allen wasn't sure why he was volunteering so much information. Allen took the opportunity to ask the question of Don Tulio's whereabouts.

"Where is Don Tulio now?"

"He is away from the village. He leaves each year about this time for a couple of weeks. Some believe he is visiting Nando, the chief *hechicero* of Nicaragua. Some think he is gathering the herbs and other ingredients he needs for his cures and spells. I really don't know, but if he was here, he would oppose what we are doing."

"Why is that?" Allen was hoping for insight from Roberto.

"Without the bridge, the village is in greater need of Don Tulio. I believe that is what he wants."

"So why do you want to see the bridge built? Aren't you afraid Don Tulio may bring a 'curse' upon you?"

"I told you, I am not afraid of Don Tulio," Roberto remarked firmly. He acted as though he wanted to say more, but contained himself. He chose rather to turn the questions back on Allen.

"When you prayed this morning, you said something about this bridge providing a way to God. What did you mean?"

Allen took a breath and lifted a silent prayer for wisdom. He wasn't sure if Roberto would be sympathetic to the mission behind the project or not. Till now he had not shared his work as a missionary with any from the village, though he felt confident that Don Tulio knew exactly why they were there. He decided to trust God with his honesty.

"Actually what I said was, that the bridge 'will provide THE Way to God for *Pozo Negro*'."

"I don't understand," said Roberto. "Any bridge built here will simply make it possible for people to get to the other side of the river without swimming or taking a canoe. How can a bridge possible reach God?"

"Again, I didn't say that the bridge would 'reach God', but that it would provide 'THE Way to God'. There is a difference."

"I still don't understand," said Roberto, squinting his eyes in confusion.

"THE Way to God is through His Son, Jesus Christ," Allen said plainly. "The reason *Pozo Negro* does not know Jesus Christ is because of what we have been talking about. Don Tulio does not want the people to know Jesus Christ, because that would free them from his power."

"What do you mean, 'free them'?" Roberto asked sincerely.

"The power that Don Tulio possesses over the people of *Pozo Negro* is a power of darkness. Jesus came to expose and overcome the darkness by being the Light. The Bible says, 'In Him, (speaking of Jesus) was Life and that Life is the Light of men. The Light shines in the darkness and the darkness is unable to overcome it'. Throughout his life, Jesus demonstrated power over demons, sickness, curses, and even death. Have you ever read the Gospel of Mark in the Bible?"

Roberto shook his head no.

"My grandmother has a Bible. I have seen it, but I have never bothered to read it."

"In the second half of the Bible, you will find four different sections that begin with the words, 'the gospel of...' There is one from Matthew, Mark, Luke and John. Matthew and John were actually men who walked with Jesus and saw the things that he did while on earth. Mark and Luke are men who heard the stories from others who walked with him. Each of these 'gospels' present the story of Jesus Christ – his life, his ministry, his teachings, and his final days. Mark tells about all of the miracles and healings that Jesus performed while on earth. You will also read about him overcoming demons. I suspect that much of what Don Tulio is able to do to frighten people, he does with the help of demons, but Jesus is stronger than even the strongest of demons. In fact, in one story he commands a thousand demons to leave one man."

"A thousand demons?" Roberto replied, his eyes growing large.

"Yes. But that is just part of the story. You will want to read about how Jesus was treated and why. May I suggest you read the gospel of Mark tonight, and we can talk more about it tomorrow?"

Allen stopped and watched Roberto's eyes. The young man was obviously hearing some things for the very first time, but he didn't want to overwhelm him. Allen decided to pull back and let the Word of God till the ground overnight. If Roberto had an ulterior reason for helping his men lay the foundation for the bridge, he would certainly return the next day. In the meantime, God was laying a foundation of His own.

"I will do just that," Roberto finally responded. "And I will talk with you more about this tomorrow."

Allen smiled. The two men finished their lunches and took a few minutes to lay back and rest. There would be plenty of work for the next two days.

"Dianne!" Rusty called from behind his desk. After a moment, she appeared in the doorway.

"You call?" she replied sweetly.

"I'm sorry," he said looking up from his Bible and notes spread out before him. "I didn't mean to yell. I need to know if you have already done the bulletin for Sunday."

"I have the layout, but I haven't run them off yet. Do you need to change something?"

"Yes, I need you to put a different title in for the message. I had planned on preaching about the Passover as we observe the Lord's Supper this Sunday. I knew we would be gone on the 9th, and the next Sunday that I am back in the pulpit is Palm Sunday."

"So what do you want to amend?" Dianne asked, trying to keep up with his reasoning for a change.

"I want to focus on prayer this Sunday. It will be the last time I address the Sunday morning crowd before the trip and I want to appeal to the church to pray for the team while we are away."

"That's a wonderful idea," Dianne agreed. "Do you have a new title?"

"Yes…just put, 'In the Garden'. I'll mention the change to Steve and maybe he can include the hymn in the opening part of the worship."

"I'll need that change as well," Dianne said, making a note on her pad.

As she pivoted to return to her desk, Rusty called again, a bit softer.

"Dianne," he said, almost swallowing her name.

She quickly turned back.

Rusty struggled over his words. "I just wanted to say, I enjoyed lunch the other day, and...well, if you don't have plans for lunch today, maybe we can get something together again."

"Without Steve?" she asked, her tone more serious than Rusty expected.

"I think he is making hospital calls today. He wouldn't be able to join us, I'm afraid."

"Oh, that's too bad," she said playfully. "I better get those changes from him before he leaves then. See you at lunch."

She quickly turned back toward her office so Rusty wouldn't see her smile. She left the doorway too soon to see his.

Allen was glad to see the four from *Pozo Negro* waiting on their side of the river again the next day. They obviously felt it would be needless to cross if they were to work on the *Pozo Negro* side. Allen was anxious to talk to Roberto and to discover if he had actually read any of the Gospel of Mark the night before. He shared with Becky about their conversation and they both agreed that Roberto had the potential of becoming a key person in reaching the village.

The team divided the materials and began transporting them across the river. Beto had learned that the missionary was generous in his hiring practice. He made a point of being ready and waiting when the group arrived. Allen was glad to see that Don Tulio still had not returned from his trip. Roberto greeted the missionary as they reached the opposite side. His uncle and the other two men didn't speak, but did extend their hands in greeting.

"Rest well?" Allen asked.

"Yes and no," Roberto replied. "I was up late reading."

Allen smiled at Roberto, who refrained from saying any more. It would be best to talk at lunch, he thought.

"But you're ready to go to work?" Allen said, averting the subject.

"Of course," Roberto acknowledged. "That's why we are here...*a su orden.*"

"We're in this together," Allen replied, picking up a shovel.

The task for the day was to mix concrete using the bags, sand that had been sifted the day before, lime and some gravel that they carried in with them that morning. Roberto's uncle cleared a place on the ground and began building a small volcano of mixture. Buckets of water were carried from the river and poured slowly into the center of the volcano. With their shovels, the three men began turning the sand, lime and concrete on top of itself, letting the water work into the mix while maintaining a wall that held the rest of the water in. As the mixture moistened, more water was added and the shovels began working the outer layers inward. With one man adding water and three men turning shovels in the pile, Allen began to add in the gravel till the mix was just right. Each man then took a shovel full and poured it into the hole. Roberto, who had been adding the water, now began using a steel pole to pack the mix into the hole. Once a layer covered the bottom, Allen and Roberto took one of the six foot posts and positioned it so that it was buried about four feet into the ground. Allen used his level to straighten the post and Roberto helped hold it in place while the other three men began pouring shovels full of concrete into the hole. Occasionally, a large rock was thrown in to brace a side and the concrete was packed around it. Using rocks also lessened the amount of concrete needed.

Making concrete on the ground always fascinated Allen. He had worked the shovel before, but could never do it as fast as the nationals. He knew when it was time to step out of the way. Allen held great respect for the simple techniques of the people that he served among. He never tried to introduce a "better way" when theirs was more than sufficient for the task. Being a "learner" meant a great deal to Allen and those who worked with him soon recognized his sincerity and accepted him in their midst. That was the mark of a good missionary – to incarnate the message of Christ within the culture of the people he was sent to reach with the Gospel.

Lunch seemed to come quickly. Roberto's uncle and friends quietly made their way to the village leaving Allen and Roberto alone to eat from the bag of sandwiches again. Becky had prepared enough for them all, just in case they changed their mind and stayed. That just meant extra sandwiches for Roberto and her husband – again.

"What is this?" Roberto asked, opening the slices of bread.

"It is called tuna-fish. Not everyone likes it. There is a ham sandwich in here if you prefer."

"No, I will eat the fish," Roberto replied.

"Tuna-fish," Allen corrected. "I wouldn't really call it fish."

"Neither would I," Roberto joked. "I have never caught a fish with pickles in its belly."

Allen laughed and together they began their sandwiches. After a few bites, Allen had to ask.

"What did you stay up last night reading?" he asked innocently.

"I found the area of the Bible called 'The Gospel of Mark' and I read the entire section. All sixteen chapters."

"That's great," Allen congratulated him. "What did you think?"

"I found it very interesting. I have known about the person of Jesus Christ all of my life. But I have to admit, I knew only small stories about his birth and death. I knew He died on a cross and that he supposedly rose from the dead."

"Supposedly?"

"No offense. I just have trouble believing that someone can rise from the grave like that."

"You're right – it is troubling to believe that someone could rise from the grave."

"What do you mean?" Roberto asked confused.

"I mean, the biggest issue that Christianity has ever had to face is the fact that the world finds it hard to believe that God raised His Son from the dead. But if you can accept that Jesus was God's Son, then it shouldn't be hard to accept that God would not leave His own beloved son in the grave after dying for the sins of the world, especially since it was God who sent His Son to die in the first place."

"What are you saying, 'God wanted Jesus to die'?"

"God wanted man to know Him. Man wanted to live his life without God. Man chose life without God and as a result, sin entered the world and changed the way man thought and acted. You have seen the result. Lying, stealing, murder, sexual sin, addictions, abuse, you name it – man does it. That's not the way God made man to think or act. So Jesus came. He came to both show the way man should think and act and to BE the way for man to be changed."

"What do you mean, 'BE the way'?" Roberto asked.

"Jesus said, 'I am the Way, the Truth, and the Life. No man comes to the Father except through Me.' We can only know God the Father through His Son, Jesus Christ."

Allen paused for a moment and looked across the river. José and his men were seated on the ground eating unaware of the discussion between he and Roberto.

"Do you see José over there?" Allen asked.

"Yes, I think he is eating one of your 'fish' and pickle sandwiches," Roberto joked.

"Can you get to him from here without getting wet and without using a boat or canoe?"

Roberto thought for a moment.

"Not easily. I would have to go either up the mountain or down to the sea to find a place to cross."

"Let's say the river is sin and that you are not allowed in José's presence with ANY of the river on you. Can you get to him?"

"No, I can't."

"Sin separates us from God in the same way. We cannot come into God's presence with any sin on us."

"But the world is full of sin," Roberto protested. "There is no one who can say that they have not been touched by sin."

"You are right," Allen agreed. "In fact, the Bible says, 'for all have sinned and fall short of reaching God's glory'. There is a great gap between us. But the Bible calls Jesus the Way. He is the Way that bridges the gap between God and man. Peter, one of Jesus's disciples, said, 'there is one mediator (or bridge), between God and man – the God/man Jesus Christ'."

"Jesus had to die to make the bridge across sin. He had to rise from the grave to give to man the Life that will change the way he thinks and acts. The proof of a Christian is a changed life."

Roberto listened intently. He still had questions, but he was beginning to understand more about the meaning of the death and resurrection of this man Jesus.

"So God wanted Jesus to die, because He knew it would build a bridge between Him and man?" Roberto asked.

"Just as God wanted Jesus to rise from the grave. You don't have one without the other."

"What about all of those stories of Jesus performing miracles, healing the sick and casting out devils?" asked Roberto, shifting to the other part of his reading.

"Those stories help us to know that the death and resurrection are real. If Jesus had power over sickness, the world and the demons while he was living, how much easier it is to believe he had power over sin and death," Allen explained.

"It sounds complicated," Roberto sighed.

"The Devil would want you to think so. He will do anything – even display power, to confuse someone about the death and resurrection of Jesus. Believe me. It is not that complicated."

"I will think about this some more," Roberto conceded. "And I will read more."

"I hope you will," said Allen. "And if you don't mind, I am going to pray for you and your family."

Roberto nodded, but said nothing more. This was not part of his plan in helping the gringo with the bridge. He now had much to think about.

The work resumed following lunch and a brief siesta. The posts were completed and the frame for the platform was constructed. The remaining work would only take a half of a day. Allen wasn't sure if he and Roberto would have another lunch hour to discuss things before the team arrived. He could only pray that a foundation for faith had been laid in the heart of one seeking truth…only time would tell.

Chapter Fourteen

"The Prayer Chain"

Bro. RUSTY nodded to Steve, who in turn motioned to both the pianist and organist that they could continue the hymn softly, but that the choir and congregation were to refrain from singing. The morning message had been directed toward the believers of the congregation with an emphasis on prayer. As the musicians played quietly, Rusty tapped his lapel mike gently to make sure he had not been muted by the soundman.

"Before the Deacons come to assist me with the Lord's Supper, may I take just one more moment to extend a special invitation for prayer," the pastor began. "As you know, a team from this church will be leaving in less than a week for Nicaragua. Many of you have been very helpful in providing scholarships for the team members, and for donating supplies and tools for the trip. I have to admit that there is not a material need that the group lacks. We are ready. But we have one more important request. We need a chain of prayer warriors that can lift the team before the throne of God during the time we are there. We have been preparing ourselves spiritually for this trip with Bible study and prayer. Three weeks ago, the team shared a day of fasting and prayer marking one month from the travel date. We are taking this trip seriously because of the news that we received about a witch doctor who is opposing the team's efforts. We would like to enlist as many as are willing to commit to an hour a day in prayer for the team and the project."

"I'm going to ask the team members present here today to come forward and kneel beside me here at the altar. If you are willing to come and stand around us here and to say 'I will pray for you and the team', then I invite you to come as the instruments play."

Rusty turned and kneeled before the Lord's Supper Table as Arnie and Alex made their way out of the choir to join him at the front. The Beaman's stepped out from their pew and walked forward. Stan and Ty joined them at the front from opposite sides and took their place kneeling next to Rhonda and Willis. Peter made his way from the balcony leaving his wife Angelina with their children. He no sooner stepped towards the stairway leading to the lower level, when Angelina took the hands of their children and followed him down. By the time he reached the lower section, they were right behind him. Betty Johnson saw Angelina following her husband and rose from her seat to join them as they reached the main aisle. Others began to rise from

174

their seats. Robert Winston had to make his way from the very back of the church where he was positioned after taking up the offering. As he walked down the center aisle, more stepped out before and behind him.

Bro. Rusty could feel a hand on the back of his shoulder and was relieved to know that at least one person had come forward in response to the need for prayer. Within a full measure of "*Wherever He Leads, I'll Go*", the nine team members from the Coronado Baptist Church were kneeling at the front with their heads lowered. Family members spaced themselves around them as choir members shed their robes to take a place in a line that was beginning to form on both sides of the team. The line continued to grow through the next stanza. Bro. Rusty began to think that Eric should bring the hymn to a close, but the music continued. The sound of footsteps began to surround them as they kneeled together. Finally, the music stopped and Steve's voice could be heard from the pulpit.

"Father, we praise You this morning as You have obviously been present in our midst. We praise You for calling us to prayer and for these who have responded to that call. We commit ourselves to lift up this team faithfully in the days to come and then during the time of their trip. May we not falter in our commitment that we are making before You this day. We pray that your light will shine in the darkness of *Pozo Negro* and that the darkness will not be able to put it out. We pray for safe travel for the team and protection from disease and injury. We pray for their boldness and the opportunity for them to share the love of Christ, dear Father, and we pray for souls to be saved."

"Amens" could be heard scattered about the sanctuary as well as from the team members huddled together at the front.

When Steve concluded his prayer, the pianist began to play "*To God be the Glory*" as an instrumental dismissal. The team members rose to hug their family members and to shake hands with those around them. Rusty was curious to see just how many came forward in a commitment of prayer. He opened his eyes and stood to two surprises. First of all, the pews were empty. Every person had found some place to stand near the front or encircling the walls, including the choir loft and pulpit area. The church as a whole had committed itself to praying for the team. His second surprise came when he turned around to find the hand on his shoulder belonging to Dianne.

"That is incredible," Billy Eldridge exclaimed. "The whole church?! That's tremendous."

Billy paused while Rusty continued on the other end of the phone line. Helen watched her husband's eyes glow as he talked to the pastor.

"No, I completely agree," Billy commented. "I can't think of any greater support that they could give."

He paused again while the excited young pastor talked on the other end.

"Yes, I think I know a few," Billy responded. "In fact, I know just the person, but I'll have to write her this week. The letter should reach her before the time we leave."

Pause.

"I don't think you know her, she lives on the east coast. I don't even know her personally apart from a couple of letters. You see, she prayed for my brother during the time of his accident. I wrote her after his death. I received a very nice letter in response. She told me about her prayer vigil for him for ten days. Her name is Gertie Baxter. From everything I can tell, she is a real prayer warrior."

Pause.

"Roger that. I'll make sure she has the name of every team member."

Pause.

"Sure, I can make a team meeting this afternoon," Billy glanced over to Helen to confirm his availability. She nodded. "Three o'clock will be fine. See you at the church."

Pause.

"Yes, I am excited. I can't help but think that God has some huge things in store for us. See you at three," Billy closed and hung up the phone.

"That sounded exciting," said Helen.

"Bro. Rusty invited the church to commit themselves to praying for the team leaving Saturday and the whole congregation responded!"

"That is exciting," Helen agreed. "So you're going to write Miss Gertie?"

"I think so. We are also going to meet this afternoon for one final orientation."

"Bro. Rusty has certainly been thorough on his preparation for this trip."

"He has," Billy confirmed. "This makes four team meetings now. We have met about logistics, planning, Bible study, packing and today he wants to give us some final instructions about culture. He's asked me to share some of my insights about visiting a third world country.... You know, the sites, the sounds, the smells, and the smiles."

"Like you're an expert!" she said sarcastically.

"They just want my impressions from my earlier trip. I think I have a few things I can offer."

"I'm sure you do," Helen said lovingly.

Billy looked down. His last trip to Central America was the last time he saw his brother Carey. He hadn't realized how much the memories would come when he started focusing on that trip. It would be bittersweet relating his experiences to the group.

The excitement was evident as the team members all arrived early for the meeting. The Beamans were met at the door by "little" Billy who was showing off his Spanish greetings. Alex and Matt made fun of him from their seats in the circle. They hadn't been practicing their phrases. Peter Moralis stepped over from the coffee maker and began rattling off several phrases to "little" Billy with perfect Spanish diction and quickly quieted the young man.

"What did you say?" Willis Beaman asked laughing.

"I just said, 'stop bothering these good people and take your seat so we can start this meeting'." Peter whispered back, trying not to embarrass "little" Billy any further.

"I heard that!" he called from his seat. "And I understood most of it," he lied unconvincingly.

The group laughed together.

Rusty took out his yellow pad and welcomed the group.

"Well, gang, just six more days! Are we all ready?"

Nods around the circle.

"I have asked Billy Eldridge to address us today about some culture elements that will be helpful to know. He is the only one in the group that has traveled in Central America on a mission trip before. I know it will not be easy for him to talk about his time with his brother, but he has agreed to share what he can. So without any further introduction; Billy...you have the floor."

Billy Eldrige stood slowly and took a deep breath.

"Let me say, first of all, that it is an honor for me to travel with you all. I wasn't sure I wanted to return to Central America after Carey's death, but God has been working in my life on many levels. I think this trip will help me bury any bitterness I may have harbored for losing Carey and will honor his memory at the same time. More importantly, it will involve me in the Great Commission as I believe God desires to involve all believers."

"Rusty has asked me to talk about some of the things we should expect to see, and how we should be prepared for responding to those things. I'm not sure I know where to begin."

Billy paused, looking at his feet.

177

"The first sight you will see getting off the plane will be the poverty. Beggars abound, many of them children. It's not easy walking past them. You will want to empty your pockets and give them everything you have. My brother had to explain to me how many are forced to beg for their parents and that the money is often used for drink or drugs. Some of the children themselves are inhalers, and will take your money and buy glue from nearby shoe repairmen. You HAVE to be discerning."

"The bottom line, is that giving without discernment simply perpetuates a lifestyle that you would rather deliver them from. Better to give food, than money whenever possible. This is especially true of children who stand at busy intersections asking for money from cars. Ask yourself if you would want your child to be darting between vehicles every day to find money. There are other ways and definitely other places."

Rhonda raised her hand.

"Are you saying that we should NOT give money to anyone while we are there?"

"No. I'm saying to be discerning. For example, if you must give, give to elderly women who have children with them – these are more likely widows on the street. The missionary can help us know about real needs. There will be opportunities for us to help while we are there, but it is best to do it at the end of the trip so that we can focus on the job."

"A second temptation you will face will be to patronize the people while you are there."

"Patronize?" Matt asked.

"Look down upon them because of the poverty, the illiteracy, their living conditions, and the seemingly lack of technology. If you are not careful, you will convey a sense of superiority. Remember, we can't even speak the language."

Billy glanced at Peter and corrected himself.

"Well, most of us can't. We will appear to be the ones who don't even know how much money to give a taxi driver, how to order a meal from a menu, or even to find the bathroom on our own. There will be things that they have done for generations that we do not understand, but that does not make them insignificant. Their culture is DIFFERENT, NOT INFERIOR to ours."

"And while I'm on it, let me share about the "Superman Syndrome".

"The 'Superman Syndrome'?" exclaimed Ty. "What is that?"

"The 'Superman Syndrome' is the thinking that I am invincible BECAUSE I am an American. I am above their laws and customs. My passport guarantees me respect and proper treatment. At the same time, I have come to make their 'planet' better – to enforce 'truth, justice, and most of all – THE AMERICAN WAY!'"

Peter laughed first. The others followed suit.

"Seriously, we need to see ourselves as strangers in a strange land. That's what the Bible says we are. We must be respectful and not critical of their customs especially in their presence. Just as Jesus humbled himself when He left His home to come to earth, we must walk humbly in Nicaragua."

"Amen," added Rusty.

"Moving in that direction, let me say that you will most likely face some vulnerability and modesty issues."

"Such as?" asked Arnie.

"You may remember Rusty and I mentioning about collecting the passports and airline tickets when we arrive. That is a real possibility. It should be the missionary's call. For some of you, that is going to leave you feeling a bit vulnerable."

Winston winced. He remembered the discussion and still wasn't comfortable with the idea.

"You will have little control during our stay about your lodging, transportation and menus. You will not be free to drink from any source you choose. We will have bottled water with us all the time. You will want to be careful, if we have showers, not to take any water in while you are showering."

"Did you say, 'IF' we have showers?" Rhonda interrupted. "I thought we were staying at a hotel in León."

"We are," Billy replied calmly. "Sometimes the hotel has water and sometimes it doesn't. Just be prepared."

"Flexible, right?" 'little' Billy chimed.

"Exactly," replied Billy. "Which brings me to modesty issues. Rhonda, with all due respect, this will affect you more than the rest of the group. At the worksite, there will not be a 'Porta-Johnny'. There are some homes near the river on the highway side, but we're not sure if they will be available to us. You men know how to take care of yourself in the woods, but we will need to make some kind of arrangement for Rhonda."

"Or I can try to wait till we are back at the hotel," she offered.

"We'll do what we can. But that's just one side of it. Be prepared to see others not being so discreet."

Billy turned his attention to the young men.

"We will be working at the river. I'm not sure what we will find, but I passed many rivers in Honduras traveling with my brother, where women would go to wash clothes and also bathe themselves while there. It is not uncommon. At the same time, it is important that we maintain the same level of moral propriety as we would in our own country. It may be natural for them, but it is not natural for you to stare – not here, not there. Plan now to avert your attention should the occasion arise. Don't give the Tempter the opportunity to undermine your witness and your character."

The young men looked Billy in the eyes and acknowledged his instruction.

"While I'm at it, I guess I should mention one other 'syndrome' that Carey told me about. It is called the 'Brown Eyed Syndrome'. It refers to the dark brown eyes that will steal your heart. You have seen the pictures. From babies to 'babes', there is the danger of 'falling in love' with a particular person while on a mission trip. It could be an infant that needs a family…"

Billy glanced back at the Beamans.

"…a young child that needs help with their schooling, a sick child in need of a special operation, a young pastor who would like to come to America and prepare for the ministry, or even an attractive person who wants companionship and a relationship. It is easy to lose focus for a people group by focusing on a single person and becoming emotionally involved. This can lead to some real problems. Please watch yourself in this area. Do not make ANY promises without consulting the missionary. And even then, don't make a promise. It is always better to provide personal assistance through the missionary after you are gone without telling the person in advance, than it is to promise assistance and never follow through. The Wests will probably talk to us more about this when we arrive."

Billy Eldridge paused for the information to sink in. He looked around the group for questions. No one's hand was raised, so he changed the subject.

"Now let's talk a little about using a translator, or I should say, an interpreter."

"What's the difference?" Stan asked honestly. "Aren't they the same thing?"

"Yes and no," Billy replied. "Both have the responsibility of conveying your words into another language. A translator is used for written work and must be careful to reproduce the wording exactly. An interpreter will try to express your intended thoughts into the other language. When we use phrases like, 'I'm tickled pink to be here', there is no real translation that would make sense. So the interpreter might say, 'I am very glad to be here'. See the difference?"

Stan nodded.

"As best as I can tell, the missionary will be our primary interpreter," Billy continued. "He will help us. There are some simple rules to remember. First of all, leave your jokes and most of your illustrations in your suitcase – they don't translate well. Second, try to speak in short complete sentences. An interpreter can't remember a paragraph. After a few times, you'll begin to feel a natural rhythm for pausing and your thoughts will flow. My brother and I got into a groove together and it seemed so natural. Most of all, don't plan to 'wing it'. Have something definite in mind before you begin. Interpreted rambling is really hard to follow."

"I'll be able to help as well," Peter offered.

"That will be helpful," Arnie added.

Billy directed his next comments to Rusty.

"Whenever possible, try to give the missionary an outline of what you plan to speak about, including the scripture passages. That allows him to use the Bible with the people."

"One last thing. Some gestures don't mean the same in other cultures so be careful of using ANY gestures while speaking. In Honduras, you point with your lips. Try doing that in this country and you might get slapped."

The group laughed.

"Bro. Rusty, that's all I have for the group, so let me turn it back over to you," said Billy respectfully and returned to his seat.

Rusty looked down at his legal pad and sighed.

"I don't know about you guys, but I'm excited about what is going to happen. Thank you Billy for sharing your insights. I took some notes and I'm sure I'm going to have to refresh myself about some of those things when we get there."

He turned his attention to the rest of the group.

"I have just a little more to add – on a spiritual note," he began. Rusty glanced back at his pad and began.

"We are going to Nicaragua to build a bridge in more ways than one. We are going to construct something that will help the people of *Pozo Negro* cross a river, but we are also going to build a bridge for the Gospel to reach *Pozo Negro*. This means we need to stay focused on two levels. We need to balance our productivity with our relationships. We need to work hard each day, but we need to take the time to get to know the people we are there to help. We will ask Bro. Allen to help us 'talk' with those we come in contact with. That is why you received instructions about interpreting, even though you may not have occasion to speak before a large group. We may all have the opportunity to share a word of testimony, either in a service or even at the work site. Let's be ready."

"We also need to balance our expectations between the experience of going and the task we are there to perform. This trip is not a vacation. I want you to experience the land, the people, the culture, but I also need you to be ready to work. There will be time for us to do some shopping, but that is not our purpose in going. On the other hand, I don't want you to just 'show up for work' and not see the richness of a different land. Balance your experience with the task. I honestly believe we will not come back to San Diego the same people we are today."

"Now let me talk a little about prayer," Rusty said seriously. "You heard me this morning ask the church to commit to praying for the team. Let me direct that to us now as emphatically as I can. You need to be praying every day between now and the time we leave for this trip. If you are comfortable with the idea, you may want to even observe a fast between now and then. We are going into an area of strong spiritual warfare. We have heard about the witch-doctor and the cloud he seems to hold over the village. I don't know if we will come into direct contact with him or not, but I do know that we need to be ready. If you have someone special you can contact to be a prayer partner while you are gone, I would encourage you to do that."

"My Sunday School class is going to be praying for us," Arnie commented.

"We have a Bible Study group on campus that said they would take turns each day praying," Matt Preston added. "And there are some believers on the football team that I have asked to pray for me while we're over there."

"Good," Rusty affirmed.

"Our parents have promised to pray for us while we're gone," Willis Beaman shared taking Rhonda's hand in his.

"There's a little-ole-lady in Virginia that I plan to write this afternoon about the trip," stated Billy.

"Can't find someone closer?" Peter Moralis joked.

"Not any closer to God," Billy quickly responded. "It's a long story – but a good one."

"That's great, gang," Rusty inserted. "Why don't we close with a special time of prayer together this afternoon. When we're finished, I have some forms for you all to sign about the insurance for the trip and I have your tickets to hand out. You all are clear on the luggage restrictions. We will meet here at the church Saturday morning by 5:30am and Steve, our Worship Director, will carry us to the airport in the church van. Are there any questions?"

The group looked around the circle and each one seemed at peace. A special bond was taking place and they each recognized it. The team had come together well. They felt prepared. The excitement of the trip was beginning to settle in. It would be an anxious week for most. They had no idea how important each one's role would play in the week to come. They had no idea the force of darkness they would be facing. They had no idea that one of them may not return. But they had prayer.

Rusty instructed the group to join hands and then asked who would care to lead out.

"I will," Ty said softly. As they bowed their heads, Ty talked to God. "Father, thank you for including me…"

––––––––––––––––––

"What are you looking for?" Helen Eldridge asked her husband as he emptied the middle drawer of the living room desk of its contents onto the desktop.

"I'm looking for your stationary," Billy replied in frustration.

"Bottom drawer," she said calmly. "There's at least three different boxes. What are you planning to do?"

"I'm planning to write a letter." He tried not to sound sarcastic.

"Why don't you use the computer? I can't remember the last time I saw you handwrite a letter."

"I know," he smiled finding a box of beige stationary. "But I'm writing Miss Gertie and I want it to be personal. I just hope I remember my cursive."

"Just print," she suggested. "Your cursive was never very legible."

"You're right…I'll print."

Billy chose a good black pen, replaced the pencils, paper clips and envelops back in the middle drawer, and got comfortable.

"Be sure to tell her that Karen is doing well in college," Helen commented before heading to the bedroom.

"I will. This shouldn't take long - wait up for me?" Billy asked.

"Don't take long," Helen teased.

Billy automatically wrote in the date at the top right corner and paused. He remembered the letter Gertie had written to his brother the week before the accident that took his life and how much that letter had meant to Carey. He glanced at his watch and carefully printed the time under the date. She would appreciate the gesture.

"Dear Miss Gertie," he began. "I'm sure you remember me. My name is Billy Eldridge - I am Carey Eldridge's brother. I wrote you shortly after Carey's death in the fall of 1998. I am sorry for not writing more often. I trust this letter finds you both doing well."

"The purpose for this letter…" Billy stopped writing.

"That sounds too formal," he said to himself. He looked at the ink on paper and remembered why he didn't handwrite very many letters. Taking another sheet of stationary, he quickly reproduced his date, time and greeting.

"I wanted to write and ask you to pray for me and several others from the Coronado Baptist Church. This is the church where Dr. Howard Pennington was pastor. I believe you prayed for him and his family. By the way, his daughter Karen is attending college with our niece, Anna (Carey's daughter). Both girls are doing especially well."

"Anyway, I am part of a mission team from the Coronado Baptist Church that is going to Nicaragua this Saturday. We will be building a bridge for a community that lives across a small river from the rest of civilization. We have learned that a witch-doctor may be present and is opposing the group's coming. We will be working with a missionary named Allen West. Would you please pray for our team while we are there? I believe you have a genuine call to intercession and I would covet your prayers on our behalf. I believe God has some tremendous work awaiting us."

"Thank you for all you have done for missionaries around the world. I hope to someday meet you in person."

Billy closed his letter and carefully folded it to fit in the special envelop that matched the stationary. He addressed it to her home in Carrolton, Virginia and affixed the stamp. Before placing it with his day planner to be mailed the next day, he bowed his head.

"Lord, thank you for Miss Gertie. May she receive this before we leave. Please give her the strength and wisdom to pray for us as we go to Nicaragua. Thank you for women like her. Amen."

Billy glanced down the hallway and could see a faint glow from under their bedroom door. He was glad it didn't take long.

"What'cha doin', Karen?" Anna Eldridge called to her roommate, who was bent over her desk in serious contemplation.

"I'm writing my little brother a letter," Karen replied proudly without looking up. "He's been on my mind a lot since the beginning of the year. I just feel he could use some encouragement."

"I bet you're right," Anna agreed. "I remember being in Costa Rica with my parents. It was not an easy time. Everything was strange. Grownups seem to deal with it better, because they feel it is part of their job to learn the new culture. An MK doesn't always see it that way. They will either adjust or not. When they don't, it's hard making them feel good about anything. They feel trapped in a world they didn't choose. It's one thing if it's the only world they have known, but it's altogether different when their world gets changed on them. My brothers came along after we were on the field, and for them, it was all they knew. I, on the other hand, had been around American stores and fast food and those things aren't easy for a kid to give up."

"You sound pretty wise on this stuff," Karen stated, looking up. "Would you mind adding a line or two to my letter?"

"I would be happy to, if you think it will help."

"I just feel like Terry needs some real encouragement right now," Karen said thoughtfully and turned back to her stationary.

"Sounds like God is trying to tell you something," Anna offered.

"I'm wondering if God is trying to tell Terry something."

CHAPTER FIFTEEN

"IN COUNTRY"

PREPARATIONS FOR Semana Santa start early for many in Costa Rica. The schools become preoccupied with practice for their participation in the pagents and parades that would adorn the celebration. Many businesses shut down for the entire work week – especially government offices. As the time draws close, those with any vacation time or senority duck out early. The beaches of Manuel Antonio, Puntarenas, and over a dozen more scenic spots on both coasts overflow with bathers and drunkards alike. Aside from the religious parades and reenactments of the Passion of Christ on Good Friday, it would be difficult to tell that Semana Santa was a religious holiday.

In contrast, the Language Institute of San José seemed to become more intense as the Holy Week of vacation approached. The school schedule called for the close of the January trimester near the end of April. Most years, it fell pretty close to Semana Santa. In the year 2000, the match was perfect. The week before Holy Week was the time of finals and ECO's that would determine the level of the student. For most language students, this was the most stressful time they spent "in country". The Penningtons were no exception.

Howard was enjoying his weekly visits to the University, but with finals approaching, his time was getting tight. Donna was experiencing a bit more stress. Her second trimester had been difficult with learning the subjunctive tense, her concerns for Terry and receiving the news of a death in the family. In some ways, Donna was envious of Howard's extra-curricular activities at the University. At least, he was able to get away from the small house, engage in ministry, and see results. She was beginning to feel her life consisted solely of walking to school, stretching her abilities to learn, walking home and doing homework. She was glad to have Juanita to take care of the arduous task of keeping the small house dust free and the clothes clean, but she wasn't enjoying herself. She couldn't remember the last time she enjoyed herself. The stress of the upcoming oral exams worried her the most. She was somewhat comfortable with the written assignments she was doing in grammar, but the ECO would be a timed and taped conversation between her and a professor where she would be expected to use as much vocabulary and tenses as she could remember. The professor would then replay the tape and listen for mistakes. Donna hated oral exams.

Terry had made friends with Eric, whose family was going to Venezuela, but that friendship would soon come to an end. Eric's family would be leaving at the end of this trimester. They had arrived in Costa Rica a trimester before the Penningtons. Terry didn't have any close friends to turn to when he felt bad, and so much of his frustrations were bottled up inside. Juanita watched Terry when he came home from school. She knew he was not happy. She knew Mrs. Pennington was not happy. She knew more than she was willing to talk about. She struggled with the thought of approaching Mr. Pennington, but she had to be careful. She had to find the right time.

Mateo walked Howard to the bus stop. The lines of young people had formed early that Tuesday as more students were making their preparations for Semana Santa. Buses, already full with shoppers two weeks before the big holiday, swung quickly into the lane and picked up only small numbers of riders before leaving again, bloated with passengers.

"I think I will take a taxi today," Howard thought aloud.

"I don't blame you," Mateo agreed. "It will take over an hour for you to get home at this rate."

"Now, don't forget, I won't be back for at least three weeks. We have exams next week, the University is closed the following week, and then I have orientation for the new trimester the next Tuesday. But don't worry, I will be back."

"I know you will, *hermano*," Mateo smiled. "And I will be here, too."

The two shook hands and Howard waved down a taxi. The ride home was much more enjoyable than the bus would have been. After giving his directions, he leaned back and closed his eyes. There would be no long walk from the top of the hill today. He would be delivered to his own front door.

Donna looked at the clock on the wall and sighed. Supper would be ready in less than ten minutes, and Howard was not home yet. She could imagine him standing shoulder to shoulder on some smelly bus trying to get back to the stop in front of the Language Institute and then have that fifteen minute walk home. He was always late on Tuesdays. It was getting easier for her to find something to complain about she thought. Terry had gotten home from school and went straight to his room and closed the door. Since he had lost the Game Boy, he would read, nap and wait for dinner to be called. She knew he was unhappy, but it's hard to throw out a life line when you are fighting the same waves.

She never heard the taxi drive up and if she had, she wouldn't have paid much attention to it. Howard was through the gate and opening the screen door before she realized he was home.

"Did I make it in time for a warm supper?" he called out pleasantly.

Donna looked out from the kitchen where she was straining off the spaghetti.

"Well, well," she replied surprised. "You're just in time, I was just about to put it on the table and wait."

"No waiting today," Howard continued in a good mood. "I decided to take a taxi – the campus was full of bus riders today. Anyway, I'm home in time for supper and I am glad."

Donna smiled. She was also.

Howard finished setting the table and knocked on Terry's door.

"Hey, bud – time for supper. Get washed up."

Terry was surprised to hear his father's voice. Like his mother, he had grown accustomed to eating without him on Tuesdays. He bounded through the door and hugged his father, then obediently followed through with a trip to the bathroom to wash his hands.

By the time they were both seated, Donna had placed the pot of sauce and bowl of noodles on the small table and was ready to serve. It was good to have the family together.

Howard gave thanks for the meal and began filling his plate with pasta.

"I told Mateo that I wouldn't be back to the campus for three weeks," he announced.

"Really?" Donna sounded surprised and a little relieved. "Why is that?"

"Exams are next week, followed by Semana Santa. Then we start the final trimester. I figure we will be too busy with the orientation week for me to fit in a trip to the University."

"You really enjoy your time there, don't you?" Donna asked.

"It has made this past trimester seem more productive. I feel like I am actually doing some ministry while learning the language," Howard responded proudly.

"I'm glad you have something meaningful to do," Donna replied half-heartedly.

Howard took the cue and changed the subject.

"Have you thought much about our time off after exams?" he posed.

"What do you mean?"

"I mean, maybe its time we thought about taking some time off for ourselves," Howard offered enthusiastically.

"And do what?" Terry suddenly entered the conversation.

"Yeah," Donna added. "What do you have in mind?"

"I don't know," Howard replied cryptically. "Maybe a trip to the beach?"

"The beach!" Terry exclaimed.

"What beach?" Donna asked, not believing they were even talking about a vacation.

"Oh, I don't know," taunted Howard. "There's Puntarenas, Guanacaste, maybe even Manuel Antonio!"

"Eric's Dad took them to Manuel Antonio," Terry quickly inserted. "He said it was beautiful and there are different beaches depending on how strong you like the waves."

"You know, I heard the same thing," Howard said smiling. He glanced up to see if Donna was smiling. Her lips were quivering.

"Could we really?" she asked.

Howard turned his full face toward her and gave her his strongest look of reassurance.

"We can, and we will – just as soon as we finish exams next week. We'll try to beat the crowd, stay a couple days and then head back before the Holy Week activities get rowdy. How does that sound?"

"Great!" yelled Terry.

"Me, too!" said Donna. "I could really use the time away from here. What will we do about the house?"

"We'll ask Juanita to watch the house over the weekend and try to get back on Monday as the holiday week gets started. We should be able to leave by Wednesday morning and get back on Saturday before the official vacation time for Juanita."

"How will we get there?" Terry asked, knowing they had no car of their own.

"We will take the bus – we'll see a lot of the countryside that way."

"How long will it take?" Donna asked.

"Who cares?" Howard said, dismissing the challenge. "Getting there will be part of the adventure. Who's in?"

"I am," Terry said firmly.

"I'm ready!" Donna added excited.

"Then it's settled," said Howard finalizing the proposal. "Now let's eat."

"Let's pray first," Terry remarked.

"You are so right," his father replied. "Terry, would you return thanks for this meal?"

"Yessir," said Terry bowing his head. The memorized prayer was still a step forward. Howard whispered his own expression of thanksgiving for the evening. He knew his family needed this time away. The Enemy had just lost a battle. The spirit of discouragement had just been driven from the table. But another host was soon to strike his blow.

———————————

Fridays were hectic on the campus of the language institute as students rushed to get home and start their weekends. Howard Pennington waited patiently for the language students to clear out of the president's outer office. It was common knowledge that Don Raul's secretary knew the best places to take the family on vacation. She could recommend beaches, white water rafting, tours of the volcanoes, or tourist shopping in Sarchí. She knew where the terminals were located for the direct buses that would make the trip in less time. For those who could afford the ticket, there was a small airfield that provided commuter planes that could make the three-hour bus trip in forty-five minutes.

Doña Marta acknowledged Howard's turn.

"Don Raul is out till about 3:00 this afternoon," she began automatically.

"Actually, I came to see you," said Howard pleasantly.

"Oh, really," Marta smiled back. "And how can I help you?"

"After exams next week, I want to take my family to a nice beach before the crowds start arriving for Semana Santa."

"Well, good luck," she started. "the beaches usually start filling up a week before Semana Santa, but I think we can find something that you can get to easily that won't be overwhelmed with people that early."

Marta pulled a folder from her bottom drawer and began leafing through the sheets and brochures. Howard watched her work the sheets with familiarity. She pulled two sheets and a couple brochures out and slid from behind her desk. She trotted to the copy machine and quickly ran off a B/W copy of the brochures and then made copies of the separate information sheets. Returning to her desk, she handed the sheets to Howard.

"There are five possibilities there, three of which are in the same area of Puntarenas. I have a brochure on Manuel Antonio with the bus information there and one other obscure place where tourists seldom go. It is not as built up and hotels may not be the best, but you can decide," she offered.

"This is great," Howard said, looking over the sheets. "We should be able to make a decision from this – thank you!"

"*A su orden!*" Doña Marta responded, indicating her willingness to serve.

Howard took the information and carefully folded the sheets to place into his backpack. He would show Donna and Terry the choices that evening.

It was gratifying to think that this vacation may be just the opportunity for Terry to enjoy himself in this country. Howard was well aware that his son was still struggling with the adjustment. Something had to happen if Terry was going to make the transition to living in a Latin world. Something was about to happen, but not what Howard was planning.

"Whoa! What was that?" Matt Preston cried out loud enough to be heard by passengers seated two rows in either direction.

"Chill, Matt," Little Billy said calmly seated beside him. "It's just turbulence. We had some coming out of Houston, man, remember?"

"I don't remember my CD player skipping from the bumps."

"Trust me, its normal."

The first-time flyers were all trying to mask their anxiety – except Matt. He questioned every procedure, every movement of the flaps, and almost every flight attendant as to whether there was anything to be worried about. He was finally given his own can of Coke and told not to worry by a six foot male flight attendant.

The flight from Houston was a little less than three hours, but seemed like an entire day for the team. The excitement of leaving the United States for the first time for most of them was an adventure to be savored. Keeping the group together in Houston had been a challenge for Rusty, but Stan and Arnie helped tow the line. Crossing the Gulf of Mexico was turbulent at times, but finally the pilot announced their final descent in approaching Managua, Nicaragua.

On the ground below, missionary Allen West and José Moralis stood in the small waiting room that allowed them to observe the arriving passengers. Separated by large panes of glass, they could only watch as they emerged from the winding corridor of immigration to their final point of customs, but could not assist them until they passed from customs to the outer sidewalk. At least the waiting room had air conditioning.

Spotting a team of twelve North Americans with bewildered looks on their faces was not difficult. Allen saw the red hair of Arnie Johnson followed by that of his son Alex and imagined that the rest of the group was not far behind. A young couple appeared and quickly took their place next to the father and son. As each one emerged from the corridor, they huddled close to the group. Finally, a young man with a look of confidence completed the group and began giving instructions. They each began to grab bags and plastic totes and move as one toward an awaiting customs agent.

Volunteer teams were no novelty to airport officials, especially since hurricane Mitch, though their numbers were beginning to wane. The customs agent looked hard at the group and tried to determine what kind of team this one was. He could give them a difficult time in hopes that they would offer something in their luggage to let them through. He could make them open every case and see if he could accuse them of something serious that would require a monetary fine. Or he could simply wave them through taking the chance that they were just another group of North American religious volunteers that had come to "help" his country. He glanced at his watch. He decided that it was too near lunch time to get into an involved confrontation. They looked harmless enough. He motioned to Rusty to carry his bags and lead the rest on to the front doors.

"He's not going to make them open their bags," Allen said quickly to José as they observed through the glass. "Come on. Let's go help them get their things."

Unsure of what was happening, Rusty looked back at the team and shrugged.

"I think he is motioning us to go on," Rusty said to the group.

"He is," Peter said quietly. "I heard him tell his partner it was too near lunch to bother."

Peter had decided not to use his Spanish in the airport for fear that it would complicate their entrance, but he did keep Rusty informed as to what was happening.

The group gathered their bags and began pushing the totes toward the door.

"Welcome to Nicaragua!" Allen called as Rusty stepped through the glass doors. José rushed forward to help carry bags. "Try to get all of your luggage to this spot," he said pointing to an open area near the curb. "José and I will bring the vehicles here and we will avoid using any of the baggage handlers. If they come by, just wave your finger and say, 'no'."

It all seemed so rushed, Rusty thought, but Allen was trying to stave off the inevitable flood of beggars, merchants and airport workers seeking tips. He knew it would become a circus in a very short time if the team did not move fast.

Rusty relayed the instructions and the young men began moving plastic totes and the heavier suitcases quickly to the spot. Arnie and Stan stood watch over the luggage while the others maneuvered their bags and carry-ons to the designated location. Once the bags were all gathered and accounted for, Allen and José went for their vehicles. Allen had his Land Cruiser emptied to handle most of the luggage and about four passengers. José brought a van his brother owned for the rest of the passengers and luggage that would not go inside the Land Cruiser. It took them less than five minutes to retrieve their vehicles.

Five minutes was long enough for Matt Preston to break off from the group to explore his new surroundings. He was fascinated with the sights and smells. No one noticed he was gone until the missionary had arrived and they needed the strong hands to start loading the luggage.

"Where's Matt?" Little Billy asked Alex.

"I don't know, maybe he's with Bro. Rusty getting the bags that are going in the Land Cruiser."

"There's Bro. Rusty talking to your Dad," Little Billy replied with concern. "He's not with either of them."

"He's got to be here somewhere – surely he didn't just wander off," said Alex, focusing on the bags he was carrying.

"Well, I don't see him near either vehicle," Little Billy stated.

The boys handed their bags to José, who was loading the smaller suitcases under the seats of his van. They looked around the stack of luggage, and then checked inside both vehicles.

"What's wrong?" Billy Eldridge asked, seeing the two young men looking around.

"We haven't seen Matt since we started loading luggage," said Alex.

"I saw him at the stack while we were bringing bags out," Billy remembered. "Did you check there?"

"We just came from there," replied Little Billy. "That's when I asked Alex where he was."

"And he's not in either vehicle?"

"No, sir," they said in unison.

"Let's go tell the missionary," Billy stated, leading the boys towards Allen.

Rusty and Allen were getting acquainted while Allen gave him a quick itinerary for the afternoon. As soon as they could load the vehicles they would start the journey out of Managua. Given the distance and time frame from León, they would need to stop and eat at a McDonalds on the way out of town. It would be faster and provide a small buffer between the change in cultures for the team. There would be plenty of time for them to taste typical Nicaraguan dining.

"We can't find Matt," Billy Eldridge reported.

"Since when?" exclaimed Rusty.

"Sometime between getting the bags together and the vehicles arriving," stated Little Billy.

"Don't worry," said Allen calmly. "He's probably checking out some of the vendors on the other side of the building. I'll send José to find him. Why don't you start assigning seating to the group."

Allen waved for José, who had just finished tying down the last of the plastic totes on the top of his van. The top carrier was fashioned for loads and provided a safe transport for the sturdy containers.

"One of the young men has wandered off. I suspect you will find him with the *vendedores*," Allen informed José as he came running.

José nodded, smiled and took off around the building.

"He'll find him," Allen said reassuringly. "Better for José to go than to send another one of your team – then we would have two wanderers."

Rusty accepted the news reluctantly. He was still concerned about a team member getting separated from the group. He could tell this was not going to be an easy week.

Rusty placed Stan and the Beamans in the Land Cruiser with him and instructed the others to load up in the remaining seats of the fifteen passenger van. Arnie decided to ride "shot-gun" in the van and took the front seat. As the rest took their seats, Arnie began counting heads.

"We should have eight – whose missing?" Arnie called out.

"Matt," replied Alex sheepishly. "José has gone to get him."

"Get him? Where is he?" Arnie replied, raising his voice.

"We're not sure – the missionary thinks he went around the building where some sellers hang out."

"That boy is going to have to stay with the group," Arnie nearly barked.

"Here they come now," Peter said, looking out the back van window.

The two jogged up to the side of the van and Matt slid into the seat beside Alex. Arnie held his tongue.

"You guys won't believe what I found," he said excitedly.

"Matt, we were worried about you," Alex interrupted. "You shouldn't take off like that. We could have left you."

"Yeah, right!" he replied sarcastically. "Like you could forget I was with you."

"Or think you were in the other vehicle," Little Billy added.

Matt stopped and thought that one over.

"Oh, yeah. Hey, sorry – but look! I made a great buy on some sunglasses!"

Matt passed his purchase over to Alex.

"They're Ray Ban, and I only paid fifteen dollars for them," Matt announced proudly. "He even took American money."

Alex admired the shades and handed them back to his buddy.

"Matt, they're imitation."

"How can you tell?"

"Because 'Ray' is not spelled – 'R...E...Y'!"

The van burst into laughter as José followed Allen out of the parking lot.

The terrain of northwest Nicaragua is relatively flat compared to the mountains that backbone the central region. The road to León seemed endless for the band of volunteers. They took in the scenery with wide-eyed wonder. In the van, Peter served as an interpreter for the many questions that the young men posed to José concerning everything from rainfall to roadside bandits. Robert Winston asked José about the Sandinistas and the revolution. José was a little guarded with responses, not wishing to engage in a political discussion. Much of his family had been involved with the Sandinista movement, though he had distanced himself from the ideology. José had found his Savior in the greatest revolutionary of all time – Jesus Christ.

In the Land Cruiser, Allen and Rusty talked about the progress that had been made on the platforms. Allen had hoped that Arnie could have been part of the discussion, but Arnie had insisted that Stan have the comfortable ride from Managua. Rusty was interested in hearing about the young man that Allen had had opportunity to witness to while they were building. The topic soon turned to the witch-doctor.

"To be honest, he hasn't been around since we began work on the platforms," Allen explained. "I'm not sure what to expect. The best information I have is that he disappears for a couple weeks each year about this time. The village isn't sure where he goes or why. They don't ask many questions, if you know what I mean."

Bro. Rusty nodded. Inwardly, he was a little relieved to think that they may not be meeting Don Tulio face to face.

"Do you expect any other opposition from the village people?" Rusty asked.

"It's hard to tell. Only a few came out to help us build the platforms. I suspect if Don Tulio had been around, that they may not have come. Even the mayor was hesitant at first. Don Tulio holds some real power over the people."

Rusty settled back in his seat and began taking in the scenery. In the distance he could see small mountains. He knew the village was in the mountains. They must be getting close.

In the van, the questions finally died down. The effects of the trip were settling in. The team was beginning to feel tired. They would arrive in León with just a short time to unpack, freshen up, and be carried to the missionary's home for dinner and orientation. It was to be a full day.

José took advantage of the lull in conversations to address the North American whose Spanish was so good.

"Where are you from?" José asked Peter directly.

Taken by surprise, Peter fumbled with his words.

"Uh, originally from Arizona, but my family moved to California when I was very young."

"You are from the United States?" José responded surprised. "But your Spanish is so natural."

"My grandparents are both from Mexico, but my parents were born in America. My grandmother never stopped speaking Spanish and wanted her grandchildren to know her language as well."

"That's good," José replied. "Family is important. What was your full name?"

"Pedro Alejandro Betancout Moralis," Peter announced proudly.

"You're kidding!" José exclaimed. "My name is also *Moralis.*"

"We could be cousins!" Peter joked.

"You never know," José laughed. "I'll just call you *Primo*, cousin."

"Ok, *Primo*. Sounds good to me," Peter returned.

The two continued talking in Spanish while the others napped.

El Pinolero was not the largest or most modern hotel in León, but it was clean. The rooms would accommodate two comfortably and each room had a shower with running water – most of the time. Its greatest advantage was its distance from the town square where weekend activities were loud and late. The price was also more reasonable than the larger hotel where most American tourists stayed. Allen's commitment to good stewardship compelled him to make arrangements that would leave more funds available for the work. Rusty agreed. The team had not come as tourists, and didn't need to be treated as such.

Check in was smooth. Each team member paired up. Alex decided to stay with his father and let his buddies room together. He hoped to get more sleep that way. The Beamans took their key and headed for their room. Stan paired up with Ty. Winston and Peter were already acquainted from their Sunday school class. Rusty shared his room with Billy Eldridge.

Allen and José paid for the rooms and informed the desk clerk that one of the team members could communicate in Spanish. Allen left his phone number in case of any problems with the front desk. He asked about the water situation and was assured they would have plenty for showers.

Rusty rejoined Allen in the front lobby after getting his bags to the room.

"Everything looks fine," he said with a smile. "I'm sure we will be alright. What are the plans for evening?"

"Becky has prepared a simple meal at our home," said Allen. "We will shuttle you over there around 6:30, eat, then have a time of orientation and prayer."

"Sounds good. I'll have everyone down here and together at that time."

"Even Matt?" Allen joked.

"Especially Matt!"

"We are glad you are here," Allen said seriously. "You are an answer to prayer. José and I have been praying for *Pozo Negro* these past eight months. I believe God has some tremendous plans for that village. I don't know what the next seven days will hold, but I know the One Who does and I trust Him."

"So do we," Rusty agreed. "We are here for Him and for you. Just tell us what we need to do."

"Again, thank you for coming."

Allen and José left Rusty in the lobby and headed for their vehicles. Rusty looked around. Check-in had been smooth, but hurried. While the others had scurried to their rooms, Rusty wanted to drink in the warmth, the smells, and the sounds. He stood in the doorway of the front office and looked out on the nearby streets of León. It was a definitely a different world, and he was glad he had come.

"Welcome to Nicaragua!" Becky greeted, as she opened her home to the line of volunteers filing out of the two vehicles.

"Thank you," responded Ty politely, as he stepped past her into the living room.

"Just find a chair. Allen is going to have a time of sharing with us before the meal."

The group streamed through the doorway filling rocking chairs, kitchen chairs, the couch as well as empty places along the wall. Rusty was the last of the group followed by Allen. Both wanted to make sure Matt Preston was inside before they closed the door.

"Before we sit down to some typical Nicaraguan food that Becky has prepared, I want to take a few minutes to share about our schedule for tomorrow. Being Sunday, we will be attending worship services in José's Church – Mount Hermon. Some of their men have been helping us with the preliminary work on the platforms. The church is just a few kilometers outside of León. We will eat together at the church and then make the trip up the mountain to the river where we will be working."

"Will we be going over to *Pozo Negro*?" Bro. Rusty asked.

"Not on Sunday," Allen was quick to reply. "We will prayer walk this side of the river and let our contractor look over the platforms. We don't want to overwhelm the village."

"Do you expect the witch-doctor to be around on Sunday?" Billy asked.

"That's an interesting question," said Allen. "When we went to build the platforms last week, Don Tulio was not in the village. We encountered no resistance at all in the building of the platforms. The locals said that he is usually away from the village this time of year for a couple of weeks. He's been gone for over two weeks. We're not sure if he will return this weekend or sometime next week, if at all, while you are here."

A quiet sigh circled around the group.

"Before we go much farther, let me share some 'in country' rules," Allen began changing the subject. "I'm sure Bro. Rusty has shared some items with you, but it doesn't hurt to reinforce them. Let me get you to do something with me. I think this will really help. I'm going to make a statement and you are going to respond with the following phrase – 'but we are not in America right now!' OK?"

The group sat up. Allen had peaked their interest.

"OK, here goes," Allen started smiling. "In America, you can drink water from a water fountain or any faucet without worry."

Allen paused as the group looked at him. He motioned for them to respond.

"But we are not in America right now," about half of the group responded. The others realized what was expected.

"Let me add," Allen inserted with emphasis. "Try not to take water in when you shower and use your bottled water to brush your teeth."

The missionary paused and then went to the next statement.

"In America, you can expect to find a public restroom in most areas you travel."

"But we are not in America right now!" the group responded in unison.

"We will be in an area where we may or may not have access to a restroom while we are working. I see we have at least one female among us. I trust you are aware of what this means?"

Rhonda nodded.

"In America, you can flush your toilet paper in the commode."

"But we are not in America right now!" the group chanted automatically.

"What?" Little Billy exclaimed.

"I thought someone would question that one," Allen laughed. "Even in homes where there is indoor plumbing, realize that the sewage system is not as developed as it may be in the states. For that reason, most bathrooms have a little trash can near the commode. Please place your paper there. You will be saving the owner of the house a great headache. Trust me."

The group nodded.

"In America, you can drive to wherever you want to go."

"But we are not in America right now!" the group replied.

"We will be carrying our materials, our tools and our supplies from where we will leave the vehicles about one quarter mile to the river's edge. Remember, we are building a bridge, but even after we are able to cross the river, we have to walk to the village of *Pozo Negro*. We will be the only ones driving to church tomorrow. Most people around us will walk, ride a bus or an animal."

"One more," Allen stated. "In America, you can easily be understood by the people you are around."

"That's debatable," Peter joked.

"BUT WE ARE NOT IN AMERICA RIGHT NOW!" the group stated in strength.

"These are just some of the issues that you may or may not have discussed before coming. There are more things that I will be sharing along the way, but water, bathrooms, transportation and language are the biggies. Does anyone have a question?"

Like most small groups, no one volunteered to ask a question. Allen took their silence as permission to move them toward the dining room where Becky was busy filling glasses with ice.

"Is the ice here safe?" Matt Preston asked sarcastically.

"Good question," Allen replied. "The answer is 'yes'. We make ice from pure water. We have a water filter that your Woman's Missionary Union made available for us several years ago. But keep up that attitude and you should make it through the week."

Becky had prepared two extra tables on the patio to handle the overflow from the dining room table. The outdoor air was pleasant. The young men quickly took seats on a patio table. They were joined by Peter. The Beamans invited Ty and Winston to sit with them at the other table. Bro. Rusty, Arnie, Billy and Stan took the chairs around the dining room table with the Wests.

This would give them a chance to talk more about the project during the meal.

Each table found a large bowl of black beans and rice, a stack of warm flour tortillas under a dish towel, a plate full of sticky fried bananas, and several pieces of fried chicken. The chicken was a concession for the team members. Becky wanted to blend something familiar with the typical dishes.

Conversations varied around each of the tables. One topic that wasn't discussed was that of Don Tulio. Concerns of water, communication, and bathrooms seemed to push out the trepidation of possibly meeting a witch doctor. The best orientation – on or off the field - could not have prepared the team for their encounter with Don Tulio. The last thing they needed was a sense of false security and in the back of his mind, Allen West knew better, but he knew the team needed to enjoy their first night in country.

Chapter Sixteen

"The Prayerwalk"

Sunday MORNING in León was anything but quiet. The morning market crowd was busy picking through the vegetables, fish, and cheeses. The smell of cooking beans, tortillas and platanos wafted through the narrow streets around the market. Heavy trucks rolled past the hotel long before dawn waking the older men first. Billy half expected the noise and was prepared for the early rise. The group was told to be ready to leave the hotel by eight o'clock. This would give them time to eat at a local *comedor* and make the Sunday school time at *Monte Hermon*. José was needed to drive his van and still make it to his church before the services began.

Surprisingly, the three college students were ready waiting when Stan made his way to the hotel lobby. Arnie was still in the room dressing having let Alex take the first shower. The Beamans followed Stan. Rhonda was not about to be the woman that held up the team. One by one, each set of roommates made their way to the lobby till all had assembled a good ten minutes before eight.

"Did everyone sleep OK?" Rusty asked.

"Pretty good," Stan replied first.

"I did fine till the roosters went at it about three-thirty or so," Ty said tired.

"Is that what those things were?" Little Billy asked. "They sounded like they were all over the place."

"It's called 'singing'," Peter Moralis commented. "A rooster calls out and other roosters call back. It can go on for over an hour sometimes."

"I don't call *that* singing," Little Billy complained.

"Just think, by the end of the week, you won't even notice it," said Peter trying to encourage the young man.

"We'll see," Little Billy muttered to himself.

The team huddled quietly near the door and waited. After fifteen minutes had passed, Robert Winston asked Rusty for the time.

"I have about five after six, but then I haven't set my watch back from Pacific time yet."

"No wonder I feel so tired," Matt Preston sighed. "I knew it couldn't be eight o'clock already."

"Don't worry," said Stan reassuringly. "You'll get your two hours back when we go home."

Somehow, the news couldn't hold back the yawns. This was definitely not going to be a vacation, the young men thought.

Allen and José pulled up to the curb and quickly herded the volunteers into the two vehicles for a quick breakfast at a local *comedor*. The menu was simple – rice and black beans, corn tortillas, eggs scrambled with tomatoes and strong black coffee. The young men ate heartily. The Beamans pulled out packaged breakfast bars from their backpacks and shared a bottle of water.

The meal was followed by a twenty minute drive to *Monte Hermon* where José pastored. As his van pulled up in the front yard of the small building, children suddenly appeared, running from all directions toward the van.

"Oh, look at the children!" Rhonda commented excitedly.

"Remember what Mr. Eldridge said," her husband cautioned. "You can't take any home with you. Beware of the 'brown eyed syndrome'."

She playfully hit him on the shoulder.

The team emptied from the van and the Land Cruiser and stood conspicuously together before the church entrance awaiting instructions. The children gathered around them like excited fans, some reaching out and taking the hands of the bewildered North Americans. It was a welcome that none fully expected and before they realized it, several eyes welled up with tears, not the least being Arnie Johnson.

"Please come on inside," Allen motioned from the doorway of the brick building.

The church had been constructed two years earlier by a volunteer team from North Carolina. The flooring was still dirt, but the space was adequate for the fifty to sixty members. Benches filled more than two thirds of the single large room leaving space for people to gather near the door. Wooden window shutters were opened from the inside to allow in the light and what breezes may be blowing. Ceiling fans circulated the air. Several fluorescent fixtures had been placed strategically in the exposed rafters, but they were not turned on in the daytime unless there was a need to shut the windows.

Sunday school classes were conducted in different locations around the main church building. Adults met in the sanctuary. Older Children were carried to a house of one of the members who lived next door to the church. The younger children were usually taught under the large tree just beyond the building. When it rained, they were brought in to sit on the floor at the back of the church near the front door, but had to study their lesson quietly so the adults could have their class in the same room.

"Folks are still arriving," Allen explained. "We had to get Pastor José here in time to begin Sunday school. You are welcome to divide up and sit in on different classes, though you will just have to watch. I won't be able to translate from all three locations. After Sunday school, we will all come back here for the worship service."

Turning to Rusty, Allen continued with his instructions.

"Bro. Rusty, you will be preaching this morning, and I will be your interpreter. Is there someone who would like to share their testimony in the service this morning?"

The team looked about the room at each other waiting for a gallant volunteer to step forward. After a moment, Alex raised his hand.

"I would like to share," Alex said humbly. His father smiled.

"That would be great!" the missionary affirmed. "I will call you when it is time. OK, feel free to explore. Classes will start in about fifteen minutes. Afterwards, just come back in here and we will sit together on the back benches."

"Like true Baptists!" Little Billy joked.

———

The Pennington family sat more relaxed than usual through the morning worship service of the Baptist Church of *Moravia*. Even Terry attempted to sing along with the praise choruses. His mind kept racing ahead three days when they would be taking their trip to the beach. It was hard to be excited and look bored at the same time. Howard half-listened to the pastor while often drifting into the conjugations that he would be tested over the next day. He was pleased that he was picking up more of each sermon as the weeks passed. Donna had successfully closed out her surroundings mentally and was day dreaming of anywhere away from the school, the house, and even the church.

After church services, they all agreed on pizza for lunch and made their way to the bus that would soon have them traveling into downtown San José. The familiar red roof of the Pizza chain was a welcome site, even though the ingredients were not the same. Terry had gotten used to the difference in taste and didn't complain about the pepperoni tasting funny anymore. The Pennington family was looking forward to their vacation and nothing was going to spoil it.

Just two days of intense exams, Howard thought, and then they could unwind as a family. This second trimester had been their greatest challenge so far, but it would soon be behind them. Donna didn't talk about her classes like she had the first trimester. Howard could only hope she was doing well in them. Without realizing it, they had slid into the most pivotal point of their own culture shock. If there wasn't a breakthrough soon that brought hope to their learning experience and bonding to their new relationships, the Penningtons would be in danger of failing more than a Spanish class. For Howard, he hoped that breakthrough would come in the form of some family recreational time together away from the classroom. He would never get to know.

Alex shifted nervously as he braced himself behind the small wooden pulpit. Allen gave a nod of encouragement and the young man swallowed nervously.

"My name is Alex Johnson," he began slowly looking to Allen for the translation.

"You can make your sentences longer," the missionary whispered.

"I am very glad to be with you all this morning," Alex continued, looking back at the congregation. "I want to tell you how Jesus has made a difference in my life."

He paused and Allen gave the interpretation.

"I became a Christian as a young boy, but I didn't always make Jesus first in my life."

Allen repeated each of his phrases in Spanish.

"I began resisting God's will for my life and inwardly I quit going to church. I still went with my parents to services, but not to worship God. After a while I even quit going to services. I know this hurt my parents. My father is here with me. That's him standing over there."

Alex pointed at the broad-chested man with the red hair leaning against the wall. Arnie smiled and waved.

"I guess I forgot how much my parents loved me and that made me forget how much God loved me. Anyway, I ended up with the wrong crowd..."

Allen held up his hand. Alex stopped mid-sentence. Allen struggled for a moment to find the right expression to describe the "wrong crowd". It took several words. He then motioned to Alex to continue.

"I knew I was doing wrong, but I couldn't help myself. I am glad that God doesn't give up on us when we get away from Him. I am also glad that my earthly father and mother didn't give up either."

"A little over a year ago, I was arrested for stealing a car with some guys I thought were my friends. It was in a jail cell that God showed me how much He really loved me. I found true forgiveness from both my heavenly Father and my earthly father. I wouldn't be here today, if it were not for both of them."

Arnie inconspicuously wiped a small tear from the corner of his eye. He was proud of his son. Alex finished sharing and sat down. Allen motioned for Rusty to step up on the platform. Rusty quickly joined the missionary. This was the moment he had been waiting for.

"Good morning. My name is Bro. Rusty Patterson. We are very glad to be with you this morning."

"Muy buenos dias. Mi nombre es Hermano Rusty Patterson," Allen began, repeating the phrases at the close of Rusty's final syllable. Allen had prompted Rusty on how to keep his sentences brief and concise, so that he could translate them smoothly. He finished the introduction and Rusty continued.

"We have come from California," Rusty blurted and then paused. Allen waited for more before interpreting.

"That sounds too corny," Rusty said aside to the missionary. "Let me start over."

Allen just nodded.

"Like you, we love the Lord Jesus Christ. We are here to worship with you and to learn how we can serve Him with you while we are here."

Allen smiled and then began speaking the young pastor's words into the ears of the Spanish congregation. Rusty's sincerity was inescapable in any language. The people waited for each phrase.

"This is the first time for most of us to travel away from our country. It has been exciting so far."

Allen translated.

"We have been told we have come to build a bridge. We have been told that there are those who may not want to see this done."

Translation.

"But we are trusting God's grace to do through us what is pleasing to Him. The Bible says in Philippians 2:13 – 'For it is God who works in you, both to will and to work of his good pleasure'."

Rusty waited on Allen to finish and then began sharing a story from the Gospel of Mark. He spaced his statements so that the missionary was able to develop a smooth rhythm between the two of them. The team listened in English and was as encouraged as the small Nicaraguan congregation.

Taking his Bible in hand, Rusty directed the congregation through Allen to join him in looking at a story that illustrated God's grace. It was the familiar story of the feeding of the five-thousand.

"In Mark, chapter six, we find the story beginning at verse thirty-one. Christ invites his disciples to come away from the crowd into a boat and to make their way across the lake. The crowd decides to follow them by running around the edge of the lake. When the boat arrives at the far side of the lake, the disciples discover a group of over five thousand men plus women and children. When Jesus saw the multitude, he was filled with compassion in his heart. The disciples didn't see the people that way. The disciples were hungry and tired. In fact, after Jesus had taught the crowd most of the day, the disciples asked him to 'send the people away'. The disciples looked at the crowd and saw a nuisance. Jesus looked upon the same multitude and saw a need."

"What happened next was a surprise to the disciples. Instead of sending the people away, Jesus commanded his disciples to feed them. He said, 'you give them something to eat'. They didn't even WANT to feed them. They soon told him that they didn't have enough food to feed them. Sometimes, we tell God we can't do what He asks, when really we don't WANT to do what He asks. Sometimes, we may want to do what He asks and sincerely believe that we can't. Grace is God's answer to both excuses."

"Grace begins when we say we CAN'T. God smiles and says, 'I never said you could – but I can. Would you like to join me as we do this together?' Grace is God giving us what we lack to please Him. That includes the desire as well as the ability. The disciples had neither the desire to feed the multitude or the ability. Jesus gave them both. He said, 'what do you have – go and see'. They came back with five small loaves of bread and two very little fishes that a little boy had brought. Peter must have laughed. He could eat more than that!"

The crowd laughed politely as Allen translated the line about Peter.

"Jesus told Peter to get a basket. He then told the rest of the disciples to get baskets because they were going to need them."

Even the children listened as Rusty told the story with such feeling.

"Then Jesus took the bread and fish and held them up and blessed them. 'Thank you Father, for what you are about to do' he said, and then began to break the bread and fish and fill each basket. He sent each disciple to a different part of the crowd and told them to pass out their food. As each one came back, they found Jesus still breaking bread, still dividing fish, still filling baskets. That is grace. Jesus gives us what we need to complete the task He gave us to do. In addition, he is able to give us the desire. Jesus puts the desire in our hearts to serve Him and then gives us the ability to complete the task He has asked us to do."

Amens were heard throughout the small room as Allen interpreted.

"Speaking for the team," Rusty stated, motioning to the rest of the group seated together on the back row. "I can honestly say that the Lord has given us all the desire to come to Nicaragua to be with you today. And we trust Him to give us the ability to build a bridge in *Pozo Negro* along with your missionary and your pastor. For 'it is God Who works in us both to will and to work of His good pleasure'."

Allen repeated the scripture as Rusty turned the pages of his Bible.

"After the feeding of the five thousand," Rusty continued. "Matthew's version of the story tells us that he sent his disciples away in a boat, dismissed the crowd and then went on the mountaintop to pray. During his prayer time, the Father must have told His Son to rejoin his disciples, even though He had sent them away in the only boat they had. The scripture says that 'in the fourth watch of the night, Jesus went out to them walking on the water'. You know that must have been frightful to see. The disciples responded with great fear, but Jesus reassured them by telling them it was Him. The opposite of faith is fear. Fear keeps us from believing what is true by filling our minds with our own imaginations. The devil knows if he can make you afraid, you will not turn to God, because 'perfect love casts out fear'. Fear keeps us from believing that God is in control."

Rusty found his words coming smoother. He had not planned this part of his message, but the words were almost saying themselves. Allen had absolutely no trouble with the translation.

"Jesus simply said, 'take courage! I am. Fear not!' The presence of Christ is all we need for any situation. We do not place our trust in our abilities or our personality. We place our trust in the person of Jesus Christ. Peter recognized this and called out from the boat, 'Lord, if it is You, call me to come to you walking on the water'. He looked Peter in the eye and said, 'come on'."

No one stirred as the words were spoken in their language. The people waited anxiously for Allen to bring them the next statement. This man from the United States was speaking God's word in a way they could understand.

"I trust you see that it was not the amount of Peter's faith that allowed him to walk on water – it was the object of his faith, Jesus Christ. When Christ calls you to join Him, He gives you the desire and ability to do whatever He has called you to do. That is why the Apostle Paul will write in his letter to the Thessalonians that, 'faithful is He Who calls you, Who also will do it'. When we embrace grace with faith – God does some amazing things both in us and through us. But He will always get the glory, because it will always be Him through us, and not we ourselves."

Rusty waited for the translation, took a breath and looked at Allen. Allen smiled and nodded. The eyes of the people were clear. They understood the message and more than that – they appreciated the word and the messenger. The Holy Spirit was evident and the people of *Monte Hermon* had heard from God.

The team loaded back into the van and Land Cruiser after the service. Arnie took a moment to put his arm around his son.

"That was a wonderful testimony you gave, son," he told Alex.

"Thanks, Dad. I really meant it. If you and Mom hadn't loved me through all that trouble I got into, I wouldn't be here today. And if the Lord hadn't be gracious in giving me a new start, no telling where I would be."

Little Billy and Matt stepped up alongside Alex and his father.

"Yeah, man, you did good," Matt said simply.

"I knew you had some trouble before college, but I had no idea how hairy it got," Little Billy added. "Sounds like you have a pretty solid relationship with your folks. They really love you, man."

Arnie smiled.

"We sure do!" he said, tightening his grip around his son's shoulder. "We sure do!"

Allen West stood between the vehicles to make an announcement.

"That was a great service. Thanks Alex, for sharing your testimony and Rusty…you did an awesome job preaching. You really connected with the people – good work, both of you. Following lunch we will drive over to the platform on this side of the river of *Pozo Negro*. We will go over the work plans for Monday and then prayer walk the area."

"Bro. West," Stan interrupted. "I heard you mention the prayer walk last night at the orientation meeting, but I'm still unclear what that is. Could you explain just a little?"

"Certainly," replied Allen, welcoming the question. "Prayer walking is praying with your *eyes open!* By that I mean, we will walk around the area of the project and pray at the same time. We will let God *show us* what to pray for. I could mention things, you can think of things, but God can show us even more. We haven't talked about it much, but the threat of some serious spiritual warfare lies before us. Jesus taught his disciples that areas of spiritual darkness need to be met with prayer and fasting. Now my wife, *hermano* José and I have observed some seasons of fasting for *Pozo Negro* and we have been in prayer consistently for the past several months. Now that you are here, I had hoped we could engage the team in prayer as well."

"Why not the fasting?" Rusty interjected.

"Yeah," echoed Little Billy.

"Speak for yourself," Matt whispered.

"No, Rusty is right," Billy Eldridge added stepping forward. "We are here to do mission work. The demands for each trip are different. This trip requires some spiritual preparation that we need to consider. If we were not able to get lunch today for some reason or another, we wouldn't complain. Why don't we voluntarily set this meal aside for prayer and fasting?"

"Are you sure?" Allen asked, looking around the group.

"I am!" Ty said first. "Count me in."

"We're willing," Willis Beaman said after getting the nod from Rhonda.

The others responded with nods of affirmation and similar comments – eventually even Matt.

"OK, then!" Allen said impressed. "I'll tell José. We'll just travel from here to the riverside. May I suggest that those riding in the van prepare yourselves together through some time of worship, singing and prayer. If you need a time of personal reflection and confession, do it on the way. It's very important though that you draw near to God and that you put away any other distractions. Prayer walking doesn't begin at the work site, it begins at the throne of God. Between here and there – find your way to the throne."

The group divided quietly according to their vehicles and took their seats. There was a solemnity that could be felt in the van as it pulled out onto the highway heading towards the mountain. Some bowed their heads, some looked out the window without seeing the landscape. Some fumbled through the pages of their Bible as they rode seeking Psalms of worship. After about twenty minutes of silent running, Rhonda lifted her head without opening her eyes.

"Lord, you have brought us to this country for a purpose and task that we may not completely understand, but we ask you to prepare us for what lies ahead," she prayed aloud.

"Amen," her husband responded.

"Lord Jesus, I've never done anything like this before," Peter Moralis prayed from the front seat. "I pray that my life be clean of sin. I confess to you my fear, I confess to you doubt, I confess to you impatience and even a critical spirit over the past couple days. Please forgive me of these and other sins that I may not have even been aware of. Cleanse me with the blood of our Lord that was shed upon Calvary. Thank you for accepting me as your own, now please use us I pray for your Holy Kingdom. In the blessed name of our Savior, we pray…"

"Father God," Robert Winston began as Peter finished. "I too must confess my sin before you today. I have never felt more unworthy for what I have been asked to do than I do at this moment, but I humbly believe you are able to use me and these others to confront the very gates of Hell in the power of your Spirit that dwells in us. We are but simple people, but you are an extreme and awesome God and you go before us. We commit ourselves to your purpose…to your will…to your glory. We take your name as a banner before us. We praise you this day."

"Yes, Lord," came several voices from the back of the van. Sporadic expressions of praise began to burst from among the passengers.

"We do praise you, Lord."

"Open our eyes to your holiness, we pray."

"You are King!"

"You are Lord!"

"You are my Shepherd!"

"You are my Redeemer!"

"You watch my going out and my coming in."

"You are God and there is no other!"

"You alone are worthy of all praise and glory!"

José sensed the worship going on around him and became overwhelmed. Though he couldn't understand all of their words, he felt the presence of God's Spirit filling his van. He found a gap in the praise and added his voice to theirs.

"*Gracias Señor por tu misericordia, tu gracia, tu amor. Bendice éste grupo grandemente con el poder de tu Espíritu y sea glorificado.*"

"*Amen!*" Peter Moralis added in his own family accent.

There was a brief moment of silence and then Rhonda began to sing softly, "*I Love You, Lord.*" The words of the praise chorus were familiar to all. They sang it often at the Coronado Baptist Church. Yet, there on the van, the chorus took on new meaning. It was not simply a song sung from a screen on the wall – it was a prayer from the deepest regions of the heart. The group sang the chorus through about three times and then moved seamlessly to "*Have Thine Own Way*". Other choruses and hymns followed as each one felt led. The hour drive to the small community outside the river seemed far too short.

The group assembled on the side of the road near the small community nestled near the mango groves. The sight of over a dozen North Americans sparked the interest of several as they watched from a careful distance near their homes. Allen stepped up to address the team.

"Folks, this is where José and I first discovered the existence of *Pozo Negro*. We were stopped at this very spot for a funeral procession. We discovered that about a hundred yards or so through those trees was a river that had taken the lives of several villagers, including a small girl being buried the day we were driving by. I don't believe that it was a coincidence. I felt God move in me that day to begin praying for this village and if possible to bring a team from the US to rebuild them a bridge. I stand here today looking at the answer to that prayer."

The team glanced about at each other humbly. They had never considered themselves an answer to prayer.

"We will walk together through that small grove over there and come to the riverside where many of us have already been working on the platform from which we will begin building the bridge tomorrow. I can't tell you how full my heart is today. I hope you are ready to go to work."

They all nodded, still humbled by the words of the missionary.

"OK, let's go see the river."

Allen led out. Rusty followed the missionary and the team fell in line behind them. José took the position at the rear of the parade to insure that no one strayed. Matt looked back at José and the Nicaraguan pastor just smiled at him and motioned for him to stay in line. Several sets of eyes watched the group from the dark safety of their homes. Where were they going, many thought. What were they doing? Even the children stayed close to home.

The group emerged into the light on the other side of the mango groves and they could see the two platforms and the river between them. Arnie walked first to the platform and began inspecting the structure. Allen West chose not to interrupt him as he looked over the strength of the platform and the foundation posts. Without calling attention to himself, Arnie kneeled at the base of one of the support posts and bowed his head.

"Lord, thank you for bringing me here," Arnie began praying. "I pray for those who will use this bridge. I pray that this bridge will help provide a witness of your love for these people. I pray that we will be safe as we begin construction tomorrow. Lord, I don't know what else to pray, but I just ask you to work through me. May I be a tool in your hands while I am here. In Jesus' name I pray…Amen."

Winston began walking down river. As he walked, Stan followed a short distance behind him. Winston paused near a large rock and climbed up on it to sit. Stan came alongside and stood with him. Together they prayed for the families that had lost loved ones in this river and prayed that no more lives would be taken by this river. They prayed God's mercy over *Pozo Negro* and the small settlement they had traveled through to get to the river. As they prayed, Stan rested his arm on Winston's shoulder in agreement.

Alex, Matt and Little Billy decided to venture in the opposite direction. They traveled up river about thirty yards and came to a small bend. Up ahead they could see activity in the water. It looked like children were playing near the bank where two or three mothers were washing clothes.

"Shall we go any further?" Matt asked.

"No, we may disturb them or worse, stumble on someone bathing. Remember what Mr. Eldridge told us," Little Billy replied.

"That's right," Alex agreed. "We're fine right here. Let's just begin praying for the people of *Pozo Negro*."

"Let's pray that they get a chance to hear the gospel," Matt offered.

"Yeah, and that the witch doctor gets saved," Little Billy added.

"That may be asking quite a bit," Matt countered.

"Maybe not," Alex injected. "There is no one God can't reach. We've been looking at this witchdoctor like he was some 'Goliath'. Maybe we need to start comparing him to God. John says, 'greater is he that is in you than he that is in the world'. We just need to start seeing him that way."

"I agree," stated Little Billy.

"OK, we'll pray for the witchdoctor," Matt agreed reluctantly.

"Why don't we just have a seat here near the bank," Alex suggested.

"Sounds good," said the other two in unison and the trio eased onto the rocky bank.

The Beamans invited Ty to join them as they retreated halfway between the river and the mango grove. Rhonda wanted to pray for the two communities on both sides of the river. It was obvious to her that the people they had just passed were not as open as the ones they had just left at *Monte Hermon*. She had seen the shadow figures of curious children peering through darkened doorways and knew there was more than suspicion in their minds – there was fear.

Finding a small patch of shade, the couple and the welder stood in a tight circle and joined hands. Willis led out in prayer.

"Lord Jesus, we come together to join our spirits in prayer for this entire area. It is evident that the darkness of *Pozo Negro* has affected this community as well. These people seem so fearful. We pray that the light of your Son will be allowed to shine in their hearts and throughout their community in a powerful way. We sensed the darkness walking through this area. We can only imagine the depth of that darkness. Lord, dispel that darkness with your light, we pray."

Rhonda and Ty quietly whispered their agreement as Willis prayed. Each one then took a turn lifting the two communities before the throne of grace.

Allen watched as Peter invited José to join him in prayer. The two walked off together towards the direction of Winston and Stan while speaking Spanish in low tones. They stopped just short of the other two men and both kneeled in the dirt. Allen knew this meant a great deal to José to be included in the prayer time with one of the team members and he thanked God for sending a volunteer that spoke Spanish.

"Shall we join Arnie," Allen said to Rusty and Billy Eldridge.

"That would be good," replied Rusty.

The three men walked to the platform and took positions around Arnie who was still praying.

"Lord God," Allen led out. "We come to this river side seeking your face. We believe you have brought us here for more than a construction task. We pray for those who will be serving the next few days on this project that you will make their hands strong and fruitful. But we pray more for the people of *Pozo Negro* and of the community that we have just walked past. This project is not about the death of a dozen people in a river. This project is about the eternal second death of every person in this village that has been prevented from hearing the gospel. So for this reason, we come to you to go before us and to stand with us as we seek to build a bridge for the gospel to *Pozo Negro*. May the forces that strive to stand against us not be allowed to stand against You! May your Spirit confound the principalities that are already at war against your will. May the power of the resurrection overcome the power of sin and death. May your name be heard and glorified at this river and beyond."

The more Allen spoke, the stronger his words grew. Each man punctuated the prayers with his own personal agreement and amen. When he finished, Allen lifted his hands in praise in the direction of the river. Rusty took the banner and continued to march in prayer.

"Father, we come to you - the Most High God, the Creator of Heaven and Earth, the Lord of Lords and King of Kings. We know that it is not your will that 'any should perish, but that all should come to repentance' and we believe that includes *Pozo Negro*. We know that you can do 'exceedingly, above all that we can ask and think' and that 'there is nothing too great for you'. We know that 'the heart of the king is in the hand of the Lord and that you can turn it whithersoever you will' and that includes the heart of this witch doctor who has set himself against you and your will. We pray this day that your will and purpose will prevail. That nothing can stand against you. And we offer ourselves as your instruments, Lord."

Rusty paused and immediately Billy Eldridge stepped in.

"Lord, Rusty is right. We are your instruments. We are your vessels. Help us to understand that the treasure we bring to these people is in earthen vessels. That the excellency of the power may be of you and not of ourselves. And may we understand that you may need to break the vessel for the light to be seen. Father, I have often questioned you about the death of my brother, Carey, but right now I understand - as your instruments, we must be prepared for whatever it takes to win the lost. God, I pray for my fellow laborers that we will truly offer ourselves as living sacrifices to you this day and commit ourselves to whatever it takes for your name to be lifted up."

"Amen," Arnie said, opening his eyes and looking directly at Billy. "That's right."

Dr. Howard Pennington sat on the small living room sofa with his grammar books opened around him. Last night cramming was never his style while in seminary, but Spanish was different. Not all of the exams would be objective tests of fill-in-the blank or list conjugations for various different kinds of verbs. There was also going to be an oral exam where he would be asked to role play with the instructor over any topic she chose and to use as many grammar examples, vocabulary, and expressions as he could while sounding natural and relevant at the same time. He would be evaluated on his pronunciation, his tense, his agreement between subjects and verbs, maintaining the proper gender usage with definite articles and the fluidity with which he spoke. Howard knew that Donna had called it a night and couldn't help but think that she was "giving up". They had studied some together that afternoon after church, but she was not in the same level as Howard and wasn't familiar with some of the grammar he would be tested on.

Howard leaned back in the corner of the sofa and rested his eyes. This was definitely the hardest time he had ever spent in his entire academic career. He wasn't just expected to learn a subject, he was expected to adapt to a new culture, a new language and a new lifestyle while carrying his family through the same experience. Language school was proving to be greatest test of his relationship with God and his family – even greater than the lesson he had learned with Karen over the priority of family in ministry. For Howard, so much was riding on the exams of the next two days. How he wished they were behind them and they could be focusing on just having some enjoyable time together at the beach.

He took a deep breath and leaned back over his books. The Lord had brought them through tough times before and He would be faithful to do it again. But Howard had no idea just how tough those times were about to get.

CHAPTER SEVENTEEN

" THE DREAM "

ADAM BAXTER pulled up in the driveway and quickly turned off the engine. He scurried to the passenger side to grab the two bags of groceries in the floorboard that he had just purchased and then scooped up the mail on the seat that had just retrieved from the mailbox at the end of their drive. He trotted to the front door. Letting himself in, he rushed to the kitchen to put the milk away and leave the other bag on the kitchen table. He knew better than to call out for Gertie from the kitchen. She didn't like him yelling through the house. He knew where to find her.

The hospital bed was a little large for their bedroom, but it wouldn't fit in the guest room. That was where he slept now. Gertie had had Adam bring a recliner in for him to sit with her. There was a small TV on the dresser which they seldom turned on. When there was important news or weather, he liked to watch it with her. The special bed could be adjusted for her to sit up and crochet – when she had the stamina. Her walker stood unused in the corner. As long as Adam could care for her, he was going to. When she could no longer walk on her own, he bought a wheel chair and built a ramp to the front door. When it became too hard to climb in and out of the chair, he got her the bed. A health care nurse came by each day for special needs. Adam was taught how to help with the basic ones. Gertie had been confined since the past December, but she was still as lucid as ever.

"Gertie, you have a letter from California!" Adam called out excitedly as he bustled through the doorway. Gertie was sitting up reading.

"Oh really!" she mused. "Who do you suppose is writing us from California?"

"Lets see," replied Adam, opening the letter for her. "It is handwritten. It must be personal." He passed it to her without reading even the greeting.

Gertie took the letter, adjusted her bifocals, and began to read to herself while Adam sat patiently waiting.

"It's from Billy Eldridge," she revealed.

"Billy Eldridge?"

"Oh, you remember, he is the brother of the missionary that I was praying for back in the fall of '98 – the one that was later killed in an automobile accident."

"Oh, Carey, yes…I remember."

"It seems that Billy is about to go...no wait, they are already there!"

"Where?" Adam asked confused.

"This was written last week and mailed on Monday, why did it take so long to get here?" Gertie asked.

"I forgot to tell you," Adam confessed. "I forgot to check the mail on Friday and Saturday I didn't go out, remember?"

"So this could have been sitting in the mailbox all weekend?" Gertie said.

"I suppose so," Adam admitted. "So where is he?"

"Billy is with a team of volunteers that have gone to Nicaragua for a construction project. According to the letter, they arrived on Saturday. They have been there for two days now. Billy is asking our prayers for the team while they are there. And listen to this part, '*We will be building a bridge for a community that lives across a small river from the rest of civilization. We have learned that a witch-doctor may be present and is opposing the group's coming. We will be working with a missionary named Allen West*'."

"Do we know Allen West?" asked Adam.

"I don't think so. His name doesn't sound familiar to me," replied Gertie, squinting her eyes and trying to think. "It is the part about the witch doctor that burdens me. This team is in definite need of prayer."

"Are you up to it?" Adam asked concerned.

Gertie looked into the loving eyes of her husband and smiled.

"As long as I have breath – I have prayer," she replied firmly. "We have some work ahead of us."

Monday morning was filled with anticipation. Most of the team members were ready and waiting on the curb before the van and Land Cruiser arrived. The side streets were much more active than they had been on Sunday morning. Less of León was sleeping in. The Sunday khakis and knit shirts they had worn to church had been replaced by working jeans and t-shirts. The young men had tied dark red bandanas around their necks. By mid-day they would convert them to head scarves that would cover the back of their necks while tucked in back of their ball caps. The Beamans took turn applying sun screen to each other – a "husband/wife thing". Arnie rechecked his plastic tote of tools, squares, levels and plumb lines. There would be no coming back to the hotel for forgotten equipment.

The van pulled up right on time followed closely by the Land Cruiser. Peter greeted José while the others began finding their seats from the day before. Arnie and Alex carried the tools to the back of the Land Cruiser.

"Rest well?" Allen asked Arnie.

"Better than the first night," Arnie replied positively. "I don't think I heard as many unusual sounds."

"I think your snoring scared them off," Alex joked with his father.

"Very funny," Alex snorted.

"I can tell you guys are going to make great roommates this week," Allen said lightly.

"We wouldn't have it any other way," Alex laughed. "I expect this to be a real bonding experience."

"Then how about bonding with me in lifting this tote into the back of the Land Cruiser?" Arnie suggested.

"Sure thing, Dad."

Donna Pennington looked at the exam on her desk for several moments before turning it over. She didn't feel nearly as confident as she had hoped. Ever since the Reddings had returned to the states, the prospect of not finishing language school had been more than a possibility. The truth was – not all who start would finish. It wasn't talked about much, but it happened. It had happened to two of their friends. Donna tried to shake off her feelings of inadequacy. Why couldn't they just go on to the field and learn the language there, she had often wondered? She knew the answer, but it didn't make her exam any easier. This was indeed the hardest work she had ever done in her life. "Please, Lord Jesus," she prayed. "Help me through this test!"

Literally two levels above her, Howard was preparing for his own grammar exam. He would be tested on the subjunctive as well as the past and preterit tense. This was so beyond any of his college Spanish. He knew the usage in conversation, but declining the verbs and knowing the rules was different. You just couldn't say it because it "sounded right". You had to know why it was right.

Howard picked out the familiar verbs first and began declining them on paper. The irregular verbs took more thought. After several minutes of rehearsing the forms in his mind, he began writing them down. It was coming to him. He turned the page and found a large section of sentences that he had to provide the correct verb and form. This was the easier portion. His practice with Mateo on the University campus helped him "hear" the correct form. In this section, he didn't have to know why it was right – he could rely on his ear. The exam was thorough, but not exhausting. He completed the grammar exam in about forty-five minutes.

Howard turned in his paper and walked out of the classroom with his chin high. He was the second to finish. He walked up to the snack bar and picked out a well-deserved pastry and a coke. Leaving the snack bar with his can in hand, Howard walked down to the lower level to look in on Donna. He peeked around the open door frame to not draw attention to himself. He didn't want either the *Maestra* or Donna to see him. Donna sat on the second row near the window. Howard eased in position to see her. He wished he hadn't. She sat at her desk with her head and pencil down. She was wringing her hands in a way all too familiar. As he watched helplessly, she wiped the corner of her eye and picked up her pencil. Taking a deep breath, she poised herself defensively over her exam and began writing slowly. After scribbling a few words, she sighed, turned over her pencil and began erasing.

Howard quietly slipped away from the doorway before she chanced seeing him looking in on her. He knew she was struggling and could almost feel her panic. Part of him wanted to rush in to the room and whisk her away from the torment and assure her it would be alright. Visions of Richard Gere marching into the factory at the close of *An Officer and a Gentleman* came to mind. But he knew he couldn't. She had to work through this area of growth herself. It was more than a language test, it was the challenge of the call – and only the strength of the call could see her through. Howard walked down to the post office to wait for her to finish. Maybe there would be a letter.

"Nobody goes to the river empty-handed!" Arnie called out from the back of the Land Cruiser. "There are plenty of things to carry down, so line up."

The team jumped to attention at the command of their foreman. The enthusiasm level was at its highest. This was going to be a good day for work. José instructed the two workers from his church that met them there to carry whatever the large North American gave them and they got in line. Peter Moralis took the opportunity to introduce himself to them.

"Can we make it all in one trip?" Allen asked Arnie.

"I hope so," Arnie smiled back. "It's quite a little hike to come back for just a shovel or a hammer."

"What can I carry?" the missionary offered.

"Why don't you take this tool box and one of these rolls of rope," replied Arnie, passing one of the large rolls of heavy rope on to Allen.

Arnie's plan was to construct a suspension bridge utilizing the four large posts as towers through which to run steel cables across the river. The ten-foot posts would absorb the compression and anchoring the cables to stakes at a set distance from the platform would handle the tension. The actual bridge would be formed by cables affixed to the beam at the base of the two platforms that would serve as an under support for a horizontal trellis of meter lengths of two by ten slats. The width of the bridge would be connected to the four-foot opening of the platforms. In addition, thick rope handrails, strung from the support posts of each platform, would provide the needed safety in crossing.

Arnie surveyed the distance between the platforms and then stepped off half the distance up the bank. When he was satisfied, he instructed the men to start digging holes for the stakes. Special four foot stakes had been prepared with welded eyes at the top. The holes would need to be dug, the stakes placed and concrete poured to refill the holes.

"What are these for?" Allen asked, picking up one of the heavy stakes.

"They will serve as anchors for the steel cable. They are distanced here to handle the stress of the bridge by spreading the weight over the posts you guys built. We'll lock down one end of the cable here…string it through the top of the post on the platform, allow it to arch to the other post, and then secure it the same distance from the other post. When we run the expansion cable from platform to platform, we will then use rope to attach it to the arching cable."

Allen nodded as if he understood.

The first half of the morning was spent preparing the anchors for the bridge. The team broke into two groups and Beto helped to shuttle half of the group across to the other platform. Arnie briefed Peter on the procedures necessary so that he could oversee the work on the *Pozo Negro* side of the river. This gave a knowledgeable person on each side of the river who could communicate with the national workers. Arnie relied on Allen to speak for him.

The young men carried supplies to each side. Stan and Winston worked with Arnie while Ty assisted Peter and the two workers that came with José. Billy Eldridge and the Beamans took turns relieving the other men in their digging. Rhonda also made sure the water bottles were full. It didn't take long for the sun to rise overhead. Without much shade to retreat to near the river, the team members took turns taking breaks near the mango grove. The villagers from the highway side watched curiously from their homes and yards as the North American workers rested and then returned to the river.

———————————

"That's everything, *Señor* Bayardos. Your money will be deposited today."

Don Tulio shook hands with the man in the suit, collected his bag, his staff and walked out of the bank office relieved that his business was finally complete. He hated coming to the capitol. He would spend the rest of the day gathering herbs from the open market and stay one more night. He was anxious to return to *Pozo Negro* – more anxious than usual.

———————————

"Well, looky here," Howard exclaimed gleefully, finding a letter in the familiar thin airmail envelope. Quickly scanning the return address, he was overwhelmed with joy. "It's from Karen!..." Then, looking at the mailing address, he added to himself, "and it's for Terry!"

Howard placed the letter on top of his books and started for the lower gate.

———————————

"How about a break?" called Little Billy.

"We just took one!" replied Matt.

"That was lunch – and that was over an hour ago," Little Billy complained. "It's getting hot out here."

"Little Billy has a point," said Allen. "We want to watch ourselves in the afternoon. This is the hottest part of the day. Why don't we call the group together for a break and prayer time."

"Prayer time?" inquired Stan. "Things have been going smooth, so far. Why we haven't had a problem one."

"Exactly," replied Allen. "I can't believe Satan has just decided to leave us alone. Something is building – and I don't mean our bridge. We can't afford to let our guard down now."

Turning to Winston, the missionary gave a humble order, "Mr. Winston, would you call the folks on the other side to join us."

Stan looked over at Arnie who simply nodded in agreement. This project was about more than getting a structure completed – it was about building a bridge for God.

"Why don't I swim over and tell them," Little Billy offered, wanting an excuse to cool himself off in the river.

"I'm afraid you wouldn't make it," warned Allen. "I know it doesn't look it, but this river is pretty deep in the middle and there is an undercurrent. José tells me they have had rains in the mountains and the river is a bit swollen right now. That's why none of the villagers have been down here trying to cross while we have been working. Beto's canoe cuts through the current, but not without effort. I'm afraid you would tire before you realized it and could be carried under. We would find you about a half of kilometer downstream."

"I'm a pretty good swimmer, you know," Little Billy protested.

"I'm sure you are, but I'm afraid you will just have to trust me on this one," Allen replied frankly.

Winston walked down to the river edge and motioned for Peter and his team to make their way across the river. The four men waved and woke up Beto, who was resting in his canoe. After a few minutes they were all together and gathered at the mango grove for shade.

"Bro. Allen thought it a good time for a break," Rusty began.

"Amen!" Matt interrupted. After a couple stares from the older men, Rusty continued.

"...and that it would be a good opportunity for us to pause for a time of prayer. I am going to ask if any of you have a special request or leading from the Lord that we could pray about."

There was stillness as the group waited for someone to speak.

"I don't know if this is worth mentioning," Ty began softly. "But I had an unusual dream last night."

The team looked in his direction. This was not a typical response in taking prayer requests.

"I dreamed we were working in the hot sun much like it's been today, when suddenly a huge dark cloud came over us. At first we were relieved to have shade, but then the cloud grew darker and darker. There was something wrong about the cloud. It made the air feel heavy, but not with rain. Instead, it was as though it was full of wind waiting to explode. We stopped our work to look at the cloud. That's when a lion came rushing us from the woods. It began chasing us to the river. I remember climbing on a rock to escape the lion. While standing on the rock, the cloud seemed right over my head. Then with a huge blast, wind came from the cloud and..."

Ty paused.

"Well, don't leave us hanging," said Rusty anxiously. "What did the wind do?"

"It parted the river, and the lion ran across to the other side."

"That's strange!" commented Little Billy

"That's what I thought," said Ty. "I'm not sure if the cloud was something good or something bad. And I have no idea what the lion is about."

"But you think the dream is meaningful?" asked Allen.

"I don't know," said Ty honestly. "I just know I don't always remember my dreams and this one has stuck with me through the day with almost every detail."

"Well, the Bible talks about the devil being like a roaring lion. Let's pray that God will protect us from the lion and that, if the cloud is evil, that His light will overcome the darkness," Allen offered.

The group bowed their heads and Allen led them in prayer. It was soon obvious that this was the reason they had taken the break. God was preparing them for something that they didn't fully understand.

Juanita worked quietly around the house while Howard read his latest novel. He was determined to not concentrate on anything Spanish for at least two hours. That included talking to the maid. Normally, Howard was very conversational with Juanita and she was appreciative. Donna didn't talk much to her. Juanita could tell Mrs. Pennington was not comfortable using her Spanish, but such was not the case with Mr. Pennington. Juanita was much more relaxed around him. Because of that, she had to be careful. She also found herself understanding more English around them.

Howard glanced at his watch. He had been home a little over an hour and a half when he heard Donna at the gate. Howard set aside his paperback to meet her at the door.

"Well, how was it?" he asked cautiously.

Donna waited to answer till she was almost to the door, then she began to cry openly. Howard quickly put his arm around her shoulder and escorted her through the doorway.

"I went blank," she sniffled. "I panicked. You name it...I experienced it. It was the longest two hours of my life."

"Oh, honey," Howard consoled as they stepped over to the couch to sit. "I'm sure you did better than you think."

"I hope so, but I doubt it. I can't wait to get to the end of this week so we can get away."

Howard held her for a few moments.

"Could we leave any earlier than Wednesday?" Donna asked softly.

"I'll see."

"I just feel like one more pressure is all it will take..." her voice trailing off into the inevitable.

"You have one or two more exams tomorrow?" Howard asked.

"Just one – the phonetics teacher has already decided we are all doing well enough to forego a final. I think she's being gracious. I know how bad I sound."

"You don't sound bad," Howard contradicted lovingly. "I've heard you talking to Juanita."

"Not lately, you haven't," Donna corrected. "That's the other problem. I'm starting to avoid natural conversations with Spanish speaking people around me. I don't feel like I'm bonding, and here we are two trimesters into the process. When is it going to happen? What is it going to take? Howard, I'm getting concerned. God is going to have to do a major work on me in this next trimester for me to be ready to minister in Honduras."

Donna was being brutally honest with herself and Howard. The events of the past eight months were beginning to mount. The break-in, the thief on the bus, the death of her aunt, the pilfering of their Christmas package, the Reddings leaving at the beginning of the year and the attack on Terry all rushed together in her mind. She knew it would be different and difficult, but this was almost more than she could shoulder. She just wanted to get away with her family.

"I can't believe God has brought us this far, to allow us to be overcome by pressure," said Howard, trying to reassure his wife. "I agree that this past year has been a stretching experience. It has tried us in many ways. But if God has called us to this task, His Word says, 'faithful is He who calls you, who also will do it!' "

"IF God has called us," Donna repeated sharply.

Howard refrained from commenting. He saw hurt, not defiance in her eyes. Donna needed reassurance from God, not words from her husband. Whatever God was about to do, Howard knew it would either strengthen her calling to stay or her resolve to seek a way back home. Howard held her close and prayed.

"Father, like David, there are times we feel your absence and we cry out. We know in our hearts you are here, but we need you to confirm your presence and to affirm your purpose in our lives. God, I believe you brought us here. I'm not sure to what end. If it was to this point alone, we need to know. If you are leading us forward, we need to know. We cannot go without you. We dare not consider any other course without you. Please God, show us your way."

As they prayed, Juanita watched quietly from the hallway. She turned and entered their bedroom to put away the clean clothes she had just taken down from the line. She knew they were praying. She knew something was wrong. She wondered if there would be much more time with this family. As she put away the clothes, she found herself looking around. Her time may indeed be shorter than she had planned.

Adam brought Gertie's evening meal on a tray and set it beside her bed.

"What time is it?" Gertie asked, looking up.

"A little after five – is it too early to eat?"

"No, I was just wondering. I've been praying for the team and found myself praying for other needs as well. I was just wondering what time it was in Central America."

Adam thought for a moment.

"We're in Daylight Savings Time now, aren't we?" Adam asked.

"Yes, first Sunday in April since Reagan changed it in '86" Gertie remembered.

"But Central America doesn't observe the time change does it?"

"I think you are right," Gertie agreed.

"Then they are two hours behind us rather than just one hour," Adam calculated.

"You are so smart," Gertie smiled.

"So I guess it's a little after three there," said Adam proudly. "Why?"

"I was just trying to see where in their work day they were. I was also praying for another family God brought to mind. You'll never guess," she teased.

"The Penningtons." Adam said matter-of-factly.

"How did you know?" Gertie replied, surprised.

Adam bent down and kissed her forehead.

"I've learned much about prayer from you, including how to hear from God. You aren't the only one who intercedes in this family. Besides…I heard you call their name when I walked by the door just a few minutes ago."

Gertie laughed.

Arnie Johnson inspected the anchors. They seemed to be solid and the concrete was setting up well. He had shown the young men what he had in mind for the cables that would extend from platform to platform and they used the canoe to carry the heavy lines across the river and to prepare the base for affixing the cables. Allen brought out a small generator and Winston and Stan began using a portable circular saw to cut the two-by-tens into the one meter lengths. It was looking like a very productive day.

"Is it my imagination or is it not as hot as it was last hour?" Stan asked Winston.

"I think you're right," Winston answered picking up a new piece of wood for Stan to cut. "It's probably only about ninety-five degrees now."

Stan chuckled.

"No, I'm serious – it feels cooler."

The two men looked up together. A large cloud had passed in front of the sun and was providing for cooler temperatures. As they lowered their heads, their eyes met.

"That's a pretty big cloud," said Stan slowly.

"Yeah...but it's not real dark," Winston remarked.

"Not yet!" said Stan half-seriously.

"We'll keep an eye on it," said Winston emphatically.

"And I'm going to watch the tree line for lions!"

Across the river, Peter gave instructions to the men from José's church on how to clasp the steel cables under the platform using a special metal plate that Arnie had brought. Little Billy helped Peter while Alex and Matt supported the cables from inside the canoe.

"What did you think about Ty's dream?" Little Billy asked Peter.

"I believe in dreams," responded Peter matter-of-factly. "My grandmother talked much about how dreams are like God's windows into our inner being."

"How do you mean?"

"They allow God to look in and they allow us to look out. Sometimes we see what He sees around us. Sometimes we see what He sees about us."

"I still don't follow," Little Billy said confused.

"Some dreams show us what is going on around us that God sees that we miss due to our own personal blindness. It's like getting God's perspective on life. Sometimes that includes things that haven't happen – like when Joseph saw the seven years of plenty and the seven years of famine. God saw them already. He showed Joseph, so that Joseph could prepare and save his people and family."

"Yeah, I remember that story," Little Billy nodded.

"Sometimes he shows us things about ourselves – like when Peter had his dream about the sheet coming down from heaven. He needed to know that he had personal prejudice that would get in the way of God's plan for the gospel going to the Gentiles. God used the dream to speak to Peter about himself, not the future."

"Do all dreams mean something?" Little Billy asked honestly.

"Sure, some dreams mean that you shouldn't eat Pizza after nine-o'clock at night!"

"I'm serious," said Little Billy.

"So am I. Some dreams are just a result of our own thought processes working through the problems and highlights of the day or reacting to some physical discomfort. I doubt we should try to read meaning into all of our dreams. But I do believe that God is able to speak to us through dreams. We just have to be discerning," Peter concluded.

"Do you think Ty's dream is a message from God?"

"I don't know, but I do think Ty believes it is and that alone is worth consideration."

"I suppose so," Little Billy conceded.

Little Billy went back to working on tightening the cable like Peter had shown him. He found himself trying to remember his dream from the night before. It seemed like it had something to do with roosters.

By the close of the work day, the team had successfully hung cable from one platform to the other and had tightened it to support the wooden slats that they would begin laying the next day. Allen didn't want to overtax the team, but they certainly had come with a heart to work. From a distance on the *Pozo Negro* side of the river, Roberto Espinal watched as the team gathered their tools and began making their way back towards the mango groves and on to the vehicles. Roberto admired the work they had accomplished. Maybe he would join them the next day to help, he thought to himself. These men truly came to work. As Roberto watched the last of the team disappear from sight he glanced over his shoulder towards the approaching sunset. What will happen when Don Tulio finds out what they are doing? Will he try to stop it? Would there be a fight? Who would win? Which one's power would prove stronger? Roberto was determined to be around to see. He would not have to wait long.

"When is your last exam tomorrow?" Howard asked at the dinner table.

"I have my phonetics exam at nine, and then I am free," Donna quickly replied.

"Terry," Howard turned his attention to his son. "When do you get out of school tomorrow?"

"Many of the kids have already gone. There is just a handful of MK's. The teachers are just giving us busy work because so many have already taken off for Semana Santa. Why?"

Howard took a breath. He had been working out the logistics in his head since the afternoon.

"I think we can get a head start on our vacation, but it means packing tonight," he announced.

"Are you serious?" exclaimed Donna gleefully.

"But what about my school?" Terry asked.

"I'll send a note with you to school in the morning asking permission to dismiss you about ten o'clock. You come home and Mom and I will be ready to call a taxi as soon as you arrive. That way we can at least say you went to school."

"I'll run all the way," promised Terry.

"Then it is settled, I'll talk to Juanita in the morning about staying over beginning tomorrow instead of waiting till Wednesday. It will give us an extra day."

"I'm for that," responded Donna excited.

"Me too," Terry almost yelled.

Howard felt good for the decision. It would take more money for the extra day, but it would be worth it. His family was happy. Soon the cares of language study would be behind them. Soon they would not have to worry about anything except remembering to put on the sunscreen. It was time to put away the Spanish books for a short season. Unfortunately, Howard forgot. He had placed the letter from Karen for Terry on top of his books.

"*León, León!*" the voice shouted in the dark.

The inn keeper pounded several times on the locked wooden door.

"Señor, Señor…are you OK?" he called frantically.

Don Tulio bolted up in the small bed. He was covered with sweat, even though a fan was aimed right at him. He looked around disoriented for a moment and then answered.

"*Si*, I'm ok,"

"What is wrong, you were shouting horribly in the middle of the night?" the voice called from the other side of the door.

"I'm sorry, it was a dream. It was just a dream. I am ok," Don Tulio repeated, assuring himself.

"Are you sure you are ok?"

"Yes," replied Don Tulio sharply. "I am sorry to have disturbed anybody. I will be leaving first thing in the morning for León."

CHAPTER EIGHTEEN

"THE CLOUD"

"LOOKS LIKE it could rain some today," Matt commented, as the rested group emerged through the mango groves.

"I suspect it is already raining up beyond the mountain," Allen West replied. "See those dark clouds to our east. It also looks like the river has risen some. That usually means rain above the area."

"Will it interfere with the work for the day?" Rusty asked.

"I doubt it, as long as it doesn't come down where we are working," said the missionary with a voice of confidence. "Still, I would stay clear of the water. The current will be a bit stronger today."

The group gathered at the platform for prayer. The clouds continued to darken in the distance.

"León?" the little man asked the bus driver for reassurance. The driver nodded and Don Tulio gave him the necessary Cordova for the trip. It would be three hours counting the stops, before they would arrive. Then he would have to find a bus going up the mountain. That could take another hour or longer. He wanted to reach *Pozo Negro* before the storm. Don Tulio could see the clouds as well. He lifted his staff as he boarded so as not to hit anyone behind him. He was still uneasy about his dream the night before. He would try to sleep some on the bus.

The morning sky was overcast as Howard and Donna walked to the language institute. Howard could tell Donna was anxious. He kept himself from asking if she felt ready. He didn't want her to have to express her apprehension. They both knew that once the morning was over, they could focus all their attention on getting ready for their trip to the beach.

Terry fidgeted in his chair at school. He, too, was anxious to complete the two classes that would finish at 10:00 and to rush home as soon as he could. He let his mind wander as the teacher drew math equations on the green board. The teacher was also killing time till he could vacate his classroom and join his friends for the holidays. Terry couldn't wait to try body surfing.

Karen had taken him to the Strand outside of San Diego with some of her friends and taught him how to catch a wave with his upper torso and ride it in to shore. Terry was bigger now and knew it would be easier. He couldn't wait. The teacher finished his equation and looked over his shoulder at the clock on the wall. He was not alone.

———————

"Looks cloudy outside," called Adam from the kitchen. He knew Gertie couldn't hear her from the bedroom, but he didn't mind repeating himself when he carried in her breakfast.

"How's that?" she called back, looking up from her Bible.

"I'll tell you when I come in," he yelled back a little louder.

Adam marched in like a dutiful butler sporting his tray. The eggs were fried and runny, the bacon crisp, and the toast dark without butter.

"I said, it looks cloudy outside," Adam repeated softly.

Gertie placed her crocheted bookmark at the Book of Numbers chapter nine where she had been reading.

"You don't say," she said amused and smiled to herself.

"I know that look," Adam teased, placing the tray over her lap and handing her the cloth napkin he had brought. "What has the weather got to do with what you were just reading?"

Gertie sighed and took Adam's hand.

"Pray with me for the breakfast and for the team in Nicaragua," she coaxed gently.

The two bowed their heads as God joined them for breakfast.

———————

Howard watched the classroom door anxiously as students would one by one open and leave having finished their phonetics exam. Usually this was not one of the harder exams. There was a little written portion and then the one on one session with the professor, so that she could grade your pronunciation. Four students had already exited the classroom and walked away briskly. No one showed any great concern for their performance, just relief to have finished that part of the trimester.

Suddenly, Howard had a thought. If he hurried, he could run to the front gate where the flower lady had plastic tubs of fresh flowers cut and ready to sell. He could pick up Donna a fresh rose and return in less than five minutes. Moved with inspiration, he jogged up the two levels of steps and sprinted past the administration building to the gate. He nodded to the guard and quickly passed through the opening to where the little woman sat on her green wooden stool.

"*Una rosa, por favor,*" he announced and produced his *Colones.*

The woman looked over her tub and selected a deep red bud in full bloom. For a man to buy a flower in a hurry meant something special was about to happen or he was already in trouble. Either way, he needed her best and he received it.

Howard thanked her and dashed back to the front gate where the guard had been watching and was ready to let him in. The guard was often humored by how the students made such a fuss over having fresh flowers. Howard trotted back to the stairway trying not to disturb the petals. As he reached the top and began to descend, he saw Donna. She was at the lower level stairway looking around for her husband. She thought he was going to wait for her. As she was about to take the stairs down towards the lower gate feeling the disappointment of having to walk home alone, she heard quickening steps behind her.

"*Señora,*" Howard called from behind, disguising his voice.

As she turned, her mouth dropped and then her lower lip began to quiver.

"*Ju look like ju could juse a rose,*" said Howard in his most romantic Latin accent. "*In fact, ju look like a rose, absolutely beautiful!*"

"You have no idea how much I needed that," Donna cried.

Howard joined her on the steps, presented the rose and kissed her sweetly on the cheek. His lips tasted her salty tear. He gently wiped it away and kissed her again.

"None of that, you two!" came a familiar voice above them.

Howard turned and waved at his former grammar professor who had just finished an exam for a group of first trimester students.

"We're entitled, we are finished and about to go on vacation," Howard announced proudly.

"Enjoy yourselves, and be careful," he called back, waving.

"We will," Donna said softly looking to her husband. "We will."

Together they turned and walked hand in hand towards the lower gate. Donna already felt a hundred miles away.

Arnie Johnson's goal for the second day was to get the cables hung that would support the wooden slats that would serve as the footbridge itself. The arching cables that had been stretched from platform to platform and anchored on each shore side would be joined to these support lines with heavy rope. The suspension bridge should be strong enough to hold several crossing at the same time. They would be using Beto and his canoe most of the day. Allen didn't want anyone venturing into the water with the current having been increased by the rains. Beto worked hard to transfer men and materials across the swollen river. Once two teams were set in place on each platform, they began pulling the cable through the drilled holes prepared in the platform. Arnie brought cable tighteners to pull the lines taut on each side.

The men worked through the morning to their break tightening the first of the cables. Peter, Matt and Alex worked on the *Pozo Negro* side. Both Billys worked in the canoe feeding the cable across. Arnie directed Stan, Winston and Willis in tightening their side. Ty experimented with the small welding machine that Allen had borrowed from a member of José's church. If they could weld the cable supports on opposite sides of the platforms, they would hold longer. Rhonda kept the men watered and took pictures. Her opportunity would come the next day when they started securing the wooden slats.

From a distance, Roberto watched. He considered going down to offer his assistance. After all, he did help build the platforms. The bridge was for his village. Surely he would be welcomed. But what if Don Tulio returned? Would he try to make him leave the village for helping the North Americans? These men had no idea what power Don Tulio had over the people. Roberto wondered if Don Tulio would have power over them. That was what he wanted to know. That was what he wanted to see. And he could see just fine from where he stood.

Terry stood nervously before the large counter that separated the students from the Director's office. The secretary took his note without reading it and carried it behind the closed door of the Director. He, too, was counting the hours to freedom. He wasn't about to begrudge this young boy a five hour head start. The secretary returned smiling and nodded. She was about to offer him his note from his parents, but he was already out the office door, skipping through the small courtyard to the front gate. He figured he could make it home in about fifteen minutes if he hurried and walked real fast. Until today, he had never had the motivation to try.

Howard and Donna were still holding hands as they reached the top of the park at *El Bosque*. Just a brisk downhill walk to the bottom and then four more streets to go. Their pace was relaxed. Their minds were clear for the first time in weeks. This vacation was so needed, Howard thought. Donna glanced at her wrist watch noting the time.

"You know, Terry should be on his way from the school about this time. He comes down the other side of the park. Why don't we go over and wait for him and all walk home together?"

"That will be fine with me," answered Howard casually. "There are some benches we can wait at. I'm sure we'll see him coming."

Now was the time for spontaneity - no worksheets to fill in, no vocabulary to be memorizing, no grammar rules to be practicing, nor assignment to carry out into the community. They were just another couple in the park. It seemed like a lifetime since they had just walked together down the streets of Coronado and watched the sunset over the Pacific. God had surely brought them a long way – together. Donna sighed. She hoped there would be more moments like these. She squeezed Howard's hand and he squeezed her's back.

SCREEEECH...THUD

"Oh my gosh, that sounded like a car hitting something," said Donna alarmed.

"It sounds like it was just around the corner," Howard added, letting go of her hand and hastening his pace to reach the end of the sidewalk. Donna hurried behind him. By the time they rounded the end of the building on the corner a small crowd had indeed gathered. Howard could see the rear of a small pickup angled diagonally in the road nearly taking up both of the narrow lanes of the side street. The crowd was encircled at the front right bumper. The driver was gone. Howard could hear shouts of angered voices. Then he heard the word, *"gringo"*.

First he thought there had been an accident where a North American had been driving and then fled the scene. He was still walking towards the group when he heard the word, *"niño"*. Surely the truck wasn't being driven by a boy, he thought. As he reached the edge of the crowd he could see the twisted legs and jeans of a young child. It must have been a boy that was hit. Then a wave of nausea swept over him – "a *gringo boy!*" Howard Pennington stopped moving. The upper torso and face was still hidden by the crowd. He had to look, but inwardly he couldn't.

"What happened?" Donna called from about six feet behind him.

"Stay there!" Howard shouted. Now he had to take the next step.

"Esta vivo!" shouted one of the women just in front of Howard. Whoever it was, they were still alive.

"Call for an ambulance," yelled a man.

Howard pushed his way around the angled bumper and looked down at his son.

"Oh God, no!" he cried.

Donna ran to join him. Seeing her son on the pavement, she grabbed her husband and began to weep.

"He's alive," Howard quickly informed her.

The crowd made room for the parents to kneel beside their young son. He was unconscious, but breathing. Howard knew not to move him. He checked for bleeding. Aside from the cut on his face from hitting the ground, there appeared to be no sign of injury.

"You are the father?" a woman asked in Spanish.

"*Si*," Howard acknowledged.

Donna was now weeping openly, stroking her son's hair.

Another man stepped forward to address Howard.

"Do you speak Spanish?" he asked.

Howard nodded.

The man began to explain slowly. He had been across the street and had seen the accident.

"Your son was coming down the street on that side," he said, indicating the direction with his head. "The truck was coming up the hill from the park and going fast. The boy tried to run across the street but didn't see the truck. The truck tried to stop. It slid from back there, but couldn't stop. The boy was knocked down by the front side of the truck, not the bumper. If he had been hit by the front, I am afraid it would have killed him. The driver ran away. But we can find out who it was. Right now you need to get your son to *Hospital Escuela*. I have a car we can take him in."

"What about the ambulance?" asked Howard.

"It will take them time to come and then to get back. I am a taxi driver and can get you there now."

"What about my wife?"

"She can ride in the back with him. You ride up front with me," he said firmly.

Howard had to decide on moving his son or waiting for an ambulance that may take more than thirty minutes to arrive and get his son to the hospital. He knew in America what he should do, but he wasn't in America. He was kneeling in the middle of the road with his injured son who needed to get to the hospital as quickly as he could.

"Do you think we can lift him without moving him much?"

"Yes," replied the taxi driver, who quickly motioned to three other men around them.

Immediately they gathered around Terry and gently lifted him, supporting him on all sides. Howard and Donna made their way to the taxi where Donna slid across the backseat to receive her son. They gently placed him on the seat. Donna resisted the temptation to place his head in her lap. Through a steady flow of tears, she gently rubbed his back. Howard jumped into the front seat as the taxi driver made a U-turn in the street in front of the truck. The driver called out to one of the men that had carried Terry to the car to wait for the police and give a full report, and to tell them that the child had been carried to the *Hospital Escuela*. Howard began praying silently, his hands trembling.

"Dear God, please spare Terry. Please God, help us get to the hospital and help me know what to do when we get there. Oh God, I am so afraid."

Lunch time seemed to come early for the team of workers. Becky and Rhonda had made sandwiches the night before at the West's home. It wasn't easy being the only girl on a twelve "man" team, but Rhonda had been able to keep up with the best of the men. Right or wrong, it just seemed natural to add "kitchen patrol" to her responsibilities. It did have its advantages. Willis would have his ham sandwich without mustard and Rhonda would see that he got the right one. The college boys waved from across the river.

"Time for lunch?" called out Little Billy, with obvious longing in his voice.

"Come on over," Allen yelled back to the crew on the *Pozo Negro* side.

"Let's go, before they get all the sandwiches," said Matt anxiously to his fellow-workers, who were already setting their tools aside and making their way to Beto's canoe.

It took almost ten minutes to get them across. The current was stronger than usual.

"What's left?" Matt called out, running up the bank.

"There's plenty of ham and cheese, bologna and cheese, and just cheese if that's what you prefer," responded Becky.

Alex helped Beto tie up the canoe.

Arnie Johnson tarried, checking the cables from the platform. Ty's welding was clean and professional, he thought.

"You ready to eat?" Alex called out to his father.

"Be right there," he called back. "Don't let all the ham and cheese get taken."

"I'll pull you a couple," Alex reassured him.

"I forgot the cooler of ice," Becky suddenly remembered. "I'll need a couple strong men to help me get it."

Billy Eldridge and Ty stepped forward. Following Becky, they passed through the dark tree line towards the road where the Land Cruiser was carefully parked off the main road. Neither one took note of the little man with the stick that passed them at the edge of the tree line.

The rest of the team gathered in the shade of the mango grove. Rhonda and Willis decided to take a short walk along the river during the lunch break and find a secluded spot. Many found seats among fallen logs. Some stood. Most were focused on their sandwiches, chips and were waiting for their bottled drinks. They divided into small groups comparing notes on their part of the work. The little man with the big stick wasn't even noticed till he had quickened his pace down the bank from the mango grove walking deliberately towards the river. Arnie was now on his knees inspecting the connections beneath the platform.

"Where do you suppose he's going in such a hurry," Stan mentioned to Allen, motioning to the small figure accelerating his stride toward the platform.

Allen turned to look and felt a sudden knot in his stomach. It was Don Tulio.

"That's the witch doctor," he said, with great concern in his voice. "He's headed toward Arnie – we better get down there."

Alex saw the little man coming towards him down the bank. He was about to wave to him when suddenly Don Tulio's eyes flared. With a single swoop of his staff, he knocked young Alex aside and continued his pace to the platform. Alex picked himself up stunned by the sudden attack and turned around to see the little man heading straight for his father, the large stick now brandished in both hands above his head.

"DAD!" Alex called out just as Don Tulio's feet reached the platform.

Arnie Johnson turned his head toward his son's voice only to see the figure of a man standing over him with something in his hands posed to strike. Arnie suddenly filled his lungs in preparation for the blow that would come across his back. He prayed his strong frame would protect him.

WOOOSH...THUD!

"DAD!!!" Alex called again, this time directing his shout toward the little man. He broke into a run towards them before his father could be struck again. Allen, Stan and Peter began rushing in the direction of the platform as well, but they were about twenty yards behind Alex. The others were too involved in their sandwiches to notice all the commotion. By the time Alex reached the platform, Don Tulio had raised the staff for a second blow. He was too focused on the big man below him to notice the young man running up behind him. Alex grabbed the stick while it was in the air and tried to jerk it out of the witch doctor's hands. Don Tulio pivoted around to face the young man that was interfering with his efforts to stop the building. Alex looked into his face and saw the contorted countenance of evil staring back. Alex was amazed at the strength the little man possessed as he held firmly to the base of his staff. With a sudden thrust, Don Tulio successfully broke Alex's grip. He lifted the rod high to bring it crashing down upon the boy's skull, when Alex charged him. The self-defensive move was not intended to injure the little man, but adrenalin drove Alex into Don Tulio's mid-section with enough force to carry them both to the unfinished edge of the platform and over the side into the raging river below.

"Alex!!" his father yelled, but the current had already pulled them both under.

"How much farther?" Howard asked the taxi driver desperately.

"We are close," he replied in a calming voice. "I will see we get there in time."

In the back seat, Donna had stopped crying and just watched Terry's little body breath. She told herself, as long as she could see his chest moving, he had a chance. She was also praying to herself.

"God, please don't take Terry. Not here. Not now. Please let him get better. Please let him see his home again – his sister, his grandparents…Please don't take him here."

The taxi driver was accustomed to taking unorthodox maneuvers as he darted through the side streets. He knew the closest route and was barely regarded by other motorists who were accustomed to taxis ruling the roads. He pulled into the hospital entrance and headed straight to the emergency area. Rolling to a stop, he quickly jumped out and ran inside to find someone who could bring a gurney or stretcher to the car. He knew the boy couldn't be placed in a wheelchair. He left Howard in the front seat wondering what he should be doing. He didn't want to leave Donna and Terry, but at the same time, he wasn't sure how long the driver would be gone. He fumbled with his door and stepped out on the sidewalk watching the emergency door expectantly. Seconds felt like minutes.

"Howard, where is the taxi driver?" Donna asked anxiously.

"He's gone inside to get help – he'll be back soon," Howard offered, trying to convince himself as well.

"You've got to do something!" she cried. "We can't just sit here. Terry needs help, NOW!"

"I know, sweetheart, I know," Howard replied, starting to pace by her door.

Howard was feeling helpless and vulnerable. He kept looking back at the entrance praying that the doors would burst open with doctors and white smocked orderlies rushing to their assistance. Eight long minutes later the doors opened. The taxi driver held one of the doors for two street clothed men as they passed through carrying a cloth stretcher between them.

"Over here," Howard shouted, hoping the men would break into a run towards the taxi. They acknowledged his wave and quickened their step. The taxi driver rushed past them and joined Howard at the door where Donna was gently rocking her son.

"They will take him in," the driver explained slowly. "I found a doctor and he is getting a room set up to examine him. He won't have to wait long. They know what happened."

"Thank you…Thank you," said Howard.

The men stepped up. Howard and the taxi driver quickly moved aside. Donna helped to pass the injured body of her son into the hands of the strangers. They carefully placed him on the stretcher and lifted him. Terry moaned. That was the first hint of consciousness he had made.

"Momma's right here," Donna quickly responded, standing over him.

But Terry didn't speak.

The hospital workers led out. Donna walked beside the stretcher. Howard and the taxi driver followed closely behind.

"Alex!" Arnie yelled again rising from his knees. Allen reached the edge of the platform.

"Arnie, wait!" Allen shouted, anticipating Arnie's next move. "You can't fight that current. Alex is young and strong. He will surface in just a moment."

The two men watched anxiously from the platform.

Stan and Peter joined them, huffing.

"Shouldn't we try to follow them along the shore?" Peter asked.

"That would be best," replied Allen quickly. "Let's go."

The four men jumped from the side of the bridge and began running along the river edge. Rusty, Little Billy and Matt noticed the men running along the bank and decided to follow. They weren't sure what had just happened, but they knew it was important.

Unaware, Winston had walked towards the treeline to wait for Billy and Ty to bring the ice and drinks. He had no idea what was taking place along the river.

About ten yards from the bridge, a head surfaced.

"There," pointed Allen, as the four continued to navigate along the bank, dodging small stumps and rocks. "I see one of them."

Suddenly, a splash was heard on the far side of the river. Their heads turned, but no one could make out the figure fighting the current to reach the two struggling in the water.

"I see Alex!" Arnie yelled. The red hair bobbed up just a little downstream from the first appearance. The two had surfaced, but Alex was drifting deeper towards the middle of the river. They were about to disappear around the bend as the four ran desperately to catch up with them.

"If they get too far around the bend the current will pick up," Allen shouted. "The river will start a down hill run."

———————————

Adam Baxter cleared the dishes from Gertie's tray that had been left since lunch. He paused before leaving the room with them and turned. Gertie was deep in prayer. He could hear her whisper.

"Lord, may Your cloud protect the team. May Your glory be seen in them today. Overshadow them with Your presence. May the enemy be overtaken like a flood. I lift this team before you, Oh God. Be with Billy and those that have traveled with him. Show Yourself mighty on their behalf, I pray."

"Yes, Lord," Adam whispered as he turned back toward the door.

———————————

As the four men reached the bend in the river, Arnie feared the worse. He could only imagine seeing the body of his son being pulled farther from them and their efforts to rescue. He wasn't even thinking about the little man that had attacked him. But he couldn't lose his son. To their surprise, Willis and Rhonda could be seen dragging a form from the river. In their effort to find a quiet place to eat, they had traveled around the bend and were in a perfect position to assist the drowning men. Rhonda had held Willis by the belt as he waded out to catch the arm of one of the passing men. Together they pulled him to shore. As the four reached them, Arnie's heart sunk. It was the little man.

"Did you see Alex?" he yelled to Willis. "Where's Alex?"

"He was further towards the middle, I couldn't reach him," replied Willis, focused on the little man. Then, pointing over his shoulder down river, he said, "But I think he was able to reach him."

"Who?" asked Stan.

The four looked up and saw the struggle of two more bodies in the river. About twelve more yards down river, a young man was grasping at the shore with his arm around Alex's chest. Peter took off running to help him. Arnie fell in close pursuit.

Allen and Stan paused with the Beamans to see how Don Tulio was doing. Rhonda was feeling his neck for a pulse.

"Is he breathing?" Allen asked first.

"I don't think so," Rhonda replied. She rolled him the rest of the way onto his back and called her husband to help.

"Willis, I'm going to give him two breaths and then start chest compressions. When I have reached five, I want you to give him another deep breath. Pinch his nose and breathe into his mouth. Make sure his head stays tilted back so that we can see if his chest begins to rise."

Willis kneeled across from her at Don Tulio's head and watched carefully. Rhonda gently tilted his head back and gave two steady breaths into his mouth. Then, moving her hands down to his chest, she began CPR. His small frame was easy to work with. Marking the distance from his sternum with two fingers, she overlapped her hands and began compressing his chest with the bottom of her palm, pumping blood into his heart.

"One one-thousand, two one-thousand, three one-thousand, four one-thousand, five one-thousand," she called out loud. As she reached her fifth compression, she looked up to her husband. "Now, give him one breath!"

Willis complied, pinching the nose of the little man and breathing into his mouth. Rhonda resumed her compressions and counting.

"I can help," Stan offered. "I instructed CPR while in the Navy."

"Great," replied Rhonda. "When I say switch, you can take over the compressions."

Down river, Arnie grabbed Peter's shirt as he stepped off of the bank to help the young rescuer. Neither men knew Roberto Espinal, but that didn't matter. He was holding Alex with all of his might. Together, they pulled the two young men up on the bank.

"Rhonda! We need you!" Arnie called from down river. "Hurry! Alex is not breathing."

Rhonda looked up at Stan.

"I can do this – you go help Alex," he said reassuringly.

"Ok," she said completing her fourth set of compressions. "Switch!"

Willis continued to breathe between compressions. Rhonda and Allen ran toward the others as quickly as they could.

Alex Johnson lay on his back, motionless. His face was pale and his lips were blue. Rhonda checked first for a pulse. Arnie could feel the tears forming. There was no time for that, he thought to himself. He had to be strong to be able to help.

"I don't feel a pulse, we'll need to do CPR. Who can help me with the breathing?" she asked as calmly as she could.

"I will," Peter replied, kneeling next to Alex's head.

Roberto looked on, not understanding either the language or the activity. He had seen men drown before. This is what they looked like.

Rhonda repeated the process of clearing the mouth, tilting the head and giving two strong breaths into Alex's mouth while holding his nose close. She moved her hands to his chest, found the position, and began her compressions while counting aloud. After the fifth compression, she called to Peter, "breathe once!"

Together they began to labor on young Alex. Allen put his arm around Arnie's shoulders for encouragement and strength.

Stan had completed five cycles with Willis when suddenly Don Tulio coughed violently. Willis expected to see water pour from his mouth like it did in the movies. He was surprised to see just a small amount of water trickle, out followed by some serious gagging. Willis pulled back from breathing and gave the little man room to vomit to one side.

"He's going to be ok," Stan commented. "Vomiting is normal for those who have ingested water. The trauma of the CPR is bringing it up. He'll be ok. I'm going to see if I can be of any help with Alex."

With that, Stan left Willis with Don Tulio, who was now coughing and trying to catch his breath. Willis was trying not to gag himself. He wiped the little man's face with his shirt-tale and told him to relax. Don Tulio didn't understand his words, but knew this man was trying to help.

Little Billy, Matt and Rusty came up on Willis and the little man.

"What happened?" asked Rusty. "We heard the commotion and saw Allen, Stan and Peter take off running. We thought they were headed for the bridge, but then we saw them and Stan heading in this direction."

"I'm not sure what happened," Willis said honestly. "All I know is that we heard yelling and when we looked up, we saw two men in the river. Rhonda and I could reach this one, but we missed Alex. Then we saw someone else in the river swimming toward Alex. About that time, the missionary, Arnie, Stan and Peter came running. The missionary and Stan stayed with Rhonda and I, then Rhonda had to go down there. Stan stayed with me till this guy came around."

"Is he going to be ok?" Rusty asked.

"I guess so. Stan went down to help with Alex."

"ALEX!" said Matt surprised. "Alex was the other one in the river?"

"I guess so," replied Willis. "That's what the guys were saying when they ran up."

"Then who is this guy?" asked little Billy. "And why was he and Alex in the river?"

"I don't know, but I'm guessing he may be our witch doctor, and he and Alex got into it and they both fell in the river."

"And he's ok?" Rusty asked again.

"Yeah, they're all down there working on Alex now," Willis added.

"Let's go!" said Little Billy excitedly.

"I'm with you," agreed Matt, and the two took off running.

"I'll stay here with you while this one comes around. There are more than enough helping down there," said Rusty calmly.

"Give them room," Arnie yelled. It had been over twenty-five cycles of compressions and his anxiety level was climbing.

Stan had stepped in for Peter and now he and Rhonda were switching every ten cycles. Matt ran up to the group and peered over the shoulder of the missionary.

"Is he ok?" the college student asked.

"Not yet," Allen said softly, so as not to agitate Arnie. "He still isn't breathing."

"How long can he go like that?" Matt asked.

No one tried to answer.

"How is the other man?" Allen asked.

"He's stirring. Taking his time getting up, I suppose," offered Matt.

"Then he's alive?" said Arnie, with a tone of disappointment.

"Arnie!" snapped Rhonda.

The rebuke was sufficient. Allen pulled Arnie to one side.

"Do you want to help save your son?"

"You know I do," said Arnie with a broken voice.

"Then help me get these other men together for prayer. Our watching Stan and Rhonda isn't helping, but prayer can."

Arnie nodded reluctantly. He didn't want to leave his son's side, even if he couldn't help those trying to restore his life. The missionary was right. They could and should pray.

Howard paced as Donna sat on the hard wooden bench just outside the examination room. He didn't want to leave his son's side, but they had asked them both to wait patiently outside.

"We need to call Juanita," said Donna, after several moments of contemplative silence.

The thought had not even occurred to Howard, but she was right. Juanita was expecting them before eleven o'clock for lunch, before they were to leave on their trip. It was well after one o'clock now.

"You're right, I need to call," Howard replied. "Will you be ok here while I try to find a phone."

Donna nodded. He reached out and squeezed her hand. It was hard to be reassuring when he was just as afraid. Howard looked around to get his bearings and then made his way to the front reception area.

The desk clerk was extremely helpful. She offered the phone lifting it up onto the counter for Howard to reach. He paused for a moment to remember his phone number and then began to dial.

"*A-lo*," came the voice on the other end.

Howard began to explain to Juanita that there had been an accident and that they had brought Terry to *Hospital Escuela*. It suddenly occurred to Howard he lacked the vocabulary to explain the seriousness of the accident to her without confusing her. He held his hand over the receiver and turned to the desk nurse.

"Could you explain our son's condition to our maid?" he asked.

She nodded and took the phone.

Howard listened as the young woman spoke professionally and yet with the tone of true compassion in her voice. He recognized some of the words, but she spoke too rapidly for him to catch the full explanation. She obviously knew the condition of his son well enough to provide sufficient information for Juanita. The nurse paused, commented and answered Juanita's obvious question. After a couple minutes, she handed the phone back to Howard.

"*Gracias*," he directed toward the nurse who responded with a smile. Turning his direction to the phone, Howard continued, "I am sure I will need to pick up some things for Terry. I don't know when that will be yet."

Juanita assured him that she would be available to help in any way. She added that she would be praying for little Terry. Howard thanked her, said good-bye and passed the phone back to the nurse.

He walked slowly back to the corridor to wait with Donna. When he found the room, she was gone.

CHAPTER NINETEEN

"THE LION"

"WHERE IS everybody?" Billy Eldridge asked Winston who had met them in the mango grove to help with the cooler of ice.

Winston turned around to see the clearing empty.

"I don't know, some had walked off, but many were over there where the food was unpacked."

"We better go see," said Ty concerned.

Becky eased by the three men and walked quickly to the place where she had set up the food containers. No one was with the food. No one was at the platform. No one was in sight. Suddenly Beto appeared from the rocks up river where he had carried his sandwich.

"*Que pasó?*" asked Becky, inquiring what had happened.

Beto explained that he had seen three of the men run from where the food was down river, but he didn't know where the others had gone.

"Down river?" Becky confirmed.

He nodded and then pointed. Becky turned to Billy and the other two.

"Something has happened! Everyone seems to have gone down river in a haste. That can only mean that someone was in the river."

"Maybe there was an accident on the platform," Ty suggested. "Maybe one of my welding joints gave way. I'm going to go check."

Ty immediately left the group and trotted down to the platform.

"Should we try to find them?" Winston asked Billy.

"Why don't you and Becky stay here with the food, in case some just wandered into the tree area. If they come back, you can tell them where the rest of the group has gone."

"OK," agreed Winston.

Billy took long strides as he made his way down the bank to follow the river's edge. Ty reached the platform and began checking his welding connections. Everything seemed to be intact. As he started for the edge of the platform he nearly tripped and fell. Catching himself, he looked down and picked up the object that had been carelessly dropped on the wooden platform. It was a long stick.

"How long has it been?" Little Billy called out.

"About twenty-five minutes," Peter whispered, standing next to him.

"How long can he go?"

"I'm not sure," Peter admitted.

"Switch!" yelled Rhonda.

With military precision, Stan moved to Alex's chest while Rhonda took her position at his head. Stan called out the compressions. The two worked well together, but they were getting tired.

Arnie looked on in anguish. With each failed cycle his hope lessened.

Allen continued to pray under his breath pleading with God for intervention. Matt stood next to him with his head bowed – as much in prayer as in his inability to watch his friend die.

Roberto stood respectfully at a distance. He had never witnessed such an effort to revive a drowned man. His mind raced to that night when his friend Daniel had been swept into the river. The night the bridge fell. He blinked his eyes. He could almost see Daniel's face on the young man lying on the ground before him. Could he have helped Daniel that night? Roberto felt a lump rise in his throat.

The five watched helplessly as Rhonda and Stan continued to work over Alex. The minutes seemed like hours. Rhonda knew that less than 5% of drowning victims responded positively to CPR if medical attention was unavailable, but she didn't say a word. As a nurse, she would work until exhaustion should overcome her. Stan was not as young. He would tire sooner.

"We'll cross that bridge when we come to it," she thought in her heart, ironically.

"How is he doing?" came a voice from behind the group.

Allen turned to see three men approaching - Rusty, Willis and Don Tulio.

Arnie slowly turned. His large frame bristled. His eyes met those of the little man. He could feel his cheeks redden and his chest tighten.

Howard tapped on the door of the examination room. A nurse opened the door. The room behind her was empty. A wave of panic passed over him. He reached out to steady himself in the doorframe.

"*El niño?*" was all he could muster.

The nurse pointed down the hall towards the end of the corridor.

"*A la derecha, cuarto uno, cero, siete,*" she said slowly.

Howard quickly turned and headed to the end of the corridor where he turned right and began looking for room 107. He passed several people in the hall, some waiting in wheelchairs, some laying on gurneys. Family members gathered around doorways, some crying and some talking. It was hot without air conditioning and the smell of medications and human odors was almost more than Howard could stomach. How could his son receive the treatment he needed in this place. He found the room and the door ajar. Knocking and entering at the same time, he saw Donna bent over a single bed against the wall.

"Donna!" Howard called out.

Turning, he could see the tears on her cheeks again.

"Is he . . ?"

"He's stable," Donna finished his difficult question. Then motioning to the doctor standing at the foot of the bed, she introduced the physician that had been working with Terry.

"This is Dr. Peniel. He speaks English."

Howard turned his full attention to the Doctor and braced himself.

"Your son has suffered some internal trauma. I have examined his skull and found no evidence of concussion or damage that would hinder him from regaining consciousness. In fact, he called for his mother while being examined."

Howard relaxed his stance and took Donna's hand in his.

"Right now he is sedated to avoid much movement," Dr. Peniel continued. "The X-rays showed at least one broken rib and a fracture to his right arm. These in themselves are not serious, but I felt firmness in the abdomen which suggests some internal bleeding."

"Will you need to examine him more? Will you need to operate?" Howard asked pointedly.

"Most likely," replied Dr. Peniel. "I need to see if that rib has punctured something. I'm confident the major organs are intact, but we need to find the source of that bleeding and soon."

"How soon can you begin?" asked Howard.

"That is the problem," Dr. Peniel said firmly. He paused and removed his glasses. "When we operate, we are going to need to give him blood. Your wife has just informed me that your son is *A negative.*"

"So use one of us for the transfusion. One of us should be a match."

"No, Howard," Donna interrupted. "I'm *A positive* and you are *B positive.* I have our blood types in my purse."

"How could Terry be *A negative* then?" Howard asked, confused.

"*A negative* is the rarest of blood types and it IS genetic, but it also can skip a generation," the doctor explained. "One of your parents must have had *A negative* blood."

"Howard's father did," answered Donna. "I remember him telling us how he almost died in a M.A.S.H. unit in Korea before they found a soldier with his blood type. They became life-long friends – remember Howard?"

Howard nodded, but found it difficult to make the comparison between that story and his son. His father had been in war.

"What about the blood supply here at the hospital," Howard asked half-heartedly. He suspected the answer.

"We do well to keep small amounts of common blood types," the Dr. replied. "We require the patients or their family to provide donors to replenish any used blood. In your case, you would have to find an *A negative* or *O negative* donor."

"*O negative?*" asked Howard.

"Just as type O is universal for most blood types, *O negative* can be used to substitute for A negative. But it is just as hard to find," explained Dr. Peniel.

"But either way, WE have to find the donor?" stated Howard, trying to clarify what he had heard.

"Yes, I'm afraid so."

"What do we do?" asked Donna, turning to Howard.

"How much time do we have?" Howard asked the doctor.

"I believe he will be stable tonight. If complications set in, they will set in quickly. I would suggest one of you stay with him at all times."

"I will stay," Donna announced. "Howard, you must go home and get our numbers for the other missionaries and begin making calls. We can only pray that someone in our mission or at the school has *A negative* blood."

"The school is closing down today," Howard remembered. "I need to hurry and try to catch our friends before they head out for their vacations."

"The phone directory is in my blue folder that I keep on our chest of drawers," instructed Donna. "Please hurry, Howard!"

Howard looked into the desperate eyes of his wife and swallowed hard. He leaned over to kiss her and then bent down to kiss the forehead of his resting son.

"Dear God," he said aloud. "Please spare my son!"

"You!" Arnie yelled into the direction of the startled little man. "What have you done? Who are you?"

Immediately, Rusty and Allen positioned themselves between Arnie and Don Tulio. They knew that Arnie's size and state of mind would make it impossible to keep him off of the little man, if that was his objective. They hoped that the barrier of their bodies would give Arnie enough pause to consider what he was doing. Matt and Little Billy saw the danger of the confrontation and tried to grab at Arnie's arms.

"Mr. Johnson, wait!" they said together.

Don Tulio's eyes grew wide at the thought of defending himself against the large man without his staff. The six figures froze in position for a moment.

"This is the witch doctor, Don Tulio, that I told you about," Allen tried to explain calmly. "He was attacking you – not your son! Alex, in his effort to rescue you, caused them to fall into the river. Please, Arnie, turn your attention to Alex, not this man. Alex needs you. Speak to him!"

Arnie relaxed his stance. The young men let go of his arms. He turned back toward the team performing CPR. Arnie walked over and knelt at the top of Alex's head so as not to get in the way of Stan who was currently giving the alternating breaths.

"Oh, God, please spare my son!" he cried.

"Switch!" Rhonda called out.

She moved up to the head and Stan took a deep breath and began compressions. He was losing his momentum. Rhonda could tell he was tiring.

"How long can he go?" Arnie asked Rhonda quietly, fearing to hear the answer.

"I have heard of some responding after thirty minutes," she offered positively.

"But not many?" Arnie questioned, his tone demanding realistic expectations.

She looked up into a father's eyes and couldn't answer. She looked back down at Alex in preparation for his next breath. Arnie thought he detected a small shaking of her head, intended for him alone.

Arnie watched Stan labor over the compressions. He thought that if he could watch carefully enough he could learn and take over. But he couldn't stand the thought of being the one who couldn't revive his own son. The others watched both Arnie and the team. Someone was going to have to make a decision.

Roberto stared at Don Tulio. This man was the blame. He was there when his friend Daniel died. He was the one that resisted the rebuilding of the bridge that caused so many others to die. Now he was responsible for this young American to drown. Maybe, finally, someone will do something about him. This was what Roberto had waited for.

"Switch!" called out Stan.

"Wait!" said Arnie.

Rhonda placed her hand on his shoulder.

"We can try a little bit longer," she said sympathetically.

"You've done all you can," replied Arnie, with resignation in his voice.

The group watched motionless. The clouds darkened overhead. Without warning, a rush of wind swept across the team. It was more than the climate that was changing around them.

Allen West turned around to see how Don Tulio was responding to the changing setting. A cryptic smile was forming on the thin lips of the little man. Allen knew what he was thinking. This was a battle of principalities and powers, and this witch doctor was feeling victorious.

"Greater is He that is in you, than he that is in the world."

Allen recognized that voice. It was the same voice that had called him to build this bridge.

"For the weapons of our warfare are not carnal, but mighty through God to the pulling down of strong holds; Casting down imaginations, and every high thing that exalteth itself against the knowledge of God, and bringing into captivity every thought to the obedience of Christ."

"The weapons of our warfare," Allen said aloud.

"What?" asked Rusty, standing closest to him.

"Eutychus!" stated the voice. Allen understood.

"Listen, everyone," Allen stated authoritatively. "Join hands and make a circle around Alex."

No one questioned the missionary. Arnie looked into Allen's eyes for understanding.

"Trust God! Your son's life is still in him," Allen said firmly.

Arnie stood and reached out his hands. Rhonda stood on his left. Matt took his right hand. The others quickly took a place encircling the body and joining hands. Allen wasn't sure what he was about to do. He was sure of only one thing. God was not through on that river bank.

Allen slowly walked to the circle and stepped between Stan and Little Billy and knelt beside Alex. He took a deep breath and looked around at the faces of those wondering what was going on. His eyes fixed on Peter.

"Peter, I want you to translate for me," Allen stated. "We're going to pray."

Peter nodded, expecting to speak in Spanish for Don Tulio and Roberto, who both stood mesmerized by the spectacle of this group surrounding the young dead man.

Allen took hold of Alex's hand.

"Bendito Padre celestial, El que da vida a todos..." began Allen.

Peter's eyes opened in surprise. He was to translate for the group.

"Blessed Heavenly Father, who gives life to all..."

"Quien nos da la respira de vida…"
"Who gives us the breath of life…"
"Quien ha vencido la muerte…"
"Who has conquered death…"
"Pedimos tu miserdicordia sobre éste joven…"
"We pray your mercy over this young man…"
"Que tu mano sea sobre él…"
"That your hand may be upon him…"
"Restaure la vida a Alex, pedimos…"
"Restore life to Alex, we pray…"
"Muestra tu Gloria, Señor. La Gloria que resusitó tu propio hijo…"
"Show your glory, Lord. The glory that raised your own son from the dead…"
"Levante a Alex, Señor. En el nombre poderoso del Señor Jesucristo – Amen!"
"Raise Alex, Oh Lord. In the mighty name of the Lord Jesus Christ, Amen!"

Silence overcame the circle. Heads bowed. Arnie held his breath. Once again, a sudden rush of wind swept across the team. No one moved.

"Look at his lips!" yelled Little Billy.

Rhonda released Arnie's hand and reached for Alex's neck.

"I feel a pulse!" she cried. "It's getting stronger."

Arnie finally began to cry.

"Thank you, Lord! Thank you!" he wept.

The team began shouting and praising God. Allen kneeled in awe beside Alex, waiting for him to open his eyes. He had never experienced such a mighty manifestation of God's presence, and he knew this was greater than himself. The whole experience had been humbling to the missionary.

Peter walked over to Roberto and asked him if he understood what was happening. Roberto shook his head no. He had never heard of a man awakening after drowning and now he had seen it with his own eyes.

"What you have seen is the power of our God who raised his own son from the dead, and now has raised this young man," said Peter, seizing on the opportunity to witness. "In the same way, God offers you the power of his resurrection to give you new life in his son, Jesus Christ."

"The missionary was talking with me about this life before you came," Roberto confessed.

"What is your name?" Peter asked.

"My name is Roberto, and yours?"

"My name is *Pedro*, they call me Peter!"

"You are a disciple of Jesus?" Roberto asked, remembering the name from his conversation with the missionary.

"Yes," replied Peter. "I am a follower of Jesus Christ. He is my Savior and my Lord, and has been for many years."

"Why?" asked Roberto honestly.

"I have learned that God made me for a special purpose, but my decisions to live my life as I want, brought about sin and kept me from knowing both God and his purpose for my life. Jesus came to provide a way for me to be forgiven of my sin and to change my life so that I could know God and find his purpose."

"Is that why he died on the cross?" Roberto asked.

"You know about the cross?" Peter questioned.

"The missionary talked with me about the cross. He said it was like a bridge that made it possible for God to receive me. Is that right?"

"That is right, Roberto. Jesus died for your sin and for mine. He did it by taking your sin and mine upon himself. He lived a perfect life, but on the cross, he took all sin upon himself and died in our place. They buried him, but three days later, he rose from the grave showing his power over both sin and death."

"Like this young man today," Roberto interrupted.

"Not quite like this. God has given Alex back his life on earth for now, but someday he will die again and then will spend eternity with the Lord. When Jesus rose from the dead, it was to conquer death for all time. He still lives. And Roberto, you need to know…he is coming again to earth – soon!"

Roberto's eyes widened. He had never heard this before. He thought the stories of Jesus and Mary were simply to keep people obedient to the Church. He never thought of Christ as a real person who loved him, who died for him, and someday would come back to earth.

"You see, he came once like a lamb to take away the sin of the world, but he will return like a lion to rule and reign forever," Peter found himself explaining.

While the two continued to speak, Don Tulio listened and stared in complete bewilderment. He had no explanation for what he had just witnessed. He could not deny the response of the young man to the prayer. And he could not believe what he was hearing.

"León!" whispered Don Tulio to himself.

Allen asked Arnie to compose himself and to begin calling Alex by name. Arnie bent down beside his son and gently addressed him.

"Alex. Wake up…Alex, my son, I love you. Wake up."

Alex's chest began to rise and fall with deep breaths. After a couple more seconds, he slowly opened his eyes. He saw the glowing face of his father smiling above him.

"Dad," he said coarsely. "Are you OK?"

"I am now," Arnie said, beginning to cry again.

"What happened?" Alex asked.

"We'll tell you all about it later," his father laughed, between tears.

The group stepped back to give Alex room to stand up. Billy Eldridge had arrived just before the group had formed for prayer. He was relieved not to have to report another death from the field to his family. He paused and gave thanks to God personally and then thanked God again for the life of his brother that had been given on the field. God had been glorified in both life and death.

"Is everyone OK?"

The team turned to see Ty Wilson approaching the group.

"You missed it, Ty," shouted Matt. "It was awesome!"

"Amen!" resounded several of the team.

"Winston and Becky are still as the work site," he said nonchalantly. "They thought someone may have fell into the river."

"They did," responded Rusty. "Alex and this man here. There was a scuffle and they fell off the platform of the bridge."

"Oh, then this must belong to him," said Ty, holding up the staff he found on the platform.

The team froze as though Ty had just waved a gun before the group.

Don Tulio saw his staff and straightened up. He moved towards Ty and took it from his hand. He stood poised with his rod and slowly turned toward the group. Walking deliberately towards Allen, he grasped the rod in both hands and faced the missionary.

"*León!*" stated Don Tulio.

"What did he say?" Little Billy asked Peter.

"He said, 'León'. That's the town we are staying in. I don't know what he means."

"*León!*" repeated Don Tulio.

"I don't understand," said Allen humbly.

"*Jesús! El León!*" Don Tulio declared.

"Oh, my gosh!" said Peter in complete surprise.

"What?" replied Little Billy.

"Watch!" exclaimed Peter.

In a slow deliberate move, Don Tulio crouched to his knees, laid the rod at Allen's feet, bowed his head and repeated.

"Jesús! El León!"

"What is he saying?" questioned Little Billy again.

"He's saying, 'Jesus – The Lion!' 'León' means 'lion'. He is referring to Jesus as The Lion. He is giving up his rod to Jesus. This is incredible!"

"The Lion?" remarked Ty. "Do you think he is referring to the lion in my dream?"

Don Tulio rose and began to talk rapidly to Allen.

"What is he saying now?" Rhonda asked, as the others leaned in close to Peter. Peter translated as the little man spoke.

"He's saying that last night he had a dream. It frightened him, because he thought it was about his death. He dreamed a lion took his staff from him. He looked the lion in the eye and knew the lion was stronger than he was. While I was sharing with Roberto, he heard me refer to Jesus as the Lion who is coming again. If I'm not mistaken, I believe he is giving his life to Jesus."

Allen refrained from picking up the staff. He knew it was not being offered to him. He listened respectfully and waited for the opportunity to lead the witch doctor in a prayer of repentance and faith. As Don Tulio confessed his desire to know the Jesus that could raise a man from the dead, Roberto stepped up beside him.

"I, too, would like to know this Jesus," he said humbly.

Arnie and Alex sat together on the ground. The rest formed their circle around the missionary, Don Tulio and Roberto. As they bowed their heads, Allen led the two men in a simple prayer confessing their sin and their need for God to forgive them and to take full control of their lives. He led them in yielding their lives completely to the Lordship of Jesus Christ, the Lion of Judah.

"Amen!" agreed the group in unison.

CHAPTER TWENTY

"MAR'S HILL"

THE TAXI driver had left, but Howard was able to quickly hail another cab that carried him back to their house in *El Bosque.* He fumbled with his gate key while calling out to Juanita to open the front door. When she didn't answer, he became agitated.

"She better not be on the phone," he thought to himself.

He opened the screen and tried the front door. It was locked. He searched his key ring for the front door key with one hand while beating on the thin wooden door with his other.

"Why won't she open the door?" he said to himself.

"*Juanita*!" he called again. No response.

Howard finally opened his front door, bursting into the kitchen/ living room.

"*Juanita*!" he called out several times while moving from door to door. No answer.

She was not in the house. He glanced out the back door and quickly surveyed his small backyard. She was not hanging clothes either. She was gone. There was not even a note on the kitchen table.

Howard was near furious, but he couldn't allow her negligence to deter him from his mission. He rushed to their bedroom to search for the blue folder Donna had described. As he entered their bedroom, he was seized with shock. The drawers had been pulled wide open. Important papers were scattered across the bed, their passports had been tossed on the floor. Donna's second purse had been emptied, it's contents also scattered across the bed.

"Juanita has robbed us!" Howard fumed. Again he couldn't let his emotions pull him from the task at hand. He found the blue folder and carried it to the living room. He sat down near the phone trying to calm down. He needed to be able to talk rationally to people about one emergency without worrying about the other. How could this be happening now? How could Juanita take such advantage of them? This was indeed the last straw.

Howard began by dialing the language school coordinator for the mission. He waited through seven long rings. No answer. He waited through four more rings hoping at least the maid would answer. Nothing.

"Where was their maid?" He thought. "Probably stealing them blind as well," he remarked to himself.

Howard tried another number.

"*Halo!*" a voice replied. Howard asked for the husband or wife. Neither was there. The one who answered said they were out for the afternoon and evening. They were going for dinner in San José, and would not be back till late. Howard thanked her and hung up.

Two more "no answers".

"I thought everyone kept people watching their houses while they were gone," Howard mused to himself. Then he remembered that some hired watchmen to stay outside the house. They weren't needed inside as long as they could walk all the way around the house and check both front and back entrances.

Howard called the next family on the list – Bob and Linda Cartwright. Their son Eric was the one that had befriended Terry after the incident with the *Gameboy.*

"Hello!" came the man's voice on the line.

"Hello!" Howard almost shouted, relieved to hear another American voice. "This is Howard Pennington. Is this Bob?"

"Yes, Howard," came the cheerful reply. "How's it going?"

"Not too good, Bob," replied Howard. He suddenly realized he would have to relate the story. He needed to be brief, but at the same time give enough details to inform Bob of their need. "I don't know how best to say this. Terry has been in an accident and we have carried him to *Hospital Escuela.*"

"Oh, my goodness! Is he Ok?"

"He's stable, but he has suffered some internal injuries. We don't know how extensive yet. They need to operate and they say we need to provide the blood for the transfusions."

"Yes, I've heard that before," Bob acknowledged. "What can we do?"

"Bob, Terry is *A negative.* Neither Donna nor I can give blood to help. *A negative* is a rare blood type. I am calling on the chance that I may find someone from the institute with either *A* or *O negative* type blood. Either one will work."

"Sorry, Howard," replied Bob. "I know none of us are either. We're all either *A positive* and Linda is O. That won't help. But let me ask you – who all are you calling?"

"I have Donna's mission directory and I'm going down the list."

"Let me help you make calls," offered Bob. "I'll start at the 'N' and call to the end of the list. If I find someone, I'll call you."

"If my phone is busy, keep trying, I'll be calling the others on this line," pleaded Howard. "It won't hurt if we find more than one donor."

"That's right," Bob said optimistically for Howard's sake. Bob knew the chances of finding one would be slim. "I'll call as soon as I have something."

"Thanks, Bob," Howard said relieved.

The two hung up and both began dialing numbers as quickly as they could.

Donna sat silently in the room next to the hospital bed. Terry was still unconscious. She was amazed they had gotten a private room. She could still hear people outside the door. It was anything but quiet.

"Dear Lord," she whispered. "I don't know what to think. It seems like our worst fears are coming to pass. We have endured the loss of personal property, our money, even close friends since we have been here. I have lost a loved one that I couldn't tell good-bye. I have been frustrated in learning this language. It doesn't seem like I am ever going to get it. And now! Just when Terry was excited about doing something here, this happens. I'm scared God. I don't mind saying it. I'm scared of being here. I'm afraid for my son. I don't think I can do this. Please help us, God. Please help us."

The door opened and a nurse stepped in. She stepped around the bed without speaking. She checked one of the monitors, wrote down a quick note and headed back to the door.

"Has my husband returned?" Donna asked wistfully.

"I just arrived," the nurse replied curtly and turned to leave.

Donna looked at her watch. It was after three already. Howard had been gone for over two hours. She was beginning to feel very much alone.

Suddenly, the door opened again. The doctor stepped in, looking down at his clipboard.

"I have some news on your son's condition," he said slowly.

Donna braced herself for the worse.

Howard finished his part of the list with no success. Of the families that he was able to speak with, none had a member with type *A negative* blood. Howard placed his head in his hands and sighed. He walked to the kitchen to pour himself some water before calling Bob Cartwright.

"Please God, may Bob have found someone who can help us," he prayed.

Setting the glass on a table beside him, Howard slowly dialed the number for the Cartwrights.

The line was busy. He held the receiver for a several seconds before laying it back down.

"Lord, please give me some indication of Your presence in this. I am doing all I know to do and nothing is happening. Please show me Your way for Terry."

Howard noticed his Bible on the sofa still open from his devotion that morning. He picked it up and reread the passage. His Bible lay open to the seventeenth chapter of Acts. He had been reading about Paul in Athens. Somehow his address on Mars Hill just didn't seem to fit the occasion. He began rereading the verses, when he decided to turn back to the story of Abraham and Isaac. That seemed more appropriate. He remembered the account was around Genesis twenty-one or twenty-two. He began thumbing back through the pages of his Bible when the phone rang.

"Hello," answered Howard quickly.

"Howard, this is Bob – have you had any luck?"

"No," Howard responded disappointed. He could tell Bob was hoping that he had.

"I'm afraid I haven't either," said Bob reluctantly. "I didn't find many at home, I'm afraid."

"I guess I should make my way back over to the hospital before it gets late. I'm sure Donna is worried to death to hear something."

"I would offer meet you there," said Bob apologetically. " But Linda and Eric have gone out and I am here alone."

"You don't have to say anymore," replied Howard. "I understand completely. You've done enough in helping make the calls"

"I'll check on you later in the evening," Bob promised.

"Thanks, Bob," said Howard before hanging up the phone.

Howard took a breath and decided to make some sandwiches for them to snack on. He picked up a plastic bag from the cabinet and began filling it with snacks, fruit, bottled water and then set it on the kitchen table to make the sandwiches. After finishing the food preparation, he picked through his stack of books in his backpack. He pulled out the novel he had been reading and then remembered the mail he had picked up the day before. He had completely forgotten about the letter for Terry from Karen. It was still on the top of his Spanish books where he had left it. He picked it up to carry with him. Then he noticed another letter under it that had been pressed against the thin envelope. It had completely escaped his attention before. It was addressed to Donna. It was from her parents. Howard swallowed hard. He prayed it was not more bad news. He wasn't sure how much more Donna could take. The thought of bad news reminded him - he would have to tell Donna about Juanita and the bedroom. Maybe that could wait, he thought. Better to focus on Terry at this time. After all, he didn't even know what was taken yet. If they were lucky, it was just the extra cash that they kept in the drawers. He would look for it later.

He gathered the bag of food, the books and the mail and headed out the front door, being careful to lock it behind him. He closed and locked the gate and walked to the edge of the street to find a taxi. This time of the afternoon, they should be running back and forth along the main route. He figured it would be quicker than calling. He was right.

As Howard sat quietly in the back seat of the taxi, his mind raced ahead to what he would have to tell Donna. This had to be the breaking point. No mother could endure any more than what they were facing. Her son was injured, blood was needed, the prospects were not presenting themselves. Their trusted maid had taken advantage of them at this most vulnerable time. And now there was possibly more bad news from home. Howard had to face the fact that this day may very well mark the end of their efforts to become missionaries. He thought about Al and Leanne Reddings. They knew the difference between their will and God's. Maybe Howard was just being too proud to see what this was doing to his family. Terry had never embraced the people or the country. Donna had been struggling for a long time. She was giving it her best effort, but Howard needed to be sensitive to what this would do to her. He had to prepare himself for the worse.

The taxi arrived at the front door of the hospital. Howard paid the driver and faced the front doors. His steps were heavy and slow. He dreaded facing Donna more than anything he had ever had to do. The sun was setting behind the hospital. It would soon be dark. Howard felt a great oppression surrounding him. He knew it was satanic. The devil was obviously hitting them with every weapon in his arsenal. He had attacked them on every side since they had arrived. He was now touching the flesh of his flesh. How much would God allow? Maybe Howard should have looked in the book of Job for his encouragement.

"God," Howard whispered in prayer. "I still trust you. I don't know why we are having to go through this – but I believe it has not caught you by surprise. I don't ask for answers, I only ask for mercy upon my son. I know that you are greater than the prince of this age. And I know that you can intervene at any time. Dear Lord, make your way clear for our lives. Whether we stay or go, I just pray that you are the one that is leading and that we will be found faithful and not fearful."

Howard walked through the crowded corridors and began checking room numbers.

"103, . .105,...107!" he said to himself. The door was closed. He tapped and then slowly opened the door. He was not prepared for the next sight.

Howard stared into the dimly lit room. Donna sat in the chair beside the hospital bed weeping. The bed was empty!

"We have to go now," Allen explained to Don Tulio and Roberto. "The team is staying in a hotel in León and it is getting late."

The team had spent the rest of the afternoon with their two new brothers in the faith. Don Tulio had many questions as did Roberto. Many questions were directed towards Alex, who was still dazed, but gaining his strength. There appeared to be no damage to his mind or his body. Rhonda was especially amazed.

Different team members took turns sharing their personal testimony through Peter and Allen and Becky. Rusty handled some Bible questions about spiritism as did Allen. Very little work was accomplished the second half of the day.

"You will return tomorrow?" Don Tulio asked.

"Yes, very early. We didn't get much work done today," Allen explained.

"Don't worry," Don Tulio smiled – something Roberto could not remember ever seeing. "There will be many hands here to help tomorrow."

"Praise the Lord!" said Peter, and then informed the rest of the group.

"I thought I was a powerful man who could work many wonders – but I see that you are a man of a powerful God who can work greater wonders and does so for our good. I cannot say that everything I did was for good," Don Tulio confessed. "Now I want to be a man of a powerful God."

"I believe you will be," replied Allen, extending his hand towards him.

The two clasped palms and shook vigorously.

"You will have your help tomorrow," Don Tulio stated firmly. "I promise it."

"And I will help him keep that promise," Roberto added.

The team took turns shaking hands with the two men and then made their way through the darkening tree line to the vehicles. Before Ty left the bank, he glanced up at the sunset sky. The clouds were gone.

"Donna!" Howard called out. "...Terry?" He couldn't bring himself to say anymore.

Donna Pennington turned, her eyes swollen from tears.

"Oh, Howard!" she almost screamed. "Oh Howard, I can't believe it!"

"Where's Terry?" Howard tried again, swallowing hard.

"He's in surgery!" she said through her sobs. "The doctor took him about fifteen minutes ago."

"Surgery? How?" asked Howard confused.

"They found a donor!" she exploded.

"THEY found a donor? Where? Who?" Howard knew she couldn't answer his questions, but he had to ask them aloud.

They embraced tightly.

After a needful moment, Donna looked up smiling.

"The Doctor doesn't think it will be a serious operation. He expects to find just a small bleeding problem, and he is going to reset the rib. The biggest problem was the blood. Where do you suppose they found a donor?"

"Maybe Bob Cartwright found someone after I left the house," mused Howard. "But I don't see how they could have gotten here and prepared for surgery before I arrived. I talked to Bob about twenty minutes ago, at the most."

Howard didn't need answers, he was just glad his son had found mercy. They would spend the next two hours pacing and holding each other.

After the first hour, Howard decided to offer Donna a sandwich that he had prepared. Taking the food from the bag, he suddenly remembered the mail.

"I almost forgot, again," Howard said apologetically. "I have a letter for you. I picked it up yesterday without realizing it. It was attached to a letter for Terry."

"A letter for Terry?" Donna asked.

"Yes – it is from Karen. Should be just the thing he needs when he wakes up."

"Whose my letter from?" inquired Donna, taking a sandwich half while they talked.

Howard paused while picking up the letter. He remembered that this could be more bad news. But God had been gracious with Terry.

"It's from your mother," Howard said softly.

"Oh," responded Donna with similar concerns. She took the letter and opened it slowly.

Unfolding the single page, she began to work her way through the handwriting. She read silently and then stopped, placing her hand over her mouth. Howard feared the news.

"What is it?" he asked gently.

"I don't believe it," Donna replied, but not disturbed. She was almost excited. "It's about Aunt Clare."

"Aunt Clare?" Howard asked confused.

"Well, not Aunt Clare personally, but about her estate," Donna explained.

"Her estate? I thought she lived with your folks."

"No, she lived NEAR my folks. She had her own house," Donna corrected. "And according to this, she had more than that."

"What do you mean?"

"Howard, I have been named in her will. Because we were so close, she put me in her will! After we decided to come to the mission field, she was so proud, she amended her will and has left us...let me see...Oh, my gosh... forty-five THOUSAND dollars!"

"You are kidding me!" exclaimed Howard.

"No. Mom said the estate will be settled this month and they will open a special account for us in Texas," Donna went on reading.

"Well, that is some good news," admitted Howard. "Now let's just wait and see if we hear some good news about Terry."

The next hour passed more quickly. Howard sat on the bed and read his novel. Donna reread her letter several times. It still seemed unreal. While she was reflecting on her memories of her Aunt Clare, there was a knock at the door.

Howard and Donna both rose to their feet.

"Come in," called Howard, toward the door. Donna stepped over and took his hand.

Doctor Peniel stepped in alone.

"Where is Terry?" Howard asked.

"He's fine," the doctor assured them. "The surgery was minimal. We'll be bringing him back here to the room in the next thirty minutes. We did need the blood, though. The donor was young and it took a lot out of her."

"Her?" Donna asked curiously. She would like to meet the person that saved her son's life. "Is she still here?"

"Yes, in fact, we're about to bring her in here to recover."

"Recover?" asked Howard. "Is she ok?"

"Yes," the doctor smiled. "She just fainted. She'll be fine. Since you had the space in your room, we thought you wouldn't mind. After all, she said that you know her."

Dr. Peniel pushed open the door wider and an orderly maneuvered a gurney through the doorway.

Howard and Donna stepped back to make room. The gurney was wheeled in and placed against the wall opposite the bed. The dim lighting made it difficult to see the face. Donna was determined. She led Howard across the room to the side of the gurney. Whoever this person was, they owed them their son's life.

"Juanita! Howard, it's Juanita!"

The Penningtons stared at the young woman lying asleep before them. Howard suddenly realized that everything he thought had been bad was turning to good.

"Thank you, sweet Jesus," Howard said, indicating more than Donna would ever know.

"Yes, Lord," Donna agreed.

Mar's Hill.

Howard unexpectedly remembered the Biblical passage he had looked at earlier. What did Mar's Hill have to do with what they had just been through? He walked over to his books, found the Bible he had brought and opened it to Acts 17. He read through the account again and suddenly saw it.

"God was trying to tell me something, and I wasn't listening," he said aloud.

"Pardon?" Donna questioned.

"I'll show you later," Howard said smiling. "Everything is going to be Ok."

Howard and Donna waited in the warm glow of the dimly lit room and experienced a peace they hadn't felt in weeks, maybe months.

Adam Baxter turned off the den lights and joined Gertie in the bedroom where she was now reading.

"Through watching TV?" she asked without looking up.

"Nothing on," he sighed. "...as usual. I thought I would just join you in some reading."

"That would be nice," she replied.

Adam looked through the books on his desk that he had been meaning to read. He picked up one and eased into his recliner so as not to disturb Gertie. After a couple of pages, he looked up from his novel.

"Can I ask you something?"

Gertie laid down her book and smiled.

"Sure dear, what is it?"

"This morning I commented about the weather and you seemed pleased that it was a cloudy day as though that had something to do with you praying for the team. Why is that?"

"It has to do with my morning Bible reading. Many times I find a connection between God's word and the events of the day. Today it just hit me that way."

"I don't understand," Adam replied confused.

"Get your Bible and read to me from Numbers chapter nine, starting around verse 15."

Adam obeyed and began reading about the Lord leading the children of Israel in the wilderness by a cloud. The cloud would rest over the tabernacle. When the cloud moved, the people moved. When the cloud rested in one spot – so did they. Then he read verse twenty-one and twenty-two:

"And so it was, when the cloud abode from even unto the morning, and that the cloud was taken up in the morning, then they journeyed: whether it was by day or by night that the cloud was taken up, they journeyed. Or whether it were two days, or a month, or a year, that the cloud tarried upon the tabernacle, remaining thereon, the children of Israel abode in their tents, and journeyed not: but when it was taken up, they journeyed."

"You see," Gertie interrupted. "The cloud was the presence of God for Israel. We look at clouds and only think they obscure the sunlight. Today, I saw God present in the clouds. I prayed that the team would also. I prayed that the team would experience God's mighty presence in their midst today. I hope to get another letter or a call from Billy Eldridge when they return and find out just how today went. I can't help but believe that it was an important time for them."

"I'm sure you're right," said Adam lovingly.

CHAPTER TWENTY-ONE

"THE BRIDGE"

THE TEAM squeezed together into the West's living room after their meal at the hotel. The prevailing mood was that of rejoicing. No one had expected to see what they had that day. It was a true miracle apart from any human explanation.

"Team, I don't have to tell you the importance of what took place today," Allen began as the group settled down. "Words cannot express our praise to God for demonstrating his power over death in giving life back to Alex. And yet, equally important, is the life that he gave to two other men today. He may have resuscitated Alex, but he resurrected Don Tulio and Roberto from sin and death."

"Amen," commented several around the room.

"We weren't sure if we were going to encounter Don Tulio while you were here. Part of me was hoping we wouldn't. But deep down I knew that this confrontation was inevitable, either during or after your trip. The darkness in this man stood as a stronghold against this project as well as the gospel itself, and it would have resisted it even after its completion. Don Tulio was what we call a 'gate-keeper'. He had the authority of preventing the gospel from entering *Pozo Negro*."

"I have to ask," said Billy Eldridge, raising his hand. "Was what happened today in any way typical for you in ministry here?"

Allen West bowed his head and smiled humbly.

"No, it wasn't," Allen confessed. "To be honest, it has never happened before. I am just as amazed as you are."

"What led you to take such a bold step of faith?" Rusty asked.

"God," Allen replied simply. "I was praying like the rest of you, and quite honestly feeling defeated by the situation. Then as clearly as I can explain, I heard a simple word – *Eutychus*!"

"Eutychus?" questioned Little Billy. "What is that?"

"Not 'what', but 'who'," Allen explained. "In Acts 20, there is a story of a young man who fell out of a window while listening to Paul preach. The group went down to find the young man had died, but Paul told them that the young man still had life in him and he proceeded to lie across him and he arose. His name was Eutychus."

"That is incredible!" said Matt, looking over to Alex who was seated quietly next to his father.

"What God did today was His idea, not mine," Allen quickly added. "I would never have stepped out on something so bold without God's direction. I can only think that God chose to do this in the presence of Don Tulio to demonstrate His power."

"What do you think will happen now?" asked Rusty.

"Now," Allen said strongly. "I think Don Tulio will serve as a bridge – someone who can help carry the gospel into their specific community and culture. For years, *Pozo Negro* has been a closed community. Don Tulio can make the difference."

"Isn't that sort of ironic?" Stan asked. "The bridge he sought to destroy – he became."

"Only God!" declared Allen.

"That's right!" said Billy Eldridge.

"So what happens tomorrow?" asked Arnie.

"I don't know," admitted Allen. "But I can't wait to find out."

The Penningtons waited anxiously for the door to open again. Juanita began to stir. She slowly adjusted her eyes to the room and saw the Penningtons seated together on the hospital bed.

"*Señora* Pennington," Juanita called out.

Donna immediately rose and walked over to the young girl who had saved her son.

"Juanita, it's ok, don't try to get up," instructed Donna reaching to take her hand.

"Terry, is he ok?" Juanita asked weakly.

"We're waiting to see," said Donna gently. "They should be bringing him in soon."

Juanita fumbled with her left hand to fish something out of her pants pocket. She finally pulled out a crumpled yellow card folded in two and held it out for Donna to take.

"I went through your bedroom to find this," she said slowly. "I had seen it before putting your clothes away. I thought I could find it again and help."

Howard realized why their bedroom had been ransacked. Juanita was looking for a special document. That also explained why the passports were not taken. They were the most valuable things in the room. Howard walked over to see what was so important.

Donna took the folded card and began to cry again. She handed it to Howard, who opened it. It was Terry's shot record, which included his blood type.

"The nurse on the phone told me there was a problem with his blood type and that neither of you could serve as donors. I was curious to see if I could help," Juanita explained.

"You are *A negative*?" Howard asked.

"*Sí Señor*," said Juanita. "It is not something you forget easily when you are in need of blood. When I was thirteen, I had a bad accident on my bicycle and needed some blood. It took them two days to find me a donor."

"Juanita," cried Donna. "I don't know how we will ever be able to thank you."

"You have saved our son's life," added Howard.

Juanita smiled.

"*A su orden*," she said simply, something they had heard several times a day when asking her to so something for the house. It simply meant, "at your service or command".

There was a tap at the door and it slowly began to open. Another gurney was maneuvered into the small room. Terry Pennington lay on his side with his eyes closed. The orderly wheeled him beside the bed so they could transfer him easily. For a moment, Terry lay facing his parents, who were standing next to Juanita, who had raised up on her gurney. Terry opened his eyes and started focusing. In the dim light he could make out the three figures. He smiled recognizing his mother first. He then looked to his father and finally to the third figure. His smile grew even larger.

"Karen!" he said weakly.

Donna looked at Howard surprised and then back at Terry.

"No sweetheart, this is not Karen," she said soothingly. "This is Juanita."

"Oh," replied Terry disappointed. "I thought it was my sister." He rolled over on his back as the orderlies lifted him onto the bed and arranged his covers.

Howard looked at Juanita and realized how Terry could make the mistake in such a setting. He suddenly remembered the letter from Karen as well. He would have it ready when Terry was fully awake, which would be the next morning. For now, they were just relieved that God was working all things together for the good.

Wednesday morning marked the third day of work for the team, but they had only completed a day and a half so far. The project was behind. Arnie was anxious to arrive. Alex was looking strong and was also excited about getting back to the worksite. As the group made their way through the mango trees, they were met with a tremendous surprise. Twenty men stood on the bank with tools in hand. Don Tulio stood on the platform where he had attacked Arnie. Next to him was a taller man that Allen recognized. He was the *Alcalde* of the village, Solomón Garcia. Next to him stood Roberto. The missionary walked to the platform and greeted the men.

"*Buenos Dias,*" said Allen offering his hand first to the mayor.

"*Buenos Dias,*" replied Solomón smiling and extending his hand in return.

Allen greeted the other two men in kind.

"Don Tulio told us of what happened yesterday," began Solomón. "Roberto confirmed his story. I must say we had trouble believing them, but I had to admit that I had never seen these two men agree on anything before. You see, the night of the rains that caused the bridge to fall, Roberto was trying to cross the bridge with another young man. His name was Daniel. He was my son. Daniel fell into the water and died. Roberto said he saw Don Tulio there that night just watching. Roberto has always blamed Don Tulio for Daniel's death. I, too, believed that Don Tulio was powerful and may have had something to do with the bridge being taken away. I have been afraid of Don Tulio ever since...until yesterday."

Don Tulio stepped up. He spoke with a confident humility.

"I have used my power and presence to control *Pozo Negro*. Yesterday, I met a greater power and a greater presence. Yesterday I gave my control to Him. These men are here today, not because I asked them to come. They are here because I could no longer forbid them. Roberto helped many to understand why you are here. They are here to help you finish OUR bridge, or should I say, 'God's bridge'?"

"I, too, found something yesterday," stated Roberto. "I found forgiveness for myself and love to forgive another. I can't explain it. I wanted to see Don Tulio dead. I thought maybe outsiders who didn't know him could defeat him. I knew this bridge would stir him to fight. I had hoped he would be driven from the village by men who were stronger than he was. When he survived the river yesterday and the young man had drowned, I began to lose all hope. Then I saw a miracle. God brought the young man back to life right before our eyes. Then I saw another miracle. Don Tulio humbled himself before God. I knew then that I needed to humble myself also. I was drowning in my own pride and hate. I too, needed to be rescued from the river in my own way. Just as God saved the young man – He has saved me."

"That is quite a testimony," responded Allen. "Would you be willing to tell others your story?"

"It would be my privilege," affirmed Roberto.

"*Alcalde*," said Allen, stepping to one side. "Would you like to meet the young man that God saved from the river yesterday?"

"We all would," Solomón stated loudly. The men on the bank began to cheer.

"Arnie," Allen called out. "Would you and Alex join us on the platform?"

The two walked proudly down the bank to the platform. Arnie kept his arm around his son's shoulders. The group of men from the village began to crowd around them on the platform as they stepped up to meet the mayor.

"May I present to you Alex Johnson and his father Arnie," introduced Allen.

The men exchanged greetings. Solomón's eyes began to tear up. He could see Daniel in this young man's face. Roberto saw it as well.

"So this is what a resurrected man looks like," Solomón finally said out loud. Allen translated for Arnie and Alex.

"I guess," replied Alex. But then he stepped over and laid his hand on Don Tulio's chest. "But, from what I understand about God, this is what a resurrected man looks like also."

Arnie smiled proudly at the depth of his son's understanding.

After a couple more comments, Solomón changed the topic of conversation.

"So this is the master builder?" he asked pointing to Arnie. "Sir, I wish to present you these men to help build the bridge if you can use them."

"That would be great," Arnie smiled big. "We got a little behind yesterday and could use the help. But more than that - we want this to be YOUR bridge. If you take part in building it, then we know you will continue to maintain it. We have come to help you."

"Good word," said Allen, before translating the statement to the *Alcalde.*

Solomón smiled at the translation and then motioned to the other men on the bank. Cheers went up again.

Billy Eldridge had made his way toward the platform during the exchange of conversation. He removed his backpack from his shoulder and motioned for Allen. The two spoke softly for a moment and then Allen nodded. Billy followed him back onto the platform where the missionary presented him to the group.

"This is Billy Eldridge," Allen began. "He had a brother who did the kind of work I do, but in Honduras. He died over a year and a half ago in an accident. Billy was able to visit him shortly before his death. He was able to give Bibles to the people his brother worked with. With your permission, he has Bibles to give your men with you here today. They are in Spanish and come from a group called the Gideons that seek to give God's Word out around the world. He would like the privilege of giving your men the Word of God today and especially to Don Tulio and Roberto."

"We would be honored to receive it," stated Solomón proudly. "May I have one also?"

Allen translated to Billy who burst out smiling.

"Tell him I have a copy for everyone here, and more for those in the village that would like a copy."

Billy reached into his backpack and took out one of the brown pocket New Testaments he had packed. He stepped up to Don Tulio and handed it to him respectfully. The little man cupped his hands around the little Bible and bowed his head.

"I now have something to replace my stick," he said firmly. "I promise to read it and to help others read theirs."

"I'll help you get a larger one," Allen promised. "One that you will be able to see easier and that will have both Old and New Testament."

Roberto took his with equal anticipation. He had never seen a Bible he could carry with him. He proudly fit the New Testament in his shirt pocket and then quickly took it back out again.

"I will carry it wherever I go," he promised.

Billy then presented one to Solomón who also received it with reverence.

"*Señor West*," said Solomón. "When this bridge is completed, would you come and hold a special service to dedicate it? And then maybe you could come and teach us this Bible."

Allen nodded humbly. He was feeling his throat tighten with emotion. He searched for the words. They seemed so natural.

"*A su orden*," he said simply.

Solomón smiled.

Peter Moralis was called to the platform. He would be given responsibility for coordinating the men from *Pozo Negro*. Arnie gave Peter his instructions and assignments. The team broke into their small work groups and together they sawed, hammered, strung line, wired, welded and built a bridge.

———————————

Terry awoke hungry. The hospital didn't provide meals. That was brought by family members. Juanita had returned to the Pennington house the night before. Howard made an early trip to the house the next morning. He gathered some fruit, applesauce, and then cooked up a small pot of oatmeal. He poured it into a thermos and sealed it for the trip back to the hospital. On his way back to the hospital, Howard took a small detour and picked up breakfast for himself and Donna at McDonalds. As Terry began to stir, he could smell the sausage, biscuits and hash browns.

"Can I have some," he pleaded.

"I'm sorry, sweetheart," his mother soothed. "We have some oatmeal for your stomach. I don't think you could handle too much solid food just yet."

"Some vacation," he replied sarcastically.

"Well, sweetie," Donna continued. "We're just so glad you're ok. You had quite an accident and gave us quite a scare. You had surgery yesterday. Do you remember anything?"

"Not much," Terry said, trying to concentrate. "I remember seeing you last night and someone else was here."

"That was Juanita," his father inserted. "You thought she was Karen, remember?"

"What was Juanita doing here?" Terry asked.

"You needed blood for the operation and you have a very special kind of blood. We couldn't help you, but Juanita had the kind of blood you needed."

"Juanita gave blood for me?"

"Yes, she did," Donna answered. "And what's more, she did it on her own. We didn't know she had the special blood, so we didn't ask her. It was her idea."

"Wow," exclaimed Terry. "That's cool."

"Which reminds me," said Howard, remembering the letter again. "You have a letter from Karen. It came the day before yesterday. I just forgot to give it to you. You can be looking at it while I get you some oatmeal and fruit."

He handed the envelope to Terry who quickly opened the thin airmail envelope. He read the first few lines to himself.

"Would you like to read it out loud?" Donna asked.

"Ok," Terry agreed and started over.

"Dear Little Brother," he started. "I have been thinking about you a lot lately and I thought you might like to get a letter in the mail. I know I could call, but letters are funner and you have something to read over and over…even from your older sister."

"How do you like Costa Rica?" Terry paused and winced. Howard and Donna understood, but they nodded for him to keep reading. "I hear they have neat fruit drinks and great beaches."

Terry stopped. He wanted to say something sarcastic, but decided against it.

"I have heard you have had some rough times lately. I guess that is another reason for me to write. Don't worry about the *Gameboy*. It's only a toy. There are more where that came from. I'm just glad nothing serious happened to you. You mean a lot to me and I really miss you. If anything ever happened to you, I don't know what I'd do."

Donna took Howard's hand. This was getting too close to home.

"I know it has been hard with the language also. Anna told me she had the same problem when she was there. In fact, she is going to add a few lines to this letter when I'm through. I just want you to know that I am proud of you. I would give anything to be in your shoes – seeing a different country, meeting people from another culture, discovering different ways of doing things, and experiencing a world bigger than Southern California. It's more than learning Spanish, it's thinking Spanish. I'm told that after this first four years, you will start calling Central America home."

"Yeah, right!" Terry responded out loud. Donna squeezed Howard's hand tightly.

"What else does she say," coaxed Donna.

"Let me see," Terry continued. "…will start calling Central America home. You don't realize now what an opportunity you have, but someday I think you will. Most kids your age in San Diego think the world consists of video games, music, and fast food. They know nothing of strange animals, exotic tasting meals, volcanoes, and wild taxi rides. Don't let these months slip by you. Experience all that you can."

"Yeah, like car accidents and hospital stays!" Terry interrupted himself again. He looked at his parents apologetically. "Sorry! Let's see, where was I?"

"Lastly, I thank God you are experiencing this as a believer in Jesus Christ. I got away from God and Mom and Dad for a couple years and you saw what road that almost took me down. I would give anything to have those years back. Use this time to draw close to God as well as Mom and Dad. They love you very much. They would give their lives for you."

Terry paused and looked into the loving eyes of his parents.

"Yeah," he said again, only softer. "I know that's right."

"Is there anything else?" Howard asked.

"Here's the part Anna wrote," said Terry looking back down at the letter. He began reading the different handwriting.

"Dear Terry, I have two brothers that have been able to do what you are doing now. They were born on the mission field, so I guess it was a bit different for them. They didn't have anything to compare their lives to. But if they were here, I think they would agree. Growing up in a foreign country has some great advantages. Your sister has named some of them, but I can add one more – the people. Not just their differences, but their devotion. I have never been around more loving people. Your family is heading to my old home – Honduras. The Honduran people were so warm and friendly, even before they got to know you. They would give you their food, even when they didn't have much for themselves. They would give you their bed when you visited and they would sleep in a hammock or on the floor. They would dig your vehicles out of the mud. They would carry your loads great distances without complaining. They would walk for hours to come to your service. I could go on. I believe that my father gave his life for people that would have given their life for him. If you were hurt, they would do everything they could to get you help…"

Terry stopped reading again. He looked up at his parents. Donna was beginning to cry. Howard put his arm around her. Terry's eyes began to brim with tears as well. Through a cracking voice, Terry formed the words, "Juanita did everything she could to help me, didn't she?"

"She sure did, son," answered his father.

"I have Costa Rican blood in me now, don't I?"

"Yes, you do."

"Think maybe I'll start liking rice and beans better now?" he joked.

Donna exploded with a tearful laugh. She rushed over to hug Terry.

"I love you, son," she cried.

"Is there any more?" Howard asked. He wanted to share something he had read the day before himself.

"Let me see," said Terry, looking back down at the letter and wiping his eyes. "Just this…"

"Whatever you may be going through, know that God is in control. He has not left you alone to work it out. He has put some good people around you, including your parents. Trust Him and trust them to help you through. And look for those special people who can help you cross the bridge into your new culture – believe me, they are there. Signed, cousin Anna"

"Cousin Anna?" Terry asked.

"Now that you are an MK, other missionaries are called 'aunts and uncles'. Since Anna is another MK, I guess that makes her your new cousin," explained his father.

"Cool!" Terry said closing the letter.

Howard took his Bible from the small table against the wall. He wanted to share with Donna and Terry what God had showed him the day before.

"I realize that all of this has caused us to stop and think about why we are here," he began. Donna stood by Terry. She had been feeling her doubts for some time now. "To be honest, I was ready to throw in the towel yesterday afternoon. I couldn't think of anything worse than having one of you hurt and in danger of dying. I did everything I could and it wasn't good enough to save my son. Then God tried to tell me that it was not up to me. While I was busy making phone calls, trying desperately to find someone with the right blood, He had already found her and had sent her to the hospital to get ready for the operation. While waiting for a phone line to clear, I picked up my Bible and started reading. It was Acts 17. I had been reading there that morning. At first I didn't think it had anything to do with the crisis we were facing, but let me read one of the verses now."

He turned the pages till he found Acts 17, verses 25 and 26:

"Neither is worshipped with men's hands, as though he needed any thing, seeing he giveth to all life, and breath, and all things; And hath made of one blood all nations of men for to dwell on all the face of the earth, and hath determined the times before appointed, and the bounds of their habitation;"

"Those words made no sense yesterday until I learned that it was Juanita who had come to give blood for the operation," Howard explained. "God didn't need me – He gives life. For Terry that life need was blood. I had only called other North Americans to help. But God has *'made of one blood all nations of men'*. There was nothing wrong with Juanita's blood being used. In fact, it was the only one that was right. Costa Ricans may talk different, live different and even think different, but we are all *'one blood'*. She has proven that. Also I learned that it is God who determines where we live and for how long. The decision to leave is not ours but His. I believe he has used Juanita to tell us now is not the time to leave! What do you think?"

Donna rubbed Terry's shoulders.

"What do you think, son?" she asked.

"I agree," Terry said firmly.

"So do I," said Donna, as though a huge burden was being lifted.

Howard took a deep breath. He felt like a huge chasm had been crossed for the Pennington family and Juanita had been the bridge. This next trimester would be different. He could tell. And he was right.

Pozo Negro had not celebrated *Semana Santa* for nearly two decades. Don Tulio would not allow it. That would now change. What would also change would be the way they would celebrate it. From now on, *Semana Santa* would mark the anniversary of their new bridge. It would also be a time to recall the story of the young man who drowned in the river and was restored to life. Don Tulio would see that the story was passed to the next generation along with the story of God's own Son who gave His life and was raised to never die again.

Arnie Johnson looked upon the bridge with deep satisfaction. It would not have been completed without the help of the village. Allen West knew just how important that was for the village. Fraternal missions were always the best – treating the nationals as brothers and equals – not as children. Arnie and Allen stood together with Solomón and Don Tulio on the very platform where they had stood two days earlier. Only now the expanse was complete with beams, cables and ropes for handrails.

A special worship service was scheduled in the town square for four in the afternoon. In preparation, the entire village had assembled on the bank of the river with the volunteer team for the dedication. The *Alcalde* spoke first thanking the team for coming and for providing the materials and plan for the bridge. He referred to the blessing the bridge would mean to those wishing to visit *Pozo Negro* as well as for those who needed to cross for their work and supplies. Allen, Becky and Peter stationed themselves so they could translate for the group. When he finished, Don Tulio was offered a chance to speak.

The little man stepped forward. Many had heard the story of his conversion and had their doubts. As he lifted his head to speak he held a little book in his hand.

"This bridge is a gift from God," He began. "But His greatest gift came in the form of His Son Jesus Christ. This book says, 'For *there is* one God, and one mediator between God and men, the man Christ Jesus.' He is our bridge to God. I pray that those who cross this bridge into *Pozo Negro* will find the bridge to heaven."

"Amen!" came a voice from the back of the crowd. The people turned to see Roberto holding the same book.

"In fact," Don Tulio continued. "I believe it is time we changed the name of our town from *Pozo Negro*."

Solomón turned and looked squarely at the little man.

"To what?" he asked cautiously.

"*Rio de Luz!*" Don Tulio pronounced proudly.

The crowd cheered. Solomón smiled. He would begin looking into what it would take to change their name.

"What is *Rio de Luz*?" Arnie asked Allen.

"It means, 'river of light'," said Allen.

"Amen!" bellowed Arnie.

The team members took turns sharing. The missionary interpreted from the bridge. No one was in a hurry. The groups began to mingle together till it was a single gathering. After all the speeches, they formed a line and began crossing the bridge in small groups. As they all reached the other side, Allen looked back across the bridge.

"Thank you, Lord," he said quietly to himself. "Thank you for what you have done."

EPILOGUE

<u>Coronado Baptist Church</u>   *Easter Sunday - April 2000*

LIKE MOST Easter Sundays, Coronado Baptist Church was filled to capacity. The team had barely been back a full week. Rusty was excited over what was about to happen. He had never heard of a pastor giving up his pulpit on an Easter service. But then most pastors didn't have a guest speaker like he did. Even the church bulletin didn't list the speaker by name. After the special music, Rusty stepped up to the pulpit as expected.

"I too, would like to welcome you to our service this morning. I realize that we have many visitors with us today, most with family members. You don't know how badly I want to preach, but God has given me other instructions."

"As most of you know, several of us have just returned from a mission trip to Nicaragua. I have asked one of our team members to speak this morning. He may have some things to share about the trip, but I believe his story will be more fitting for this glorious Easter morning than anything I could have prepared from my study. May I present to you, Alex Johnson."

Alex walked nervously up the platform steps to the pulpit and thanked his pastor for the kind introduction. He propped a heavy twisted staff against the side of the pulpit – the only souvenir he brought back from the trip. Taking his Bible in hand, be opened it and began to reading from the New International Version of Philippians 3:10:

> *"I want to know Christ and the power of his resurrection and the fellowship of sharing in his sufferings, becoming like him in his death."*

Alex laid the Bible on the pulpit, took a deep breath and looked over the expectant eyes of the congregation.

"Let me start off by saying, 'be careful what you ask for'..."

<u>Baxter Home – Carrolton, Virginia</u> *Wednesday after Easter - April 2000*

"Got the mail," Adam called from the hallway as he made his way to the bedroom. "And guess who you got a letter from?"

"They got back on Saturday," Gertie giggled. "We should be hearing something from the mission team to Nicaragua."

"Here it is," he announced, just as excited as she was.

Gertie opened the letter and began reading aloud.

"Dear Gertie and Adam, I have some exciting news from Nicaragua. It was so much more than just an encounter with a witchdoctor. Let me start by thanking you for your prayers during our trip. You have no idea what they meant to us, and particularly to one of our team members. I hope you are sitting down…"

Language Institute – San José Costa Rica *Graduation Day – August 2000*

"I still can't believe you are here!" Donna squealed.

"Why not, Mom!" Karen squealed back. "You came to my graduation! It's not like you CAN'T afford it now. After all of the things you guys have been through, I guess I should be saying, 'I can't believe YOU are here!"

"You have no idea how true that is," said Howard.

"It was hard, but I helped them get through it," boasted Terry. "At least we will FINALLY be able to go to the beach, and you will get to go with us!"

They all four laughed.

"When do you start back to classes?" Howard asked Karen.

"The Monday after I get back from this trip."

"That doesn't give you much time," said her mother.

"I think I'll have enough time to get settled in," Karen assured her.

"I hope so," said Donna with a tinge of concern. It was a mother's job to worry.

"Oh, that reminds me," said Karen, searching through her handbag. She retrieved a small envelope and handed it to her father. "I meant to give this to you at the airport when I arrived, but we got caught up in the greetings."

"That's OK," said Howard. "I've been known to forget to deliver mail a time or two, myself."

Donna smiled.

"Oh, it's not a letter," replied Karen smugly. "It's an invitation."

"An invitation?" said Donna suspiciously. "To what?"

"…the exchanging of vows between Samuel "Rusty" Patterson and Dianne Marie Winters" announced Howard. "Rusty is marrying the secretary!"

"When?" asked Donna.

"Two weeks from now," read Howard. "We'll send a card back with Karen and a nice wedding check. After that trip to Nicaragua Karen told us about, no telling where he plans to take her."

They all laughed again.

The graduation service was long, but they were in no hurry. Karen was relishing every minute seated next to her little brother. With uncharacteristic charm, Terry was enjoying every minute with her as well.

The refreshments following the graduation exercise was the moment Howard had been waiting for. He had used the final trimester to do some homework with Mateo on the University campus. Mateo was waiting for them in the back of the gymnasium.

"You have it?" Howard asked.

Mateo nodded, patting his shirt.

"Follow me," Howard instructed.

Donna had gotten two cups of punch and went looking for another special guest.

"Juanita, thank you for coming," said Donna extending a cup of punch. "Would you join us for a moment?"

Juanita was surprised. She knew that the family would be moving soon to their field of service in Honduras. She had only one more week of work to be with them. They had been very gracious since the accident. She had learned much from Mr. Pennington about the Bible in the past three months and felt her spiritual life had improved alongside his Spanish. She had no idea what they wanted to ask of her now.

The Pennington family gathered around Juanita with huge smiles. Juanita had met Karen two days earlier when she arrived, but she didn't recognize the young black man with them.

"Juanita," began Howard, taking the lead. "This is a special day for us as a family. We have not been together for nearly a full year. We wanted to share it with you, because in many ways, you have become like family to us."

Juanita blushed.

"I'm going to ask Mateo to translate for me, because I have some things to say that I don't know the Spanish words for YET!"

Juanita nodded and Mateo stepped up next to Mr. Pennington.

"You saved our son's life and your blood runs through his veins today. You helped us adjust to our new culture and language in ways we'll never fully understand. You became our bridge. We are better prepared to go to Honduras now because of you. Language school can only teach you how to communicate. You have shown us how to relate to people. For this we thank you."

Juanita nodded humbly accepting the appreciation.

"When Terry was brought in to the room that night, he called you 'Karen', his sister. We knew it was a mistake, but in some ways, he was right. You have become like a family member that we can trust and love. While we were here, we lost a family member, Mrs. Pennington's Aunt Clare. And yet, while we were here, we have gained a family member – you."

Juanita began to look confused.

"I know you can't go with us to Honduras. That is not what I am saying. I know you have your own life. I know you have your own dreams. I know you would like to go to college, but your family can't send you. I'm just saying that we would like to be the family that can. To thank you for all you mean to us, I have worked with Mateo to establish an education fund at the University of Costa Rica and we have provided enough funds to pay for your entire education and books and some spending money while you study so you won't have to serve in homes for the next four years."

Mateo completed the translation and pulled out the account information from his shirt. Juanita stared with unbelief. She looked up into the smiling faces of the Pennington family and began to cry.

"I know how you feel," said Karen. "They did the same thing for me!"

Mateo translated for Karen and Juanita suddenly hugged her. She then hugged Donna and Terry. As she turned to Howard she paused. Composing herself, she began to speak slowly...in English.

"Mr. and Mrs. Pennington. God bless you and your family much. I will miss you much. I will..." She looked to Mateo and asked him for a word. She wanted to say it herself. He whispered it back. "...*study* much. You are good people. You will find good people in Honduras. You help me much about God. Thank You."

Then looking to Terry, she placed her finger on the inside of his elbow where they had drawn blood and smiled. "We are brother and sister by blood – *A negative!*"

They all laughed. The Penningtons were now ready to move on.

About The Author

Randy Pool is a believer, a husband and father, a missionary and a storyteller. Born into a military family, his travels carried him to both coasts and Puerto Rico while still a young child. Then at the age of fifteen, his life was eternally changed by Jesus Christ.

Pursuant to a call to ministry, Randy received a B.A. degree in Religion and Greek from Union University. He later earned his M.Div. from Mid-America Baptist Theological Seminary of Memphis. While at Union, he met and married the love of his life, Cindy.

After ten years together, three children and pastoring two churches, Randy and Cindy went to the mission fields of Central America. They served as Church Planters in Honduras and Nicaragua for eleven years with the International Mission Board of the Southern Baptist Convention. Randy writes from his experiences in ministry and missions with a keen eye to detail.

Randy and Cindy now live back in Tennessee where Randy serves with the Mississippi River Ministry connecting churches to poverty areas within their community. He is still a missionary, now working through the North American Mission Board, SBC. He sees writing as a channel of information, inspiration, as well as entertainment.

Randy has written for several Baptist publications, including Dimension Magazine, Missions Leader Magazine, Nuestra Tarea (Spanish Baptist Magazine), and The Baptist and Reflector (State newspaper). He has two other books in print, The Breach, and Poolside Reflections – both bearing the mark of missions.

Randy enjoys life. When time allows, he relaxes with family and friends in hammocks beneath a gallera built on their small homestead in Gibson County – a touch of Latin culture in West Tennessee. He enjoys telling stories that bring humor to life and Christ to heart.

Printed in the United States
45782LVS00004B/292-324

9 781425 912772